Land
Barons

A. Dru Kristenev

Land Barons

E-edition, ChangingWind.Org: November, 2008
Second Edition: 2012

ISBN: 0615640389
ISBN- 13: 978-0615640389

A. Dru Kristenev

Can there be anything so evil as
to steal a child's future through fear?
A. Keller

Land Barons

Author's Note...

The idea for Land Barons first came to me in 1999 as I witnessed the steady disenfranchisement of landowners, farmers and ranchers, as well as public land users, their rights whittled away by the incursion of government regulation via executive order and legislation.

It is imperative we conserve the resources of this country, however it should not be enforced to the ruin of good stewards of the land, those communities, families, and individual owners who have managed their charge with dignity and wisdom. Yet we have seen government agencies and the rise of private conservancies insert themselves into the arena of land management, often without the knowledge necessary to administer that land appropriately. It has been demonstrated, time and again, that bureaucracy lacks the accountability needed in order to oversee property with perspicacity.

It behooves us to suitably observe property rights, be they of individuals, companies or tribal agencies and to understand how national forest land was initially set aside for the benefit of the public, the true owners: the people of this great country. We should continue to be vigilant in protecting our resources yet respecting private property rights.

I was reliant on experts in their fields, news reports, environmental impact studies and anecdotal evidence to craft the basis for the story, which is of course, fictional. As usual, all mistakes are mine and I must thank the many friends who took the time to read the manuscript and offer their suggestions and criticism, much of which I incorporated into the text. I am forever in their debt.

Although it was not my intent to offend anyone, it is likely that I have. It appears to be my nature to do so. In all, I pray that we, as a nation, learn more how political agenda crafts environmental policies that affect every aspect of our lives. I adjure all of us to pay attention and not relinquish the rights that were so hard-won by our forebears.

A. Dru Kristenev
November 7, 2008

Land Barons

[3]...saith the Lord: and I will cause them
to return to the land that I gave to their fathers,
and they shall possess it.
Jeremiah 30

Land Barons

Chapter 1

Closing the door behind him, the farmer stopped to gaze at the expanse of vivid yellow blooms that covered much of the acreage within sight. Looking more closely, off-color patches could be seen interspersed among the healthy plants. Not that it mattered. He wouldn't be coming back and there wasn't anything he could do to improve the health of his crops…they were dying with or without all his years of care and patience. He could no longer afford to till the ground that had passed from father to son for almost a hundred years.

Today was closing day. Closing up the house, closing the escrow and closing down his heart's desire to stay and be the good steward of the land that he had promised to be. This land that had been the stabilizing force in his life throughout all of his 45 years. No longer.

Crop failure for three years on end and his wife's steady decline had left him with no alternative but to sell and close off this part of his life. His children wouldn't have the opportunity he had had to finish growing up in their, and his, childhood home.

Sighing, he crossed the front porch and, descending the steps, he went over to hold his wife's hand as she looked up at him from her wheelchair. Her fingers trembled with an ague that they couldn't understand. As young as she was, her nervous system was shutting down and all the doctors and clinics they had visited hadn't been able to make a definable diagnosis.

She was dying and he couldn't help her, same as his family's heritage. They were both dying and no one knew what to do except sell and cut their losses. Well, if it were just things, the material goods that were being lost, that would be no problem. But they were losing their livelihood and Mary's life all in one fell swoop.

May as well finish packing up, he thought. He checked to see how the kids were doing with loading up the rest of the household goods. They'd sold all of the heavy equipment and some of the furniture. Even so, this was the last of three loads and the house was empty, as quiet as a tomb except for the scratching of a few field mice in the attic. They had always been a part of the family, enough so that the old mouser, Rocky, even gave up on them.

Rocky was already settled into the new place in town. They were fortunate to find something comfortable that they could afford. A ranch style home in the Orchards where Mary wouldn't have to deal with the stairs. He had already installed a ramp up the front entry to make access easier for her. His son and daughter would be registering at the high school in town and he had already hired on at a farm equipment repair shop. Their needs were covered, all but the need for home…this home and this land.

•••••••

He lifted his wife out of her chair and tenderly placed her in the passenger seat of the ten-year-old Buick. Every time he held her he was again surprised at how light she had become in his arms. All of the sturdiness that she had exuded not six months before had dissipated with her dwindling strength. He pulled the seat belt down within her reach so she could clasp it across her steadily wasting form. As much as he wanted to let the tears fall from his eyes, he knew that he couldn't. Even as Mary's strength was waning, his had to be visible.

Everything had been cinched down in the truck bed and his son, who'd be seventeen in two weeks, would follow them into town with his younger sister riding shotgun. The oldest son wasn't due home from college for another week, so he would meet them at the new place, where he'd have to share a room with his brother during his visits home.

Well, he mused, things sure do change, whether or not we like it.

"Time to go," he called to the kids. And they climbed into the truck. He turned the engine over and started down the long drive to the road, swiveling his head side to side, taking in his last look at his home.

•••••••

As they crawled out onto the county road and headed down the hill, a line of three rigs with flatbed trailers fired up their diesels and grumbled up the drive toward the old house and the hay barn. One of them was hauling a Caterpillar with a backhoe. The homestead wouldn't be standing much longer.

Land Barons

Chapter 2

Brisk steps, soft breeze, easy sunshine.

This is what I've been waiting for. The words were unspoken, playing through her mind as she watched an otter skimming through the water, fifteen feet from the footpath that she followed along the river.

This was the first time she'd encountered an otter this far inland. Growing up in California and spending many years in towns up and down the West Coast, she'd come across otters gamboling in the Pacific bays. For Idaho, this was a 'lifer,' as she liked to borrow the term from bird watchers.

Keeping an eye on her hiking partner as he dove into the waters and then came back up to watch her progress, she wondered what took her so long to make the break. All kinds of reasons stole through her thoughts, and she finally settled on the one that she had kept at bay for the last few hours.

Today was the first anniversary of her father's passing. She had avoided giving over any time to memories until just now, when the realization of the date hit her hard enough to make her stop in her tracks. Standing by the waterside, she followed the otter's progress down river, curious as to why she had been evading this train of thought. As the momentary sadness washed over her, she knew why. She missed him. And she still questioned herself about how he had spent his final hours, wondering what she could have done differently to make his passing easier.

Oh, he'd had a good life. Hard, but rewarding. The family had weathered many difficult years and losses, but they had always muddled through. And Pa, well, he had made his small fortune and had the opportunity to enjoy it in retirement. Not everyone's wishes are answered in that way, but he was fortunate. That still didn't make it any easier knowing that he was gone.

She'd talked to her brother who was getting ready to light a yahrzeit, a memorial candle, for their father at sundown and she remembered that she had one stashed away at the house. Didn't know when she had purchased it or why, but she could see it in her mind's eye sitting on that lonely shelf. She decided that she would light it for him tonight.

Continuing down the riverside trail, she noticed that she was alone again, the otter having abandoned her to her reverie. Two more miles to go, so she quickened the pace and started batting ideas around for fresh news angles for one of her clients.

Over the past year, she had been ramping up her efforts to create a larger clientele for her one-woman public relations show. As a former newspaper publisher, having been thrown to the dogs when the new corporate owners moved in – 'downsizing' is *such* a misleading euphemism, she knew what editors wanted when it came to press releases. She'd edited and rewritten enough of them in her time. One of her 'folks,' as she liked to refer to her customers, was a radio talk show host in a small market, looking to expand his airtime exposure. His provocative view of the world wasn't exactly what many of the markets were willing to experiment with, but she was planting his basic, down and dirty viewpoint in front of enough program directors that she felt sure they'd open a door somewhere soon.

As she mused over what made this talk jock interesting, she kept the rapid rhythm of her feet going on down the trail. One, two, three, four; one, two, three, four, until she reached her vehicle stationed under the broad leaves of sycamores lining the parking lot.

Reinvigorated, she pulled her visor off her head and shook her curling, sable hair free from the clip. Attempting to arrange the unruly mop while peering in the sideview mirror, she quickly gave up, reckoning the effort to be a lost cause. She climbed up on the running board and settled herself into the driver's seat, turned the key over in the ignition and drove home.

•••••••

Home. A new experience, in a manner of speaking. She hadn't really had a place that she had called home for quite some time. The last year and a half had been spent living as a virtual guest, caring for her father as his illness took him through his decline and finally to his death. Then staying on to try to help his wife as she worked her way through a painful loss and chemotherapy all at one time.

14

After meeting her other obligations, she knew it was time to go. The situation in California had come to feel like stagnation. No career opportunities were opening and her personal life was empty aside from the few friends she had there. Although she missed them greatly, they were busy people and she had a gut feeling that it was time to move on.

The last few years she'd been playing emotional ping pong. Her husband, a prominent doctor, left for fairer shores, literally, and she filled the hole with caring for ailing parents. Not that it wasn't something of a relief to be done with a marriage dying of disuse, she conceded that starting from scratch wasn't high on her list of fun things to do. Age was also a factor, as much as she hated to admit it. Although she was relatively young for all the professional experience she carried in her beat-up briefcase, she was beyond the 'looking for romance' stage of life, having entered her fourth decade.

The question was, where to go? She'd enjoyed her stay in Idaho and had made some interesting friends there while her husband had briefly operated a small clinic in rural Idaho County. Other friends Back East had entreated her to move there. After packing everything she had into the back of her Expedition, she jumped behind the steering wheel and motored across country only to end up back in Idaho.

So far, it had seemed like a good decision. She pulled her sneakers off in the utility room, dropping the sweat-dampened socks into the hamper. Tromping through the kitchen, she stopped at the sink to get a glass of purified water and took it onto the deck, where she settled into one of the two patio chairs. She put her feet up on the rail, wriggled her toes and sipped the refreshing water.

She hadn't been in the house more than a month. It was a bargain with a cock-eyed view of the river that needed a bit of fixing up. Not much, mind you. She wasn't all that handy aside from a little painting and the basest of plumbing skills. It was coming along, though. She'd replaced some of the windows, changed some fixtures and removed some god-awful wallpaper. Maybe that was the wrong term. 'Satan's bordello' might have been more fitting in describing the velvety stripes of crimson, gold and violet that had garishly painted the walls. The thought of it made her wince. It happened to be simpler to actually remove one of the non-weight bearing walls rather than fuss with stripping off the paper. The contractor even let her wield the sledgehammer for a while. Wasn't *that* a therapeutic way to increase the light in the living area.

She didn't plan on doing much more than that. It was tidy and roomy enough to have a master suite, office and a sewing room that could be converted for receiving guests. Who needed more than that?

Finishing her drink and odd reflections, she pulled herself out of the chair, strolled back to her office and settled herself in front of the computer to check her e-mail. Nothing much on the correspondence side, just her ex-husband, whose odd sense of fairness was to throw her a business bone, checking in on the progress of a brochure for his office. Hey, a buck was a buck and she wasn't about to turn away work even from a clueless clod. The other message was from Uncle Mike with his occasional feed on life in the New York suburbs, i.e. Philadelphia.

As she closed up the program, her phone rang.

Sue Shuler was on the line asking what she was planning for Friday.

"Thea, you ought to drop by. The weather's been cooperating, and you haven't been up to visit for weeks."

"Oddly enough, I was planning on driving out because I need to take care of a few things at the bank. You two can put up with me coming by afterward?"

"Why else would I badger you to make the drive," Sue cajoled. "Azy's barbecuing and you're coming for dinner."

"Sounds like a plan in need of realization. And I need to see some friendly faces. I'll be there around five if that suits your schedule."

"It's a date and bring the wine."

Chapter 3

Traveling up the river road to her old haunts was always a pleasure of combined stimuli. Breathing in the orange-tinged fragrance of the honey locusts that bordered the banks, cleared her mind and refreshed her energy level. Negotiating the turns at a speed five to ten miles above the limit (sometimes more than that, but she wouldn't admit that lawlessness aloud), she found it relaxing and exhilarating at the same time. Driving was her favored pastime aside from reading just about anything she could lay her hands on. The road gave her time to fathom her place in the world and indulge her fantasies. When she was younger and single, she had owned a swift little sports car, built to handle mountain roads. After taking one of her buddies on a back-road banked for speed, he had dubbed her 'Ricky Racer,' a moniker she thought rather suitable at the time. Steering with alacrity, she still enjoyed taking the curves at the top end of safety, which was somewhat limited in a full-size truck.

Within the hour she was entering the reduced speed zone of the small town she had lived near for a time. Making a right turn into the miniscule business district, she went down the street lined by storefronts dressed in facades that gave the impression of a 19th century western movie set.

She parked in front of the bank and went inside to conduct a few transactions, though it seemed to be more of a social call. Even while living out-of-state, she continued to keep her accounts with the institution not only because she had considered the manager and employees friends, but they also made certain a customer's needs were met. After trying to deal with a few bankers in California during her brief tenure back there, she had just thrown up her hands and called her pals in Idaho for help. No waiting. They took care of everything by phone and fax. She couldn't feel more thankful. She figured that spending the day upriver once in a while was a bit of a lark and a good excuse to visit. Since most of the town's residents kept accounts at this little branch of Silver Savings, she was awash in her former neighbors' activities, silly and serious, within ten minutes of her arrival.

Land Barons

Anthea dropped into a couple of Main Street businesses to say hello before they closed up for the day before she needed to head up to Sue and Azy's. Always happy to shoot the breeze a little, she caught up on more of the local news. Around here there was always something in the air, from the arrest of some local genius trying to create a fuss over the government's so-called financial fraud to preparations for the Memorial Day activities at the city park.

Sharing farewells, she popped into her rig, checked her list to make sure she had handled all of her business and putting the truck in drive, pulled away from the curb. Waving at one of her friends, she rounded the block and went on her way up the hill.

••••••••

The Shuler's lived about 11 miles out of town and up the Harsdale Road which wound in and around farms as it climbed 2,000 feet out of the river valley. They had been neighbors while she and her husband had resided in Idaho a few years back, when they thought that a fresh start might revitalize the marriage. Anthea missed the community feeling of living on the hill, folks always being available to help each other. What she didn't miss was the strained marital relationship that left her demoralized and ready to move on in the end.

Rounding the hairpin turns and waving at the drivers headed in the opposite direction brought back the happier memories. When she had first moved back to Los Angeles for a short time, on their final countdown, she was so trained to automatically wave at neighbors on the road that Angelinos looked at her cross-eyed when her hand came up in greeting as they passed. It didn't take long to lose the habit in that environment, and she wasn't heartbroken to leave the city behind when the time came to move again. She'll never understand her ex's need to get back to the urban jungle. *Well, he can have it. You can't find paradise breathing the diesel fumes of the city bus you're stuck behind in bumper-to-bumper traffic. Who cares if the beach is two miles away?*

The middle of May in central Idaho could radically shift weatherwise from balmy to downright cold and rainy. Today, however was a perfectly sun-drenched day with the sun still high overhead, as the solstice was a month from reaching its yearly zenith. Turning the corner

18

into the Shuler's drive, she made her approach slowly over the gravel, trying not to kick up too much dust. Their dog, a friendly Rottweiler, which adjective when applied to most members of the breed might be an oxymoron, came over to the driver's door and eagerly wagged his stump of a tail as she stepped down from the truck. Scratching him behind the ears with both hands, she savored the welcome of an unprejudiced animal.

"Come here, Nancy," called Sue. The dog, a male, had been saddled with the name by their five-year-old who had wanted a little sister so badly, she'd wrap the pup in lacy doll clothes until the dresses wouldn't fit over the dog's head. Unfortunately, the appellation stuck and Nancy was now a 140-pound papered stud that was in demand for siring litters throughout the region. When his master called, he trotted away from their guest and, circling his rug by the side door, plumped down in a dusty cloud and dropped his huge muzzle onto his paws.

Sue was standing by the open door with her hands on her hips.

"Are you coming in or not?"

"Your herb garden is almost too inviting to leave," said Anthea as she stooped to smell the pristine, white blossoms just springing up from the raised beds. After getting her fill of the fresh scent, she walked briskly up to the porch and gave Sue a solid hug.

"We've missed you, girl. It's great having you back, but we don't get to see you anywhere near as often as we'd like," complained Sue. "The only drawback with this state is that it just takes too long to get anywhere."

Anthea returned the hug, leaving her arm around the slight woman's shoulders as they entered the house.

Inside was an eclectic mix of decorative miscellany stemming from their mixed history of life on the beach and in the mountains. Anthea had once asked what had brought the Shulers back from the idyllic shores of Hawaii to settle among the pines and meadows of the foothills in North Central Idaho. Azy, an Idaho native was homesick enough that they had made the change in geography some 15 years earlier. Between the willow chairs, mixed with the rough-hewn coffee table, the room was strewn with hunting mementos of the islands and the local terrain. In the den, the wall was shared by trophies of both a tusked boar from the leeward side of Maui and a moose taken in the mountains just a few miles from their present home. Décor centering around palm fronds and seashells melded in an oddly pleasing fashion with the forest motifs displayed in the wall art.

Sue, a hapa haole from the Big Island, relished her home and spent her days gardening, tending her few sheep, home schooling the last of her three children, and getting involved up to her elbows in local politics. Despite her size, she was a powerhouse that most of the locals refused to cross when she had her back up. Shorts, a bright pink, button-down blouse and the ever present flip-flops, that lit-up across the heel when she walked, were her costume for the day. Her dark hair was straight cut at her jawline, which exaggerated her mood when she jutted her chin in disapproval. This evening though, her smile was wide and a sparkle in her golden, brown eyes emanated a warmth of welcome.

Azy, tall and rangy in his jeans and t-shirt emblazoned with a Hawaiian sovereignty slogan on the front and "Ku" boldly imprinted on the back, was wiping his hands on a dishtowel as he came in the back door. His hardy constitution was belied by his name, Assael, an attorney by trade, who decided long ago that he preferred the semi-lawlessness of the north woods to the metropolitan atmosphere of Honolulu.

He came up to their guest and swallowed her in a tight squeeze since this was the first opportunity he'd had to see his former neighbor since her return to the state.

"Don't you look a sight to an old bear," he grumbled.

"Just so long as I get the bearhugs," she gibed. "I think that's what I miss most about my dad," she added a little more somberly. "I don't get the requisite three hugs a day."

"I guess you ought to visit more."

"I'll see what I can do about that," she said.

Sue pulled three Molson lagers out of the refrigerator and, popping the cap off each one, handed them out.

"Where's Lindy today?" Anthea swiveled her head around, checking out the interior for signs of their youngest daughter, age 12.

"Staying with a friend for the week-end. They're going camping down at the river," answered Sue. "School's not quite out for the other girls and they want some time to goof off. I'm not sure I envy Ellie's parents taking five pre-teen girls. What a handful."

"Looks like your weekend will be quiet then."

"Not hardly. Tawny and Christie are due back from school tomorrow and Sunday. This is the only time for just us adults," put in Azy. Lifting his beer in the air and toasting the general surroundings, grinning, he said, "Make the most of it. Peace is a precious commodity."

The two ladies joined him in his salute.

Settling down on the sofa, with Sue in her favorite rocker and Azy backwards on a dining room chair, forearms crossed on the high back, they got reacquainted with one another's daily activities. Azy had been in court more than he'd like during the last two weeks with a civil case. He was representing a naturopath who was prescribing concoctions that had supposedly caused a reaction for a client. They were suing for damages.

"She hasn't much to stand on aside from unsubstantiated hives and nausea. They're trying to show that her leg problems are related to the doctor's work. Looks more like it stems from the auto accident she had two months before. A good chiropractor would help her more than a silly ass lawsuit. But then, there's no adjusting some people's attitudes," he quipped.

"Will you win?" asked Anthea.

"I don't see it going for the plaintiff. There's no evidence that I can see. Not much more in the way of excitement in these parts, but, you know, I kind of like it that way."

Sue was going over her run-in at a Chamber of Commerce meeting with some environmentalists that were trying to push business owners to support a ban on fishing in the local waterways. They weren't going for it because so many of them make a living off of the anglers visiting the area.

"Some people think that everything with gills or wings is an endangered species even though their own statistics don't back their bluster. Those folks need a life besides meddling in our livelihood," Sue stated flatly. She then segued into a running narrative on the local gossip. Who's been sick, who's selling their home, who's building...all the underlying information about a small, tightly knit community.

They spent the next hour talking back and forth while Azy managed the barbecue. Sue, having gone into the kitchen to prepare salad and side dishes, continued the banter over the counter to where Anthea had restationed herself to listen.

•••••••

The meal was a satisfying blend of conversation, seasoned venison and a choice California varietal wine that Anthea had supplied. Afterward, the ladies cleared the table and washed-up the dishes while Azy tended to the outdoor grill.

When he reentered the back, he brought the utensils in for cleaning and was followed by a man that Anthea had not seen before. She hadn't noticed the sound of any approaching vehicle, so when she thought she heard voices on the back deck, she assumed Azy was listening to the radio. Turning around from the duty of drying the salad bowl, she was met with a steady gaze from a pair of incisive gray eyes. Standing a couple inches taller than Azy's six-foot frame, an easy smile lit his rugged features as he held out his hand while his friend introduced him to her.

"Anthea, this is an old friend of mine, Gary Mathers."

Anthea took his hand, which he offered for a single, solid shake, clasping her fingers for a brief few seconds afterward.

"How old a friend," she inquired.

"Old enough for me to know better than to introduce him to someone I wouldn't trust him with."

"Meaning?" she asked, arching her eyebrows.

"Let's say we were buddies in the navy and he was enough of a hell-raiser that were I you, I would watch out for him. Or maybe it's that he ought to watch out for you?" Azy said with a cocky grin.

"Happy to meet you, whatever it is that our lawyer friend just said. Because, as usual, it was just twisted enough to make no sense." She offered him a small smile and he gave her one in return telling her that whatever Azy said wasn't true anyway, considering his chosen profession as an attorney.

"Hey, you ladies are finished in there, aren't you?" Azy asked. "Come on out to the porch, we can finish this superior vintage among friends."

"Sure," said Sue. "Thea, I can finish this later since we have unexpected company. Put your towel down." She took the cloth from her hands, laid it across the drying dishes and pulled Anthea by the hand toward the door.

22

Azy and Sue nestled next to each other on the swing while Anthea pulled her feet under her in an oversized deck chair, comfortably upholstered with plush cushions. Mathers leaned against the railing after accepting a glass of wine from his host.

Studying the newcomer, Anthea said, "After your remark, might I be correct in assuming that you and Azy don't share the same occupation?'

"You would, indeed, Miss, uh…"

"Keller, and you can call me Anthea or Thea."

"No way," said Sue. "Thea is reserved for family and I'll let you know when you've met the requirements," she told him with an intimidating glare.

He raised an eyebrow and smiled indulgently at his friends as he conceded.

"Anthea," he finally finished his address to her. "I'm only a school teacher who doesn't dabble in such lofty subjects as the law."

Sue rolled her eyes and leaned out to look across at Anthea. "No, but he enforced enough of them in the past."

"A retired police office, Gary?"

"For a while after leaving the navy. Teaching suits me better. And you?"

"I'm just a worn-out newsmonger."

"You look a little young to be worn-out."

"As they say, 'it's not the years, it's the mileage.'"

"Goodness, Thea," interrupted Sue. "You'd think you were a thousand years old from the way you talk." Looking at Mathers, she added, "Thea's retired from newspaper publishing but she keeps her hand in the business as a press rep for others."

"PR, then," he concluded.

"Yes, along with independent publications and graphics, editorial and the like. I enjoy doing independent work, though the paycheck isn't as regular."

"That seems to be the price of autonomy," he concurred.

"You must be a teacher. It's not often someone actually uses their vocabulary to capacity."

He shrugged his shoulders with a small grin.

"I try."

The conversation continued in an affable atmosphere that moved from professions to the usual local politics and even a smattering of religion since their area was heavily peppered with a variety of churches. Churches that taught everything from polygamy to end times. They managed to keep the discussion objective without touching too much on their personal doctrines. In all, the time sped by rapidly and it was after ten o'clock when Anthea checked the time and finally said that she had to move along.

"I've got an hour's drive back to town, so I'd better say my thank yous and ply the road soon, or I'll never get home."

She turned to Mathers and offered him her hand.

"It was a pleasure meeting you."

"I agree," he said as he held her hand. Taken by the vibrancy of her blue eyes, he had a difficult time relinquishing her gaze.

She turned and gave Azy a hug and let Sue walk her to the car.

"Nice guy, huh?"

"You didn't set this up, did you?" she looked at Sue accusingly.

"Me? Not on your life. Azy, now…that's another story."

Anthea wagged her head in mock disgust. "Does *he* know it's a set-up?"

"Who knows what men think." She gave her a hug and sent her on her way down the mountain.

Chapter 4

Meandering through the aisles at a home improvement center, Anthea stopped in the electrical section. She had to make her decision on which light fixture she preferred for the breakfast room.

Standing with her arms crossed under her bosom, her head tilted back to see the choices, she contemplated the two finalists.

"Having trouble deciding?" The sultry voice next to her ear made her jump. She whipped around to see Gary Mathers standing behind her, a couple of plumbing components in his hands.

Placing her hands on her hips, her eyes flashed dangerously.

"Do you make it a habit of sneaking up on poor, defenseless women who are already cowed by the very thought of entering this male sanctum?"

"Not intentionally," he chuckled lightly. "And I can hardly believe that the redneck crew of home improvement neurotics could ever instill you with fear."

"So far, I've managed to beat them off with a stick. At least, until you materialized."

"Sorry about startling you. I just couldn't pass up the opportunity to say hello." He had a rather beguiling smile that took her more by surprise than the initial words he had spoken in her ear. Loosening up some as a result, she made a good-natured offering.

"It was only because I was concentrating on the two light fixtures. I guess I just blocked out everything else. Bad habit." Noting the items in his grip, she said, "Plumbing problems?"

"Just finishing up some work in the half bath. Getting close to finishing the majority of the house. Though I've been told that a house is never finished. There's always one more project cropping up."

"The joys of home ownership are never-ending," she agreed. "I'm engulfed in a similar undertaking...more light for the breakfast table. Since you're here, what's your opinion." She pointed to the two candidates.

He raised his eyebrows and pulled back defensively.

"You don't seriously think I'm foolish enough to offer an opinion?

I've been trained to know when to shut-up and simply admire the view."

"Ah, you've been married before," she cocked her eye at him playfully.

"Widowed, actually."

"Oh, I didn't mean to appear callous."

"You didn't. I've been on my own for three years now. We all have challenges in life"

"Tell me about it," she halfway muttered under her breath.

"Pardon me?"

"Oh, nothing, really. Changes happen with or without our consent," she offered in contrition.

"Anyway, I hope that I haven't disturbed your concentration with my idle banter."

"Of course not. It was good to see you again." She gave him a shy smile and was almost disappointed when he nodded and turned to go. Then she wagged her head in disgust with herself. *What am I think-ing? This is no time to be getting foggy-brained about a man, even a handsome, respectable, interesting one that sets my hormones on edge. Shut up, will you? You're too old for hormones.* As she watched him turn the corner, he briefly peered over his shoulder, caught her looking and nodded with a self-satisfied smirk that brought her up short, realizing she'd been staring, before he disappeared up another aisle.

•••••••

Pushing her cart into the checkout lane, she inadvertently parked herself in the line next to Mathers as he was just pulling out his wallet. He picked up his bag, and turning to exit saw her in the next queue. Walking over, he made certain that she saw his approach.

"Could you use some help getting that out to your car, ma'am?"

She looked up into the clear gray irises that seemed to be rimmed with gold. Catching his grin, she almost answered him with a negative, but rapidly changing course, she said, "Sure, a little assistance is always welcome."

She turned back to the clerk and paid her bill, then pushing the cart out the door, Mathers walked by her side.

"Where's your rig?"

She nodded to the left. "Over there, the blue Expedition."

His vision followed where she indicated and he recognized the vehicle that had been parked at his friend's the week before. She already had her keys in her hand, having extracted them from her purse before exiting through the sliding doors, and she pressed the button unlocking the doors. Gary went around to the tailgate with her, and placing his own bag in the cart, lifted out the large box and placed it in the truck. She grabbed a smaller bag and deposited it next to the box. She closed the door as Gary picked up his own package. While she pushed the cart to the collection area, he followed her.

"How do you feel about getting a cup of coffee with a virtual stranger?"

"We were introduced properly by trusted friends, so I would hardly classify you as a stranger in that sense," she said.

He raised an eyebrow, and a corner of his mouth curved upward. "So, is that a yes?"

"That is affirmative. I'd enjoy some coffee. Got a place in mind?"

"Right over there, Blackbird Cafe. The espresso's not bad, either."

"Well, you got me. Mocha lattes are my weakness," her smile widened and they dropped off his purchase at his truck on their way across the parking lot.

•••••••

Driving back to the house, Anthea mused over the last hour and a half that she had spent with Gary. The word 'interviewing' cropped up in her head as she tried to describe to herself what had just happened.

Why would I be interviewing him? She just about kicked herself as she was unloading the truck, hoping that she hadn't been as obvious to him as she was to herself. *Jeez, don't I ever learn anything?*

Granted, she found him interesting and personable. And the ultimate factor – he was intelligent. Intelligent males have practically become relics. He was a tad reticent when it came to sharing much of his history, though she got the part about him having served in the navy for six years. Then he spent twenty years on the Portland police force, working some special unit for the last six. He wasn't exactly forthcoming about the nature of the work, though it sounded like it had worn him down enough to go back to school and finish up his master's. He didn't exactly say in what discipline he had his degree, but he mentioned that he had been teaching foreign languages at Multnomah College before he decided to retire to Idaho. From police officer to professor. That takes some doing to make such a complete change in your life.

At least he made his choices. Her own had been pretty much foisted on her throughout the last fifteen years. She still suffered from the abject fear of having absolutely no control over her life. For now, she seemed to be operating under her own power and the thought of involving herself with another human being was definitely out of the question. She had a business to jumpstart so she could finish her own master's thesis. School is expensive and someone has to pay for it. Checking herself in the mirror, she grumbled, "and you're it."

•••••••

She didn't have long to continue pondering the results of her encounter with a Mr. Mathers when a rap on the back door was rapidly followed by the entrance of two young people.

"I guess I can't say, 'don't you ever knock?' when the question is more like, 'don't you ever wait for me to answer the door?' I might not have been dressed." Anthea tried to look stern at the two tall newlyweds framed in the doorway looking not the least bit chagrined.

"We were right behind you driving up and figured you couldn't have stripped that fast," said Lainie, her deep brown, almost black hair swinging side to side as she laughingly negated Anthea's protest with her head. "We did, however, see you having coffee with a real looker at the espresso place." She raised her eyebrows and Cisco nodded his head, a huge grin stamped across his genial features.

"What, were you two dogging me on my errands?'

"Not hardly," put in Cisco. "We just happened to be fillin' up at the gas station when we spotted you and Mr. Slick at the café."

"What kind of a label is that?" Anthea couldn't help but laugh at the big kid's odd assessment of her new acquaintance.

"Well," said Cisco, dropping into a serious tone of voice. "He looked pretty smarted-up, um, sophisticated...you know, slick."

Lainie gave her husband a sidelong look of almost disbelief. Her mouth tweaked at the corner in amusement. Then she caught Anthea's gaze. "I don't know where he gets this stuff, but I thought the guy looked respectable and, let's see, appropriate. Yeah, that's the word, appropriate for you."

"And you could tell all that by looking across the parking lot." Anthea made it a statement while trying to be stern…her features betraying her with a barely controlled smile.

"Hey, we're observant," he said almost defensively.

"And, we want to make sure you don't get tied up with any lowlifes," added Lainie. "somebody's gotta look out for you."

"I didn't know that I was so helpless *and* clueless." By this time, Anthea couldn't hide her pleasure at the couple's interest in her well-being. It had been a long time since anyone had tried to protect her from anything, let alone herself.

"Well, from what you've told us, you haven't exactly been the best judge of men." Lainie cocked her eyebrow.

"No argument there," conceded Anthea. "So, you two twirps could tell exactly what kind of man I was talking to by his clothes?"

"It's more than that," said Cisco. "We learn to judge men by their actions along with their words, and even if we couldn't hear what he was saying, (*thank goodness for that, thought Anthea*) he seemed genuinely interested and a good listener. Also relaxed in his chair, not like he was trying to come on to you in a big way."

"You're right, you *are* observant."

Lainie and Cisco (that's *Franc*isco to his grandmother) Rafael were both raised on the reservation in a world that borrowed from two cultures. On the one hand, they were taught the old ways, learning about how life was in the past, often taking part in the time-honored traditions of the seasonal life – gathering, hunting, celebrations and ceremonies. They were also taught to honor the earth and her gifts. Sometimes this almost seemed to contradict the trappings of modern life, but they and their families had learned to meld the two lifestyles in a way that worked well for them.

Lainie was a student in nursing at the local college, working in the library on the side. Cisco studied in the humanities department pursuing an interest in video production. He had hopes to continue the preservation of his people's culture through the creation of educational documentaries. In the meantime, he put in hours at the ammunition factory down by the river.

The two of them had been married just a few months before and were now occupants of Anthea's guesthouse. They may be renters but it hadn't taken them long to fill the role of family members and Anthea's honorary protectors as well.

"So," Lainie leant forward and bent down a little to look directly in Anthea's eyes, "you like him?"

Taken by surprise, Anthea's face flushed pink. *How can these two babies get right to the meat of things and make a woman* twice *their age blush?*

"I hardly know, dear. I just met him last week."

"Well I think you like him," She said, straightening up. "But we'll keep an eye on this guy all the same."

"And on you," threw in Cisco as they hugged Anthea and headed over to their own place.

•••••••

Gary deposited his goods on the kitchen counter and decided he wasn't in the mood to mess with finishing plumbing the sink in the powder room. He'll get to it tomorrow. Instead, he went to the fridge and grabbed a beer, popped the cap with an opener and plunked down on one of the Adirondack chairs he had on the back deck.

Taking a mouthful, he watched the water foam over the rocks in the riverbed below. There wasn't anything else more soothing to his ears, other than the sound of the surf on a rocky shore. Although he missed the Oregon coast, he also knew that he had done the right thing in selling the house after Maddy died. His wife, Madeline, had so loved that place that he simply couldn't stay there after she was gone. He saw her in every room, under every tree and even walking on the shingle after a storm had stirred up the seaweed and left driftwood strewn along the shoreline. It was her passion to go sifting through the flotsam that would wash up after a good blow.

No, he did the right thing coming here and building this place. It was time to start over. He'd been mourning too long. So, what was he doing now? Sitting on the deck, pitying himself, that's what. No more. He was starting that book he used to tell Maddy he was going to write. And he actually had more than half of the outline finished. Who knew you had to practically write a book to write a book. He'd finish it. He'd managed to finish these other stages in his life and he certainly wasn't old enough to throw in the towel. They keep telling you life begins at fifty. Well, hell, he sure hoped so.

He took another swig off his beer and thought about the woman with whom he'd just spent the afternoon. Looking into those shockingly blue eyes definitely made him realize that he wasn't too old, not yet. Unless, of course, she disagreed with that 'life begins at fifty' business, because she hadn't caught up with him. He was guessing at her age as being ten or more years his junior, but don't women like distinguished, older gentlemen? *Man, don't start fooling yourself.*

He finished the beer, stood up and leaned out over the railing, watching the sun sink behind the hills, painting the horizon with brilliant splashes of color that mellowed to softer tones as the day melded into dusk.

Land Barons

Chapter 5

Gary was just finishing tightening down the connectors underneath the sink in the powder room. He gave the pipe wrench one last tug and crawled back out, making certain not to bump his head as he stood up. Thinking that if he had just hired a real plumber to handle the project, he would have saved himself the sore back, not to mention the headache from the last time when he hadn't been so careful and had practically knocked himself unconscious.

Rubbing his lower back with one hand, he replaced his tools in the box and carried it back to the workbench in the garage.

Well, at least it's done. He went back into the bathroom to straighten up and wash his hands. Drying his hands on his pants because he didn't want to mess with changing the guest towels, he went into the kitchen to figure out what else he should do today. It was already past noon and he'd worked straight through the morning. He opened the refrigerator and put together a quick sandwich to assuage the hunger growling in his belly.

While chewing his lunch, he promptly decided against any more physical labor and he quickly relegated the idea of writing to the 'I don't feel creative' file. That left going to town, where he didn't need anything, or taking off into the countryside for a little "R and R."

The last idea got his vote, and since it was the only one that counted, he won the election. He looked at his semi-grungy jeans, figured they were just the thing for dirt trails and went into the garage to grab his gloves and brought his ATV out onto the driveway.

Climbing on, he fired up the engine and headed up the road to his closest neighbor's house, the Stablers.

Len Stabler had told him to come on up and visit anytime. He also said that he was free to use his road across the property as an easement to the national forest land that backed his farm.

Gary determined that poking around in the woods would be cathartic after grubbing around under a wet bathroom basin. At least all the other fixtures had already been installed and he had no need to mess with the toilet. So, he passed his neighbor's mailbox, which had an old fashioned, horse-drawn plow artistically arranged next to it. He had thought that a nice touch. It brought attention to their station as custodians of the land.

The house had been built almost half a mile up the long drive and wasn't visible from the road, and Gary drove past the main drive to the back easement that went directly past the dairy barn and an old corral. As he rounded the low hill, he was surprised to see that the barn and outbuildings had a couple of large semis parked next to them and they were methodically being dismantled.

He pulled up into the construction site (or 'destruction' site as it appeared to him) and got off his vehicle. He approached one of the workers to inquire what was going on when some fella came up to him and told him he was trespassing, making sure his wording was rude and uncompromising. Gary looked at him quizzically and told the guy that he had permission from the owners to use this access at any time.

"Not anymore, pal. Not since the new management took over."

"What, a new owner? I didn't hear anything about it," protested Gary.

"I can't help what your friends don't tell ya, but the Nature's Wilds Conservancy owns this now and you're trespassing. So, turn your tail around and drive right back down that road before we have you arrested," he angrily pointed back down the hill.

"How long have you guys been here?"

"Don't matter to you. Just get out of here before I call the sheriff," huffed Hothead, as Gary mentally tagged him.

Gary got back on his four-wheeler and said, "Sure, don't get so riled. It was just an honest mistake." He roared back down the hill, wondering what the hell happened to the Stablers. He knew that Mary was really ill and apparently getting worse. Why would they leave at a time like this when she probably needed to be home and surrounded by family? He obviously wasn't going to get any answers this way.

•••••••

Arriving home after having been chased off the Stabler's family farm, Gary left his ATV in the garage and went into the house. He went to the stack of old newspapers he'd left piled up from this last week and started rummaging through them looking for anything regarding the family's departure. Nothing.

This is a small town, how could the fact that a large organization like this, what was it? Right, the Nature's Wilds Conservancy. How could it get past the local news staff that this 'conservancy' bought up one of the area's oldest homesteads without a peep? Len Stabler farmed more than 3,500 acres, which was a pretty fair-sized parcel. The thing about Len, though, was that he was tied to the land by heritage. Gary remembered him recounting the family history of more than 90 years on the property. Sitting at the table, elbows on the wood planks in front of him, he ran his hands through his hair and massaged his temples, thinking about his neighbor and how hard it must have been to give up that place and wondering what the circumstances were that could force such a tough decision.

He looked at his watch: 6:30. Figuring that the salvage crew was probably about ready to close-up operations at the farm, he went back out to the garage and rolled out his dirt bike. He wanted to go back over there and see what had been done to the place. In his mind, there was something going on that just didn't seem kosher. Maybe he had spent too many years behind a badge to take Hothead's demands to vacate the property at face value. Why the hostility? There was no call for that kind of reception. So, what else could he do but go back to the property, of course.

He hopped on his bike and went back up the road. Not as enthralled with noise as so many other off-road enthusiasts, he had made some effort to muffle the usual deafening roar of most bikes. He liked the idea that he could motor through the countryside without utterly destroying his own peace of mind by ravaging his hearing along with that of his neighbors. Not to say that the bike was quiet, but he had certainly been able to lessen the impact of the decibels it produced.

Driving out to the main entry of the farm, he turned at the old plow to go up to the house. He wanted to take a look at the status of the farmhouse, which was almost 100 years old and one of the first homes built in the region. He supposed that, at the least, the conservancy would restore it to its original state and have it registered as a historic landmark.

As he rounded the bend, leaving the stand of trees, he saw that there was nothing. The house was gone and so was the old hay barn.

No outbuildings. No pumphouse. Nothing was left aside from the lone shade tree spreading its branches over the vanished porch. They had demolished everything. As he approached, he realized that they had cleaned up the place so that only the old river rock foundation was left. Even the basement had been backfilled, the ring of smooth, water-worn stone all that remained at the site.

Looking off to the right, he saw a fifth wheel stationed by the group of maples providing a cool overhang for the temporary housing. While Gary was idling by the edge of the foundation, because even the stone walkway to the front door had been removed, the door of the camper opened and Gary recognized Hothead as he descended the steps, laughing loudly with someone inside.

Before Gary could decide what to do, the bull-necked foreman twisted around on the bottom rung, preparing to step down, and look-ing up, he caught sight of Gary across the few hundred yard distance. He yelled in Gary's direction, face mottling red in anger. Calling back over his shoulder to the fifth wheel's interior, he reached behind to grab something that his buddy inside handed him. Swiftly bringing the long object to eye level and taking aim, Gary realized the guy had a rifle. Mired in place by shock, he heard the gunfire and felt the draught of the bullet as it whizzed by his ear. Wasting no time, he gunned the engine and took off in the most convenient direction, which was up the farm road toward the forest.

A quick check over his shoulder proved that Hothead had com-mandeered the truck that was standing by the camper. His compatriot at the wheel, Hothead leaned out of the window, gun barrel trained on the fleeing figure ahead, shouting epithets as they furiously pursued their quarry.

Who the hell is this guy? At this point, Gary was berating himself for even venturing onto the property. He didn't know what he thought he would discover, because all he found out was that the Stablers were gone and so was their home. For this he gets chased by some crazy-ass construction worker.

As he sped up the road, kicking up a plume of dust, the litany of 'curiosity killed the cat' kept rolling around his brain. It was another half-mile from the cover of the trees and the truck wasn't far behind so he opened the throttle and shot into the thick, green shadows.

Knowing that the bike had the advantage on smaller roads, he kept his eyes open for a chance to break away from the main route. Finally, rounding a bend, he saw his chance to increase his lead as he neared a firebreak that crossed the gravel surface he was following.

He braked as he made the sharp turn, skidding and nearly losing his balance. As Gary hauled out, the width of the road dwindled further until it became little more than a four-wheel track. The truck was losing ground, but that didn't keep Hothead from taking a few potshots out the window. Gary, who was familiar with these woods, having driven through there often during the last year, made a quick right onto an even narrower trail and headed across a field that stretched for no more than a few acres. The truck couldn't negotiate the turn and had to back up and make another stab at it before following Gary across the meadow.

Peering back at his pursuers, he saw that the distance was closing between them. As he approached the edge of the wood, another shot whistled past his arm and he whipped the bike around on a sharp curve, heading through the trees. The trail had become too narrow for the truck to follow and they were forced to stop before they plowed into one of the pines.

Sliding through the soft dirt, Gary managed to get himself back onto a wider fire road and, giving his bike more power, made his escape as fast as possible.

•••••••

Back on the main road with the sky darkening in the west, Gary slowed down, trying to calm his heartbeat as he headed back to his house.

Damn, I am definitely too old to be horsing around with a couple of demented miscreants on my ass. Trying to kill me, no less.

The homicidal wrecking crew were lost in the trees and had no clue where he had come from, so he just drove home, pulled into his drive and put the bike away while trying to even out his breathing.

Maybe I ought to get a paper bag to stop hyperventilating like some frightened old biddy.

Stripping off his riding gloves he flopped into a high backed chair and put his head between his knees. Thinking that the reaction of these clowns was way out of proportion to the infraction, he was stymied as to what the reason could be. *Maybe there is none, and these yahoos just get their jollies shooting firearms at innocent trespassers.* Of course, he'd been too many years in law enforcement to believe that, which meant that there was something fishy about the operations of this land protection agency. Tomorrow he would do some research on Nature's Wilds Conservancy.

Chapter 6

It had taken Gary quite a while to wind down and catch a few hours of sleep, so he was surprised to find himself waking when the sun had already climbed a ways above the horizon.

Nothing like a little adrenaline to keep you up at night.

Taking in the crisp sunlight of what was rapidly becoming a warm day, he decided against making coffee, showered, dressed and went straight into town.

He pulled up in front of the Marcasite Mercantile, angling the truck into a space next to those of the 'coffee klatch' who he knew would be locked in conversation at the morning mecca on the corner. Since he had a few items to purchase in order to finish an outdoor project, he decided to get them first and see if he couldn't obtain a little news in the process.

The mercantile was one of those all-purpose hardware-cum-gift shops that are often found in small communities where the residents make the trip into the larger population centers as rarely as they can manage. The entrance opened onto handcrafted wood products that included everything from lawn ornaments to Christmas ornaments, depending on the season. The aisles were stocked with house paint, cooking utensils, personal espresso makers, plush toys and lawn mowers, even an occasional kitchen sink.

At this mid-morning hour, the store wasn't particularly busy and it didn't take him long to find the section he needed. Picking out a couple of hose connectors and examining their stock of lawn care products, he carried what he needed to the wide check-out counter, behind which the owner seemed ensconced in a voluminous desk chair.

Ginny, a diminutive woman with a wild cap of unruly red hair that she had carelessly drawn into a clip at the back of her head, was rapidly working the calculator as Gary walked up to the register. She peered up at him and said it'd be just a minute.

When she climbed out of the chair and came over to stand behind the counter, she greeted him, smiling.

"Sorry, but if I walk away from anything that involves numbers,

39

I'll lose my place and then I'll end up thinking I either found a fortune or lost one in the middle of my ciphering. And you know you can't trust the banks to get it straight."

"I suppose I'd be more apt to hire a bookkeeper than struggle through mathematic gyrations," he offered pleasantly. "So, how else is life treating you besides giving you fits over the accounts?"

"Fine, I guess. Haven't seen you in a bit. You been holed up working at the house?"

"Nope. I drove over to Portland to visit with my daughter and the new grandbaby…and her husband, of course," he threw in.

"It's okay to forget about the grown-ups once the little ones start coming along," she offered in a way of excuse. "How many you got?"

"This is the first one, so I couldn't miss the opportunity. Besides, if granddad hadn't shown up, I'd never hear the end of it. She's just a month old now."

"That's terrific. Nothing like family to keep you on track."

"You bet. Speaking of which, Ginny, I was just up at the Stabler's yesterday and everything is gone. I know I was out of town for a couple of weeks but the whole homestead was torn down," he tilted his head to catch her eye. "What happened?"

"I'm surprised you didn't hear about it. Though you're right, it happened fast," she scrunched up her forehead in concern as she talked. "You know they've had crop failures for something like three years and they'd had to mortgage the farm just to keep it going. It might've worked if Mary hadn't've come down sick like she did."

"Do you know what the problem is, why she's ill, I mean?"

"No, that's the trouble. The doctors haven't been able to pinpoint anything and she's just going downhill." She drew in a deep breath and exhaled slowly. "Mary's such a great gal, I can't believe they can't help her." She looked up at him again. "The medical bills have just beat them practically into bankruptcy and when this environmental group came back to see if they'd sell, well, Len finally threw in the towel."

Gary looked at her with a renewed interest. "What do you mean they 'came back'?"

"Seems they'd tried to purchase the land a couple years ago, but Len wasn't about to sell the family farm. I mean that was their whole life. So, he tried the mortgage angle, but that just wasn't going to do the trick after Mary started failing." She sighed again. "I just hate to see them giving up everything and moving. They had no choice, though, and now this land conservation group has taken it over."

She caught his gaze again. "I wish we could've been able to help. This town's small enough as it is without having to see some of our history destroyed. And I gather from what you said, that that's exactly what's happening." Ginny crossed her arms and harumphed at nobody in particular.

"Yeah, they definitely revamped the landscape at the farm, because everything has been dismantled, from what I could see. And they weren't exactly happy about my dropping by to watch the demolition. In fact, I was chased off in a very no-nonsense manner."

Picking up his parcel, he thanked Ginny for her time.

"See you soon. Don't get too bogged down by the numbers," he threw over his shoulder as he exited the store. He deposited his purchases in the front seat of the truck before heading to his next stop on his information gathering mission - the Miner's Gap Café.

•••••••

Poking his head in the door, Gary was welcomed by the genial discussion ongoing among the occupants of a long table. 'The boys,' as they referred to themselves, were deeply involved in a debate on the changes supposedly being implemented regarding the Roadless Act. The executive order had been enforced by the previous federal administration and was something that placed national forest land into a limbo that diminished public access by letting some current roads deteriorate and, in some areas, the forest service was restoring the natural habitat by actually removing access routes. It was a hot topic as the current administration had reversed the decision that allowed state governments to challenge current policy in an effort to regain access to thousands of wilderness acres that had been placed off-limits just a few years before. And now, some federal judge in San Francisco was trying to block the current executive decision.

"The policy is just that, a policy," according to Don Lucas, an electrical contractor and current town council member who was sitting at the head of the table. "Anything the state wants to do on their land," he said, "still has to pass the approval of the flippin' forest service,"

41

which he bluntly interpreted to mean that any request will be stamped 'denied.'

One of the other men at the table contributed his take on the executive order controversy. "It seems to me that a judge can't decide she likes one executive order better than another, particularly when the last one overrides the first. Doesn't the judge have to cite legal precedent that negates the whole idea of executive orders? Otherwise it's just a matter of preference, which isn't a legal decision, it's political opinion."

"You know, with the environmentalists challenging everything in court," Lucas declared, "the whole thing is a damn mess. But I guess that's what they want…to pull industry to a grinding halt."

Lucas was big, with a heavy shouldered frame and a florid complexion. He had thinning gray hair cut short and neatly combed back from his temples. A native of Marcasite and an outdoor enthusiast, as many of the residents, he shared the opinion of much of the local populace. There were a few liberals from back east and the left coast who had relocated to the area for its noted scenic beauty, but, on the whole, their ultra-environmentally motivated politics were shared by few other than transplants. The locals weren't particularly sympathetic to the eco-political agenda of some of them. As they saw it, the reason these folks moved out here to enjoy the continued heritage of natural splendor was due to the legacy of proper land management by local ranchers, farmers, tribal government and other longtime residents. Lucas and his chums were adamant supporters of the adage that you don't fix what ain't broke. On the whole, Gary agreed with them and didn't hold with the attitude that a few of the super-environmentally oriented newcomers brought to the community. It brought to mind the bumper sticker from the 70's he used to see in his home state – "Don't Californicate Oregon" – which he felt was a harbinger of the future, and one that came to pass.

Closing the door behind him, the boys centered their attention on Gary and broke into friendly hellos from their seats, tabling the conversation to greet a neighbor. Gary extended his hand to a number of the men to shake and good-naturedly pat a few shoulders while they offered tidbits of non-essential personal data. Asking after his well-being, he gave a brief history of his trip to the city for the family to recognize his proud, new status as grandfather. He received a few more back slaps as a sign of approval and was invited to pull up a chair.

Grabbing a chair from one of the tables nearby, he flipped it around, found the niche they had just created and slid onto the seat.

As he was lowering himself onto the seat, the owner, Pat, her dark hair pulled back in a bun at the nape of her neck, came out of the kitchen with a fresh pot of coffee and an extra cup. After setting the mug in front of Gary and filling it, she made it around the table with warm-ups while she took his order. As most of the boys had already eaten, he kept the request simple, which she committed to memory and then called through the window to the fry cook on her way to the counter.

Settling into the pleasant banter with his tablemates, Gary mentioned that he had driven up to the Stabler place and was ungraciously received by the current occupants. Although he didn't go into detail about his second encounter with the encamped ruffians, he plied his companions for any knowledge they might have of the Nature's Wilds Conservancy.

Tom Sparrow, Ginny's husband, who was always AWOL from the store two or three days a week at this hour, piped up with his general opinion that this conservancy group was invading the community.

"This isn't the first time they've moved in on the area. I hear that they purchased a pretty big ranch further upriver and were quick as rabbits to make it off-limits," he huffed.

"I don't know what their agenda is but I heard they've been checking into some adjoining properties in the area, not that anyone is interested in selling. It was pretty much a quirk that finally pushed Len into the market," said Lucas. "He told me last year that he had no intention of letting his family farm go to the auction block."

"Well, we know that sometimes we get backed into a corner," added Nate Garrity, the retired solicitor who had turned his practice over to a young attorney from Boise. "No one knows what the future holds and Len and Mary ended up in a precarious financial bind, what with her sudden decline in health and all."

"So, what do you really know about the conservancy," asked Gary.

"Not much," said Tom. "They just showed up on Len's doorstep a while back, looking to buy him out. And then we'd heard about that other, what was it six or eight thousand acres? I don't even remember.

Might've been less."

"There ain't much to know," Lucas said flatly. "They just appeared and I'd be happy if they'd disappear."

Gary finished his coffee and as the rest of his compatriots were readying to depart for their various businesses, he settled his bill with Pat and took his leave.

Opening the cab door of his truck, he decided he wasn't satisfied with the tidbits the boys could offer, so, curiosity getting the better of him and having no other pressing duties, he plotted his route down river and to town.

•••••••

Winding along the river, he noticed two boats lazily drifting along in the center of the stream. The occupants of one were passing some items to the couple in the other craft. He assumed it was some soft drink or beer as they slid past each other and slowly continued following the current at a dreamy pace.

Nice way to spend a relaxing afternoon...Friends, a little sun - shine...

He couldn't watch them but for fleeting intervals as he rounded the bend, the road demanding his attention as he came upon the next curve. Leaving the boaters to their diversion, he brought his concentration back to the highway and making it into town while he'd still have some time at the library.

He crossed the river and went to the city library where there were usually computer stations available, though that wasn't guaranteed now that school was out for the day. He was in luck, however. When he checked in at the desk, there were three unoccupied cubicles so he was able to commandeer one immediately.

As he sat down to log-on he thought that he probably could have done this on his own computer at home. The idea of waiting forever through what always seemed to be an interminable search on his own system just wasn't palatable. *The price of gas be damned.* His drive seemed justified when the machine swiftly led him through cyberspace to the Nature's Wilds Conservancy website without the exasperation that was inevitable on his own obsolete collection of mismatched components.

44

Scrolling through pages of scenic photos depicting the harsh, dramatic beauty of pristine wilderness that had come under the sway of the conservancy over the previous decade, he was astounded at the vast amount of acreage the organization controlled. He made note of the states listed that hosted land holdings now belonging to Nature's Wilds. California, Montana, Idaho, Washington, Oregon, Colorado, Utah, Arizona, Nevada and New Mexico. The story describing how the environmental group was started barely made mention of how it received its funding, which to Gary's mind must have been enormous considering its area of dominion. Although there was a map of the western United States, it didn't designate the actual regions where the conservancy owned land, nor did it indicate the size of the properties. The copy only listed the states, briefly mentioning the whereabouts of holdings while stressing the importance of maintaining ecosystems with exceptionally long diatribes that dripped insincere devotion to saving the earth's wonders.

Who writes this sappy junk? It reads like high school student essays on 'why we should honor mother earth.' The only other information he could glean was the fact that purchases were pending in Wyoming, to save the already abundant antelope, Mississippi and Minnesota. *I guess they need to protect the mosquito population, too.*

With those unflattering thoughts foremost in his mind, for which he chastised himself, although briefly, over the fact that these guys are very likely as committed as they sound, he logged off.

He had found previously that most newspapers didn't allow you to read their archives without first purchasing a password. As he wasn't interested in getting tied into a number of publications just for this search, he thought of the next best thing, which he knew was the other reason he had driven all the way to town. He would call Anthea Keller for advice and maybe a little assistance. She was a journalist, after all.

He went to the desk and asked to use a phone book, since he didn't have her number. Looking up Keller in the Paradise Valley listings, which luckily was alphabetical and not sectioned by communities, he found that her name wasn't there. Right, he thought, she said she had just moved in. She wouldn't be in this year's book. So he did the next best thing…he called Sue.

When she answered the phone, pleased as she was to speak with him, she still gave him the third degree. He should have known it wouldn't be easy wrangling a number out of Mama Sue, the protector of all her single women friends. She practically asked him if his intentions were honorable, when he slid the information in that he was hoping for her help with a little news research. Having assuaged her need to know, she gave him Anthea's number. Glibly ending the call with a bright "tell her hello," she hung up.

By this time, he was sweating. For having dealt with the criminal element and their unscrupulous advocates for so many years, Sue could be a far more intimidating adversary.

•••••••

He dialed the number, and after taking a few deep breaths, was better prepared to speak.

Anthea answered the call within four rings, using the name of her PR business, Storyline, in her greeting.

"Hello, Anthea? This is Gary Mathers," he began.

"Hey there, Gary. What can I do for you?"

"I've encountered a little bit of a puzzle and remembering what you had said about your history in journalism, I immediately thought of you for help," he said. "Did you ever do much investigative work?"

"Not really. Aside from the mundane story about municipal financing or political contests, most of the "investigation" meant interviewing involved parties," she explained. "No Pulitzer Prizes on my mantle, I'm afraid."

"You were simply overlooked by the nominating committee, I'm sure. Besides, all I need is a little assistance with some basic research. Would you be interested in discussing it over dinner? I'd like your opinion on my hunches before I make any moves," trying to make the invitation as innocuous as possible he realized the double entendre after he made the gaffe, and nearly groaned.

Trying for a comeback that wasn't awkward, she simply said, "That would be fine. I don't have anything pressing right now so, what did you have in mind?"

Practically breathing a sigh of relief, he suggested the restaurant down at the marina.

"Great. I like that place. Meet you there at what, seven?" she suggested.

"Sounds good. I'll see you there."

•••••••

When Anthea walked into the waiting area of the landing, she saw Mathers' strong profile against the sun, which was still delivering heat with more than an hour remaining before sunset. His dark hair seemed shadowed against the sunlit streaks of gray that salted thick locks trimmed neatly at the nape. He turned to catch her observing him and walking toward her, clasped her hand, saying, "Thank you for coming on such short notice."

"I certainly had no better offer for this evening. Watching "Hatari" for the 80th time wasn't as enticing a prospect."

"You like John Wayne?" His eyes widened in surprise. "Most women prefer Leonardo di Caprio or Jude Law."

"I guess I like the old movies and heroes and heroines with some character. Besides, Leo is too young for me. Sophistication and bravado ranks higher above nouveau Hollywood action, any day."

"I'm pretty much in agreement though I'll pay my few bucks for a little action now and again."

She looked at him with an amused smile and was curious to see him turn slightly red. She couldn't remember the last time she'd seen a man blush, though if he was flustered at his faux pas, he brushed past it with enviable ease.

"Shall we get seated?" he asked. "How about on the patio since it's so comfortable outside."

"I'd like that."

The hostess brought them to a table overlooking the slips where pleasure boats, fishing craft and houseboats were moored. A line of seadoos marched down one pier with a couple of jet boats tied up next to them, all belonging to a daily rental business.

The view offered a wide panorama of the Snake River stretching west between the deepening shadows of the broad cliffs. The hills tumbling down from the plateau were still green this time of year, but the grasses would soon turn brown as the rain tapered off into summer drought.

Ordering beverages, Anthea leaned forward in her chair, arms crossed on the table, and asked what 'hunch' was leading him to delve into research.

He decided that he ought to start with an abbreviated narration of his discovery at the neighbor's farm, how he hadn't been out of touch but a couple of weeks and they had sold off the property, packed up and left.

"What's so odd about that?" she asked, not seeing anything particularly sinister in the occurrences.

"Nothing, except that Len wouldn't sell his home unless he was under duress and after my experience with Hothead, the whole episode seemed forced and unnatural," he explained.

"And who is 'Hothead?'"

"I was going to bypass this part of the story, but it really is the kicker for my intuitive feeling on this whole thing," he added. "When I went over there a second time, after being invited to leave earlier in the day with a good dose of hostility and threats, and saw that the house and barn had been demolished, 'Hothead,' though I can think of a better epithet that'd fit his foul temperament, felt impelled to chase me off the property with a rifle…which he discharged in my direction a number of times."

Trying hard not to let her features display the shock that swept over her, Anthea clamped her jaw shut and just stared at him for a minute.

"I'd say that the incident would increase my curiosity a tad, as well," she finally said. "Looks like 'Hothead' doesn't think with his."

"Frankly, I'm just very happy that he isn't any better a marksman," Gary stated somberly. His face changing into a sly smile, "Otherwise, I wouldn't have had this opportunity for an evening in your company."

"No, I'm guessing that you'd be keeping company with the now defunct homestead," she said with a tinge of anger. "Why did you go back there after the guy had previously threatened you, anyway?"

"I wouldn't say that it was the most intelligent move on my part," he offered somewhat contritely. "Anyway, I want to know who these jokers are. Why on earth would they fire a gun at a simple bystander, trespassing or not? So far as I know, it's not hunting season."

"It does seem odd and a little intriguing. Tell me what you know."

He described what he had found on the Nature's Wilds website, detailing the photo journal of properties and the lame editorial content about their mission.

"There was hardly anything about their history, not even a list of the board of directors. Seems to me that most non-profits are proud of their personnel and even list e-mail addresses so visitors to the website can get more involved. The information was slim and really inadequate." He looked a little frustrated. "Do you have any idea where to look for more background on this environmental group?"

"I've got a few ideas." She brightened. "Hungry?" She indicated the waitress who was bringing their meal.

"Actually, I am. Tell me what you think after the entrée, yes?"

"Sure, we have plenty of time," she said as she laid her napkin across her lap.

Land Barons

Chapter 7

The dinner conversation sent her into investigative mode, well at least as far as the internet was concerned. When she got home she plugged into a search engine with the Nature's Wilds headline to see what would pop-up. She was expecting that with what Mathers had said about their presence in so many states, there would be a long list of references. However this wasn't the case. Her search came up with only a few mentions, and those were to specific holdings that were open to the public. There weren't even many references to news stories about the organization over the past decade, and what she did find was vague and uninteresting.

Odd that they would purchase this amount of acreage all over the west and not even make it accessible to the public they are purported - ly serving. Talk about flying under the radar.

Bringing up each website, she pored through what little information was reposited in each. There was the initial website that Mathers had found, which she saw was much as he had described it. *Boring.* Then she went to the others individually. They took the net surfer on a visual tour of the land via a barrage of photos and the few amenities each offered for the tourist. That seemed to consist of little more than a visitor center, some which were bare bones, and a few well-developed hiking trails. One site in New Mexico had campground facilities.

Other than that, she was at a loss to see what purpose the foundation served. They went into rural areas and bought up property that, in many instances, appeared to be situated adjacent to national forest land. It looked like they didn't develop it for public use or even for educational tours. They didn't even tout their intent to preserve the land in its pristine condition.

Their general purpose seemed to be acquisition, though they didn't say that in their hype. What they did say was that they were overseeing the land for posterity. *Who's posterity?*

The only numbers she could find were in regard to the one property that had built a campground and had some RV hook-ups. That property, they wrote, had been improved with the help of two other funding non-profits. One was tied to Grigor Scirras, a Romanian multi-billionaire who turned his weapons trade money over to liberal causes, and the other to a few Hollywood benefactors who cut albums warbling about the evils of modern society. A fair chunk of money was sunk into this one project however, in that it totaled over a hundred million for the purchase and development of the parcel. *Not that they developed much of it...twenty acres out of 225,000?*

This pretty much covered what was easily available. She guessed they had their reasons for not being any more specific and she began to think Mathers had a solid hunch about Nature's Wilds even if it hadn't been driven home by gunshots.

•••••••

Next morning she called Gary to give him the results of her nocturnal browsing.

"Not much in plain view, is there?" he said as he sipped his coffee, holding the phone to his ear with his shoulder.

"Afraid not. Of course that doesn't mean there aren't records. That would take quite a bit more digging to locate the counties where they've purchased property and hunt up the transfer papers or recorded deeds. Those won't give you amounts paid for the land, just who they were purchased from. But you've got to have some idea of where to look first. You know what they say, 'location, location, location.' And I've got a feeling that is what this is about. No evidence, just one of your run-of-the-mill hunches."

"All I can say is you'd better watch your hunches better than I did...might get you into trouble," he offered sagely.

She laughed. "Ah, the voice of experience. What do you want to do with this fairly worthless sheaf of papers?"

"Look through them," he hesitated, "maybe it'll give me an idea."

"I'd say you need to be careful when implementing your ideas, they could be hazardous to life and limb."

"I still think it's worth following up." He stopped to think. "Hey, do you want to come on out here? I'll show you around, give you the grand tour of Marcasite, the wonderland of North Central Idaho. Maybe get some insight into what the big draw is." A note of optimism rang in his voice.

"That's not such a bad idea. I don't have anything pressing today if you're free to act as a guide."

"That would suit my schedule fine," he said, finishing the call by giving her directions and setting a time.

•••••••

Deciding that most of their probing would probably be benign, Anthea let her mind wander while she drove to the turn-off. Leaving U.S. 12, she crossed the bridge and headed north on SR 4, passing through the Marcasite County seat, which wasn't Marcasite, but the larger town of Lathrop. The town was laid out horizontally along the river, with Main Street situated two blocks north of the banks, running in the same direction.

She passed the downtown area, which stretched for some eight blocks. Considering the metropolis was home to less than 3,000 residents, the business district was fairly impressive, housing three banks, a courthouse, sheriff's station, refurbished hotel circa 1840 and a number of cafes and bars. It even hosted two higher-end restaurants, enticing travelers and locals alike.

Continuing up the route, which followed the course of the Marcasite River, she passed one of the two local supermarkets and fringe businesses that lined the highway. The road narrowed as it began a slow climb up the straight valley, hugging the waterway on the right. A deepening forest of pine and fir clung to the hills on either side of the road, giving the impression that you were leaving civilization behind.

Just when she thought she was at the edge of the wilderness, the road curved into a widening valley, whose walls gently rolled toward the rushing water which was still coming into the full flood stage. An old wrecking yard straddled a few acres on the left and as she slowed with the reduced speed signs, the hamlet of Marcasite spread before her, covering all of three blocks fronting the highway.

She spotted the Miner's Gap right away on the left side of the street, noting Mather's truck parked obliquely, next to rigs of varied age and disrepair. *You can always tell the newbies, fancy new rigs that haven't been worn out by years of backroad travel. I guess I'll fit right in.*

53

With that thought she pulled into an open spot across the street from the restaurant, reached for the puny file of internet data, though the few sheets rendered it almost ludicrous to pluralize the term describing it's contents. Standing on the running board, she grabbed her purse, then stepped down and turned to close the door, deciding not to bother locking the car, noting that the SUV next to her was left running while the operator ran some errand.

She jaywalked to the café and entered through the open door. *Mmm, the smell of fried food and weak coffee.* She'd never been able to figure out why, in the center of espresso crazed road warriors, all the local cafes served coffee the consistency of muddy water. *I can suffer through one cup.*

Mathers had seen her arrive and was walking over to greet her as she came into the shop, which was quite busy during the lunch hour. He gestured over to the booth he'd been occupying and inquired about the drive.

"Not bad, little traffic and not as long as I'd anticipated," she answered agreeably. "I don't know why I thought this was further out. Travel time wasn't more than 35 minutes."

"Generally speaking, it doesn't take as long to get to places as some folks think. At least you're covering the mileage as opposed to the city where you might travel 10 miles in the same amount of time…or less," his affable tone relaxing her.

"I brought what little I downloaded, and I mean little. These guys either don't do much or want you to think that they are basically harmless and, well, don't do much. That is, aside from collect acres and acres, and acres, of prime real estate."

"That's why you're here today," his eyes emanating warmth despite their clear, cool color. "To show you just how superior this region is."

"I'm looking forward to the tour," she replied with a drop of hesitancy.

•••••••

They sipped their bland coffee, 'tasteless' was the word that came to Anthea's mind, and went over the few printouts she'd brought.

"You can see that they keep their financing under tight guard," she said. "It's not like it isn't available. In order for them to keep their non-profit status they must file with the IRS and the records can be accessed because it's an organization registered for public benefit. At least, that's what they want people to believe, although what it is they do that's advantageous for the likes of you and me is debatable." She looked across the table at him. "Anyway, it certainly isn't clear."

"All I could see that Nature's Wilds is about is hoarding real estate like someone would stockpile wood for a long winter," observed Mathers. "It obviously makes sense to *them* but we're not in the loop."

As they bent over a page that had the few numbers that had been revealed at one of the websites, Anthea pointed out a couple of allusions she'd missed.

"Let's see, I didn't pick up on this last night, not that it means much, but here," she placed her finger on the page, "major donors besides Scirras and EarthClear, that rock and roll backed environmental group, includes this Carl Chamberlain who has apparently taken a personal interest."

"Isn't he the other Bill Gates?"

"Not quite." She elucidated, "he's more like Disney and Microsoft rolled into one. You know, digital entertainment for the whole family. Solis Industries."

"I've heard his name but hadn't made the connection." He shrugged his shoulders, "so, fire me...oh wait, no, that's another real estate-cum-entertainment mogul."

She caught him in his meager joke, which evoked a brief grimace of pain.

"I rather agree. Bad, bad joke," said Mathers as he leaned back in his seat and looked up at the ceiling. "You know, ever since my daughter got pregnant I've been checking out the new toys and games for kids." He brought his eyes down to look at her. "Have you seen some of the video games and animated movies clogging the shelves at the department stores? The really scary ones are produced by, guess who?"

"Solis?" she raised her gaze to meet his, curious as to where he was going with this train of thought and what it had to do with environmentalism. "And what do you mean 'scary?'"

"Well, most of them are centered around how humanity is destroying the earth. Basically, they're using cute cartoons to scare the hell out of kids by having them see tornadoes and hurricanes tear up the countryside, telling them all the while that people are responsible for the destruction and practically have to live like cavemen in order to save the world. They even throw in earthquakes and volcanoes erupting. What could humanity possibly have to do with a natural force of that kind? That one's ludicrous but the games are worse."

"How can they be worse than that?" She'd seen something alluding to this on television, but she didn't watch TV much and hadn't followed up on it.

"Let's see. There's one that follows a native African child as he encounters all these fierce demons of global warming like glaciers melting to flood cities, massive icebergs breaking off Antarctica and smashing into ships, howling windstorms in the desert engulfing whole tribes of Bedouins. And, get this, the poor little boy carries the onus of the disasters on his shoulders. There are all these *weapons* that he can use to defeat the evildoers causing the problem, and *those* are, of course, characterizations of monstrous SUV's, filthy factories, rednecks on snowmobiles…that kind of thing. It's unconscionable to make little children feel like they are responsible for saving the world or that they even have any control over events."

"Particularly when what these guys are promoting is based on arguable research, and the validity of their findings is being hotly debated every day. I remember when we were all going to die in the looming ice age they were touting in the 70's. Even if they have a solid case, you don't frighten children with death and destruction." She thought back a little. "I remember the first time I went to Disneyland and got to ride the Matterhorn when I was six. They always put the smallest person in front and I was scared to death. I cried the whole first half of the ride because I thought I was supposed to be steering the toboggan, but I didn't know how and I thought we were going to die. I didn't lighten up until my older cousin yelled that it was okay and I was supposed to scream, not cry. They're panicking the kids the way I was panicked by thinking I needed to control something that I had no power over. Now *that's* evil."

"And that's just one way Solis has amassed a thousand fortunes even by today's standards. It makes you wonder about the connection, or if there is one between promoting environmental activism by indoctrinating children to despise society and Nature's Wilds land appropriations. That's a pretty wide leap."

He had noticed that after using the name Nature's Wilds, the table behind them had become a bit less boisterous to the point of near silence. At first, he supposed that they were just eating, knowing that conversation dies when one has their mouth full. When he looked over his shoulder to get Pat's attention for service, he saw that their plates had been shoved aside, apparently some time ago. Noting that the demeanor of the three younger workers seated behind him had turned solemn, he indicated to Anthea that it was time to leave. When Pat appeared with the coffeepot, he told her that they were ready to go and he needed the check.

He steered their chatter away from the subject and into more small talk. When Pat returned with the ticket he stood up, laid the money and tip on the table and guiding Anthea by her elbow, gently led her outside to the sidewalk.

"If it's okay we'll just take the truck over to my house and go overland from there," he said as he opened the passenger door for her.

"You need running boards," she suggested as she practically vaulted into the cab of the 4x4 Chevy. "We short folk prefer to retain our dignity when traveling via oversized vehicle." Getting seated, she muttered, "Thank goodness I'm not wearing a dress."

"Why do you think there aren't running boards?" he said with a touch of mischief.

"Do men ever grow up?"

"Not if we can help it."

•••••••

Mathers drove north approximately two miles on Lilliot Road to the home he had spent the last year building.

As they pulled into the drive, the semi-rustic looking ranch house sat back approximately 1000 feet on a well-maintained gravel drive. Stopping in front of the attached garage, he got out first and attempted to assist Anthea from her perch, but she'd already opened the door and was hopping down. Standing at the height of 5'4," she wasn't exactly short, but it was still a stretch to climb in and out of the elevated truck. She straightened her walking shorts and followed Mathers up the front walk.

The house was artistically landscaped with river rock and a few native plants carefully interspersed among the stones. A large wooden door, with a hand-hewn design of a pine bough, guarded the entryway. He unlocked the door and swung it wide to make room for her to enter first. *So, all of chivalry is not dead,* she thought. Stepping past him, she saw the entryway was paved with evenly laid stones that could be death to a woman in spike heels, but then, those weren't uniform wear in the woods. Hardwood floors stretched across a large open living area that housed both the requisite sofa and chairs and the more formal dining set, which wasn't so much formal as large enough to seat eight. The kitchen area beyond was obviously where Mathers ate his meals. There was a counter with a couple of stools delineating the separation of rooms and on the other side of the workspace was a smaller glass top breakfast set.

"I'm impressed," she said as she meandered through the furniture, noting the fabrics and the few bits of art on the wall. "Very homey. Do it all yourself?"

"Not on your life," he laughed. "I know my limitations and general construction is not within my list of accomplishments. Though I did carve the panel on the front door."

"Now that is definitely a work of art, and very inviting for new arrivals, too. I'm still impressed."

He took her by the arm and led her to the sliding glass doors that opened onto the deck. Unlatching them, he gestured her through. She immediately heard the gurgling of the river and, walking over to the rail, leaned over to take in the view of the vale below.

"This is what I would call relaxing," she mused aloud.

He came to stand next to her, hands on the top balustrade, and took a deep breath. "That's the idea," he agreed.

"All right, now I'm relaxed and ready to move on to phase two," she piped up. "What's the plan?"

"Aside from getting out of the Miner's Gap with those three fellas listening in on everything we said," she looked at him with a note of mild astonishment, "Didn't you notice their utter lack of discussion among themselves?"

"Yes, well…no, not really," she stuttered. "They were yapping away when we sat down."

"That lasted until they heard what we were talking about. On top of that, they looked familiar. They might have been working at the Stabler place when I went out there the first time."

"Great. Now we have spies keeping tabs on us," she lifted an eyebrow. "What else ya got? Rogue sheepherders?"

"Nope, this is cattle country and I figgered we'd go up the road apiece and get us a good gander at a few head o' longhorn," he jawed.

"I'm game. Walk or drive?'

"Four-wheel," he told her.

•••••••

Anthea was basically a city girl and this was a first. She had declared that she was prepared so when she was confronted with an ATV that was built for two, she exhaled audibly.

"Were you worried?" he asked, noticing her relief.

"Only that you might try to stick me on one to fly solo, which would have been disastrous since I've never straddled any such monster."

"I would never do that to a lady. I keep the two-seater version so I can take out my daughter, though she drives it too, or she and her husband can go off-road. It's comfortable for me either way and safer for a passenger." He indicated the rear seat so she could climb aboard. "You ready?"

"As I'll ever be," she replied with more resolve than she felt.

•••••••

They drove up the road past Stabler's farm until they came to a trail leading off to the left. This was an easement between two properties that local equestrians, hunters and ATV operators used to reach the remote high prairie and forest lands.

Skirting the private property bordered by long expanses of barbed wire, they rode over the rolling grassland toward the treed boundary of the national forest. A few isolated clusters of pines stood at intervals, most often in hollows between the gentle slopes that extended into the proximal distance. The further they traveled, a flurry of activity appeared just over the next hill. As they approached, they were able to discern a small black cloud of birds circling in a confined sector.

"Why do you think they're flocking like that?" Anthea practically yelled over the noise of the engine.

He turned his head to the side, keeping his eyes on the track. "Probably some dead animal, I'm guessing something large, like a deer," he explained.

As they came up to the field, they closed on the area and many of the crows flew off, escaping the intruder. Mathers pulled next to the fence and turned the motor off. He dismounted and helped Anthea down, then both of them walked forward to the edge of the fencing. Peering across the field, he saw a number of downed animals, and automatically covered his nose with his hand to protect himself from the rancid smell of death that assaulted him. Anthea followed him over, mimicking Mathers to ward off the stench.

"My God," she breathed.

"There must be a dozen cattle here, and they're pretty obviously dead." He was shocked at the visage and simultaneously became concerned about their own safety, not knowing what had killed the animals. Hearing another vehicle, he looked up to see a truck advancing from the direction they had just come. The rig stopped right behind their ATV and Frank Ahlsted climbed out of the cab.

Ahlsted walked over and acknowledged Mathers with a handshake, who quickly introduced his passenger and then asked about the dead steers.

"We were just on a sightseeing tour when we stumbled on this," he pointed to the macabre tableau.

"This isn't the first group we've lost in the last week. My boys are on the way out to prepare the carcasses for burning," said Ahlsted, clearly distressed by the loss.

"Any idea what's killing them?" asked Mathers.

Looking at his neighbor, the rancher replied shaking his head. "No idea. Some disease or poison, maybe. The vet has a couple of 'em in for necropsies, tryin' to figure it out. He's pretty sure that it won't jump species, though." He directed the comment to Anthea, making sure she understood that there wasn't any danger, aside from the attack on the olfactory nerves. "We've got more than 20 head down already."

"I'm sorry to hear that. I certainly hope the cause is determined soon before you suffer any more losses," condoled Mathers. "Have you noticed anything out of the ordinary, lately?"

Ahlsted looked puzzled. "Can't think what you might mean."

"Say, some odd folks hanging around or unknowns driving through like we are...you know, people you don't recognize. Like that..."

"Nah, it's been pretty quiet. A couple of local kids out on their horses now that the weather's good, maybe a few four-wheelers. The usual." He stood contemplating the carcasses for a minute. "We did have a visitor a while back. Some kid from one of the colleges wanted to see the spread. Said he was doing some kind of study for an ag class, or some such, on local ranches. Had one of the boys drive him around the operation. Seemed harmless enough."

"Could he have represented a conservation group?" pressed Mathers.

"Maybe. I don't really remember what he said, I had to get out and tend to some calves." He saw the other truck approaching up the dirt road, dust trailing in the clear air. "We've got some work to do here. You may want to head on home so you don't have to drive back by here later. The lady might find it, um, offensive."

"Good luck and I hope you isolate the trouble, Frank. Take care." They shook hands one more time, Anthea saying that she wished they had met under better circumstances. Mounting the four-wheeler, Mathers started it up and they turned around, departing the way they had come.

Checking both ways before he reentered traffic on the main highway, Mathers noticed a truck parked by the side of the road a little ways off. As he turned south he saw a figure standing by the driver's side, leaning against the bed, smoking a cigarette. Thinking that he'd seen the guy before, he opened the throttle and drove them back to his house.

Land Barons

Chapter 8

Reaching Mathers' turnoff, they rode up to the house, and he parked the ATV back in the garage. They entered the house through the utility room, checking their shoes for mud and manure. As he walked by the refrigerator, he opened the door and grabbed two beers.

"Want one?"

"Either that or something with a little more punch. I need to get that smell out of my nose and I'm only hoping that alcohol will help," she groaned.

"Unless you want it nasally infused, you're out of luck."

"They haven't invented a 'spirit spray' yet? Isn't that the quickest way to get drugs into your system? I'm sure I read that somewhere."

"Imbibing is your only option today," and he extended her the bottle.

"Or would you prefer a chilled pilsner to straight out of the bottle?" he asked politely.

"No thank you. I'm not quite that prissy," she sighed with a slight smile.

He slid open the glass doors and indicated a seat for her before he plunked himself into its mate and stretched out his long legs onto the matching ottoman.

Turning his attention to a hawk that was perched on a branch across the river, he watched the predator swoop down out of the tree and disappear below his field of vision.

"Did you notice that guy standing by his truck on the road?"

Catching her a little off-guard with the remark, she replied. "Wasn't he one of the trio sitting behind you at the café?"

"That's what I thought," he said halfway under his breath. "I'm still not sure where I've seen him before, probably just around town, but I don't like that he was hanging out on the road, waiting for something."

"Or someone…" she trailed off. They settled a little more into their chairs and enjoyed the clean, fresh scent of the pine forest that lined the shallow ravine directing the river's flow.

"What have you heard about purchases of substantial acreage in the region," she inquired lazily.

"Before our initial conversation, I had breakfast with the local equivalent of a coffee klatch, and one of them mentioned a large acquisition by our environmental friends. They didn't have any real information, either," he lamented.

"You know, if you're really interested, you can check the assessor's office for recent title changes. They ought to be recorded," she suggested.

"I could probably do that tomorrow," said Mathers. "The county offices are just down the way in Lathrop. I only have a few things to do around here, so, I guess I'm free to do as I please," He grinned at her.

"Nice life to have," she reflected. "I, on the other hand, must be getting back to work. I've got some releases to prepare for tomorrow, so," raising her bottle to Mathers, she added, "I think I need a ride back to my chariot."

"Of course," he said as he rose and collected her discard. "I'm just sorry our excursion wasn't a little more refreshing."

"It was informative, however. Never a dull moment around here, eh?" she said, goosing his attention with an amiable chuckle.

"Not lately. Maybe we can try it another time," he offered with a smidgen of optimism.

"I don't see why not." Anthea merrily tossed the bait as she walked back inside the house.

•••••••

Motoring down the river, Anthea checked her rear view mirror to make certain she wasn't being tailgated or, more importantly, a cop wasn't in close range. Seeing nothing but a maroon and white pick-up in her wake, she confidently powered out of the curve and let the numbers climb just a little more on the speedometer. As always, she kept her eye on the mirror for traffic changes and saw none…just the same truck, hanging back a few hundred yards. She didn't pay any other attention to him.

As the two-lane highway merged into U.S. 95, she kept a vigil for faster, and slower, vehicles while taking the quickest route home.

Since she lived a couple of miles from town, she had to go through a fair amount of traffic, and continuing to look back, as always, she saw that same truck not far behind.

Thinking about it a little more, she realized that the truck parked by the side of the road had been similarly marked. *Not like there aren't a hundred Chevies like that one around here.* The thought of someone following her still rattled her enough that she decided to deviate from her regular route and make a rapid turn at the next street. She quickly turned again and pulled into a convenience store on her right. Stopping, she watched to see if her imagined tail would drive by.

She waited a couple of minutes and seeing nothing, got out of the car and looking down the street, went inside to pick-up something she didn't need. She exited the store and checking both sides of the street again, hopped back into the Expedition and went on home, scolding herself for being paranoid.

Land Barons

Chapter 9

Sunset was just beginning to sizzle on the horizon as she closed the garage door and dropped down from the running board. Passing through the kitchen, she stopped to get herself a glass of iced tea from the fridge and opened the doors onto the deck. Seating herself at the patio table, she watched the dramatic display of color swiping the sky before she looked down onto the legal pad that she had brought outside with her. Between making a few notes about their experiences of the day and her discussions with Mathers, she kept watch on the changing backdrop of the hills on the other side of the Snake River. The vermilion-tinged clouds shifting into magenta were outlined against a wash of brilliant blue.

After rapidly outlining the day's events, she concluded that there really wasn't much to them aside from a minor case of paranoia between both she and Mathers. *Lovely as it is out here, I've got work to do.*

Taking her glass into the kitchen, she raided the vegetable bin for greens and made herself a quick salad with some leftover grilled salmon, splashed some dressing on it and took it with her to the computer.

Anthea gnoshed on the lettuce and pink fish in between drawing up a couple of press releases for a client who was getting ready to depart for an engagement in Branson, Missouri. A veteran ventriloquist from the Bible belt, she was preparing for a week of entertaining at one of the theaters in the glitzy atmosphere of the country-western's Vegas-style venue. Rapping out a couple of story angles took her awhile as Anthea re-read the client's history to make sure the information was correct, most importantly, show times and where to purchase tickets.

She read over the material for mistakes, fixing a few here and there and closed down the program with the knowledge that she needed to re-check them in the morning before sending them out. Picking up the dirty dishes, she deposited them in the sink, went to turn on the radio and came back in to wash-up.

It didn't take long to finish cleaning the kitchen then go into the living room to resettle herself into one of the chairs to read with the radio droning in the background. She looked up from the book to catch the news, saw the time and decided to watch it on the television so she could get the latest weather update.

Calling it a night, she closed up the entertainment center, put her glass in the sink and went in to prepare for bed.

The usual ablutions being completed, Anthea, with the ever-present book, climbed into bed and flicking on the light, read for a little more. As always, she fell asleep, book in hand.

•••••••

She was startled awake by a scratching noise at the back door. Listening for a minute and hearing it stop, she assumed it was just a raccoon and, reaching over, turned out the light that had been left on, rolled over and went back to sleep…or, at least tried to. Thinking that there were some other odd sounds emanating from the kitchen, she determined to investigate anyway.

This paranoia is getting to be annoying but I know I won't sleep until I look.

Walking into the dining area, she turned on a light and grabbed the big Maglite she kept on the counter, 'just in case.' That's when she felt a breeze on her back and turned to see the glass door wide open. *I know I closed that.* Though she really wasn't sure she had, so, she slid it shut, *again.*

Holding the flashlight as a weapon with both hands curled around the casing, she slowly made her way toward the other rooms. Opening the extra bedroom, she led with the Maglite raised above her head and switched on the overhead lamp. *Nothing here.* But as she turned around to go check her office, she caught the stomping of running feet coming from that direction and before she could see who or what it was, she was slammed in the chest and fell backwards over the arm-rest of a low chair.

Scared to death, she tried to catch her breath as she heard footsteps dashing along the deck until everything was quiet. She just sat there, with her feet dangling over the arm of the chair for what seemed like hours, frozen into inactivity.

Finally, Anthea forced herself to her feet and warily making her way into the living room, she again closed the glass slider and locked it. As she began to shiver almost uncontrollably, she picked up the phone and dialed 911. *Lotta good that'll do. The guy's gone.*

•••••••

As small as this town seemed to be, it still took twenty minutes for the police to arrive. By this time, she had wrapped herself in a light robe thinking that it was a good thing she didn't sleep sans nightie. *Of course, then I might've scared him off quicker.*

Reaching the front door, she peered through the peephole and saw the uniform. Figuring it couldn't happen twice in one night, she opened the door a crack and asked for his ID, which he promptly held for her to examine.

He identified himself as Officer Craig and she invited him in the house.

"Don't you usually travel in pairs?" she asked.

"If we can, but there was a pretty bad accident on the bridge. That's what took so long. Sorry ma'am." *At least he was polite.*

"No problem. I didn't have anything else planned for tonight," she tried the comedic routine. "Not that I had sent invitations to burglars, either." He didn't laugh. Guess it wasn't funny.

"Would you like to tell me what transpired, ma'am?" he asked, hoping to push the interview along.

As she sat down, taking a ragged breath, the inevitable knock on the back door came. Looking up, the policeman and Thea caught the vision of a big man, long braid trailing over his shoulder, leaning into the glass door with his hands cupped around his eyes attempting to see into the living room since she hadn't yet turned up the lights. The officer jumped up and started to pull out his weapon when Thea screeched, "Don't! That's my neighbor from the guesthouse."

Pulling herself out of the chair, she went to the door with the officer right behind her and let Cisco inside.

"Now what? Did you see something?"

"Hunh, what?" The big kid looked confused. "We just saw the cop come into the driveway and Lainie told me to go make sure you're okay." He looked down from his 6'5" height to the top of her head,

69

concern on his amiable features.

At this the officer relaxed and moved aside so Cisco could step further into the room.

"What happened? You all right?" he asked.

"That's what we're trying to find out," said Officer Craig as he walked back toward the sofa. "Can we get to the report now, ma'am? Or do you expect any other visitors?"

"Not unless your wife shows up on the doorstep, too," she said peering up at Cisco as she plunked back down on the sofa. Of course, just as she said that Lainie came pushing through the door with a mirror of Cisco's anxiety pasted across her brow.

Before she could open her mouth, Thea said, "just sit down and we'll get Officer Craig the information for his report and you two can go back to bed."

At that, Thea led him through the incident, what little there was of it…from invisible raccoon to large breaker and enterer.

"Did you get a look at the suspect, ma'am?" This 'ma'am' thing was beginning to abrade her nerves.

"I'm afraid not, Officer Craig. He ran past and knocked me on my ass before I could see anything but a dark blue t-shirt and jeans, I think."

"Hair color, height, age, weight?"

"Not really. Dark, taller than me, who knows and fast enough that he's probably not obese. Other than that, I didn't have the guts to follow him."

"Did you check to see if anything was missing?" he ignored her near snottiness, chalking it up to shock and anger, like most B & E victims.

"Actually, I don't know how I managed to think that much, but I did look around in the office where he was and none of the equipment was tampered with. Frankly, I don't know what he wanted, because it all looks pretty much untouched." Anthea looked up at him, wondering if she should have bothered calling after all. He stood there, immobile and stone-faced, just like they teach them in cop school.

The officer turned to look at the two Indians lined up on the sofa next to Thea. "Did either of you see anything before my cruiser drove up?"

They looked at each other querulously and then, turning back to the policeman, mutely shook their heads side-to-side.

"If you don't mind ma'am," *there he goes with the 'ma'am, again,* "I'll just have a look around and see if I can find anything. Is that all right with you?" his face showing a touch of concern.

"Sure, officer. Be my guest, since I haven't any idea what he'd want."

He walked through the house and asked her a couple of things about where the intruder had gone, etc. When he finished, he wrote a few more notes on his pad, made sure he had her name and address correct, wrote the name of the two non-witnesses, and prepared to leave.

"I'm going to go out your back door here, where he exited, and take a look around outside before I go make a report, but I doubt I'll find much, particularly since others have been over the same ground." He looked not quite accusingly at the couple on the sofa. "Don't forget to lock up after your guests leave. I won't bother you anymore tonight. You try to have a nice evening."

"Thank you for coming, Officer Craig. I appreciate the effort," she tried to smile as he nodded and she locked him out on the deck.

If there ever was a time that I could use a drink, it's now.

"I don't exactly want to blow my image with my young, admiring public," she said to Lainie and Cisco, who were still a little bemused by the proceedings, "but I'm going to have a drink. Anyone want to join me?"

In unison, the two of them shook their heads again while they watched her get up and go to the liquor cabinet.

Reaching inside, she pulled out a very nice single malt that she almost never drank and poured herself a shot. Immediately, Cisco shot to his feet and started pacing the room.

"There was something that you didn't tell Officer Craig wasn't there?" he asked as he trod back and forth across the carpet.

Thea looked over her shoulder as she recapped the bottle, eyebrows nearly to her hairline. "How'd you figure that?"

"Oh it's just that you can't lie to save your life...your face gives everything away."

"So, how come the cop didn't come to the same conclusion?" she asked.

"Oh, he probably did, but decided it wouldn't go anywhere since

71

the guy didn't take anything anyway. So what was it, that you were holding back?"

Taking the glass to the sofa, she curled up in a corner, sipped her scotch and glanced over at Lainie, who still had an expression of worry on her face but was keeping quiet, anticipating the answer.

"Well, I was on my way back from Marcasite..."

"What were you doing up there?" cut-in Cisco.

"None of your business, Mister Nosey."

"She was visiting that man we saw her with," stated Lainie matter-of-factly.

Thea swung her head over to Lainie, surprise slapped across her features and her mouth slightly open.

Lainie negligently flipped the back of her hand through the air. "Cisco told you how obvious you are," she grinned.

Thea dropped her eyes and groaned as she bobbed her head sideways in disbelief. "Ah well, I may as well tell you the whole story. Well, at least, the short version." With that, Thea described briefly her trip to Marcasite, not disclosing the basis of Mathers' and her interest, deciding that if there was any real danger she didn't want the kids involved. She mentioned her uneasiness about the possibility of being followed and her abortive attempts to shake off the imagined tail.

When she was finished, she took another swallow of the scotch and just looked back and forth between the two newlyweds who had both schooled their faces into a stoic expression.

"There's clearly more to it than that," said Cisco, whose size had a tendency to mislead people as to his astuteness, a trait he used to his advantage since he felt it was better to be underestimated. "But I'm not going to press you for the details. You must have good reason for staying close-mouthed." He didn't look happy about her reticence to divulge more information but thought better of trying to get more out of her.

Thea got up and started toward the door, waving the two of them out. "That's all you're gonna get from me tonight. You sure you don't wanna be a cop, Cisco? You've got the demeanor, not to mention the ability to intimidate. Now, shoo, both of you."

They leaned down and hugged her one at a time with Cisco saying into her ear, "No one can intimidate the opposition like you can, little dragon."

After pushing them out and re-locking the door, she pulled the drapes, grabbed a blanket throw off the arm of the couch and wrapped herself up in it. Curling up in the corner of the sofa she watched the darkness and finally dropped off to sleep, still clutching the Maglite.

Land Barons

Chapter 10

It was after 1 a.m. when the maroon and white pick-up pulled in and parked behind the row of offices and businesses lining Main Street in Marcasite.

A young man dressed in a t-shirt and jeans, exited the truck and quietly approached the back door of the Rural Resources office, knocking softly.

A trim woman in her thirties, light brown hair pulled back and held in place by a chopstick, carefully opened the door and admitted him.

Walking to the back room of the office, she sat on a desk, one leg dangling over the edge and anxiously asked how it went.

"Could've been worse. I barely got out of there without getting caught. The owner came out of nowhere just as I was leaving," he told her, handing her a slim manila folder which she placed next to her on the desk.

"You weren't recognized, were you," she asked in an exasperated tone.

"I doubt it. I was out of there like a shot. No way could I be identified," he explained feeling as if she was unfairly jumping down his throat. He stood there, pouting.

"Yeah, yeah. And what is it you're studying at the U?" she needled.

"Environmental law, I don't have any classes entitled 'The Finer Points of Breaking and Entering 101.'" He was pissed.

"Fine." She pursed her lips momentarily. "It was a simple enough task, and even this got screwed up, Christ…"

"Look, I got what you wanted and I got out without any real trouble," he complained. "What else do you want, man?" He dropped down into a secretarial chair, equipped with casters, and leaned back, hands in his pockets and legs stretched in front of him, crossed at the ankles.

"What I don't want is trouble and I'm afraid that's what we're going to get soon enough." She was hugging herself and had started rubbing her hands up and down her upper arms in uneasiness. She then abruptly dropped her hands and picked up the folder, opening it.

"Did you look at the contents?"

"I didn't really have an opportunity, but, by the size of it, there's not much there. Frankly, I don't think there's anything to worry about. All they're doing is speculating about land purchases," he said as he was beginning to relax.

Leafing through the few papers she remarked, "This is basically stuff they downloaded off of a few websites. For once I think you may be right." She breathed a sigh of relief.

"As they say, that's why I get paid the 'big bucks.'"

"Every summer job should be so lucrative," she sneered.

"You know damn well I was being sarcastic," he said, sounding hurt.

"Look, I'm sorry. I'm just under a lot of pressure from these guys and I shouldn't be taking it out on you. Why don't you go home and get some sleep. I'll see you later today, this afternoon. Okay?"

"Yeah, later." He stood up from where he'd been sitting, pushing the chair away.

"And…thanks," she opened the rear door and let him out, turning the lock as he left.

She leaned her shoulder into the door, chin dropped to her chest, going over this morning's call and the worry that it had caused her. She'd prowled the office for hours, alternately debating the aspects of what they were doing and drowning in misgiving.

She didn't understand what was expected of her. She had taken this job believing that she was here to develop community awareness of the environment and promote its protection from the dangers of development and industry. She hoped that she wasn't wrong and that this cloak and dagger stuff wasn't going to become a trend. What was expected of her?

Exasperation and a feeling that she was losing control of what had been a well-planned career, a purposeful life, washed over her.

Hell, what have I gotten into…

Chapter 11

Rolling her head to look up at the ceiling, Anthea found herself examining a different ceiling than usual. It took a minute before her disorientation subsided and she realized that she had fallen asleep on the sofa, knees tucked up under her robe and her Maglite rolling across her lap.

I guess that scotch did the trick.

She rubbed the sore spot on her sternum, remembering the impact that had flung her into the chair. Raising her arms above her head, she stretched like a cat as the flashlight fell off the couch and clunked onto the floor. She sat up, noticed some soreness in her low back and planted her feet on the large, patterned rug that trickled jewel tones across the living area. Standing, she elongated her limbs above her body one last time and padded into the kitchen to start her coffee, thinking how much she should give in to adding more caffeine to this morning's pot. *The evils of caffeine are far outweighed by the need of the one - me.* Eschewing health for one day, she made it a fully caffeinated brew.

As the coffee dripped, she flicked on the radio to catch her morning fix of talk radio while she went into the office to bring the computer on-line. Picking through her papers from her work yesterday, she noticed that the thin folder of the downloads wasn't where she thought she'd left it. Anthea supposed she'd mislaid it, as she often did, usually by wandering off to some other part of the house and changing work modes and thoughts in the process, leaving objects in her wake. She knew she'd find it later.

She pulled up her program, opened the files of the new press releases and then went back to collect her mug of coffee, doctor it and bring it back to her office.

Thinking she'd just get these documents checked before she does anything else, she sat down to make corrections. Locating three mistakes, she fixed them and printed out copies for her paper files. Double checking the hard copy to see that the content, construction and presentation was right, she e-mailed the documents to her client first for her perusal, to make sure the information wasn't misleading. That done, she went for a refill and back to her suite for a shower.

She turned on the water, running her hand under the spigot until the temperature had reached a comfortable level. Dropping her night-clothes on the floor in a heap, she stood under the spray and sighed as the warm freshets ran down her back where she languorously rubbed the stiffness away.

Just as Anthea was finishing the task of drying her hair, and she did consider it work trying to get the unruly curls to follow some plan that she made rather than their own, the phone rang. Turning off the appli-ance and examining the result in the mirror, she grimaced thinking that another bad hair day is just the norm, so what's new?

She got to the phone by the fourth ring and, answering it, found herself speaking to a representative from the police department. Apparently, they feel compelled to follow-up on B & E's at lonely middle-aged women's homes by calling to make sure they weren't fur-ther harassed by gremlins or offenders that visit twice in one night. Assuring the voice on the other end that she was perfectly fine, they concluded the call with stiff pleasantries.

After finishing the call, she realized that there was a message on the machine that must have come in while she was showering. Listening to the recording, she heard Lainie's voice calling to check up on her, too. *Must be an epidemic.* She dialed the kids' number and left a return message telling them that everything was fine and the police also had followed up with a morning call. She thanked them, told them to work hard and hung up.

Returning to the sink and gazing in the mirror, Thea gave up on any attempt to improve the hair situation, opting to use combs to hold the majority of her mop up and off of her neck, then finished getting dressed.

Toying with the idea of a third cup of coffee, she went back into the office and retrieved her portable handset and called her client, the ventriloquist, while she made her way back to the coffee maker.

Three hours time difference lay in between but she still lucked out and her client, and friend, answered the phone. She confirmed receiv-ing the e-mail and was just in the process of proofing the copy when Anthea called. For the first bit of jollity this morning, she was delight-ed with the content and told Anthea to send it off.

Anthea told her it's going to be a great show to a sold-out house and after going through the "wish I could be there to see it," and meaning it, they said their farewells. *Maybe next time*, Anthea thought.

Taking the phone and her last cup of joe into the office she settled herself behind the computer one more time to e-mail and fax out releases to the news media in and around Branson, plus a few outlets near the performer's regular haunts. As an afterthought, she threw in a few addresses in Vegas and Nashville. *Got to build for the future.*

•••••••

A while later, the duty of 'reaching out' accomplished, Anthea began picking up her purse and a list of errands she needed to run in town. Halfway to the door, she stopped and thought about the spotty information she and Mathers had been able to glean about Nature's Wilds.

I don't know why this is nagging me so much, but... she put her things down and went back into the office to look up a friend at the San Francisco Chronicle, Dan Rennselaer.

One of the bits of information they had noticed was that Nature's Wilds was headquartered in the city by the bay, so who else would be more appropriate to call for help than Dan? Digging through her address book, she located his number and dialed.

When all she got was his voicemail, she let a single expletive go before the beep and then left a brief but to the point message i.e. what did he know about Nature's Wilds Conservancy and could he e-mail her with anything he might be able to dredge up. Thanking him and promising to call back soon, she hung up.

Before she left she wanted to leave some notes in the file she was beginning to compile on the environmental organization. So she started a diligent search for the folder. It wasn't anywhere on her desk and after systematically tearing through everything in the office, she confirmed that it simply was not in the room. She took the hunt through the rest of the house, room by room, only to come up empty handed. Finally, she concluded the obvious: it wasn't here.

Land Barons

Chapter 12

Gary started his day just as he said he would, by going down to Lathrop to visit the assessor's office.

The county offices were located in a grand old, granite block building that brooded over the south end of town across from the locals' favorite watering hole, the Elkhorn. Parking in the lot in the back, Gary strode into the rear entrance noting how nice it is to walk into a courthouse and not have to stop at a security station, stand in line to go through a metal detector and empty his pockets into a basket. He was beginning to savor the freedom of living in a really small town. Funny, he thought, how people don't realize what an enormous, urban center Portland had become over the decades. It had definitely become too large for him and each day he was more thankful that he'd pulled up stakes and left altogether.

Although he and his wife had managed to purchase a weekend cottage on the coast, even that had become unbearable filled as it was with memories. *Best decision I made in years was to come out here. Well, at least until someone started shooting at me...*

He found the directory and saw that the assessor's office was in Suite 2B. Bypassing the elevator, he climbed the stairs two at a time and noticed that the office was right in front of him as he emerged from the stairwell. He peered in the glass portion of the door and saw only one clerk, but no lines, obviously another advantage of living in the sticks.

He pulled open the door, approached the counter and plastered his 'I'm confused and helpless' grin on his face, the one he'd used successfully for so many years as a cop. Of course, it worked again because as soon as he said "Miss?" the matronly keeper of the records waddled over to assist the poor, good-looking but apparently lost, man.

In her most motherly tone, despite the fact she was approximately the same age as he, she asked, "What can I help you with today?"

Giving in to the helpless act, he explained what he was looking for and wanted to know if she could assist him with a basic search.

As she wasn't particularly busy, she directed him to the computers and brought up the proper files for him.

"Now, you just scroll through these deeds here to find what you're looking for. Now, you realize these are only for our county," she raised her eyebrows in concern to be certain he caught on.

"Yes, indeed. Thank you, Miss...?"

"Sally, you can just call me Sally."

"Thank you, Sally. But I have one other question before you go."

"Sure, hon', what is it?"

"Do you have a book of the plat maps that I can compare the property descriptions to?"

"Of course. I'll get it for you." She happily moved back through the swinging door, latched it behind her and went to find the long, flat books. She brought them up to the countertop and said, "Now here they are, you just let me know when you're done with them. All right, dearie?"

He stood up to get the books and smiled ingratiatingly. "Thank you again, Sally. Your help has been invaluable."

She looked infinitely pleased and went back to her work.

•••••••

As he plowed through the deeds recorded over the last two years, it took him longer than he had expected. He hadn't realized how bustling the real estate business had been in the county. The majority of sales were closer to Lathrop so it made his search somewhat simpler. He was looking for large parcels of a few thousand acres or more in the Marcasite/Lilliot area. What he found were five purchases within the last eighteen months amounting to almost 30,000 acres.

When he pulled the plat maps up in the elongated book that Sally had lent him, he located the five parcels as being all within a close proximity of each other, with three abutting the national forest. Not all listed Nature's Wilds Conservancy as the new owner. Only three were held by that entity. The other two were deeded to some other corporate entity called Protectorate Inc. which he presumed to be related to the non-profit in some fashion.

After he finished making his notes, he deposited the books on the counter. As he laid them down he asked Sally whether or not it was possible to get printouts of the five deeds he had located, to which she sweetly answered, "Of course, but it will cost you...all of 50 cents a piece." She winked and he thought her harmless flirting lent her a strangely unique charm.

"That'd be just terrific. Thank you." And he gave her the page numbers he needed.

•••••••

Taking his paperwork with him, he crossed the street and strolled up the block to the Blue Heron Café, a popular gourmet eatery specializing in tantalizing baked goods and espresso. He enjoyed taking the time to visit the restaurant, with its eclectic atmosphere, it was almost out of place in the old lumber town.

He stopped by the pile of newspapers stacked on a chair by the front door and fished out today's edition. Tucking it under his arm, he took a seat at a table so he had a view out the front window. The owner, Tricia, was exceptionally tall and full figured, dark blonde hair falling below her hips that she kept tied back with a fanciful, beaded clip.

"How're you doin' today, Gary? What can I getcha?"

"Some of that exceptional house blend and that special you've got listed on the board. It sounds like one of your more scrumptious creations." He gave her a playful half-smile.

"Whatever you want, you got it," she laughed as she flicked her hair over her shoulder and went to get his coffee.

When she brought back his steaming mug and set down some cream, she sat across from him and inquired about what had roped in his attention in the paper.

"This story about Frank Ahlsted's cattle losses. I was just up at his place yesterday with a friend and we came across about a dozen head that were downed on an upper range. That's a bad business he's got to deal with and I notice that a few deer were found dead of the same mysterious illness." He frowned in concern for his neighbor.

"I'd read that. They haven't been able to figure any of it out, from what I could tell." She clucked her tongue in sympathy. "Said they don't know if it's parasites, disease or some poison."

"Have you heard any related talk from locals?"

83

"Nah. No one seems to know much about it. Frank was in a few days ago, didn't know he fancied vanilla lattes. He's sufferin' with all this gossip."

"Sure wish there was something we could do to help," he said wistfully.

"Well, you could find out what the problem is, didn't you used to be a cop?"

He laughed. "A lifetime ago. Besides Fish and Game is in on it now. They'll figure it out."

"I hope so. Let me go get your lunch."

As she pushed away from the table, he read through another page and came across the obituaries. The second listing was for Mary Stabler, who died at age 41, leaving her husband, two sons and a daughter. All it said was that she'd been ill for six months before passing on two days ago. All that grief her family is experiencing, first the crops, then their home, now a wife and mother.

Tricia arrived with his prosciutto foccacia, elegantly presented with a few sprigs of parsley tracing the edge. She set the plate in front of him, but he found that he had lost his appetite.

•••••••

Carrie DiMarco, the new director of the Rural Resources Center in Marcasite County had traveled into Lathrop for a morning meeting at the local elementary school to sketch out plans for their Environmental Trek Day. Much of DiMarco's work was the coordination of educational programs for local schools and organizations, guiding them with ecologically friendly learning projects for the children. Day camps, field trips and on-campus projects filled most of her schedule.

Today, she was organizing a daytrip for fourth through sixth graders to the newly instated nature trail near Lilliot, a project close to her heart. Although she had only been moved to the outlying office three months before, she had worked diligently with the local volunteer organization and the forest service in developing and designing the waystation.

The meeting had eaten up her morning, leaving her drained and famished, particularly after last night's late hours and closely averted disaster. Caffeine was a necessity to get her through the rest of the day and the Blue Heron offered some of the finest blends available in town.

Leaving her paperwork in her copper colored Honda Civic that had seen better days, she closed and locked the driver's door before crossing the street and entering the quaint, fern filled establishment.

Her eyes momentarily widened when she noticed Gary Mathers seated by himself at a table for four, examining the paper. Without looking up from the printed page before him, he sipped his coffee and seemed oblivious to everything else. Just as well, she thought, considering she really didn't want to make eye contact or share pleasantries.

She stopped by the stack of discarded papers and found a duplicate copy of the day's Journal, which she took with her to a table situated on the other side of the café near a couple of casually dressed business owners. Their discussion centered around the refurbishing of the National Guard Armory and whether the work would be completed in time for the hospital benefit that was six weeks away.

Keeping Mathers in her scope, she requested a house blend and Tricia's incomparable French toast, knowing that she would continue to watch her 'quarry,' as she was beginning to think of him. When the coffee came, she added cream and a packet of raw sugar. Stirring, she looked despairingly up at the ceiling. *I don't need this.*

After serving DiMarco her beverage, Tricia sat back down with Mathers and, from her vantage point, she could hear their conversation about the Stablers and the wife's untimely demise after a relatively short illness. She also heard him question her about some large ranches changing hands over the last year. Tricia knew about a conservation group looking into purchasing some property, but hadn't heard anything positive. At which point their words were muffled and she couldn't make out much of what was said.

Returning her attention to the paper, Carrie skimmed the stories, picking out the one that appeared to be of interest to Mathers. Reading the local angle on the rancher's woes made her wonder about the dilemmas that had cropped up in the vicinity. She'd picked up some gossip about the cattle dying and now this new twist that a few deer had been affected. Puzzled by some of the developments, suspicion was creeping into her awareness. She couldn't put her finger on the culprits or their possible rationalization, but she had a notion that people she knew were involved.

Despite her worries, she managed to swallow the majority of the generous portion on her dish… *hunger wins out over anxiety*…noticing that Mathers hardly touched his food. She asked Tricia for her check so she'd be ready to exit when he did. Taking her time, she doled out some cash with a generous tip, leaving it on the table while she lounged over a refill of coffee, waiting.

When Mathers finally paid his tab, Tricia moaned plaintively, "You hardly ate a thing, boy. Doncha feel all right?"

"It sounded so good and looked so inviting, Tricia, but for some reason I just wasn't as hungry as I thought. I didn't mean to disappoint you."

"I'll wrap it for you to take home. Maybe you'll feel like eatin' later," she gave him a wistful smile.

Gathering up the neat little package and the copy of the Journal, Mathers strode out the door and down the block to the courthouse that he'd visited earlier. DiMarco climbed behind the wheel of her car and followed him up the street, while she waited at the curb, she saw him pull out and turn onto the road heading back up to Marcasite. She trailed behind his Chevy keeping two vehicles' distance.

Wending his way up SR 4, she stayed within easy sight of him without appearing to draw his attention. When they reached the outskirts of town, traffic slowed and the van and beat-up old pick-up that had served as a buffer pulled into the parking lot of the grocery store. No longer having the advantage of intervening cars for cover, DiMarco hung back even more as she continued the low-key pursuit up the hill.

About two miles out of town, Mathers slowed and swung left into a drive that disappeared around a cluster of tall pines. As she passed, she saw the mailbox, his surname printed in simple, bold characters on the side. Releasing a sigh of relief, she continued up the hill until she could comfortably execute a u-turn and proceeded backtracking to town and her office.

•••••••

Letting herself into the office, she dropped her purse on the desk and slumped into the executive's seat. Propping her elbows on the wood surface, she cradled her forehead with her splayed fingers, procrastinating for a few minutes. Rubbing her temples with one hand, she lifted the handset of the phone and reluctantly placed a call.

An assistant promptly answered after three rings and coolly asked her to hold while she accessed her administrator's office. While holding on the line, Carrie turned to look up at the ceiling of the old building which boasted antique, embossed copper plates dating the edifice to early in the last century. She could picture the dirt streets lined by shops and businesses whose wooden facades resembled what Hollywood tries to reproduce for modern cinema…the classic western milieu. Imagining the scene more thoroughly she could see the oxen or huge Belgians, their shaggy fetlocks slogging through the mud, burdened with mill-bound wagons piled high with timber. She wondered if she would have been more comfortable living in that world when the automobile was a new invention and gaslights lit the avenues as darkness fell.

Startled out of her reverie by the satiny, and sometimes what seemed a slightly menacing, sotto voce on the other end, her salutation was stiff and awkward.

"What can I do for you today, Ms. DiMarco?"

"I assumed that you would want me to inform you of any developments, sir," she managed to say.

"Certainly. You learned something of interest?" he inquired.

"Possibly, sir. I happened to be in a small café in Lathrop when I overheard the subject who has been turning up at rather inopportune moments, was asking about recent appropriations of large land parcels. Apparently he had spent the morning at the county courthouse and although his purpose there isn't confirmed, it sounded as though he may have been investigating title changes."

"Well, I wouldn't worry about that. The records are public and there is nothing illicit in the transactions. You don't need to fret over someone's inquisitiveness," he purred. "Your job is just to continue your educational programs." He slightly accentuated the last two words. "Leave the annoyances to us, we'll handle them."

"As you say. Thank you sir."

Land Barons

Chapter 13

Gary was taking the rest of the afternoon to finish constructing a tool shed that he had situated under the deck that ran along the river frontage of the house. Most of the work had been done. All that was needed was to screw the hinges in place in order to hang the doors, then he'd be able to move his lawn equipment into the new housing and get it out from underfoot in the garage.

Bending down to extract his drill driver from the toolbox, he stopped to look at the northern horizon as he straightened up. His attention was arrested by a growing cloud of smoke fanning across the sky. Putting his tools down, he quickened his pace back up to the house and placed a call to 911 only to find that the fire had already been reported.

An active member of the volunteer fire department, Gary rummaged through his tools, grabbed his heavy work gloves, an ax and shovel, and tossed them in the truckbed. He hopped in the Chevy and whipped around in the driveway, racing to find the fire.

Judging from where the smoke was emanating, he sped up the mountain. The cloud appeared to grow as he traveled north, filling the sky. Coming upon a ragged row of pick-ups about five miles from his place, he pulled in at the end of the line. Just as he was reaching behind the cab lifting out his tools, the engine from the fire station in Marcasite roared onto the scene, sirens blaring. A backhoe was already working over at the raging blaze digging a firebreak around the acres of cut timber, logs piled high and dancing with uncontrolled plumes of flame. As he surveyed the damage, he realized that the fire must have been burning for some time because all of the log heaps were ablaze and the efforts to douse the flames were accomplishing little.

How could he have arrived so late, he wondered, because the mill was already fully engulfed and no one could get close enough to wage a useful attack. The attempts by the line of volunteers, who manned the fire hose, shooting a thick spray of water siphoned from the pond with the portable pump, were obviously inadequate. Not waiting any longer, Gary jumped into the fray to help wherever he was directed.

Land Barons

Spring was well advanced and it had been a dry one so some of the wood was tinder dry, lending itself to feed the fire faster. The mill had been built primarily of wood, which due to its age was well seasoned and nothing more than fuel. Gary was later told that it went up like a torch and there had been nothing they could do to save it.

The fire continued to burn so fiercely that no one could get within 100 feet of the flaming structure without being seared by the intense temperature. At least 30 volunteers were tackling the blazes from numerous angles, only to be beaten back by the blistering heat or scorched for their trouble. Sweating, ash coated men and women were flinging shovel after shovel full of dirt on the stacks of smoldering wood attempting to bank the fire, but the devastation was total.

Gary was overwhelmed by the destruction the fire had wreaked in so little time. He felt helpless amid the all-consuming blaze that seemed to burn in every direction. All that was left standing was, iron-ically, the kiln. It stood off to the side of the mill and, although it too was constructed of wood, the firefighters were able to abate the flames on the nearest stack of logs so the building wasn't susceptible to fly-ing embers. The kiln stood quiescent amid the ash deposits growing around it. A silent witness to the flash and fury of fire when it isn't har-nessed inside a structure built for the purpose of containment.

As the volunteers were heaving with the backbreaking work of damping the smoking cinders, a clamor arose from the ranks as notice spread that another fire was burning not too far distant. They split the crew and Gary jumped in one of the trucks making for the newly dis-covered blaze.

As they pulled up to the fire line, they were halted by the forest service employees that had formed a ring around the area. The new fire was landlocked inside national forest land and the rangers flatly denied the volunteer fire crew access to help fight the blaze.

Gary approached one of the men who appeared to be directing the flow of assistance, or non-activity, by what he could discern.

"What's the problem with the community helping fight the fire," he yelled above the ruckus.

"Sorry, sir. USFS policy is to maintain control of the fire zone without endangering the civilian population," he replied tightly.

"That makes no sense," said the crew leader. "We're all trained to be of assistance in an emergency like this. Let us do what we can to help. At least let us help dig the fire breaks. You can always use strong backs for that."

"No can do. Our orders are clear. No one in or out that isn't in government employ. We already have our sawyers and backhoes up there. Sorry, sir, we have to follow USFS guidelines," which he said without the slightest tinge of apology.

With access denied, the volunteers stood by and watched as virtually nothing was done to put out the blaze. A government sanctioned fire crew finally arrived, to make a very minimal attempt at fighting the leaping flames. The frustration that bit at the men held at bay by the forest service employees was crushing. They couldn't force the rangers to accept their help and examining the gear sported by the ones standing guard, Gary noted that they were all armed, which he thought was odd. Having been denied access, they packed up their gear and drove back down the road to assist in the clean-up at the mill.

•••••••

The volunteers consisted of men and women from nearby farms and homes, all equipped to do what they could to help their neighbors in a time of disaster. Unfortunately, this particular fire destroyed more than the Powell Lumber Mill. When it burned it took the livelihood of many residents in Marcasite and Lilliot. What in years past had been a major employer, had already seen cutbacks in operations as logging had reached critical mass by environmentalists' standards, bringing the equation down to 'no timber, no lumber.'

As the ashes drifted on the breeze while the fire was brought under control, the last of the jobs at the Powell Mill disappeared as well. The blaze had managed to burn down the site and burn-out an important part of the local economy.

Land Barons

Chapter 14

Dragging his tools out of the back of the truck, Gary unwound the hose and proceeded to wash down his implements, feeling as though he didn't really have a chance to use them the way they were meant to be used, which was to save someone's home or livelihood. He had done neither. They had shoveled dirt and hauled logs and tempered flames with water, but none of it mattered in the end. The fire consumed everything anyway. Although no one was hurt, the blaze had still consumed lives as well. The mill was gone and so were the jobs it had harbored in an already depressed area.

In the end, Gary was bone-weary and felt beaten.

Finishing the simple task of cleaning the ash off his tools, he pulled off his boots and left them on the step in the garage. Barefoot, he walked into the house, stopping in the utility room, stripped, and shoved his filthy clothes into the washer.

Padding down the hall, Gary went into the master bath and turned on the shower, knowing that he'd feel better once he'd scraped the soot off his body. Stepping into the hot water, he just stood under the spray letting the distress and the ash slide down the drain at the same time until he was ready to move enough to pick up the soap and wash off the rest of the grime. Looking at his fingernails, he wondered if he'd ever get them clean again. The ash was everywhere, in his nose, his eyes, inside his gloves and his clothes. It seemed like it had crept into every pore of his skin.

He took his time scrubbing and then scrubbed again to make sure he was clear of all the cinders, examining and reexamining himself to be certain all trace of the fire was gone. When he was satisfied with the result, he turned off the shower and, wrapping a towel around himself, went into the kitchen, retrieved a beer from the refrigerator and stepped out onto the deck to watch the diminishing dusk. The smoke, still hovering over the mountain, caught the lingering light in a display of softening hues of crimson, violet and gold. How so much devastation could reveal such incredible beauty was hard for him to comprehend. Yet, he could see the truth of it right before his eyes and he accepted the vision as it faded with the daylight.

Pulling himself out of his maudlin introspection, he took his bottle into the study where he flicked on his rarely touched computer. His intentions had been good in setting up the tool in order to write his book (he had actually started the outline) and to e-mail his daughter. Parking his terry wrapped body into the secretarial chair, he decided to do precisely that, thinking it might be good to tell her about the day and share some of his concern, without upsetting her, of course. So, he'd make it a narrative rather than a contemplative letter. Well, she always says she wants to hear what he's doing. At least she won't think he's bored.

After he finished the e-mail and had sent it on its way, he got up to go back into the kitchen to get something to eat, but noticed his answering machine blinking at him. Pressing the button, he heard Anthea's voice asking him to give her a call. Gazing up at the clock, he saw that it was 10:30 and picked up the phone figuring that it wasn't too late to call.

•••••••

Hearing the phone ring, Anthea glanced at her watch and, shrugging her shoulders, placed her book on the coffee table and reached for the handset lying nearby.

"Hello," she answered in a fairly husky tone, her vocal cords having been off-duty for the last hour or so.

"Good evening, Anthea. It's Gary. I hope I didn't wake you. You sound drowsy."

"Only from the rapidly degenerating pace of this book I'm reading," her voice brightened.

"I apologize for the late hour, but I just noticed the answering machine's insistent blinking a few minutes ago. I've been out on a fire line with the local volunteer department and just got myself cleaned-up," he explained.

"Is everything all right? Are you?" she queried, concerned.

"Well, I'm fine but the lumber mill is toast. Everything in sight is burned or damaged beyond saving." He sounded defeated. "I just hope Bob Powell's insurance is paid up. There'll be no reopening that place anytime soon, I'm afraid."

"I'm sorry to hear that knowing how dependent some of these communities are on a central industry." She was quiet for a bit then asked for more information which he gave her, letting the disappointment roll off his chest as he also described the incident at the wildfire. At his mention of the forest service employees sporting sidearms, she was all ears.

"What did you make of the government guys with guns?" she asked.

"I really don't know. I'm not familiar with regular rangers wearing sidearms, though there are forest service law enforcement officers that you'll see occasionally and they're armed."

"Hmmm," was all Anthea answered, just accepting the explanation since she had no related knowledge on which to base further inquiry.

"That's certainly enough to chew on for now," he stopped himself, realizing that he'd rattled on more than he needed. "Tell me, what did you call about. Something I can help with?"

"This morning I placed a call to a friend of mine at the San Francisco Chronicle in hopes he might be able to round up some information on Nature's Wilds Conservancy. Since their main office is located there, I thought he may have easier access to retrieve articles or related info on the group. In any case, I went to put some notes in that file I was beginning to compile, and I simply could *not* find it anywhere." Sounding a little frustrated, she added, "I turned this place upside down. Did I leave it with you?"

"'Fraid not. You packed it up with you when you left for home."

"Great…" her voice trailed off.

"What's up?" he asked, noting the disturbed quality in her tone. "Tell me what's going on."

"I'm guessing that that's what the break-in was all about," Anthea said flatly.

He sat up, alarmed.

"You got my attention now," he forced his voice not to reveal his agitation. "What break-in?"

"Last night after I went to bed someone, well, I guess you could say they *walked-in*, since the back door wasn't locked. Traipsed as easy as you please into my office and apparently took nothing. At least, that's what I thought until I couldn't find the folder."

"Are *you* okay? Did you see the perp?"

"Falling back into cop-mode, are we?" She chuckled at his quick change from simple concern to hard-ass attitude.

"Some things die hard. Tell me."

She related the full incident, leaving out nothing since he prompted her through the whole event like any detective would. Then she said, "You sure you're retired from the force? They could've used you here last night. Officer Craig might have learned something."

He lightened up a little and fell back into a more relaxed speech pattern. "Why do you think anyone would want that file. It had virtually nothing in it other than what anyone could download off the internet." The statement was thrown out to the atmosphere as much as her.

"They must think that we're a little more than passively interested in their activities. Frankly, if that fool of a hothead, as you so endearingly refer to him, hadn't chased you with a gun, I'm sure your curiosity would have died a natural death." She stopped to think. "Did you find anything at the assessor's office?"

"Some deeds of note…change of title and what all," he decided he was too tired to open that subject tonight and, probably, so was Anthea.

"Doncha think you've had enough for one day? I'm sure you could use the rest after last night's shake-up. Bet you didn't sleep much," his tone dropped to a caress.

"No, me and the Maglite finally caught some shuteye on the couch," she admitted. "And I'm sure you're ragged out after the fire. Why don't we talk tomorrow," she suggested.

"Good idea," he agreed softly. "Tomorrow then."

Standing up, he tightened his towel around his waist, went out to the kitchen to trash the bottle that he had been clutching convulsively as she conveyed the tale of the break-in. He may not have known Anthea long but something about her was getting to him if he was that upset about her safety. He'd damn near broken that bottle when she told him what happened. He hadn't expected this to pose a threat to her as well as himself. How could such a harmless bit of gawking become so important?

Not ready for sleep, his mind muddled with concern for Anthea was making him restless. He wasn't ready to start caring about someone else. He'd only started to care about himself again. Sitting in the Adirondack chair on the deck, he forced himself to stretch his legs out onto the ottoman and listen to the water rushing below. He ran his fingers through his hair, locking them together behind his head and leaning back into the cushion. He hardly knew who *he* was anymore and he wasn't prepared to entangle his emotions on somebody else's behalf.

Laying back on his palms, elbows jutting to either side of his head, he quieted his thoughts and noticed the sound of the deer snorting in the garden that he hadn't bothered to plant this spring.

Land Barons

Chapter 15

Anthea awoke a little earlier than usual after a restless night tossing and turning so much the bed was a shambles of twisted covers and pummeled pillows. Crawling out of the wreckage, she pushed her hands through her matted hair only to have her fingers get tangled in the snarls that seemed to be a direct result of her war with the bedclothes. Sighing in defeat, she knew that the real battle was the one to be waged with her emotions and the disheveled mass on her head was only an outward symptom of the growing inner turmoil.

I'm not prepared for upheaval and I simply refuse to care. I'll be damned if I'm going to be a target for another cavalier heartbreaker to waltz off with my sanity. Pinning her rationality to this defiant resolve to protect herself, she trod down the hall to continue her morning rituals. First on the list? Make coffee.

She made a mental list of what needed to be accomplished as the coffee finished dripping. Filling her mug, she took her morning elixir directly into the office and punched up her word processing program. Figuring she'd better get as much done before she called Mathers to put their respective notes together, *and keep my head down against incoming fire,* she settled into composing cover letters for the next hour or so.

Coming up for air only for another cup of coffee, Anthea finished her task and made her way to the shower to attempt to wash the knots out of her mop of hair. Checking the time and seeing how much she had completed by 8:30, she was satisfied that her workload was under control and free to move on to other things for the next part of the day. Dropping her robe and nightgown in a pile, she slid under the reinvigorating spray of hot water and rubbed her eyes even more awake.

Unwanted thoughts flitted through her mind about the upcoming a.m. meeting with her new confederate. Beating them back with a conscious effort to concentrate on the problem at hand, she began sorting through the facts that they had begun to compile. *Facts or just imag - ined conspiracy?* She shook her head under the flowing water, wondering if they were really seeing something where nothing existed.

Then she reminded herself that Mathers had been a cop for 20 years. He wouldn't be given to fanciful delusions, and normally, neither would she.

Turning off the water, she pulled a towel through the partially open shower door and scrubbed her hair with the terry cloth. She wrapped the fabric around herself and, standing in front of the mirror, she took a largetooth comb and attacked the tangles spread across her shoulders. As she managed to ease the comb through her hair, she noticed the growing number of gray hairs interspersed among the dark curls. *Can't say I didn't earn 'em, I just don't want to look at 'em.* Accepting their presence, she finished erasing the snarls from her hair, shook out her multi-layered tresses and reached for her underwear when she heard the doorbell sound. The overly loud bong reminded her that she intended to exchange the annoying noisemaker with something less intrusive, which annoyed her even more because she had to grab her robe and tromp out to answer the door.

Glancing through the viewer in the door, she was further annoyed to see Gary Mathers' tall figure filling the small scope. Burying her irritation, she pasted a smile on her face and opened the door.

Poking her wet head around the corner of the molding, she said, "How unexpected to see you on my stoop, Mr. Mathers."

He grinned broadly, noting her deshabille, and held up a white bag, "I brought breakfast," he offered confidently.

She widened the opening and said, "As you can see I'm hardly dressed to receive visitors."

"No problem," his eyes wandered over her figure, the curling mass framing her face and settled on her blue eyes, which reminded him of clear Caribbean waters. He gently pushed through the entrance and said, "I can wait."

Standing back and crossing her arms over her chest as he calmly barged in, she burred, "I don't seem to remember giving you my address."

"You didn't," he responded roguishly. "I still have contacts with the local police." And if it was possible for him to preen even more, he did exactly that.

Anthea wagged her head in disgust and led him out of the entry-way. Pointing to the kitchen she said, "Coffee's over there," and she went back to finish dressing.

•••••••

Emerging ten minutes later in a summer dress with her hair pulled back with large combs, tendrils fell provocatively around her face and down her neck. Although Gary fully expected Anthea to catch his attention, he was caught off-guard instead. *Keep yourself in check, boy. We have work to do.*

Without giving away the pace of his pulse, he stood up from where he had been lounging at the breakfast nook and went to hold up the coffee carafe.

"I hope you don't mind that I made a fresh pot, the dregs in the previous brew were looking suspiciously like sludge," he said keeping his voice even when he was afraid that it would crack like an adolescent's.

Walking up beside him to take a fresh cup from the cabinet, she brushed his arm and coolly apologized, "Had I been expecting guests, I would have been more diligent in my hostessing duties. I made coffee early today and forgot to turn it off after I'd finished. She turned to look up at his mischievously crinkling eyes, recognizing a handsome turn to his rugged features, and losing her vexation, acknowledged his self-sufficiency. "Glad you could locate the components for such a feat in an unknown kitchen."

"I'm a resourceful guy," he replied, eyes flashing mildly.

They both moved to sit across from one another at the table where Mathers had placed a plate of croissants, delicately stacked.

"Mademoiselle?" he said, lifting the dish and offering it to her.

"Croissant du chocolat? How did you know?" she lifted her brows in mock amazement.

"I remembered your penchant for mocha lattes and took a chance that chocolate might be the key to your heart," Mathers bored his eyes into hers.

Oddly flustered, she carefully helped herself and began to pull the pastry apart while she nodded at today's newspaper.

"Did you see the story on the fire?" she inquired.

"Hadn't had a chance to look," he said as he took a bite and turned the paper to face him. "Looks like they got the gist of what happened, though it doesn't say whether or not it was arson."

"You think it was?"

"I have a suspicion. How else could everything go up at once." It was a statement rather than a question. "All of the cut lumber and the stacked timber were in flames all at the same time. A natural progression in a high wind would have logs catching in succession and some not at all. Even the mill burned fast. It looked like Dresden in the Second World War with enough flame to create its own wind."

"Do you know the owner, Bob Powell?" she asked.

"Only in passing. He seems like a nice guy and has tried hard to keep the place open because of the importance the mill has as a major regional employer. I also know what it has cost him and his family."

"But you don't think he can rebuild," she said flatly.

"No way is any insurance company going to ante up with the amount needed for that. His losses are catastrophic," a despondent trace crept into his voice. "And from reading this article, the patch of forest that went up in flames was also his property." His look turned black. "Those sons of bitches," he muttered under his breath.

"What are you talking about?"

"When we tried to get in to work on the forest fire, the US Forest Service refused us access saying that we couldn't fight a fire on federal land, some legal policy. Well according to this, it was private property that was *land-locked* by federal land." He looked up at her, the fury in his expression almost frightening. "They denied a private property owner the *right* to protect his own land." He didn't raise his voice, but the deep menace of his tone was intense.

Grasping the meaning of his words, her face went blank. How could the forest service stand aside and watch someone's livelihood burn to the ground because of a jurisdictional dispute? She began to understand Mathers' anger and obvious frustration.

"Do you have any idea how much 500 acres of prime timber is worth?" he asked rhetorically. "Those bastards let a fortune, not to mention jobs, burn without lifting a finger. I'd sue in a heartbeat, if I were him.

"You know it's bad enough that the mill couldn't get enough timber consignments with the environmental lobbies slapping restraining orders against every logging company trying to harvest in the northwest. They even block the harvesting of dead and dying trees that are nothing but fuel for the next conflagration." Mathers was burning in his own right. "But this," and he stabbed the paper with his index finger, "this was private land and it seems they made sure that he'd never be able to reap a profit. I guess it wasn't enough just to keep filing injunctions so he couldn't harvest his own timber."

Their conversation was interrupted by the ringing phone. She reached around Mathers and lifting the handset, answering the call.

"This is Thea." She was quiet while the caller identified himself and her expression softened into a slight smile.

"Hey Dan, thanks for returning my call. How're things by you?" She listened to his reply and then asked if he had had an opportunity to look into the matter she had called about.

As Gary wasn't privy to the other side of the conversation, Anthea's close proximity set his mind to wandering down avenues he thought were closed to him. The light scent of orange blossoms wafted toward him as she looked out the window, her attention engaged by the person on the other end of the line. His eyes roamed over her neat form, encased in a loose, brightly colored dress that ended in a flounce that caressed her thighs. He noticed the strong muscles of her legs, admiring the shape of her calves as she stood a mere yard away from him, intently considering the import of what she was being told. No longer hearing the content of her words, he was losing himself in the dusky sing-song of her voice pattern. Only when she hung up, turning to replace the receiver, did her gaze brush past his own which was centered on her midriff, eyes clouded, entranced.

"What are you seeing?" she inquired in a smoky tone, noticing his unfocused stare.

Shaking his woolly head loose from his preoccupation, a sinful smile slid across his lips as he answered with the noncommittal "nothing."

"Right." Her eyebrows furrowed slightly. "That was Dan Rennselaer, a friend of mine from a San Francisco paper."

"How good a friend?" The question popped out without forethought, which he regretted as soon as he asked.

"What planet are you on, Mathers?" She bent down a little to look into his eyes that met her gaze with an intensity that almost made her gasp. Pulling away quickly, she went on, "Whatever, Dan works at the Chronicle and I called him yesterday to see if he could drum up any information about Nature's Wilds, which," she added with a little grin, "he did."

She filled in Mathers on the basics that Rennselaer had just related over the telephone, walking toward her office as she talked, motioning him to follow.

"He e-mailed me his results."

Mathers trailed her light tread down the hall, the brief notion of making a detour into one of the other rooms flitting through his mind. *Focus, you jerk.* With difficulty, he returned his attention to the matter at hand.

She sat down at her computer, went online and opened her e-mail account. As expected there was a new contact waiting for her to access, which she did immediately. As the attachment opened she skimmed through it quickly, Mathers leaning over her to read the monitor from just past her shoulder.

"I'm just going to run this out so we can read it properly," she said as she hit the command to print. Even as she finished the small task, she was all too aware of Mathers' nearness. She leaned over, fished the printed sheets from the bin and managed to maneuver him back a short distance by sheer force of will. Collecting the papers, she gestured Mathers to exit the confining atmosphere of the office and follow her back to the kitchen where his presence wasn't as overpowering and she felt she could take a full breath.

Laying the notes on the table, she sorted them and gave Mathers one set.

"It looks like Nature's Wilds Conservancy is funded pretty exclusively by these three foundations, although the general information on them is pretty slim. They have to get their money somewhere," she observed. She raised one of the sheets to read its contents and saw the name of two organizations that have received some press coverage Friends of the Land and Earth Grant. The latter was a well-known ecology promotion non-profit whose board of directors looked like a who's who of corporate America combined with the entertainment industry's heavy hitters. Dan had attached biographies of the board members but aside from them being influential in the business, music and film world, there wasn't anything that was particularly interesting.

"All it seems to mean is that there's money backing the conservancy," Mathers said. "Which, of course, we already knew. How else could they be purchasing land all across the States?'

"Nothing more than the obvious here," she agreed.

"Doesn't look like this helps much." He sounded disappointed.

"We're just going to have to dig deeper."

Land Barons

Chapter 16

Billy Brogus was kicking back in a patio chair, legs outstretched with scuffed boots crossed at the ankles resting on the rail that encircled the deck, surveying a small part of his miniature empire. The view he beheld was that of forested hillsides reaching into the distant mountains. What interested him most, however, was what he couldn't see. Buried among the lush green boughs swaying in the morning breeze, were acres of crops…cash crops that couldn't be distinguished from the companion plants by the naked eye. His smile curved up a little more as he simply enjoyed the prospect that they were preparing for harvest, and it would be a healthy one.

Brogus was a man of means, not that anyone but his immediate confederates were privy to that information. His status as a businessman was low key as his legitimate crop made a modest profit. It was the illicit enterprise that made him a wealthy man, and that crop was what he was viewing without actually seeing at the moment.

An entrepreneur in the distribution of shady goods, Brogus' clandestine agricultural operations had been hugely successful. No one knew where it came from, but Wildwood Gold was a byword on the street and he had the exclusive contract. He handled everything from planting to harvest to marketing and he made a hefty profit in so doing.

Leaning back with his Sony notebook opened in his lap, he was going through the current accounting for the upcoming harvest. Sun flashed off his red-gold hair and sifted through the neatly trimmed beard he sported. Brogus finished his entries and settling his feet back on the wooden floorboards, set aside the computer and stood up to stretch his tall, well-made frame. Now in his late thirties, his physical condition was excellent due to his personal interest in the farms, hiking through the forests to reach the concealed crops and check on their progress as well as the health of his employees. Although he dealt in what some would consider an unsavory trade, he was diligent about making certain his people were properly compensated. He may traffic in illegal product but, according to his cohorts, he wasn't without a conscience. The thought of which would have made him laugh. Yeah, an outlaw with a heart, that's him.

His number one, Joe Santos, brought out the daily paper and laid it on the railing in front of his boss. He pointed out the article on the fire that covered most of the front page.

"Looks like the major story around here," said Santos.

"Well, it would be considering all those jobs just went up in smoke," observed Brogus.

"That was a pretty big blaze, the forest fire that is."

"Yeah, I was with the volunteers when the forest service drove them away from the fire line spouting some kind of jurisdictional trash," he was disgusted. "They just let the trees burn. Even if the mill hadn't been incinerated, those green goons were doing a damned effective job of shoving old man Powell into the poorhouse."

"You mean those injunctions that kept him from cutting his timber." It was a statement. "It's not like we can fill the gap here. Most of what we do is under the radar."

"Look, we make a contribution to the local economy in our own way, but we're not likely to become a major employer for precisely the reason you just pointed out." Brogus shook his head.

"Come on," he beckoned Santos with his hand. "We've got to go check that operation near yesterday's fire. I want to make sure nobody stumbled across anything they shouldn't know about."

They gathered up a few things, loaded them in the Jeep and drove off.

•••••••

In her office, facing the main drag in Marcasite, Carrie DiMarco was working the phones. She'd been on the line with the principal of the local elementary school for half an hour already, going over the details for tomorrow's outdoor workshop. Hanging her head as she tried desperately to maneuver her way out of the conversation so she could prepare her packets for the students, she heard the school secretary tell Mrs. Tabor that she had a call from district on hold. Carrie looked up toward the heavens and mouthed a thank you to any invisible deity that happened to be within silent earshot and was perfunctorily disconnected within seconds. As the new director of Rural

Resources she was making her community contacts and coordinating educational nature walks and presentations for many of the area schools and organizations. The next day's field trip was one of many she'd penciled in on the calendar.

She lifted the phone once again and dialed a new number, receiving an answering machine, she left a message reminding her assistant to meet her at the office at noon so they could travel to the school together. Before hanging up, she also remarked that she had seen the newspaper this morning and the coverage on the fire.

Traffic down the only artery through Marcasite was bustling with the usual business of a small town. Tourists strolled into the few antique and gift shops, and the café actually had a waiting line. Even the banks were encountering what could almost be considered a rush in a town this size.

She was standing in front of her desk, observing the activity when the phone rang behind her. Turning to grasp the receiver, she answered in a professional tone, "Rural Resources, this is Carrie. How may I help you?"

A voice she recognized by the subtlety of the speaker's timbre began with a blasé salutation.

"Good day, Ms. DiMarco."

"Good morning, sir," she replied with what was a growing trepidation every time he called.

"We heard about the fire that decimated the local lumber mill and that other wildfire nearby," he noted almost disinterestedly.

"Yes, it looks like Powell was pretty well burned out. I don't think he'll have the resources to reopen soon, if ever," she commented as blandly as possible.

The only response she heard was a non-committal "too bad" from the other end of the line. "We'll talk again." The phone went dead.

Replacing the handset, she stared unseeing out the plate glass window at the brisk spring trade, vainly hoping that she wouldn't hear from him again.

•••••••

Anthea and Mathers had gathered up all the materials they had and decided that it was time to do a little reconnaissance. They had a copy of the deeds that he had found the day before, and although he had looked up some of the parcels in the ledger at the assessor's office, they realized that they needed a proper map designating range and township in order to locate them.

Gary inveigled Anthea to climb into his truck, citing the lack of sense in driving two vehicles out to Marcasite. In Lathrop they stopped back by the courthouse to check through the plat book once more. Bringing a detailed county map that they had purchased at a local outfitter's, they used the descriptions to get an idea where the parcels were on the chart. The newly compiled information tucked under his arm, they went up the hill to Mathers' home where they alighted from the cab and bearing their document collection inside, they laid everything across his dining table.

Anthea spread out the map, smoothing the folds to lessen the shadows and began poring over the cartographic elements, looking from the lot description in the deeds and back to the map.

"Sometimes it's difficult to get beyond the lot and subdivision part of the legal description to find the pertinent section on a regular map. I think surveyors use language beyond our ken the same as attorneys. Oh look, here's one."

Mathers leaned forward to look over her shoulder and to fight the inclination to inhale too deeply the scent from her hair. Forcing himself to focus on the chart, he followed her finger to one of the recent purchases and checking the deed, concurred with her find.

"Let's see where this next one is. Seems to me that it will be closely situated." Reaching over to another one of the legal documents, his arm brushed hers, sending a chill up her spine. He pulled the paper close enough to easily read and didn't bother to reposition himself, staying close enough for physical contact.

Anthea felt the heat he emanated, which was muddling her thought processes, so she squirmed to get a comfortable distance reestablished.

"Here it is," he stabbed the map, uncapped a highlighter and outlined the two parcels so far located. She slipped past him to pick-up the last of the deeds and held them while they scrutinized the markings to find their placement. As each one was discovered, they drew a bright orange line around the general area. Then they stood back to examine the map. What they saw was a large block of Marcasite County, which was no longer under the ownership of private individuals, but had been swallowed by a land conservancy, sworn to protect the land from human devastation.

"Okay, now let's find where Ahlsted's ranch is and the lumber mill, see if we can't expand the picture," instructed Mathers.

"These appear to be the missing puzzle pieces, don't they?" She looked past her shoulder at him, realizing again how close he was physically. "Where's your property?"

He pointed down at an area that skirted the river shore.

"Right here, right in the midst of the usurpation."

"Do you have much acreage?"

"No, just twenty acres. Most of its trees and some hayfields. Nothing they'd bother with."

"Not unless you get in their way," she said, concerned.

"Now, why would I do any such thing?" He lowered his eyes to hers and gave her a puckish grin that generated a warmth within her that caught her unprepared. Instead she redirected her attention to the map and drew her finger along the national forest where it bordered the newly acquired land.

"Why do you think they chose this particular area and notice how it all abuts the forest." She paused and said again, almost under her breath, "why?"

"I'm sure they'd explain that it was for conservation purposes," he said.

"But to what cost for these families," Anthea opined.

"Not to mention the local economy." He looked at her and said, "I think it's time to make a foray into the forest. Let's go for a drive. Come on, we need a break."

Returning to the Chevy, they headed up the mountain to revisit the site of yesterday's fire. As they arrived at the smoking ruin, they saw Bob Powell kicking through the ashes of what had been the office. His son, Doug, the mill foreman, was using a crowbar to get into a fire resistant file cabinet that looked like the heat had welded shut.

Mathers and Anthea carefully stepped through the debris, checking the ground for potential hazards. When he reached Bob Powell, he offered his hand in condolence.

"I'm sorry we weren't able to save the mill, Bob. I was here with the rest of the volunteer fire fighters and fast as I thought the response time was, we were still too late."

"One thing's for sure, the way it went up, there couldn't be a 'fast enough.'" He looked reflectively across the moonscape of dust and burned-out buildings. "This old mill has been operating since 1907 and this is the second fire in all that time. Wood building or no, even the first fire 60 years ago didn't do this much damage. This time *noth - ing's* left.

"Have they determined the cause of the fire?" inquired Mathers.

"They're still investigating, though they've bandied around the word 'negligence.'" He had an angry cast to his features.

"No negligence could account for the way this was consumed in so short a time," offered Mathers.

"What the hell do they mean by that?" Doug put in bitterly. "Someone dropped a cigarette or accidentally fired up a flamethrower? That's just about what you'd need for this kind of absolute destruction. No misplaced cig or unattended hotplate is gonna do *anything* like this," he spat.

"What about accelerants? Have any been found?" asked Anthea.

"If they've found any, they're not talkin', at least, not to me," grumbled the father. "And until they fixate on an answer, we can't get dime one out of those damn insurers." He bent over to pick up an object that might have been a paperweight or a stapler. It was only recognizable now as an indistinguishable lump of metal.

"I don't know where my folks are gonna go now," he lamented. "We were struggling to keep our operations alive what with the eco-lobby shutting us down every time we tried to harvest our own trees. And that patch of forest that just burned? I had just gotten word that the injunction was thrown out so we were preparing to start logging next week." He looked emotionally spent. "No mill and now no timber to process. They couldn't have planned it any better."

"You think eco-terrorists might have burned you out?" Anthea ventured.

"Now, I didn't say that. It just seems awful coincidental with all the flack we've been getting from environmentalists. They were protesting at our office in town just last month."

"They're not gonna bother the big boys, are they?" added Doug. "They'll expend all their energy on folks like us but let the monster companies like Weyerhauser and Georgia Pacific slide because they have the resources to fight back." He was disgusted with the whole situation. "They'd have law enforcement haulin' their scrawny butts off to jail in no time."

"Much as it's hard to accept, it's probably true, just like any predator going for the soft underbelly of their prey," added Powell. "We're the helpless prey that can't protect itself. The easy target."

Mathers gave Bob Powell his hand again. "Let me know if there's anything I can do." He surveyed the ruin. "Though I'm not sure what that could be right now. Give me a call. I'm in the book."

They shook hands.

"Thanks for being here to help when it counted most," he raised his eyes to sweep across the devastation. "Too bad it was a wasted effort."

As they reached the Chevy, Mathers opened Anthea's door for her and helped her up into the cab.

"There's still smoke rising off of the wildfire. I want to see what the situation is out there now." He looked over at her and she nodded her agreement.

Land Barons

Chapter 17

Backtracking to where Mathers stood shoulder to shoulder with his volunteer fire district members the day before, they found that the access road was now blocked by sawhorses and yellow tape, discouraging entry from any but official personnel. No one was manning the barrier.

"This is a friendly welcome," noted Mathers, vexed at the gall of the rangers yet again. "Let's try a different route."

He turned around and drove further north another mile to exit at a dirt track that followed a line of trees.

Leaving the asphalt, Mathers said, "This is the back way in and they may not have bothered to set up barriers because the road is pretty poor." Looking over at Anthea, he notified her, "It's gonna be bumpy."

"I didn't know this was a recreational excursion," she tossed out with a smile.

This was definitely the indirect route and it was a rough track that was generally used by hunters on their ATV's. They watched as the smoke trailing into the sky appeared to get closer as they covered a couple of miles of rough road. The plume billowed thick and black as it rose from the forest just ahead of them. Fire licked up the trunks of trees as a helicopter flew over to dump its load of retardant on the recalcitrant flames. Although it was difficult to tell from their vantage point, Mathers thought that the fire might have been mostly contained.

"Interesting that they went out of their way to keep fire fighting craft away from the area yesterday and today they're throwing whatever they have at the blaze."

"And by that you mean…?" inquired Anthea.

"They just cordoned off the area, wouldn't let the volunteer fire crew in to assist and took virtually no action themselves. There certainly weren't any airdrops and no federal fire crews in sight. Gave us some tripe about USFS policy."

"What was their policy? To let it burn?" She was incredulous.

"Looks that way. Seems it isn't their duty to protect anything but government land, yet they wouldn't let locals cross public land to save a private holding." His face reflected his distaste. "But I'm guessing it's okay to fight it now since the fire is encroaching on USFS land and their liability." He was pensive. "Could be the whole basis of their 'policy' is simply to avoid a litigious situation…you know, keep the public out so there'll be no chance of being sued."

"Pretty cynical viewpoint, don't you think?" asked Anthea.

"Yeah, well, this is the government we're talking about, and CYA is the first order of business." He pursed his lips in distaste.

They had left the truck standing by the side of the track while viewing the fire and the attempt to douse the flames, which were climbing high amid the boughs. At the least, the weather was in the favor of the fire crews as it was a calm day. Even at this distance, however they could see the trees sway in the wind created by the fire itself and jumped when a dry tree literally exploded in flame, a small shockwave slapping their bodies.

A beat-up Jeep, painted the nauseating green the forest service favors, bouncing and jarring the occupants, shot out of the treeline, fast approaching their position.

"Looks like we're gonna get the boot again," said Mathers, watching the vehicle jounce in their direction.

All they received from the driver and passenger was a drilling stare as the Jeep flew by without slowing. Mathers noted their lack of uniforms and wondered who they were.

•••••••

"Who do you think they are?" Brogus asked his manager cum chauffeur.

"No idea…lookie loos, prob'ly," Santos offered, uninterested.

"Doubtful. I recognize the guy from the fire yesterday. One of the volunteer bunch, like me I guess."

"Wanna go back and have a word with 'em?"

"No. They don't need to know anything about us. No questions, no answers.

"Gotcha." Santos just kept the Jeep bouncing down the road at a brisk clip.

Mathers and Anthea kept their eyes trained on the disappearing

Jeep, the roll bar being the last part of the vehicle to slide from view.

"So, who was that? Definitely not official personnel," stated Anthea.

"He looks like a fella I've seen. I think he runs some business way off the beaten track," mused Mathers as he watched the dust dissipate.

"He's in some kind of hurry." Her eyes drifted back to her companion. "I thought everyone out here lived in a laid back heaven," she added with an amused glint.

"This is America, no one knows how to relax. We're just a bunch of workaholics, remember?" He responded in the same droll spirit. "Aren't we the poster children of leisure."

Realizing that they'd gone as far as they could without becoming an encumbrance to the fire fighting process, they climbed back in the Chevy and, with less need for haste than the Jeep's riders, returned to Mathers' home.

•••••••

From under cover of the overhanging branches, a young man of medium height and build emerged from the shadows, lowering his binoculars as the dust from the second vehicle diffused into the smoke-laden air. Not used to the duty of tracking, he found it an intriguing, albeit sometimes dull, charge but today all he'd been doing was checking the damage of one burned out ruin after another.

His curiosity was piqued as he watched the Jeep come barreling out of the trees, knowing that they were neither rangers nor local landowners. He hadn't seen them earlier when he had half-hidden his own vehicle back in the woods, but he knew they weren't strangers. He was certain that he had observed them on the street in town sometime in the recent past. The question of what they had been doing so close to the fire line obviously wasn't going to be answered today.

With nothing else to divert his interest since even the wildilfe had deserted the area, frightened of the encroaching blaze, he hiked back to his borrowed four-wheeler and rode back down the mountain.

117

Land Barons

Chapter 18

The phone jangled in her ear as she was finishing composing the handouts for tomorrow's outdoor workshop. The bleating noise grated on her already frazzled nerves, sending her heart into minor arrhythmia, not to mention the complete interruption of her concentration.

"What now," she muttered before lifting the receiver and answering in the proper tone.

In response to the disembodied but recognizable voice on the other end, she said, "Those two just seem to show up every time we turn around, and particularly where they're not wanted."

"They didn't seem to be doing anything more than the usual rubber-necking at a disaster site. Though what their interest is, I've no clue."

"Well, let them be and don't bother to follow them, we have enough to think about and need to keep a low profile."

"What's the problem?" He was ready to hop in his truck and go.

"I'm just telling you that we have to cool it if somebody's taking an undue interest in certain developments and have their nose in the wind," she explained vaguely.

There was silence on the line before he piped up with an epiphany. "Oh, you mean sniffing around."

She was getting exasperated. "What are you majoring in…deductive reasoning?"

"Amusing," he said, hurt by her sarcasm. "Hey, someone else was out here too, though I didn't see them 'til they came blasting out of the trees. I'm pretty sure they didn't notice me."

"Anyone we know?"

"I recognized their faces but I don't know who they are. I think I've just seen them around town. But they ventured much closer to the fire line than I did. They must've been checking something out," he offered.

"Terrific, that's all we need are more interested parties," She sighed into the mouthpiece. "Look, you've done fine. Just call it a day and don't worry about the gawkers."

"Sure," he signed off.

Carrie replaced the receiver, drained of energy. Turning her attention back to the computer, she wrapped up her project and sent the document to 'print.' Leaning back in the chair, she listened to the copies spitting out of the printer situated on an adjacent stand. The whirring of the gears followed by the pages dropping one on top of the next, created a cadence that began to soothe the raw edges of her emotional state. When the machine finished its task, she took her time floating back to the surface of reality, at which point she shut down the program and collected the copies. Jogging the pile, she set them neatly on her desk ready for delivery the next morning.

The clock ticked a steady beat in the otherwise silent office, drawing her to check the hour. Quitting time, she decided and hunted for her key to lock the front door. Gathering her personal effects, and throwing the strap of her purse over her shoulder, she departed out of the rear entrance, turning to secure the lock and thinking that this was supposed to be so easy.

·······

Traveling down the mountain, Anthea kept her gaze on the billow of hazy smoke that diminished as the distance grew between them and the forest that was still under the sway of unfettered flames. Bits of ash floated by on the breeze, some of it depositing on the windshield, creating a film of soot that ended up coating the vehicle until it appeared gray in color rather than the light desert tan it was intended to be. The air was beginning to clear as they neared the turn-off to Mathers' place with only occasional filmy black flakes catching the wind for a ride this far from the fire. Her hopes whirled around the firefighters controlling the blaze soon, even though it was too late for Bob Powell to benefit from its extinguishing.

Gary seemed lost in his own contemplation as he steered the Chevy almost by rote down the two-lane highway. Anthea stole the opportunity to examine his profile, noting the strength of his countenance and the solidity of character that he exuded. His presence was comforting to her as she weighed the unfortunate circumstances that others now had to confront. Not that she hadn't faced enough of her own demons over the years. Having to struggle back from abandonment after her husband left and create a livelihood for herself when prospects seemed less than nil, she had managed to carve out a niche for herself in the business world. *Mostly luck.* Counting blessings may seem quaint to some, she thought, but she was making her checklist of every one that she was lucky to have. Those folks who tell you that you've got to make your luck have obviously never had to rely on it. No contest here, she was definitely a fortunate woman.

She felt the truck slow and make the bend to the right as Gary left the macadam and followed the gravel road up to his driveway. As he braked, she brought her focus back to the present. Alighting from his seat, he came around to her door and practically lifted her to the ground as he helped her out of the suspended cab.

"Thank you." The words came out garbled as she sensed a blush beginning to creep up her neck.

He looked down at her and said simply, "You're welcome, miss."

Her head shot up with a smile. "Thanks for not saying 'ma'am.' I've begun to dread the designation and that young officer in Lewiston, although polite in his intent, was trying my patience every time he used it."

"My pleasure, *miss*," and he emphasized the word with an infectious grin.

Throughout the whole exchange he had not released her from his firm grip, but kept his hands wrapped around her waist. Reluctantly he removed his fingers and gestured to the front door for the second time today.

He tossed his keys onto the hall table and led the way into the living room, walking directly to the glass doors and opening them to allow the cooling evening air to circulate. Standing at the rail, the plume of smoke was still evident rising above the ridge. Anthea laid her fingers lightly on the roughhewn railing to take in the fresh scent of the river vale and view the myriad shades of green that colored it. Gary settled himself next to her, close enough for her to hear the sough of his breath in the relative silent surroundings. As he did so, he gently covered one of her hands with his, stroking the side of her palm with his thumb.

The warmth that channeled through her system from his touch was far more intense than she expected for such simple contact. She looked at him only to see that he had not changed the direction of his focus, but continued to view the quiet forest while touching her only in this way.

Nonplussed, she lowered her eyes and attempted to calm her pulse that had inadvertently increased when he placed his hand over hers. Finally, he turned to look at her, taking her hand in his, he leaned into the rail, his elbow supported by the wooden beam.

"Are you ready for some dinner?" If it was possible to make such a blasé inquiry sound any more sensual, she was sure no one had managed it before now and she felt the blood flush her skin as he intoned the question. Unable to find her tongue, she only nodded slowly in reply.

"Good," and he pulled her to him and kissed her lightly at first, surprising her with his lips brushing hers in a tender caress which quickly gave way to a deepening search as his tongue slid into her slightly parted mouth. She returned the ardor of his first foray inside her defenses, letting them crumble around her as he drew her closer.

Reticent to disengage himself from her pliant lips, he lifted his mouth away from hers, a smoky mien suffusing his eyes turning to hint of teasing. "Let me do what men do best… grill meat." He stood back slightly with his hands on her upper arms, kneading her muscles with a gentle but supple touch.

Anthea was mesmerized enough to say and do nothing. She stood there letting him support her with his hands because her own strength had dissipated and she needed his to keep herself upright.

Swallowing, she said, "What can I do to help?"

"Absolutely nothing more than what you're doing now, filling my sight with a loveliness I haven't encountered in a very long time."

Her eyes widened in surprise. She never thought of herself in those terms and could hardly accept his words though it was evident he meant them. Instead of answering, she smiled shyly which only encouraged him to bend forward and kiss her again before going back into the house, leaving her slightly stunned and grappling to regain composure.

Anthea readjusted her dress and after letting her hands float up to check her hair, she followed Mathers back into the kitchen.

"I'm sure you have something I can do to be useful," she ventured as he pulled steaks out of the refrigerator. She stood with her back resting against the counter as he then reached down and drew a bottle of

Cabernet out of a small wine rack. Standing it on the butcher block, he opened a drawer to remove the corkscrew and, applying it to the task, pulled the cork free. He turned to open a cabinet, brought out two crystal wine goblets and placed them on the wooden cutting surface.

"Will you pour?" he asked in a silky voice.

"Certainly, sir." She smiled as she tipped the bottle, generously filling the two glasses.

They maneuvered around each other as he directed her to the dishes and cutlery while lighting the grill. Moving in on the crisper, Anthea rummaged for salad makings and located bowl and utensils while Gary manned the outside duties.

She set the table and arranged the salad bowl. Bringing Gary his wine, she stood by the deck railing and sipped the dry, red vintage.

"Very pleasing," she said with approval.

"Me or the wine?" He faced her with a glint of mischief playing in his gray irises.

"Mmmm, you far more than the wine. Though this appears to be quite superior, " she added almost absently as she lifted the glass to examine it in the dying embers of daylight.

He left the fillets to themselves and gathered her up for another sultry kiss, which only left her even more flustered than the first time.

"Am I embarrassing you, Anthea?" He held her chin in his fingers.

"No, yes…I just feel so strange."

"Should I leave you be?"

"No…no," she said more firmly. "I'm just not used to the attention."

"That's a poor excuse. I expect men are often attending to you."

"Oh, not at all. I keep to myself, and…" she let her words float off with the breeze.

"And you're afraid of entanglement."

She looked at him, understanding that he could see through her.

His own thoughts, as he searched her eyes, were those of sympathetic comprehension. He was being drawn inexorably toward the image of her full, pouting mouth, unable to resist her sweet taste that still lingered on his lips. He lost the battle to hold back. Fully knowing that he was on the precipice of losing his perspective, he plunged over the edge and enfolding her in his arms, tenderly lowered his mouth to hers. Enflamed by the exquisite contact, he pressed her suppleness to his chest, her arms sliding up his back, encircling him of their own accord.

When they finally separated, they were both struggling for breath, the flush of longing infused them both, but it also frightened them equally. He backed off slightly, huskily pointing out that dinner will burn.

Agreeing, Anthea desperately tried to recover her dignity while the heightened awareness of every move he made in returning to the meal's preparation kept her heart hammering rather than slowing. *Oh lord, now how can I simply fall back into the small talk mode? Face it, it ain't gonna happen.* She knew that detachment wasn't going to be part of the equation, they'd crossed the line. A sweet, tender boundary, but a boundary none the less. This was the limit of walls disintegrating, from here she had to rebuild.

Mathers removed the entrée from the grill and brought it to the table. He pulled out the chair for her to sit, which she did feeling like she was swimming through pudding, her limbs moving with a languor that was unnatural.

Sitting opposite her and leaning across the table, he wrapped his fingers around her own, his desire conveyed by the smoldering look in his eyes. Working hard to slow his pulse, he wanted to allay the fear that was displayed in Anthea's features.

"Don't worry, I'm not going to ravish you, as much as the idea appeals to me. I want you to trust me and that is going to take some effort." He indicated the meal laid before them. "Join me, please."

Uncertain as to whether she could even swallow a morsel, she delicately raised her fork and smiled her reply, which was a simple 'thank you.'

The silence was drawn out interminably while they ate. Finally, the tension dispelled, they were able to engage in desultory conversation.

Anthea took the opportunity to probe a little further into his past with simple queries.

"Is Gary your given name or a shortened version of something more fitting with your aristocratic bearing?"

At that he practically guffawed. "Aristocratic? I'm as far from noble blood as a mule from a Lippizaner. But you guessed right about my name, though it has more to do with a passion for literature than heritage."

She raised her brows inquisitively, awaiting an answer.

"Mother was a fan of the Camelot fable and chose the name from a relative of King Arthur. Supposedly a son of the witch, Morgause, or as some tales referred to her as Morgan le Fay, and a brother of the gallant Sir Gawain - the second youngest, Gaheris. She was enamored with the name even as a teen and apparently pressured my dad into naming his only son after the squire who, according to legend, died in the service of the king protecting him from his own evil son, Mordred, Gaheris' half-brother. You know, the tale has been so twisted over the centuries that it gets confusing as to whether Morgan was the same as Morgause or her mother or sister, who had enchanted King Uther Pendragon, Arthur's father, creating a real incest problem when she seduced Arthur to conceive Mordred."

"She was his sister?" She asked incredulously

"Truthfully, I forget the details. Though it might be that she was his aunt."

"So, let's see if I have this right. Gaheris was Arthur's half brother and Mordred was both his son and nephew. No wait, that's only if she was his sister. Very confusing. Yet the nobility of the name breeds through your demeanor, blue-blood or not."

"Not to mention the fact that Camelot and King Arthur never existed," he corrected her train of thought.

"That depends on your view of history and the fact that the tale came down from the dark ages where only clerics and a few of the privileged could read, or wizards like Merlin. Remember the first rule of myth, it's based, however loosely, in fact. Besides, I like the idea of believing your name is descended from the annals of Chivalry."

"What about 'Anthea?' What is the origin of that unusual name?" He tilted his head in slight amusement, lifting his glass to drink.

"Mom never told me how she and Dad settled on the choice. I do remember them telling us once that all of our names were chosen according to how they sounded with our surname."

He rolled her full name around his tongue just as he had done with his wine, approving.

"But no family secret or special fancy that prompted the selection."

"No, all the name afforded me was the unfortunate epithet of 'anteater' in grade school," the recollection prompted a slight frown to pucker her brow. "I'm guessing the length of my nose didn't help that, either."

"Children aren't known for their consideration," he said gazing at her above the crystal rim.

Breaking the eye contact, Anthea placed her fork on the plate, indicating the conclusion of the meal. Then she began to stack and clear the dishes, rising to collect the dirty crockery and deposit it in the sink.

Gary stood and carried the rest of the plates into the kitchen, blocking her exit.

"Don't worry about the dishes. I'll do them later."

She shook her curls, negating his offer. "You cook, I clean. It's only fair."

"Okay, then I'll dry."

A tacit agreement in place, they silently worked side-by-side to finish the dishes. Every plate and utensil had been washed, dried and returned to its proper location, at which point an awkward moment ensued.

Brushing the tendrils of hair from her forehead, Gary leaned over to buss her temple with a light touch that made her stomach flutter. A knuckle under her chin, Gary raised her head so their eyes met. "I think it's time I took you home," and he bent to kiss her once more.

Releasing her chin, he went to gather her things as she looked at him with a tremulous mixture of yearning and relief. Shaking off the spell he had created, she followed him to the truck and he drove her to her door.

Chapter 19

"Careful as you leave the vehicle and line up single file," the young teacher, short sleeve chambray shirt neatly tucked into her jeans, reminded the children as they descended from the dented, old yellow school bus. The fifth and sixth graders, disregarding the warning, hopped and jumped down the steps, giggling and pushing once they reached the ground. Taking the arms of two boys whose playful shoving was rapidly getting out of hand, she pulled them apart and set them at opposite ends of the line.

Carrie had climbed down ahead of the crowd and had parked herself off to the side while Miss Preston did her best to control the unruly waifs. Remembering her own life at that age didn't give her any comfort, having been constantly at the butt of some bully's insensitive joke, though she never really knew why they chose her to pick on other than being introverted and a real bookworm. The purposeful hurt that would spew from one particular boy's mouth, whose ugly language rivaled the repulsiveness of his appearance, which was due more to filth than physical deformity, was the worst of her memories. Her gaze drifted across the young faces queued up next to the dusty side of the bus. Most of the children seemed well behaved enough, only a few were overly rambunctious. Nothing she couldn't deal with.

Miss Preston, a new college graduate, went down the line handing the students each a personal water bottle and advising them that this would be all they would receive. "Make sure you don't lose it, and if you finish your water before the end of the hike, keep your bottle until you can discard it properly in a recycling bin." The lack of interest displayed in her directions convinced Carrie that she would probably have to return for trash pick-up later.

"Pay attention to Miss DiMarco now, because you never know when you might have a pop quiz on what you learn here," forewarned the teacher only to be rewarded with a collective groan.

Carrie's assistant exited the bus last, a backpack loaded with extra supplies for the three-quarter mile hike hitched over his shoulder.

Carrie called out, "Are we ready?" …to which there was a clamorous response of yelled yesses and a few whistles that pierced her eardrums, threatening her with a lifelong case of tinnitus. "Great then, let's go."

She lead the motley train of pupils, knowing that the test was to keep them interested in the subject matter. They stopped at the first of the stations along the way where a type of native tree was indicated by its genus appellation that was posted on the identifying plaque. She waited for the children to gather around before she rattled off the conditions under which this particular tree thrived and what percentage of the forest it comprised. She passed around a diagram of the pine's needle type and shape of the cone and seed so they might learn to recognize them.

As the tail end of the line was finishing the examination of the diagram, they began to move on down the nature trail. Only fourteen more to go, Carrie thought.

They rounded the path to view each of the native flora specimens with some of the children exhibiting an actual interest in the topic. Others just used the free time to goof-off with their buddies and enjoy the chance to be outside rather than cooped-up in the classroom. On the whole, Carrie really enjoyed instructing the kids, particularly when she was able to reach a few of them with the enthusiasm that she felt for protecting the environment.

The flora was well designated by neatly stationed signs but the area was fairly devoid of native fauna aside from a few squirrels racing up the trees. These were kids who had grown up in the country, so they didn't respond to the everyday appearance of the like of squirrels, even the cottontail that hopped past was mostly ignored. One boy stopped and aimed at the rabbit as if he wielded a shotgun. Probably just like the one he had at home, thought Carrie disgustedly. She knew that most of her students were also raised on hunting, which she had no stomach for, considering it barbaric. She returned her attention to the job at hand, that of indoctrinating these kids to cherish the land they lived on and to keep it from being despoiled by man.

At approximately the halfway point of the walk, a glade opened up with picnic tables and benches situated under the hanging boughs of the evergreens. Miss Preston split the class up into groups that she knew she could control and assigned them to specific tables.

Carrie took her position at what could be considered the front of the classroom, a backdrop of native pines, firs and a few deciduous trees sprinkled in the mix. The late spring day was comfortably warm with the temperature hovering in the high seventies, light filtering through the branches in a soft green glow.

"Have you all learned something new today?"

No direct response was forthcoming, just a lot of head-bobbing as they all nodded an affirmative answer.

This was the part that Carrie liked best, a captive audience that is generally accepting of her opinion on the sanctity of nature and the duty of humanity to leave the wilds in its natural state, undisturbed by the greedy, gluttonous hand of those who would usurp the earth's bounty for their own gain. Not that she'd use that terminology with a passle of kids. Instead she drew a picture of the earth's perfect balance, how nature operated the way it was intended without man's interference. She talked about how the forests should retain their unchanged state so children just like them could enjoy them in the future. Leading her listeners through a scenario of her version of paradise, she culminated her little talk.

One boy, hair spiked with gel in a contemporary style, he seemed a little younger than the others. His hand shot up as soon as she asked for questions.

"If we left everything to itself, like they've been doing in the national parks for the last twenty years, won't it just all burn out with the next big fire, leaving nothing for anyone to enjoy?" he squeaked a little on the final word.

"Of course not, nature has managed itself for millenia."

"Yeah, but nature also provides natural checks and balances, like occasional wildfires to clear out the underbrush."

She was astonished at his vocabulary and was beginning to wonder if someone had set her up with a ringer. "And your point, sir?"

"My point is that the forests have been so mismanaged over the last decades that underbrush and dead timber haven't been removed. They've also had an aggressive forest fire prevention program which was altered last decade, leaving the forest, particularly the national parks in serious danger."

"Are you saying we should have regular fires?" Why was she letting this kid draw her into a debate?

"No, what my studies have shown is that if the US Forest Service hadn't instituted such an all-encompassing fire suppression plan as well as refusing to allow selective logging to clear the density of the forest, we wouldn't be in the position we are today of sitting on virtual tinderboxes." He took a deep breath and plowed ahead, his spiky do, bobbing with the waving of his short arms.

"Look what happened as a result in Yellowstone in 1988. That fire burned so hot in the northeast sector that it actually sterilized the soil. It's a moonscape and I don't think that that was the intention of the forest service's "let nature take its course" plan, because, in effect, they prevented exactly that and created the scenario for a superfire. It is true that some seeds need very hot temperatures to germinate, but that can be accomplished without the whole forest burning to the substrata. Now no one is enjoying pristine woodlands."

Carrie stood with her mouth practically agape after the youngster's tirade on forest management.

"How old are you?" The question came from a bystander who, touring the nature trail, had stopped to listen in on the class discussion.

Carrie looked up to see who had crashed her class, a stunned expression of surprise flashing across her face only to be rapidly replaced by a flat mask of indifference. She turned back to the loquacious student.

"Eminent environmentalists have taught otherwise," noted Carrie

"Eminent environmentalists need to get out more." The kids howled with laughter at the interloper's comment as he lounged against the trunk of a tree just outside the circle of tables.

"Well, I think that's enough entertainment for now," Carrie motioned the children up with her hands. "Everybody up, let's finish the tour."

Finishing the course took less time than she expected, partially due to her abbreviated explanation of the plants and partly due to her discomfiture at the earlier incident. Finally, they approached the bus and another picnic area where she stopped to speak with Miss Preston to discuss giving the children their snacks and a restroom break before returning to the school. The teacher agreed and took charge of her students, Carrie's assistant helping where needed.

Walking back to where the class had just ended their nature walk, Carrie found her intruder, this time leaning against a fence post with arms folded across his chest.

"Well, hello Billy. Do you make it a habit of popping out of the woodwork these days?"

"Nah, only when it's certain to induce shock and dismay in some old acquaintance," he offered her a grin filled with mischief.

Hesitating, she asked, "Did you plan this?"

"No, I was just checking out the new nature trail. Heard you were in town, though."

Carrie just gave him a questioning look in response.

"Nothing so conniving. I read the local paper and the new director for Rural Resources made the front page," he explained without expression.

"It wasn't any secret," she agreed.

Taking in the surroundings as he slowly swiveled his head. "Is this your doing?"

"I helped raise the funds and write the development grant, so, yes, I guess it is in a way."

"You know, a real nice family used to live on this property until about a couple years ago. The land had been in their hands for generations until some nasty misfortunes forced them to sell. But I suppose their bad luck was the gain for your supercilious organization," he added in a disgusted tone.

She just gave him a stare that could burn holes through steel.

"Much as you advocate leaving nature to itself, you never did learn to leave it or people alone. Always have to preach and meddle. They taught you well at Environmental U," his disapproval was palpable.

She was bristling. "And what did you major in at Humboldt...agribiz? At the very least your vocabulary improved. You've a ways to go yet to match that ten-year-old going on eighty back there."

"Meaning?"

"That you spent more time and effort managing that pot farm rather than deigning to enter a classroom."

He glared down his nose at her. "Must've been less important than you think to court the professors, since I still got my diploma."

She harrumphed. "So, what's the draw in Idaho?"

"Peaceful backwoods, friendly neighbors that mind their own business, at least until Rural Resources and your ilk arrived on their doorstep to instruct them on how to live among nature's wonders."

"Everyone could benefit from more knowledge on protecting the environment from overuse," she instructed.

"Protect? Overuse? Seems to me like these country folks have been living in harmony with the land for generations. I don't get your type. City dwellers with a sophisticated education, devising land use plans from ivory towers without ever bothering to live in the target zone before passing judgment. Then you collect enough money to force your opinions on the good inhabitants of the land." His aversion to their politics fueled his tongue. "Guess that nobody knows more about the ecological balance than the environmental gurus you all pray to."

"You know, I haven't had the pleasure of seeing you in years, and apparently nothing has changed. You still deal in the never-never land mentality, reality doesn't exist and Peter Pan is your idol. Not to mention your general lack of social graces."

"I dropped out of my last Emily Post class and as to reality…take a look at the hard-working families that live here, doing a damn fine job of stewardship without the assistance of your haughty foundation. Most aren't interested in your pontificating, and just like that boy, could punch holes in your logic without effort."

"What is it about pig-headed men and their penchant for avoiding adulthood," she blistered.

"You oughtta know all about that as you seem to have joined their ranks. As I remember the adage from Humboldt, it's the place where 'men are men and the women are too.' Maybe you took that too much to heart." His exasperation was taking him to the edge of patience for someone who prided himself on being laid back in his approach to just about everyone. Well, everyone but Carrie. She pushed every button without even trying. He rubbed his forehead. Years go by and some things don't change, particularly women.

"It's always hard to stand up for what's right and maybe you're correct, at least in that I display more backbone than you by holding to my convictions and not just hiding out in the woods." She lowered her hands from being jammed at her waist where she had obstinately waged her verbal battle. "Great to see you again, too."

He watched her march back to the bus, her back as straight as a sword ready to meet her next skirmish. Shaking his head at such fatuous allegiance to a creed, he was baffled at how such an intelligent person could give over their thought processes to others. The new form of brainwashing. Stuffing his hands in his pockets and bending his knee to rest the heel of his boot on the post behind him, the sarcastic remark that passed through his mind was that that had gone well.

Land Barons

Chapter 20

Banking low over the ridge, a helicopter swooped past the tops of the pine sentinels standing guard at the edge of the meadow that stretched into the misty distance. The bird came swinging in at an angle so the passengers, particularly the man riding shotgun, could gloat over the view spread below. They slid past a narrow cataract of crystal clear water spilling over a 200-foot sheer wall of granite, flanked on either side by conifers marching down the precipice, clinging tenaciously to the ledges and outcroppings of stone. The raw beauty of the falls was lost on the executive who only saw the vista as an asset, a personal possession. His pride swelled further as they flew toward a rustic mansion that resembled more of a castle constructed of northwest gold - native cedar - than a hunting lodge, which was how he referred to the estate. Circling the building site once as the passenger indicated, in order to drink in the majesty of it all, the Solis Industries Bell, made one last sweep and landed on the helipad.

The three occupants climbed out of the fuselage while the rotors slowed their steady beating of the air. The first to exit was the executive, decked out in his version of northwest chic consisting of a Pendleton jacket open over a brushed cotton workshirt and designer jeans. A gaudy belt buckle of inlaid obsidian and turquoise fashioned in the likeness of a galloping horse enclosed the slight paunch that had begun to form at his waist. Danner hiking boots encased his feet despite the fact he had no intention of trailblazing today or any other day. Stepping outside the radius of the whirring blades, his two shadows ran up to his side and accompanied him on the final approach to the wide veranda that encircled the whole of the structure.

The man leading the pack halted abruptly 100 feet from the house, forcing his two sidekicks to practically trip over their feet, first in their hurry to keep up and then by the sudden stop. Gazing from under his raised eyebrows to his assistant, who was clinging to her dignity after traipsing after her boss' inconsiderate pace, he brusquely asked how close they are to completing the construction.

"Looks like less than a couple of weeks, sir," said Laura Cane, try-

135

ing to dig through her notebook for the latest update on the work. Locating the sheet she wanted, she pulled it free and read the basics to refresh her memory. "We're waiting for the final delivery of travertine from Italy to finish the front entry. A number of fixtures are yet to be installed and we're awaiting the last of the furniture for a few of the guest rooms."

Not waiting for her to replace her paperwork, he plowed ahead to the front steps. "I take it the master suite is complete and the kitchen and common rooms are all fully outfitted."

"Yes, sir," she called from a few feet behind him as she trailed after his long stride. As they reached the veranda and he assaulted the stairs like General MacArthur on the beach, she caught up to him again. This time the proprietor turned to look back on the hayfields, acres of grass yielding to the soft breeze, swaying under his avaricious regard, the splendor of the view never entering his mind. All he could see was the monetary value and the power it represented, the fact that he beheld some of the most incredible, unsullied terrain in the country never entered his mind. This was just another acquisition.

The other visitor, Pelton Travis, renowned architect, stayed off to the side, uncertain as to whether he was ready to hear his client's comments. Even his vaunted reputation didn't afford him any more respectful treatment than the average laborer when it came to the biting comments of this particular client. He still wondered why he had ever considered accepting the commission.

Cane pulled up beside her boss and, straightening her jacket, shared the view, though not particularly the sentiment. As an attorney who often seemed to be demoted to little more than a gofer, ire often smoldered under the surface, though her outrageous salary more than compensated for her personal peeve. What she saw before her was the result of a job well done that would yield a huge bonus after the rest of the work in the region is finished. That was enough to hold her anger at bay, knowing that retirement was within reach and at the age of 34 she would be finished with egomaniacs like her present employer.

Swallowing the bitterness that was souring her tongue, she told him, "You'll be more than comfortable tonight. We've already hired a few household workers as well as the chef, so you'll also have the opportunity to test his wares."

"Good. I'm looking forward to touring the property and the facilities and relaxing for the day."

"If you'd like, we can start with a cocktail and retire to the deck overlooking the falls," she suggested. "You might like to freshen up, also. There are two guest baths on the ground floor or you may wish to use the master suite instead."

The pride of ownership sweeping across his boyish features with a spreading grin, he said, "I'll take advantage of one of the downstairs powder rooms. Just point the way, counselor. Then I want the dollar tour."

"As you wish," and she led him down the hall.

•••••••

When he emerged, Cane directed him through the cavernous entryway, which still had only the subflooring exposed. He followed her into a great room the size of the Colosseum, a wall of windows overseeing the dramatic view of woods and waterfalls. She led him past an array of leather couches and easy chairs designed for comfort, to a full bar lining an opposite wall that was paneled with rich cedar planks.

"It's fully stocked, sir."

"Just what I need on a day like this…a beer and a to-die-for view." He opened the full-size refrigerator and grabbed an Uncle Ben's, popping the top on a built-in cap remover. "Help yourself, Laura, Travis." And he headed straight for the line of French doors, passing through the beveled glass enclosure and plumping himself onto a classically designed chaise lounge.

Tall and gangly, Carl Chamberlain looked the epitome of the brainy nerd he was. Stretched out on the chaise, legs crossed at the ankles, he appeared much younger than his 38 years except for the shining pate gleaming through his fair, thinning hair. His self-satisfied grin was a mile wide as he gulped his beer and savored the magnificence of the view that belonged to him, the boy from the wrong side of the turnpike. He couldn't help himself but to cackle at what he'd been able to accomplish, pulling himself out of the trailer park and into the catbird's seat. Yep, this is what life should be.

Lifting his beer in a salute to himself, under his breath he said,

"Lookee here, Ted Turner, even you don't have digs like this in your Montana "home on the range."

Chapter 21

DiMarco was scrolling through her e-mail inbox before she opened the one from a contact that she much preferred to ignore. If she followed her inclination she would then be forced to speak with the contact instead, which of late, had become a burden that frayed her nerves. Opening the mail she read the simple message asking how the educational plan was proceeding.

Before she sent her reply she wanted to recheck the progress of owner listings that she kept in a small file on her database. She realized that there may be news of a possible success that they will be glad of, but the other prospect was becoming a thorny situation and she was very aware that her contact was not much interested in problems, only solutions. She was quite certain that there wasn't much she could do in this respect, so she would have to word her response carefully.

Sitting back in her chair, contemplating the multiple issues confounding the situation, the most recent development troubled her more, the arrival on the scene of Billy Brogus. She had no clue what his interest was in the new preserve and until today, hadn't been aware of his presence in the area. In her mind he was a wildcard. The stubborn S.O.B. that she had known in college, when they had dated for a while, always played on the edge of the law and she had no doubt he hadn't changed his lifestyle even after fifteen years. If anything, he'd only learned to flaunt the law with elán. She fervently hoped that he wouldn't become a complication, but deep down, she knew that he already was.

•••••••

Brogus was leaning a hip against his desk as he surveyed the expanse of meadows and trees that was visible from his office window at his home business center. His mind wandered over the events of the day, particularly his encounter with Carrie. If she had changed during the intervening years, he couldn't discern anything other than an even more forceful passion for her values. He was hoping that she'd have mellowed in her beliefs as he had after spending years in rural America, learning what life out here was really like as opposed to what some high-handed professors espoused in the collegiate forum.

There were all forms of maturity and one was learning to examine the facts and compare the rhetoric from all sides. He had come to understand how politics had become a minefield of misinformation that had choked the environmental movement. The well-intentioned right-thinking ecologists had been led down the yellow brick road, in his opinion, demonizing honest farmers, ranchers and loggers who worked the land and respected it. They had been lumped in with corporate greed and were painted as people who would rather see fishkills than lose a single dollar of profit. The agricultural base in this country was rapidly being emasculated by the litigation that swamped courts in states like Idaho. Much of the time he ignored the situation because of the frustration level. It was easier to isolate himself and it was a necessity considering his major source of income. Despite his intention to more fully develop the legitimate side of his operations, it had been an uphill battle to move it into the black, but it looked as if he had finally met his goal. Pinesap Farms was showing a profit and that propelled his plans into forward motion.

Brogus recentered his thoughts on the work at hand and bringing his attention back to Santos and Weeble who were awaiting orders, he asked for a progress report.

"Have operations been shut down like we talked about?" He directed the question to Joe Santos, who had parked his beefy frame in a rolling secretarial chair, boots flat on the floor except for the steady piston pumping of his right leg in a restless tattoo.

"You bet, boss. We got about seven people out at Pinesap 3, harvesting and packaging product for transport."

"Who's handling the eradication of signs of cultivation?"

"Carlos is. He's got a handle on the operation." It was Weeble who answered, decked out in his everyday garb of knife-edge creased, fitted camie slacks topped with a crisp, cotton shirt complete with epaulets and oversized pockets. Short and stocky, Weeble took pains to cast an oxymoronic image of biker sophistication with his gray-streaked blond hair pulled back into a neatly combed ponytail that hung halfway down his back. Brogus figured it was a statement to compensate for the receding hairline that revealed more of his pate as each year passed. Santos wasn't so obsessed with posturing. He was taller by several inches, sported a full head of nearly black hair that curled around his ears, and although boxy in build, he was a solid mass that would tend to fat in later life if he got lazy.

Brogus gave them both a serious brush with his eyes. "You understand it's imperative that all telltale signs of our presence are erased. That place has got to be returned to pristine condition. The other problem is that Pinesap 8 has to be moved, pronto. It's too damn close to that preserve with the nature walk that just opened. We've been lucky so far, but I don't trust folks to stick to the trail. Thank goodness that field has been so well camouflaged but it's got to be gone, tomorrow. Capisce?"

"Capisco," agreed Santos.

"Just what I need, a Mexican who properly conjugates Italian." He shook his head and half-glared at Weeble who offered a mock salute, "Surright!"

Brogus chortled. "Scram, Weeble. Just get it done."

"This is gonna be a costly move," said Santos, raising his chin from where it had been pressed to his chest, watching his cohort leave the room.

"We have no choice. All it takes is one adventuresome hiker figuring he'll blaze his own trail and end up stumbling onto the farm. For right now, go ahead and move product to the new area we've been preparing in the northwest sector, but don't transplant yet. There are other things going on and we may have to drastically alter our plans."

"Consider it done," Santos stood to comply with the charge Brogus had given him. "This time tomorrow it should all be handled."

"Thanks." Brogus turned back to the huge glazed pane, going over the implications of the changes in circumstance that had been cascading over the past couple of weeks. The encroachment of the environmental groups and the conservancy moving in from every direction was reason to cause him concern. Access to federal lands was being all but cut off.

It just may be time to think about retirement, old boy.

Land Barons

Chapter 22

Finding a parking spot in town turned out to be more of a hassle than expected as Gary prowled Second Street hunting for an open space within three blocks of the post office. The busy morning traffic was a surprise until he remembered that Marcasite Heritage Days was coming up and business owners were buzzing back and forth with preparations for the parade and the following events planned at the city park. He saw a blue pick-up backing out from the curb and he quickly maneuvered behind him, ready to snatch up the open spot as soon as it came clear. As he pulled in to snug his bumper next to the sidewalk's edge, he considered himself lucky after spending more time hunting up parking than it took to drive to town.

He stepped down from his rig in front of the Gleason Insurance Company and saw Bob Powell exiting the converted two-story Victorian home trimmed with white gingerbread and boasting a garden of rose trees. Stopping at the end of the walkway Powell and Mathers greeted each other with a handshake.

"So, what's the word?" Mathers inquired with an upbeat hand pumping. "Good news, I hope."

Powell frowned his answer. "Arson, according to the investigator and the underwriters won't cover the loss."

"I don't understand," he was flabbergasted. "Why the hell not?"

"Apparently, they found two gas cans that look like they might have come from the mill's carpool," Powell was fuming. "They're not actually saying I torched my own place, mind ya, but they're implying that the circumstances are too suspicious and are refusing to settle."

Mathers lowered his head and rubbed his temples. "Geez, Bob, it's hard to distinguish between idiocy and corruption." He looked up at his neighbor, "Now what do you do?"

Powell lifted his eyes and scanned the clear blue of the sky, as if searching for answers. "No clue. We were just about to get a reprieve because we finally got the go ahead to harvest that stand of timber that burned. Judge threw out that injunction. We've got other properties but the legal fees to get to them are killing us. Even if we could get past the barrage of lawsuits those environmental attorneys keep churning out, we've got no mill left and selling the timber to another lumber company wouldn't cover the expenses to harvest. I may have to sell the whole

kit 'n' kaboodle to save the rest of my property.

"You've got a buyer already?" Gary was incredulous.

"Yeah, that conservancy group rode in on the last of the smoke. If it were clouds, you'd think it was the Almighty Himself. They already made an offer and I may have no choice but to take it." Not a man to give in to despair, he just shook his head and let the disappointment roll off his back.

"Lord am I sorry to hear that," Mathers said in a pained voice. "Maybe there's an alternative. You have some time before you decide, don't you?"

"Some, not much. The mill wasn't doing as well these days with the artificial timber crunch. I'll do my homework, but I'm not optimistic." His expression was troubled. "Unfortunately, the situation is just about as bad as it could get."

"You gotta do what you gotta do. I just wish there was something that *I* could do."

Mathers squeezed Powell's shoulder and took his leave to head over to the post office. Then he figured he'd get some lunch at the Miner's Gap, maybe even pick-up a little gossip.

•••••••

Carrie DiMarco had just let herself back into the Rural Resources office and gone straight to the computer, knowing that she'd better check her e-mail before too late in the day. Logging on, the first notice to blip in front of her was new correspondence from Nature's Wilds Conservancy. Not always thrilled to be on the receiving end of their net connection, she opened the mail, half-wincing in anticipation.

Her contact was informing her of a probable acceptance of an offer for the Powell Lumber Mill and contiguous property. Uncertain as to why she needed to be informed of the imminent transaction, nonetheless she replied with a positive message wishing them luck. Her organization had helped with some basic investigation of the Powell Mill's economic vulnerability. Associated with Rural Resources' agency were two other environmental organizations that had been litigating to keep him from harvesting properties landlocked by the national forest. She assumed that the supportive role they had taken must be the reason for their presumption of her interest.

The fact that the injunction the coalition had filed was recently overturned made her wonder about the coincidence of a catastrophic fire engulfing not only the mill, but the parcel that had been involved in the suit. Fighting these issues via the court system did not always allow for justice, which in her mind meant that these mature forests would be off-limits to logging and letting nature have its way without man meddling in the process of life. The sudden disruption caused by the blaze that wiped out the livelihood for hundreds of workers and the Powell family would portend an economic crisis in the region, she knew.

Her consolation was that the rest of the land was now protected from the marauding of the lumber industry. The consequences of the burn were nothing to be ecstatic over but the exploitation would cease once the conservancy establishes title and for that, she was grateful.

•••••••

Gary sat by the window, finishing his midday meal at the Miner's Gap. It had been a busy morning for the staff and he hadn't picked up much from anyone aside from a few tidbits on the plans for Heritage Days. Pat, who was usually a fount of information, was swamped with orders and attending to new customers, the café being a favorite for locals and tourists alike.

Seeing that town wasn't to be a resource for him today, he folded the paper and left it in an ever-growing pile by the door for others to page through with their lunch and strolled back down the street to where he'd left his rig.

Positioned behind the wheel, he let the powerful engine idle while he contemplated the rest of his day and opted to take one last gander at the flattening of the Stabler's farm. Putting the truck into gear, he maneuvered his way around the pedestrians moseying across the streets, slowly making his way back to the main highway.

He followed the road at an easy clip, in no real hurry today, particularly after hearing Bob Powell's hardly inspiring news. As he closed the distance to the entrance of the farm, he noticed a new sign designating the property as belonging to Nature's Wilds Conservancy right next to a very imposing 'no trespassing' notice.

Real friendly folks. But then, don't I know that from experience.

He also saw a number of flatbeds loaded with old wood planks that might have come from the barn. One of the drivers was leaning against the cab door taking a cigarette break and Mathers, thinking *what the hell*, pulled up behind him and jumped down to have a word with the guy. *At least he doesn't look like he'll shoot.*

"What're you hauling?" He tried to put on a good ol' boy friendliness as he approached the cab.

"Just the last of that old barn. It's going to salvage today." He pushed away from the cab and left the bored expression in place.

"Where's that? I didn't know of any salvage operation around here and I didn't think there'd be much call for old floorboards and siding"

"It ain't around here. We haul it to Spokane to a company that re-mills and re-finishes used wood. You'd be surprised. Some of these fancy folks movin' in from the city like to outfit their place in this trendy new style of makin' everything look old." He warmed a little to having some plain conversation. Gary figured he'd been hanging around for a while waiting on the okay to move out.

"Sounds like you could save a lot of money by reusing the old wood," offered Gary.

"No way, man. By the time the lumber is re-planed and refurbished with that 'patina' these designers are fallin' all over themselves for, it costs more than new lumber." He chuckled. "These folks spend more than you and I'd make in a lifetime on this 'rustic' look just to impress their buddies from Jackson Hole. It's all the rage in Montana and Wyoming with those weekend country gents."

"I had no idea it was such big business. Learn something new everyday." Mathers scanned the drive back up to the old house that had been torn down, counting the dollars that Nature's Wilds was probably reaping off Stablers' pain and toil. "Hey, what demolition company is overseeing the sight?"

"No demo company. We're just day hirees for that conservation group. They've been doing quite a bit of de-construction around here for the past six months or so. It's been keeping some of the laid-off lumber workers in pocket money. Though this kind of work isn't around for long and I heard about the mill burning. It's gonna be hard times up here."

Mathers caught a glimpse of Hothead who he decided he'd rather not encounter again considering the last meeting was so amicable. Before the foreman could make his way down the road and take notice of Gary, he said thanks to the trucker and a brief goodbye, hopped in his own rig and rapidly swung around to head back down the road.

Keeping his eye on the rear view mirror to make sure that he wasn't noticed and subsequently followed, he pulled into his own drive and went back up to the house.

After returning home he digested what the trucker had told him about the salvage operation. Not only was Nature's Wilds stepping in and walking away with a deal on the property because of the desperation sale, they were reaping benefits from the salvage operation of seasoned lumber that would find its way to architects' plans for country estates at top dollar. He wondered what else this conservancy operation was squeezing out of their unsophisticated pigeons.

He rolled the information around in his head and was debating whether or not to call Anthea with the tidbit, knowing that it wasn't that important. What he really wanted was an excuse to call her. After leaving her home the other night he did nothing but burn up with the thoughts of their magnetism. He hadn't wanted to leave her but he knew that he was unprepared for the emotions that were sweeping through him and he could all too easily read her ambivalent reaction, both wanting and haunted in unison. He knew that he wasn't going to be able to keep his thoughts of her at bay, it was already invading his sleep as well as his waking hours.

He picked up the phone and dialed her number, already having consigned it to memory. There was no answer so he left a message for her to return his call when she came in.

Land Barons

Chapter 23

The day was spent doing domestic chores: vacuuming, dusting, scrubbing and as little gardening as possible. A green thumb wasn't one of Anthea's attributes. Keeping a neat house was. The necessity of living in scrupulously clean quarters had been ingrained as a child, mostly due to the fact that when she was small, some of the apartments her family had occupied had the unwanted roommates of the six-legged sort. That had to do more with the neighborhood rather than the lack of cleanliness. Some creatures would only exchange residency from one apartment to another according to who had most recently sprayed and the battle was a constant one. As a result, Anthea was more than careful with her kitchen duties, having almost a phobia about keeping the sink practically antiseptic. She wasn't quite so neurotic about the rest of the house and would let the dust bunnies accumulate for a week or two before she forced herself to wield a dust mop and cloth. The kitchen floor was another story altogether, swept and cleaned after most meals. She sometimes chided herself for showing signs of obsessive-compulsive disorder.

Satisfied that the basics were under control for another week, she changed to her walking shoes, pinned her hair back in a pseudo-fashionable messy twist with curls sprouting at odd angles and headed down to the riverside trail for her regular jaunt.

The sun was still high in the late afternoon sky with the temperature hovering around 85 or so degrees, comfortable weather for today. As she locked up the car and turned toward the asphalt walkway she realized that the hotter summer weather would be moving in soon and she would be forced to take her walks later in the evening.

Today as she traveled at a steady pace she kept her eye on the river to her left, watching the boaters skim over the water, some towing tubers and one circling a skier who was having a tough time with his water start. She could commiserate even though she hadn't attempted to water-ski in over a decade and wasn't about to take up the sport now. Her eye caught some movement at the river's edge and as she passed a tangle of blackberry brambles, she saw a doe was getting a drink in the lapping water. The sight reminded her how much she had to be aware of deer crossing the road even as she'd drive through town because she really wasn't interested in another thousand dollars in damage to her truck like the last time. The buck had been fine but her rig had suffered hospitalization in the shop for two weeks.

Marking time with the jabber of talk radio in her ear, she took note of the most recent scandal to light up the airwaves. One of her afternoon favorites was busy losing his cool with some nitwit who thought he'd have half a chance at making a non-existent argument, only to be yelled off the show with 'moron' ringing in his ears. *You better know what you're getting into if you're foolish enough to call these guys. You get what you deserve.*

A commercial came on and she turned the volume down, letting herself trace back through the last couple of days' events. She may be somewhat removed from the day-to-day grind of a newspaper, but her instincts were still well-honed and her nose was definitely out of joint about the implications of Nature's Wilds involvement with displacing hard working families from their homes. All of what she had been compiling pointed to the unjust crushing of people's dreams and the destruction of their heritage. as farmers and lumbermen were finding themselves without a job or a future. It seemed to her that anyone who used the land was finding themselves without access to it.

Guess it's a good thing there's not much mining going on anymore. They'd probably be out on their ass, too. Or buried in some slagpit to make room for some environmentally responsible pretender. Not that she didn't recognize the lack of foresight that had been displayed by a number of mining outfits that were now defunct or still cleaning up after themselves.

Her talk show came back on the air and she increased the volume to see who the host would chew out next when some bicyclist whizzed by and clipped her forearm hard with the handlebars. Her musings turned to swearing, cussing up a storm using the language she'd picked up in her youth hanging out in the print shop where she'd often fly the press as a youngster, jogging the newspapers and tying the bundles as they came shooting past the cutter, down the conveyor belt and into her hands. More colorful language you wouldn't find on the docks spouting from the mouths of stevedores.

Catching her breath she stopped to check the damage the jerk had inflicted and found that it didn't look anywhere near as bad as it felt. Having no choice but to finish her walk, she pumped up her pace to get back home and ice the injury before it became a massive bruise with a full palette of hues. She jumped in the Expedition and whipped out of the lot to get up the hill.

As soon as she reached the house, Anthea grabbed her stuff off the passenger seat, got down and quickly unlocked the door. Dropping her belongings on the floor she went directly to the freezer where she removed a soft ice pack and wrapped it in place with a linen kitchen towel.

"I hope that works to keep the black and blue away," she grumbled under her breath in between expletives.

Knowing that she could do nothing more but keep her arm elevated and iced, she went back to check her messages in hopes that her client, a talk radio host not unlike the one she'd been listening to earlier, had called back. They were looking for another angle for the next barrage of releases she was preparing to let loose on the media. Finding the message light pulsing on and off, she depressed the 'play' button and heard a husky voice of indeterminate sex telling her to watch her back next time she ambles down the riverside path if she doesn't curb her interest in a certain subject.

Before she could react to the threat, which teed her off even more since whoever it was had apparently left the message before the incident and not after the fact, she heard Gary asking her to return his call. Leaving the messages on the recorder, she left off caring about the bicycle-borne terrorist and lifted the receiver to call Mathers, wondering what he would be calling about as she flushed with the memory of their contact the other night. Almost preparing to hang-up because of a sudden flare of self-consciousness, she heard him answer and the sound of his baritone on the voicemail flustered her so she could barely say 'hello.'

She wasn't given a chance to speak before Mathers voice overrode the machine with a, "Got ya. This is Mathers."

"Gary, it's Anthea returning your call," she almost stumbled over those simple words, mentally kicking herself for being such an agitated filly.

The timbre of his voice changed at hearing her on the line, becoming smoother and, thinking it was her imagination, more sultry.

151

"Thanks for calling back."

"No problem," she intoned with definite problems keeping her cool. "What do you need?"

Unable to restrain himself, he said, "You, for one thing."

Oh God. Now what do I say? Her pulse sped up but her tongue stayed lodged in her mouth unable to articulate anything.

"I just garnered a little information this afternoon, thinking you might be interested although I doubt it's of much import," he quickly switched gears, sensing her discomfort.

"Shoot," was all she could spit out.

"I caught up with Bob Powell this morning and he shared the bad news that not only are the investigators talking arson on the mill fire, which we all pretty much allowed it was, but they're inferring it was an inside job. The upshot is that they won't recognize his claim, evidence or not. He'll have to fight them in court to get satisfaction."

"That is so utterly unjust," bemoaned Anthea. "He had no motive that I can see."

"I don't see one either," he agreed. "If anything, he needed his mill because the injunction on harvesting the lumber that so coincidentally burned, had just been tossed by the appellate court."

"If it didn't sound so fishy, it'd be mystifying."

"After that, I drove by Stabler's place for old time's sake and three semi's with flatbeds were lined up loaded to the gills with lumber from the dismantled buildings. They're taking everything apart, piece by piece when those buildings could have been, and should have been registered as historical landmarks, what I heard."

"I'm so sorry to hear that," the sadness permeating her voice. "That family lost everything. Now even their legacy has been erased. But why bother with the expense?"

"That was my question and one of the truckers was obliging enough to answer. Seems they're salvaging all the old wood. They haul it to a place in Spokane that re-mills the planking for resale to upscale builders. It seems that the 'retro farmhouse' is the newest fad among the elite, I think he referred to Jackson Hole as an example. Sounds like a real scheme."

"You're saying that Nature's Wilds is making a mint off of destroying vintage homes and barns and turning around and selling the refurbished wood at a profit to the nouveau riche of the range." She was beginning to fume and he smiled picturing her normally bright, blue eyes taking on the fury of storm clouds.

"Sounds like it to me. I didn't know there was such an industry getting the upper crust to customize their new digs to look old."

"I've seen architectural and design articles on the new 'rustic' styling among estates being built in the boonies. They're taking recycling to a higher level, not that it's such a bad thing, only when they destroy families to take their homes and feed the ever-growing appetite of the shameless wealthy. Me? All I care about is light and a view if I can afford one."

"Speaking of which, how would you like me to make you dinner? 'Cause I've got both."

Land Barons

Chapter 24

Daylight was beginning to soften into the golden glow that pho-tographers love so well when Frank Ahlsted received a buzz on his handheld Motorola. Depressing the transmit button, he asked what the problem was since most everyone had already finished for the day.

One of his crew said they had rounded up the cattle for preparation to move them to summer pasture tomorrow but it seemed they were missing a couple of calves in the shuffle. He said he was pretty sure where they are but he'd promised his son he'd be at his baseball game this evening and, you know the wife, she'd take the knife to the fami-ly jewels just as soon as a bull's if he didn't show up.

Ahlsted laughed at the thought, knowing his man's better half who was a plump little thing with a mean streak that'd come forth anytime she was protecting her brood. So he told him to go on home, asking where the lost calves were. He advised his boss that he figured they'd gotten themselves hung up in the ravine over at Lazy Creek, remind-ing him of that trail the cows sometimes follow in the southwest sec-tor.

Noting that there was still plenty of time 'til dark, Ahlsted said he'd go round 'em up before they become cougar feed and signed off.

Before heading off, he opened the kitchen door and called in to his wife, letting her know he had to round up a couple of strays. Then he headed out to the barn where the machinery and farm vehicles were stored, grabbed his rope and a few supplies and attached them to his ATV, mounted and ran out to Lazy Creek.

A deer trail followed the steep sides of the arroyo down to the creek and occasionally, after a rain had loosened up the rocky walls of the vale, cattle sometimes couldn't negotiate their way back up with-out help. It was rare that cows got themselves stuck down by the creek bed, but calves didn't always have the experience of their older and wiser cousins.

Ahlsted came roaring right up to the lip of the steep but fairly shal-low canyon, where there's always been a good solid base and he could tie up the end of his rope for leverage to haul the calves out. Braking hard, he felt the ground give underfoot. Instead of stopping, the four-wheeler just started sliding in the direction of the declivity and he realized that the vehicle was going to pull him over the side. He tried to jump off the ATV but he was too late in responding to the unexpected danger and both he and the four by four rolled down the side of the little canyon. The tumbling machine caught his leg and he was unable to dislodge himself as he crashed down through the brambles and stubby pines. He struggled to release himself from the churning of the vehicle, bouncing off of the rocks and through the scrub. His mind frantically searching for a way to disentangle his limbs from the wheels, he couldn't wrap it around the thought that he might die. Finally, the rolling ceased and he came to rest under the weight of his ATV, his eyes open but seeing nothing of the gurgling stream running by his side and all thought was gone.

•••••••

Taking a sip from a glass of wine, Anthea gently rocked in the covered swing that stood on Mathers' veranda, absorbing the last rays of the sun playing through a few shifting clouds. The sky was beginning to streak with the jewel tones of day's end, creating a molten glow behind the mountains. The simple peacefulness washed over her, cleansing the slight uneasiness she felt after the purposeful accident by the river and the subsequent menacing message left on her machine.

Sitting back, she watched Gary handle his duty at the grill with the chef's pride that men exude when they're in their element, and from experience she knew that this was most men's domain. She had no inclination to interfere so she just swung her feet and enjoyed the view.

"I almost feel guilty being pampered while a man does the work," she offered as an excuse for not assisting.

"Good. Loners like me don't get the opportunity to entertain very often and I avoid cooking other than firing up the grill, like a lot of guys," and he shot her a knowing glance almost so she'd realize he'd been reading her mind.

"What do you do in the winter? Shovel off the snow and grill your potpies?" she challenged.

"Nah, don't eat potpies and the oven does work in a pinch. But there's not much snow here and I'm free to barbecue all year long. Works for me." He grinned as he placed the steaks on the fire.

"May I ask the chef what's on the menu?" she turned her head in a coquettish posture, smiling sweetly.

"Local beef. You remember Frank Ahlsted, the rancher up the road a ways?"

"Yes, I do. I also remember that he was fighting some kind of problem with his cattle. I distinctly recall the most unpleasant odor of dead cow," she said as she wrinkled her nose.

"That's an unfortunate circumstance that just arose a week or so ago and I hope he's able to pinpoint the problem soon. I hate to see him lose so many head, it has to impact his financial health as well." He pointed to the meat on the grill with his fork, "This here's last year's beef, homegrown, range fed and decidedly tasty."

"I certainly hope they are able to overcome their trouble with that toxin or disease before long, otherwise there may be no 'this year's' beef."

"I haven't heard any results on their testing yet but I pray he's able to make it through these losses and come out on top." He became melancholy for a minute.

"Do you know him well?"

"Not real well, I've only been up here for a little over a year and actually only moved in a few months ago when the majority of the construction was completed. The folks up here are good people and I'm glad I made the decision to move here, even if it is a distance from my daughter."

"I understand the sentiment. It's much the same reason I moved out here permanently. The people I had come to know when I lived here for a while as well as just feeling safe in the valley. I haven't had a home in a long time, if ever, really. This is home now," she let the thought trail off into the growing darkness.

He came over to sit by her while she spoke, glimpsing her profile in the fading light, noticing an inner strength that he hadn't quite perceived during the past week that they had come to know each other better. He sat back in the swing and rocked lazily with her, silence settling in comfortably.

Neither spoke for a few minutes until Gary rose to check the grill and set the table with the final components of the meal. He came over to assist her out of the swing, pulling her to her feet by the hands and wrapping them around his waist until they stood, the space closed between them. He leaned over and kissed her lightly, bringing his hand up to brush a few curls out of her blue eyes that in the duskiness reminded him of deep wells of clear spring water. Taking her hand, he led her to a chair and settled her at the table.

They ate in relative silence, contemplating their surroundings and the evening sounds, the bubbling of the river, chirping of the crickets, croaking of the frogs and the occasional song of a night bird.

•••••••

After dinner and dishes were done and put away, Anthea and Gary resettled themselves back on the deck, a cup of coffee held by each. He seated himself next to her on the swing and when he touched her arm, she jerked it away, placing it across her stomach as a reflexive reaction to his touch.

At first, he was mystified considering her earlier acceptance of his touch and withdrew his arm.

"I'm sorry I jumped like that, but I hurt my arm earlier today and it's still somewhat painful," she apologized.

"What happened? Did you hurt yourself badly?" he asked as concern crossed his features, highlighting the misty gray of his eyes.

"No. Just some clumsy ass on a bike slammed my arm with his handlebars as he passed me. I'll survive, I assure you."

"Let me check it, see if there's anything I can do. Ex-policemen are pretty good with injuries," he tried to win her over with his smile.

"You needn't, Gary. It's fine. I just need a few days to heal," she demurred.

He continued to press her until she finally gave in to his insistence.

"You're worse than any fishwife I've ever met," she glared up at him as he rolled up her sleeve. "Where'd you learn to nag so well?"

"It's a gift." He softened her demeanor with his own tender probing of her bruised arm.

"Yipe!"

"Sorry, I guess I'm not as light fingered as I thought. Probably why I never made it in a life of crime and had to join the forces of justice instead," he grinned sympathetically. As he looked at the swelling and discoloration, the humor vanished.

She looked down and was surprised at the array of blues and reds angrily striping her arm. "I'd no idea it looked so awful. I'm afraid the drive home was too long to be countered by the icing I put it through. If you're quick enough with the R.I.C.E. application to an injury, you can avoid after-effects like this."

"R.I.C.E?" he asked, his eyebrows lifting in question.

"You know, rest, ice, compression, elevation. All the things you apply to an injury like this or similar trauma like a strain or sprain." She looked at him over her raised arm. "I thought you said you'd had emergency training?"

"Sure, I just don't remember that little acronym. I think we ought to ice it some more to get that swelling down, don't you?"

"You're probably right," she said, still stunned at how bad the injury looked as opposed to how it felt, which was sore but not particularly bad. "I didn't give it the proper attention since I was in such a rush to check messages."

"How important could they have been?"

"Well, aside from Mr. Ominous, I wouldn't be here enjoying your company if I hadn't listened to the machine," she tried to soothe him with a smile.

"Who's Mr. Ominous?" he asked beginning to feel a little uneasy at her glib description of events.

"Apparently, it was some bozo, doing a fine job of impersonating some mafioso by telling me to watch myself when I walk by the river. I'm guessing, after the fact you see, that this," and she raised her arm for emphasis, "was what he meant. Not much harm done in the long run," she said trying to blow the worry aside.

"Except that you were actually threatened. Did you save the message?" Mathers was reverting to interrogation mode.

"I didn't erase it, just in case it meant something, though frankly, I've no clue what his beef is with me."

"It could be that our showing up at most inopportune times may be getting under somebody's skin. Our little investigation may be upsetting the Nature's Wilds folks," he turned introspective as he applied the ice pack.

"The operative word here is 'little' we haven't come up with anything," she pointed out.

"It seems they may think otherwise."

They both fell silent for a few moments.

"Refill on the coffee, Thea?"

"Sure. Thank you."

As he tipped the carafe to pour he said, "You know, you don't need to travel all the way to town tonight." He was trying to cover his concern for her welfare with his offer to stay.

"Thank you, sir, for your hospitality but I think it's best if I go."

Chapter 25

Waking too early with the sun, Anthea laid in bed, covers thrown in disarray after a restless night wondering from where the next threat might come but mostly, why? For the life of her, she couldn't understand anyone getting their nose out of joint with Mathers' or her few inquiries. They hadn't uncovered anything other than the fact that Nature's Wilds was interested in accumulating property on and around the Marcasite River, unless their tactics are unsavory, which she suspected but certainly couldn't prove. All they were doing was increasing her willingness to investigate further. *Somebody's not too smart.*

After giving over another half hour to her musings, she finally threw her feet over the side of the bed and made the effort to get herself organized. She had work to do.

•••••••

Daylight hours burning away, Anthea was settled in front of her computer screen editing a cover letter for an entertainer's press packet. In the middle of reconstructing a sentence that just wasn't working, her phone rang, making her jump and lose her train of thought. Since the point she was making had slipped beyond her short term memory capacity, she stopped and answered the phone.

"Thea here."

"I'm sorry to disturb you so early, Thea, but I thought you would want to be informed right away. There's been an accident up at Frank Ahlsted's," he was reserved as he spoke.

"Oh no. What happened?"

"I don't know the details but Frank went over the side of a ravine."

"Is he all right?" The hair on the back of her neck was suddenly standing on end.

She could hear Gary take a breath and let it out slowly. "I'm afraid not. I was told he didn't make it."

Not knowing what else to say, she hesitated and then asked, "Do you know what happened?"

"Not really. I'm on my way over to see if I can help in some way and thought you ought to be informed of yet another tragedy in my general neighborhood."

"Do you think there is anything I can do? Does he have family?"

"To the best of my knowledge their kids are grown and live out of state except for one daughter, Lissa, who's home from college for the summer and working locally. I think one of Mrs. Ahlsted's friends will be coming up from town." He stopped to think, swamped with shock from the latest calamity so close to home. "I'll call you if anything comes up but I want to get there while the sheriff is still at the scene, okay?"

"Okay," she responded without enthusiasm. "I'll talk to you later."

•••••••

Gordon Curran and Sully Tyson, the two students working as assistants at Rural Resources for the summer were seated in Curran's truck, driving into the office. They'd been rooming together in a small cottage up the Marcasite-Lilliot Road for the few months they were stationed in Marcasite. Sully had trundled in during the wee hours of the morning, waking his roommate who wasn't exactly pleased with losing sleep due to the other's night owl cavorting.

"How could you find anything interesting to do around here?" a cranky Curran queried Sully with a jaundiced eye. "They really roll-up the sidewalks at night. The theater isn't even open during the week and the local bars are real dives."

"Looks to me like you're not resourceful enough to find something to occupy yourself. This is a small town but there's always action if you know where to look."

"Yeah, like where, under some moose's balls?" he muttered.

"Prob'ly, if there were any around here. I've just got a knack for finding fun." He was smug about locating extracurricular activity in what would otherwise be a boring town.

"Trouble's more like it."

"Could be," he smirked.

•••••••

162

DiMarco was on the phone when the two young men sauntered in the office door. Giving them stink-eye, her first question was why they're late.

"Since there wasn't anything special on the calendar, we thought it wouldn't be any great crime to stop for breakfast," Sully was off-hand in his disrespectful response.

"There's always something to be done around here. If you want to stop to enjoy yourselves, get up earlier so you're on time, or at the least, call and let me know of your intent to be tardy."

"Tardy. Now there's a term I haven't heard since grade school," he said as he ambled over to the coffeepot.

"Anyway, there's news."

"We heard. Gossip travels faster here than lightning. Everyone was talking about that rancher taking a header down a ledge," said Sully.

"I wouldn't use such crass terms, but that's pretty much what the buzz is," added Curran giving Sully a disapproving glare.

"Did you hear that he's dead?" asked Carrie.

Sully looked up from stirring cream into his coffee, surprised. "No, man. Just that he went over the side. Are you sure?"

"I keep informed," she said with lackluster. "It's my job to know what's going on in the area we're here to serve."

"What's your job? Secret spy for nature?" Curran asked, incredulous of her claim. "I thought Rural Resources was a community assistance organization, not an espionage network."

Waving away his comment, she went on, "Whatever. It's important that I know what's happening in the neighborhood. As for you two...we have some clean-up work that needs to be done today at the old Garrison Garage. You remember that we volunteered to help the city remove the old oil drums so the place can be refurbished." She grinned at them, "Just helping out in the community. So, get yourselves on over there, okay?"

"Sure, boss lady," gibed Sully.

The boys collected work gloves and overalls that hung on hooks in the back of the office before they sidled out the door.

Land Barons

Chapter 26

Turning onto the long gravel road that led up to the Ahlsted place, Mathers was grim about the implications of Frank's fatal accident. He knew that he had been struggling because of the losses of cattle that were rapidly adding up. Gary didn't know how many head had died in the last week and a half and he hadn't heard that Fish and Game had narrowed the field of virtual perpetrators, whether it was disease or poison and how it was introduced into the herd.

He pulled up in front of the house and walked up to the front door. Ginny from the mercantile was one of Mrs. Ahlsted's closest friends and she answered the door for the family.

"Hey, Ginny," Mathers greeted her as she opened the door. Her small face was pinched with care and worry.

"Hi Gary. Guess good news travels fast," the sardonic response was underlined by a slightly bitter tone.

He ignored her comment, knowing that she was hurting almost as badly as her friend. "I just came by to offer condolences to the family," he said solemnly.

"Vera's in the kitchen if you want to come in," and she pulled the door open wider as an invitation.

"Thanks Ginny. I won't take up much time." He entered the hall and followed Ginny's diminutive frame into the kitchen where Vera Ahlsted was nursing a cup of coffee at the old formica table which was probably a relic from Frank's childhood. She looked up at the intrusion, her eyes puffy from weeping and her forehead creased from fretting.

Gary took her hand and squeezed it with warmth and consideration, asking if there was anything that he could do.

She cleared her throat before replying, finding it difficult to speak. "No, but thank you for offering."

Again, he gave his condolences and turned to go, seeing that his presence was more distressing than helpful. As Ginny walked him to the front entryway he asked her if she knew whether or not the sheriff was still around.

"He's down at the site of the accident and I expect he'll be there for a while."

"Do you know where that is? I'd like to speak to him."

"Sure," she said and gave him directions over to Lazy Creek.

•••••••

He followed the route that Ginny had verbally drawn for him, which took him over a track that was bumpy and gritty for the better part of a mile. Finally, he saw two pick-ups ahead that sported the Marcasite County Sheriff's insignia, which only became readable as he came within the last twenty yards. An ambulance also stood near the scene. Parking a distance away to be certain that he didn't impede activity at the accident scene, Mathers walked over to join Sheriff Dave Stellenbeck, who was crouched by the trailhead, examining the edge of the ravine.

Sheriff Stellenbeck was a raw boned man standing well over six feet whose high school linebacker's frame had started to get soft around the middle. And his knees weren't as springy as they'd been in his youth, because he groaned as he pushed himself up off the ground to greet Mathers.

"Hey, Gary. This is an unexpected pleasure."

"I know you're joking," he said as he extended his hand to the sheriff's even bigger paw. "I heard about Frank's accident and thought maybe I could help."

"Yeah? You got some special knowledge of what happened here?" he looked skeptical underneath his slow smile.

"No, just neighborly interest."

"Or ghoulish curiosity?" Stellenbeck's smile grew wider.

Mathers was serious as he answered. "Hardly. I was just talking with Frank the other day about the die-off he's had in the herd. I was just hoping this didn't have anything to do with it."

"I don't see how. It looks like he couldn't stop the four-wheeler in time and it slid down the slope. Appears like he couldn't dislodge his boot from where it got hooked under the seat and tumbled with the vehicle down the hill. It ended up on top of him." He shook his big head side-to-side in dismay.

"Any idea what he was doing out here?"

166

"Not really. The missus said he got a call on the handheld, though she didn't hear the details, just something about a couple of calves. He told her he needed to check on some stock and that he oughtta be back soon." He looked over the side again.

"When he didn't come back she tried calling Bert, the foreman, to see what he knew, which turned out to be nothing. Then around 10 p.m. she called me. Said he hadn't come in and she was worried. We did what we could during the night but couldn't really start the search until first light and just found Frank a few hours ago. Unfortunately, we were too late."

"Any sign of the stock she referred to?" asked Mathers.

"Nope. Didn't see nary a hair of any calves around here."

"Mind if I take a look around?"

"Well," he was unsure as to whether he should give permission. "Be careful about muckin' anything up."

Mathers gave him a questioning glance. "Are you treating this as a homicide?"

"We have to until we've weighed all the evidence to determine positively that it was an accident. I'd guess you'd know that. You were a cop weren't you?"

"Been a while, but it's not exactly a secret. Not that I advertise the fact," he gave Stellenbeck a look denoting his wish to keep the information between them.

"Well, I could always use a pair of experienced eyes," expressing his tacit approval of Mathers' assistance.

Walking over to the lip of the ravine, keeping clear of the tire marks, he checked the head of the deer trail to see if anything struck him as unusual. He took pains to make sure he didn't muddy the evidence, if this indeed was a crime scene, and he avoided the area where officials and paramedics had already tromped through part of the setting. He looked over the edge and saw that they were down there now, rigging a harness up to the stretcher so they could bring Frank's body up the incline. They'd have to use a winch in order to get the body to the top. It was too steep for the men to carry it up without help, so they had it hooked up in such a way that all they needed to do was guide the stretcher, making certain it didn't crash against the arroyo wall during its ascent.

Squatting down to check the stability of the declivity's rim, he noticed a weakened area right at the trailhead that appeared to be where the ground collapsed under the weight of the vehicle. It seemed odd to him that the area that gave way was a good five feet from the little canyon's edge. Trying not to disturb things too much, he used a stick to gently probe the soft dirt where it began to look like there was a pocket under the sod where earth had been removed. To his eye, it looked like it had been deliberately excavated. Bending over further, he found a number of broken, rotting surveyor's stakes that were partially buried in the earth. He called the sheriff over to take a gander.

"Dave, what do make of these stakes?"

"Maybe it's left from some previous survey, though I don't think this is a property line," he rubbed his jaw which was sprinkled with salt and pepper stubble.

"Even so, I could see one or maybe two stakes, but half a dozen? The way the ground gave way underneath the four-wheeler, it looks like maybe someone had dug out a pit and re-laid the sod over some loose fill that was just barely held in place by these stakes that are rotted through. See where they broke off? There's also a broken plank half-buried here. It's rotted through, too. Any substantial weight on this and it'd disintegrate, fast." Both Stellenbeck and Mathers contemplated the scenario.

"Whoever devised this must have thought that the old wood would have been strewn down the side of the ravine and gone unnoticed," the sheriff was reflective. "I think we lucked out that the evidence didn't disappear under the loose rock and dirt. But why would anyone build a booby-trap and who would know how?"

"Those are questions you get to answer, but I'd say someone with battlefield experience might have the know-how to concoct something like this," said Mathers.

"Better get some pictures." Stellenbeck called Deputy Mark Tolman over, who had just climbed back up from the creek bed. "Mark, I need you to get the camera and get some shots of this."

The deputy kept his expression closed as he scanned the scene, wondering what the sheriff could possibly have in mind by including a civilian in his investigation. With only a year under his belt with this department, he was protective of his position and definitely disapproved of the intrusion of someone like Mathers, who he distrusted instinctively. Following directions, however, he sauntered over with the digital camera in hand that he had just been using to get images of the victim at the bottom of the ravine. He nodded to Stellenbeck as he advanced to the breach in the canyon rim.

"Don't know what this means but we'd better cover all the angles." Swinging his attention back to Mathers, he said, "What made you think to look for something like this?" His attitude taking a bit of a turn, a glint of suspicion flashing across his face.

"Just a hunch. Frank knew this land better than anyone, and he certainly wouldn't have pulled this close to the edge if he wasn't damn sure it was stable. He'd probably been up here hundreds of times. And didn't Vera say that he was looking for stock down here? Stock which haven't left any mark? Might've been a set-up."

Tolman hiked his trousers and stooped down in order to get a number of shots of the disturbed ground. He didn't say anything to Mathers or the sheriff, presenting himself as a task-oriented professional while he concentrated on the odd assortment of decaying and split stakes emerging from the earth.

The sheriff was quiet for a moment. "Don't leave town, you'll probably be called to testify at the inquest."

"So you think there'll be one," said Mathers, resigning himself to accepting the unhappy fate of his neighbor.

"There will now," and Sheriff Stellenbeck pulled down the brim of his hat to emphasize how serious the situation had become.

Land Barons

Chapter 27

Billy Brogus strolled through the aisles at the processing plant at the main campus of Pinesap Farms inspecting the packaging line of organic herbs, many of which were actually collected wild as opposed to cultivated in carefully maintained fields. Plants such as St. John's wort and chamomile grew in abundance all across meadows and hayfields in the area but the echinacea, lobelia and a smattering of others they either grew in the neat garden rows situated adjacent to the old converted barn or were ordered from other organic farms.

He lifted one of the tincture bottles and rolled it across the rough skin of his work hardened hands as he contemplated the immediate future and how he was beginning to feel that everything was caving in after years of building his little empire. He knew he'd have to deal with some tough decision making at some point soon, he had just hoped he'd have a few more years before crunch time arrived. *Even a few more months would've been nice,* he thought.

He walked through the oversized garage door that was standing open, allowing the rays of the morning sun to warm his bones. Brogus wasn't old, just 37, but he'd lived in the shadow of the law, keeping a low profile for so many years that time had burdened him with more than his share of mental aches and misgivings. He turned his face up to let the bright shafts of light play over his skin, basking like the small lizards he'd often find perched on nearby rocks, soaking up the heat.

Santos found him leaning against the wall, lost in his own meditations, staring off into the encompassing forest that formed the protective barrier between Brogus' compound and the rest of the world.

"Hey, Boss," he broached the space hesitantly, not wanting to disturb his superior's solitude. Brogus focused on his foreman with a raised brow, willing him to continue without uttering a word.

"We just got a call from Lissa Ahlsted."

"Right, the girl running the distribution division for the herbals," Brogus pegged her position within operations.

"Yeah. She called saying she couldn't come in today. There's been some kind of bad accident at her folks' ranch."

"She say anything specific?" His question a cross between interest and concern.

"She said enough before she fell apart blubbering on the phone." Santos had been embarrassed by her loss of composure when she had called, not knowing what to say or how to handle the emotion. After the fact, he was sure he had sounded rude and uncaring which made him feel like a heel.

Brogus brought him back to the present with a piercing jolt from his blue eyes.

"It sounded like she said her dad was dead." He gulped his discomfort.

"I hope you were able to convey some sympathy," Brogus gave him a mocking half-grin, knowing full well that Santos' social skills could use some grooming.

In response, Santos looked out at the view guiltily, certain that he had been no such thing despite his intentions. "I tried," was his flat response. "I did tell her not to worry about missing work."

"Well, that will have to do. I'll call back later and offer condolences, even if they are redundant. We wouldn't want people to think we were heartless S.O.B.s"

Still holding the dropper bottle in his grip, he asked Santos if they were ready to ship today.

"Of course. This," and he looked down at his boss' possession, nodding, "and the other product. It was a good crop. Good thing the weather's cooperated this year so we could begin harvesting this early in the season."

"That, at least, is good news since we'll need to offset the unexpected crop rotation. Some of those plants being moved were close to bud weren't they," he made it a statement of fact instead of a question.

"Yep. We'll actually be able to close up those sections before long," he bolstered Brogus' opinion of the fields' readiness.

"One less thing to worry about..." and he turned to go back to his office, his mind tripping over other more grave questions surrounding the circumstances of one of his not-so-distant neighbor's untimely demise. More doubts flurried his thoughts; too few answers.

•••••••

Two very large ungainly feet, decked out in the hippest new version of Nikes, were irreverently flung, toes turned out to opposite walls, on the surface of a massive oak desk that was capped with rose quartz marbled granite polished to a silky finish. The owner of those feet was reclined in a matching stone-gray leather chair, a hand-rolled Cuban Romeo and Julietta fit snugly between his fingers as his lips puffed rings of smoke that curled up to his office ceiling where a specialized air filter sucked it out of the atmosphere.

His intercom rang in a softly muted melody, programmed to inform the hearer of a call without unduly intruding into their work mode. Despite that, Chamberlain was still annoyed at the interruption of his invaluable calculations and slapped the button.

"Yes, Laura," he answered perfunctorily. "What can I do for you?"

At first put off by his brusque attitude, Cane shook off the aggravation and tamed her tongue before inadvertently lashing out at her lord and master, which she knew was precisely how he imagined himself.

"Following up as you directed, sir."

The only response she received was a grunt.

"I just received a call from the contractor, sir, and he informed me that the travertine has arrived a bit ahead of schedule. The entryway will be installed within the week bringing the finish work to completion. You will be free to schedule your gathering as soon as you like."

Chamberlain's demeanor switched gears immediately, the hyper level of delight usually displayed by a child overtook his voice with a laughing excitement. His giddiness was due to the simplest of pleasures, that of being allowed to show off his new toy. The major difference between him and a child of ten being that his new acquisition was an estate the size of a county with the seat of power sporting a price tag of $28 million.

Eager as he was, he calmed himself a little to answer in a disciplined fashion, reining in his childlike thrill. "Terrific. I'll let you handle all the details for the visit soonest. You have the guest list, correct?"

"Right here, sir. I'll inform you of the final plans." She exhaled with a sense of relief, letting the thought of submitting her resignation dance in her head. *Won't be long now, thank God.*

Leaning back in his luxurious executive seat one more time,

Land Barons

Chamberlain resettled his feet back on his desk and gloated over the newest and most extravagant of his appropriations. He understood the trappings of wealth and how it could impress even the most jaded of power brokers. He had crossed the line not only into the world of the super rich 'haves,' but he knew he had become the model to which even mighty potentates and masters of industry aspired. That just made his day.

Chapter 28

Another executive, this one a minimally paid county peace officer, sat forward in his well-worn but serviceable swivel chair, running a jumble of facts through his brain, which was beginning to feel like rapidly overloaded capacitors in a computer with too little memory. Drawing out notes on a legal pad usually helped him to narrow his wild thoughts down to some kind of order, but that just wasn't happening today. Instead, the more he attempted to make lists and coordinate evidence, of which there was damn little, all he seemed to end up with was a good man who was dead, apparently at someone's whim for no good reason. *At least no reason that makes any sense to me. But then, if this sort of thing made sense, I probably wouldn't be in law enforce - ment, I'd be out committing crimes. And likely be a lot happier.* The odd reflection almost startled him back to reality and the reality was that someone he'd known for most of his life had met a nasty and untimely end.

"Tolman, did you download those photos?" he called out in an effort to divert his woefully uncomfortable train of thought.

"Yes sir. Put a rush on the prints just as you ordered." He ran his fingers across a thick shock of an almost military-short crop of blonde hair, keeping the resentment of having to account for every gesture out of his voice.

Without looking up, the sheriff asked, "How about the crime scene investigators. Do you know if they've finished processing the scene?"

"Sir, as far as I know they're still scouring the area. I understood from their superior that it would be a long day that, because the incident took place outdoors, they've got a lot of ground to cover, literally. They've already bagged and shipped some of the major pieces of evidence, such as the stakes and the wood plank. Though he also said that there was very little chance of retrieving any prints off the rough surfaces."

"Damn," he muttered, already feeling beaten by having nothing to hang his hat on in this case. No idea of a motive was anywhere in his sight. He also knew that they hadn't even started the real investigation yet. "Well, there isn't much to be done there for now. Call Frank's foreman, Bert, to come in for an interview, will you? I want to go back over what he had to say about yesterday evening."

"Sure. Right away."

As soon as Deputy Tolman went back to the phone to make his call, Stellenbeck turned to his computer and logged on to the internet. He watched the screen as his homepage quickly built itself on the screen, then he immediately went to the new message box and began composing an e-mail to a buddy, Detective Seth Vieras with the state police in Boise. Following up on a wild hair, he typed in a request for his pal to run a background check on Gaheris 'Gary' Mathers, formerly of the Portland police force.

•••••••

When Gary drove up his gravel road, he found Anthea standing by her Expedition, which she'd parked haphazardly in front of his walkway. After he'd called this morning she was unable to concentrate on her work any longer. What were the implications of the accident? *Probably none, just a coincidence.* She knew, after years in the news business, that coincidence rarely had anything to do with the compounding elements of multiple tragedies. And Gary was smack in the middle of it all. She was out of the house ten minutes later taking the only action that was available to her, and that was to be there, on the spot, whether or not her presence would make a difference.

Before he could exit the truck, she arrived at his door and placed her hands across the felt weather stripping on the fully open window.

"It just didn't feel right futzing around the house, waiting for you to call. I hope you don't mind," she was immediately embarrassed for having jumped the gun and driven all the way out here without any provocation.

In lieu of an answer all she received was a lopsided grin and a question, "Futzing?" He took both of her hands in one of his own and gently lifted them off the door frame as he opened the cab and stepped down, keeping his gray eyes trained on her the whole time. He released her so he could step around the open door, where he confronted her and again asked, "Futzing?"

"Yeah, it's something an old friend of mine always used to say."

176

She shrugged, "habitual usage on my part and nobody else really understands it besides her and me. The fact is that it pretty much sounds like what it means."

"I guess it does, more or less like twiddling your thumbs only on a larger scale," he suggested.

"More or less," she agreed.

He had unconsciously taken her hands in his once more and letting his gaze wander across her features, he settled on her cerulean blue eyes. The depths of that well of color seemed likely to swallow him if he didn't pull himself back to reality, the reality of an unwarranted death of a neighbor.

Finding herself locked by his unrelenting stare, she almost visibly shook herself to regain composure, squeezed his hands and dropped hers to her side.

"Were you able to find out anything about Mr. Ahlsted's accident?" she asked earnestly.

"More than I wanted to know," he said, turning aside to close the truck door and lead her into the house. "It wasn't an accident," he spoke as he continued up the stone path not noticing that she was frozen in place until he had opened the door to let her step in front of him.

"What do you mean, it wasn't an accident," her voice floated to him from several feet away. "Are you sure?"

"I'd say yes. The circumstances leading to his plunging over the side of the ravine appeared a bit too obvious to me." He walked back to nudge her forward to the house.

"Why would anyone want to kill him?" The shock was only beginning to wear off as she moved toward the house.

"The look I got from the sheriff... he might think that I know the answer."

"What?" She looked up at him. "That doesn't make any sense *what*soever."

"I was the one looking for something more than just an accident and I was the one who found the signs of the pitfall. Matter of who saw it first, I think. It didn't cross his mind that it would be anything other than what it appeared, the ground giving way under the weight of the ATV and Ahlsted falling down the slope." He ushered her inside. "There's the supposition that someone who would think of looking

177

may likely be the perpetrator. And he didn't think to look, but I did."

"So, why did you…think to look, that is," she sat down at the table while he went into the kitchen to make coffee.

"Don't know," he said to the coffee maker and no one in particular. "There have been far too many shady things going on of late and the conservancy name keeps cropping up at every instance." His shoulders slumped a little in recognition of what made him examine the scene more closely. "I just felt a need to be thorough, not that the sheriff wouldn't have."

She cocked her head sideways when she asked. "How did you figure it out."

He caught her eyes from across the room, a cloud flitting across his own. "Years of not-so-overt combat experience." His smile turned a trifle wooden with a sour memory.

"That explains how you would know what to look for, but the sheriff may indeed think that your anticipation of foul play might appear suspicious," she was troubled by the possibility Stellenbeck could even entertain the idea.

Letting the concept slough off his back, he said, "He's going to think what he wants. Anyway, I'll be going in to make a formal statement since I managed to appear on the scene without an invitation. Neighborly interest doesn't seem to be reason enough these days," and he gave her a sad smile.

"It's certain to get all straightened out. He couldn't possibly think of you as a real suspect." Her expression perked up. "He just needs to get to know you a little better, like I have." She rose to give him a peck on the cheek, to which he responded by taking her around the waist, drawing her to his chest and planting a firm kiss on her mouth. Taken unexpectedly by his melting against her lips, she returned the sentiment with equal fervor.

He pulled away briefly to tell her, "The sheriff is not about to get to know me the way you have." He laughed lightly in her ear and kissed her again for emphasis.

•••••••

Prowling the office, unpleasant scenarios churning through his mind, Sheriff Stellenbeck found himself planted behind Deputy

Tolman, peering past his broad shoulders and buzz cut at the computer screen displaying lines of data he was entering at a rapid clip.

"How's the report coming?"

The deputy's back stiffened with the question coming right past his ear from such close quarters. A feeling of annoyance meshed with inadequacy washed over him and aside in the blink of an eye. "Can I help you, Sheriff?"

"No need to be so touchy, Mark. This thing has just gotten under my skin, maybe yours, too." He wandered over to another desk and hitched his hip up, leaning his weight on the paper-strewn surface. "Have you interviewed the family yet?"

"Just Mrs. Ahlsted. It's in the report," he answered a bit more brusquely than necessary.

Stellenbeck lifted a brow at the hostility beginning to seep through Tolman's usually stoic attitude. "How about the daughter? I understand she's home for the summer."

"She wasn't available when I was there. Gone into town for something for her mom." He exhaled the bitterness into the air, letting it go. Chiding himself for allowing it to become evident, even for a moment. He was better than that. "I'll get back over there this afternoon for her statement," he reassured his superior, managing a slight upturning of one corner of his mouth.

"I thought I'd heard some rumor that you two had been seeing each other socially. If that's so, perhaps I should conduct the interview."

"That won't be necessary. We've gone out for coffee a couple of times but I shouldn't think that it would cause any kind of problem or conflict of interest. We hardly know each other," he said with finality, hopefully ending that line of discussion.

"I have no compunction as to your ability to handle an interview, but we can't have even the breath of impropriety tainting this investigation since we're probably dealing with murder," he answered gravely.

"Are you that certain?" a glimmer of surprise flitting across his face.

"Two homicide detectives from the state police came in on my request to review the scene and the evidence garnered by the crime scene crew. They think that section of ground was rigged to collapse.

They seem pretty positive."

"What about that guy Mathers? Wasn't he poking around the scene?"

"Only after asking my permission first." He was silent for a beat. "He was the one who noticed the ground had been disturbed, saw the stakes. Not that they were anything like invisible. I'm just not sure that I would have thought to look myself," and he ruminated over that bit of insight.

"Odd that he'd pick up on that or think to check for it," said Tolman skeptically.

"He'll be in tomorrow morning to give his statement. We'll see what was going through his mind then." He removed himself from the edge of the desk and went back into his office, closing the door behind him.

Chapter 29

Rummaging through the odd stacks of files that had been accumulating on her worktable, DiMarco glanced up at the clock to see the time displayed on its plain, utilitarian face. *How did it get to be so late?* She finally looked out the front window and noticed that the shadows had grown long which meant that she should have closed up shop two hours past. Instead she had gotten sidetracked with all the minutiae of preparing workshops for the area schools, not to mention the new grant she probably spent five hours on today alone, compiling statistics and reports for reference.

She placed both hands flat on the table, straddling a pile of folders needing filing, and let her head hang down between her shoulders, trying to eradicate the tension that had built along her trapezius muscles and ran down between the wings of her scapulae.

After a few moments, she raised her head and gathered up a box of teaching supplies that were left over from an earlier class, hefted it onto her hip and opened the supply closet, then set the carton on a shelf. Closing the narrow door, she turned to shut down the computer and set the answering machine only to be confronted with the unbidden sight of Billy Brogus, lounging in her chair, feet propped disrespectfully on her desk.

"Who let the dogs in?" she queried the room in general.

"That's a welcome I haven't enjoyed before," a smirk slid across his lips as he locked his hands behind his head, appearing to make himself even more comfortable.

"You're *not* welcome here," she retorted.

"I see we hold grudges. What's it been, 12, 15 years?"

"Who's counting? I try not to keep track of the more unpleasant incidents in my life," she said in an attempt to brush him off.

"I guess I do, because I remember our last encounter quite well. Even with a certain fondness." His voice rumbled with a sensual burr. "Call me sentimental."

"Right. So what's the occasion today? Particularly since our individual recollections don't exactly coincide." She pushed his boots off her desk so she could reach the keyboard of her computer.

He looked up at her from her chair, hands on the armrests, as she leant past him to manipulate the keys and close out her programs. "I thought we might get reacquainted. You know, talk over old times." He raised his eyebrows and a smile played across his lips.

"What you think and what will happen are definitely two different things. Perhaps you haven't been listening, but I'm not interested in a 'reacquaintance.'" She tried to ignore the fact that he was seated just inches from her, with a very good view of her backside.

"That's unfortunate. I had figured enough time had passed that we might be able to start over." He folded himself in half so he could look directly into her eyes as she punched the last button and the screen went black.

Twisting her head around to stare back at him, she said, "You figured wrong, so you may as well clean the dirt off my desk from your filthy boots and get reacquainted with the exit."

Standing up, he brushed the surface of the desk and leaned down to get within inches of her face, his impish grin mocking her with the charm that she remembered only too well. She sucked in her breath and would have pulled back, but she was boxed in.

"Come on," his voice sultry as the dusk, "we're neighbors now. Just have a drink with me."

"Are you kidding?" She managed to wriggle around the chair and face him from the other side of the desk. "I doubt your reputation is any improved from when we last met and you were peddling weed. For all I know, you still are." She shook her head. "I can't afford to be seen with you."

"Ah, and sully your good name…it's not written that we have to go anywhere public, if that's your concern. However, I am the upstanding proprietor of Pinesap Farms, purveyor of natural herbs and huckleberry products."

She laughed aloud. "I can just imagine what 'natural herbs' you deal in."

"St. John's wort, chamomile, echinacea, native garlic, rose hips, organic apple cider vinegar…health products that even you might use." He slid around the desk, closing the distance between them he placed his hands gently on her shoulders which sent an unexpected shiver through her system, dredging up old memories. "I think your imagination has run away with you."

He brought his lips closer to hers and whispered, "Come with me."

She stepped back, catching her breath and then plunged in. "Even if you are a 'new man' and a respected entrepreneur, I frankly don't see the advantage of fraternizing."

He followed her by taking a step forward. "Don't you? We're not in the military, we're not on opposite sides of the law...politics maybe. We just won't broach that subject." He looked deep into her the green pools of her eyes. "Come on, when's the last time you 'fraternized' with anybody?"

She gulped, "That's none of your business, but you know very well that I haven't been here long enough to meet many people."

"So, come with me. You don't like the company, I'll bring you back." He drew his finger lightly down her cheek, delicately pushing a tendril of hair behind her ear.

Isolation had engulfed her for more than just the short time she had been in Marcasite. It had been years of a self-imposed lifestyle of loneliness, fearing to place any faith in friends or lovers. It was safer to wall herself off from the world, but it was an exile that drained her emotionally. On top of that, she was being bombarded with flashbacks of their volatile relationship in college. What frightened her most was the fact that she was still drawn to him like a moth to the flame. She dropped her head back and closed her eyes to try to gain some perspective. He was the same, but different. He appeared far more mature in his attitude and physically than she remembered. And he stirred something in her that she thought had been quenched. As much as she hated to admit it, the spark was still there.

Do I know what I'm doing? No, she decided. But she accepted his invitation anyway.

•••••••

Tolman finished fielding calls at the station, staying long after his shift ended, then grabbed a bite at the Mexican restaurant a few blocks down on Main Street in Lathrop. He stewed in his own thoughts about the recent events occurring around Marcasite, thinking that there was simply too much happening in such a short time span for a town that small. His mind meandered down that road, leading him to Lissa

Ahlsted. He pictured the tall, solid ranch girl who bucked hay and could rope a calf with as much ability as every other hand. She'd been the rodeo queen for the Marcasite event while a senior in high school and a champion barrel racer. She was a tough one as well as appealing, but he had qualms about getting involved with her as he thought about the complications.

He finished his meal and drained the last of his beer, paid the check with a smile when the owner's wife, Alicia, came by the table to check if he needed anything more.

"Everything was just fine," he contrived a shy smile as he got up to take his leave. "Thank you, ma'am." And he went out the door.

He drove straight over to the Ahlsted's from town, twenty minutes up State Highway 4. Knocking on the front door, he positioned himself a good foot back on the porch when Lissa peered through the glass inset that was centered in the big metal door. Recognizing his form, she pulled the door open and he moved forward placing an outstretched hand nonchalantly on the jamb, which brought him closer to her as she stood framed by the hall light shining behind her. Her blonde hair was mussed from continuously having run her fingers through it in worry and frustration. Her eyes were rimmed with red from crying and, young as she was, dark circles had appeared brought on by the sudden grief that had wracked her body and left her exhausted.

"I had to come by and see how you were coping, Lissa," he said with concern.

The simple task of answering his question almost proved too much as she closed her eyes to squeeze back the tears before they began streaming down her face for the hundredth time today. Taking a deep breath to calm herself, she said simply, "We're okay."

Taking her hand in his, he wiped away a stray tear streaking down her cheek saying, "Obviously not. And you're not expected to be after a shock like this."

"Really," she insisted. "We'll make it. Ginny just left. She's such a dear. She's been here all day. I guess Tom was forced to spend time at the store rather than in the company of his coffee mates," she tried to manage a weak smile.

"At least you've still got a sense of humor, however lame," he said with a little grin. "How about your brothers? When do you expect them?"

"Tomorrow," she was slightly wistful. "Mom talked to both of them today and Joe can't get away any earlier than tomorrow evening. It'll be a red-eye for him. I suppose he'll fit in with us women that way, huh?" He grimaced as she made another stab at comic relief.

"Can you think of anything that I can do? Will Joe need a ride from the airport?"

"No, he's renting a car. But thanks for the offer. I'm sure you're already swamped with work as it is." Her gaze dropped to examine his shoes.

"Not so much that I can't find time to be helpful," he said as he crooked his finger under her chin so he could meet her eyes. "What about the ranch? You all able to handle that?"

"Mom's working with Bert. I think keeping busy is cathartic for her, takes her mind off the immediate situation and holds her together." Another tear slid unbidden down her face.

"How about you? You'll be home for a little while, I'm guessing."

"Yes. Billy insisted I take the time for family, though it might actually be easier to stay at work and keep myself occupied. Instead, I'm going to help move the cattle to the summer range. Climbing on a horse would be good therapy. I don't get to ride that much anymore and half the time they use those damn ATVs anyway." The thought brought her back to her father's accident and she closed her eyes to try to keep the weeping at bay. "There's work to be done here."

"Look, if you feel up to it, maybe I can take you for a ride in a day or two. Let you breathe a little."

"I don't know if that's such a good idea. I need to be here when Brad and Joe come in and won't it seem a little odd since you're involved in the investigation?" She brought her eyes up to study him.

"I doubt it. It's not exactly a secret that we've gone out a few times. Let me do what I can to help even if all it is, is getting you away for a little bit."

"Okay. Call me tomorrow night. I've got to go in now and make sure Mom's all right. I'm worried most about her."

Tolman reached for her and pulled her into a chaste hug. Hesitating a little at first, Lissa gave in to the offer of comfort, crying softly into his uniform as he stroked her hair.

With his arms wrapped around her, listening to the muffled sobs, he wondered how well he had control of the situation.

Chapter 30

Opening her eyes with the light streaming in from the window, Anthea blinked repeatedly as she looked up at the unfamiliar ceiling, slightly disoriented. Rising up on her elbows, she scanned the room, denoting the earthy tones and heavy oak frame of the bed in which she was ensconced, sheets twisted around her ankles. As she flipped off the covers and set her feet on the floor, she remembered that she was not at home, but in Mathers' guest room. She had declined a place in his bed, fear and uncertainty keeping her from an intimacy that she otherwise craved. *Nope, I'm definitely not ready for that leap yet. Thank goodness he's not overwhelming me with his 'needs' like every other male I've ever known.* She breathed a sigh of relief, feeling the pressure dissipate, despite the niggling want at the back of her own mind.

They had spent the rest of the afternoon and evening comparing ideas and seeing if there was an actual puzzle or just a faint notion of paranoia insinuating itself into both their psyches. *At least it's not just me.* She tried to gather her thoughts together as she tapped her toes on the oval rag throw that lay by the bedside. Gazing into the blended tones of fall: rust, golden mustard and sienna that were entwined in the knotted pattern, she jumped at the knock on the door.

Easing the door open just and inch or two, Mathers called softly into the room, keeping himself out of sight behind it, "Are you ready for coffee?"

"Couldn't possibly face the world without it," she replied. "Be right out."

She pushed herself off of the bed and opening the closet, rummaged around until she found a robe that was far too big for her small frame. Donning the thick, terry monster, she knotted the belt around her waist, tried to run her fingers through her dark, tangled mop and trotted out to the kitchen.

"I hope you don't mind that I didn't dress for breakfast," she apologized as she joined him at the table where he sat clad in sweats and a t-shirt. Before she could sit, he hopped up and meeting her on the other side of the table, pulled out the chair for her, the gesture of gallantry bringing a small smile to her lips.

"Here, have a seat and a cuppa." He studied her as he went into the kitchen to fill a mug with steaming coffee. "You look like you're just two steps from joining the zombie population."

"Sorry to disappoint, but mornings aren't my preferred time of day. Coffee is the breath of life, keeping all zombies at bay, much like garlic wards off vampires." She gratefully accepted the cup and sipped the brew.

"Breakfast for the undead?"

She hefted the mug, "This is breakfast." She fell silent to savor her coffee.

"Well, I can see it will be a while yet before conversation becomes animated." He smirked and she stared him down with a scornful glare.

"I never promised otherwise. You want animation? Get a kitten."

"Did you sleep well?" he asked, playfully solicitous.

"As you made note of my appearance, it was the sleep of the dead," she replied, deadpan.

"Good. I'm glad you were comfortable."

"Not to be rude, but I was too tired to know the difference."

Not missing his chance, he said, "I still think you would have been better off with company. Then you definitely would have discerned a difference."

She gave him a sidelong glance. "No doubt." And she returned her attention to her coffee, although with a little difficulty after his last remark. Letting the slight flush subside, she asked what plans he had for the day.

"The sheriff is expecting me to arrive at the office in Lathrop to give them an official statement. You're welcome to stay," he let the offer drift into a long silence.

"I'd best get my act together and get back into town. Aside from the work I need to finish today, I also think it's time to start compiling more information on the local players. Not that I'm any kind of investigator, but you'd be surprised what you can find on the internet." She turned the corner of her mouth up in a mischievous curve. "Bet I could find some interesting stuff about you."

"My life's an open book," he said spreading his hands wide.

"You're obviously also a rather suspicious character. Why else would the sheriff have his eye on you as a suspect."

"Now what makes you think that?" he asked, perplexed.

"From what you said of your encounter at the accident scene. We need to find out who else would have a motive to send poor Ahlsted to his death and I don't think the law is looking in the same barn that we are."

"Highly unlikely that they've put anything into the same perspective as you and me," he agreed.

"And we certainly can't have you rotting behind bars, upstanding citizen that you are. Suspicious or not."

"You really think I'm suspicious?" He sounded hurt.

"Nah, but you're mysterious. Relatively new in the area, a secret past and way too much curiosity about neighbor's affairs. I take it back, you definitely qualify as suspicious," she added with a hint of a smile. She stood up, gave him a peck on the cheek and swept past him, the tail of the robe trailing behind like the royal train of a gown.

•••••••

The numbers were making him crazy. He didn't mind the work involved in almost every aspect of the business, but the accounting for the nonexistent side of the farm's management, was something he preferred not to do. Trouble was, you couldn't exactly hire in a bookkeeper. Too many questions that have no answers would ensue. *And then I'd have to kill him.* He laughed at his private joke, knowing that any true underworld organization might act on such a whim, but to him, it was simply an unexpressed gag, like what secret agents would quip. He went back to examining the columns of digits, and nodded to himself that it would be possible to initiate his plans soon. Good. He closed up the program and pulled out the jump drive. As he began to put away the laptop his attention was attracted to a helicopter sliding over the ridge, making its way to the new estate buried in the crests of trees beyond his property. *The enigmatic mansion in the forest that is about as real to the locals as Brigadoon.*

He placed the memory stick in the file cabinet and locked it, then reached for his coffee and downed the last of it, leaving a few grounds swimming in the bottom of the cup. Leaving the mug on his desk, he unlocked the bottom drawer on the right and pulled out his gun, checked to see the clip was loaded and that the chamber was clear, set the safety and laid it on the desk. He grabbed his jacket off the coat tree and pulled it over his shoulders, then slipped the gun into his pocket for insurance. He didn't like carrying a piece and rarely did, but today he decided he needed the extra protection, just in case. He snatched his keys from the credenza and closed the door behind him as he walked purposefully to his truck.

The road up the mountain curled through seemingly impenetrably thick stands of trees forming a canopy above that virtually blocked the sun's rays. The appearance was that of a dim, shadowy tunnel roofed by upturned pine boughs reaching for the light that danced above them. It was little more than a dirt track and was the only access route since the other two roads had been deconstructed by the forest service in an attempt to return the timberland to its untouched state. Not that that was possible as this was all second and third growth forest, having been logged out more than once in the past hundred or so years. Instead, the undergrowth was becoming impenetrable as it spread unimpeded across the dank forest floor. In areas it was so thick that even the wildlife couldn't negotiate their way through the trees. *Leave it to the environmental know-it-alls to kill a forest and have no clue that's what's happening right under their noses.* He left off that train of thought, knowing full well it would only crank up his anger quotient and he couldn't afford to be testy when he met up with his next appointment, not that they were aware of his visit.

He grumbled to himself about the poor condition of the road as he crossed a shallow brook and took note of the many rust-colored trees interspersed among the healthy ones, the bright hue indicative of the advanced stages of disease that plagued the forest. He was thankful that the number of trees affected by the mountain pine beetle wasn't anywhere near approaching the infested acreage found elsewhere in the state. However, just seeing this much of the forest discolored gave him a glimmer of concern.

Climbing up the rocky route, he rounded a corner and drove past a barracks situated on the right where the road finally improved for the last mile that it led up to the main complex. He passed a number of outbuildings, designed to enhance the overall appearance of the estate, the architecture simple but blending into the rustic nature of the rest of the buildings. Passing the cluster of buildings, he finally pulled up in front of an oversized garage constructed to accommodate six vehicles.

As no visitor goes unnoticed, a guard, who had been following him since he emerged from the dense trees, swung his green Range Rover in front of Billy's truck and climbed out to confront the uninvited guest before he could reach the steps of the house.

"I'm sorry, sir, but visitors are not allowed without prior arrangements. You'll have to leave immediately." The security representative wore a uniform similar to that of the forest service, perhaps so people would unintentionally mistake them for USFS employees and not question their authority. He was also armed, though he made no move to unholster his weapon.

These boys don't screw around. Brogus kept his hands to his side and in plain sight.

"Don't worry, Bud. Just here to see Miss Laura. She was expected in this morning, I believe." He waved his hands slightly in front of his chest, palms open, as a non-threatening gesture, hoping to ease this guy's itchy trigger finger, just in case he had one.

Dropping the menacing stare, the guard said, "Actually she just arrived a little while back." Hearing the front door groan open, he turned to check. "Looks like she heard your approach." Looking toward the main house he called, "Miss Cane, were you expecting this gentleman?"

She descended the steps, eyes widening briefly in surprise, ditching the expression rapidly before the security guard noticed. Raising an eyebrow, she replied, "I believe Mr. Brogus is welcome here."

Billy stepped forward past the bewildered guard, flashing an ingratiating grin as he reached out to shake Cane's hand.

"Always a pleasure Ms. Cane," he said and bussed her cheek in the European fashion.

She simply nodded her dismissal to the guard before turning her attention to her visitor.

"And what brings you here, today, Mr. Brogus?" she asked, keeping her voice lowered until the retreating guard was out of earshot.

"Just Billy, Ma'am. Hopefully, you have a few minutes that I might address a bit of business with you," he said, giving her one of his most charming smiles.

Without acknowledging his statement, she turned to ascend the wide stone stairs to the deep veranda that encompassed the huge house. Shrugging his shoulders, he followed her into the main entryway and into a sitting room, furnished with a warm-toned yet rugged looking couch and two occasional chairs. He sat back, noting the mix of rustic décor that was subtly influenced with refinements from civilization. *Just the picture of what city wizkids think the country life ought to look like. Trite.*

"Nice digs. I see no expense was spared in outfitting this little hideaway," he said aloud as he scanned the room. A houseman brought in a silver coffee service and a cut crystal tray displaying a nice selection of homemade muffins and breads sliced to reveal cranberries, blueberries, huckleberries and an assortment of nutmeats.

Picking up an offered morsel, he said, "How'd you know my favorite. Just like Grandma used to make," and he took a bite.

"I'm pleased you're so easily gratified. Now what is it that I can do for you?" she asked politely.

Setting his plate back on the glass-topped table that had a beautifully carved scene of bass in a stream under the surface, he picked up a cup of coffee and proceeded to explain his problem.

"I'm sure you're aware of the fire that destroyed a large stand of trees last week."

She nodded her comprehension, uttering only "mmmm."

"The clean-up operation is bringing workers within a dangerous proximity of one of our farms. We packed up for relocation immediately and the crops need to be transplanted as soon as possible."

She leaned back in her chair and just watched him over the rim of her china cup with an unemotional stare that he found slightly disconcerting.

"We had discussed alternate sites earlier this year, as you'll remember."

At this she nodded and smiled slightly, "Yes we did."

"I must move the growing area to the previously designated Site 3, as temporary placement. I wanted to confer with you to ascertain your agreement before we actually made the move. Is there any problem with that?" His eyes locked onto hers, probing for any depth of feeling within those deep brown wells. If there was, she was adept at camouflaging any personal sentiment.

"No, there's no problem. We had come to a mutual agreement some time back and there is no reason to renegotiate. Mr. Chamberlain is due in the morning and it is imperative that your company is undetectable. I can't have him alarmed by anything he deems outside of ordinary activity." She took another sip of her coffee.

"It's all under control. When will you be moving out your own workforce?" He asked keeping his tone bland and unintrusive as he probed for information.

"In about a week. The construction is pretty much complete so they will be returned to their basecamp."

"That soon? You've moved the development here along at a very rapid clip and it's impressive, to say the least. I'm sure Mr. Chamberlain will be happy to have his liability reduced with the workers finally finished and removed from the property."

"He's excited about the new lodge and looking forward to entertaining. He is also appreciative of the workmen's contribution."

He trained his gaze on her as he guessed that Chamberlain would be relieved to have the barracks cleared as soon as possible.

"Thank you for your hospitality, Ms. Cane." He stood to shake her hand. "It's always a pleasure doing business with you." As he turned to take his leave he said, "I'll just see myself out. Enjoy your stay."

Making his way over the rough terrain, Brogus knew he had a decision to make and soon. The information he'd gleaned from Laura Cane put his timetable on the fast track. He mulled over all the related data as he cautiously traversed the road down the mountain.

Land Barons

Chapter 31

Annie, who was playing the dual role of dispatcher and receptionist, pushed the button on her multi-line phone for the sheriff's private line.

"Yea-uh, what can I do for you, Annie?"

"Got a Detective Vieras on line one for you. From Boise," she sang in her high pitched voice.

"Thanks, Annie. I'll pick-up." He pressed the flashing indicator and put the receiver to his ear.

"Hey, Seth. What you got? Anything interesting?"

"Dave. I don't know what you were expecting, but he comes up clean...retired cop with commendations."

"Any reason you could find that he would know anything about traps, hidden snares and whatnot?" His tone was subdued figuring he'd hit a dead end with a fellow peace officer.

"From the looks of his military record, he served with covert ops in the garden spots of the world like Laos and Beirut. He likely picked-up all sorts of nasty technology in the more nefarious arts while in the service of Uncle Sam. I'm sure much of the learning curve was in discovering what the other side's more murderous techniques were in order to disable them. That was in the line of duty way back when. Since then he's had twenty years on the force, most of it in Portland, Oregon, some of it in an anti-terrorist unit. But the last six years he's been a college professor. I doubt he's your man."

"I haven't got any specific feeling about Mathers aside from thinking like I ought to check into everyone's history. You never know what skeletons can tumble out of a closet and most people have some kind of secret. Though it looks like his is pretty much that he'd prefer to keep his law enforcement years in the past," he said, trying to highlight his pragmatic viewpoint.

"You know, it may have actually been lucky for you that this guy came along when he did. Think you might have missed the evidence pointing to a homicide?" Vieras voice sounded distant over the phone, like he was calling from a train tunnel.

"It's possible. We just assumed it was an accident and that's what bothered me most. What made him think to look for foul play?" Stellenbeck sounded bemused.

"Guess you'll ask him when you see him. Didn't you say he's coming in to be interviewed?"

"Yeah, he's due here in about an hour." He scratched his head abstractedly. "Thanks for the info, Seth. Let me know if you trip over anything else."

"Will do, Dave. Glad to help."

•••••••

As Mathers entered the sheriff's station in Lathrop, Annie beamed a big 'hello' from her seat behind the receptionist's desk. Her rosy cheeks full under her short cropped curly bob. Her ebullient demeanor and cherubic figure were one of the office's assets and a general annoyance to Deputy Tolman who had a tendency to be sullen. Tolman, ever in an accommodating mood, nodded at Mathers with a barely concealed scowl and told Annie to buzz the sheriff that his 10:00 a.m. appointment had arrived.

"Sure thing," she bubbled and punched the sheriff's line to make the announcement.

The door opened to the sheriff's inner sanctum and Stellenbeck stuck out his head to greet Mathers.

"Morning, Sheriff," said Gary, somewhat somberly in respect to the nature of the call.

"Morning, Gary. Thanks for coming in." He ushered him into the office and indicating a chair, said, "Have a seat."

Placing his hands on his knees, Mathers asked blandly, "So, where do we start?" his pewter gray eyes probing the sheriff's mood.

"If you don't mind, I'm going to tape the interview since my notation skills aren't what they ought to be." Gary nodded his ascent. "Okay, then," and he depressed the play and record buttons simultaneously, beginning the session by stating the basic information of date and time, then name and address of Mathers with himself as conducting the interview.

"Let's start with your acquaintance with the deceased and how you came to be at the scene after the fact." Stellenbeck decided to give him plenty of latitude for his statement and sat back to hear the explanations.

"You know the grapevine in a small town," he said as a preface to his story. "I heard Frank had an accident and ran over to find out if there was anything I could do to help my neighbors. Usual story."

"How well did you know Frank Ahlsted?" prompted Stellenbeck. He settled into his high-backed chair, half reclined with his hands clasped over his comfortably round stomach.

"Well enough that we'd stop and chat once in a while. He'd given me permission to use the easement across his property to access the public lands adjacent to the ranch."

"You go out there often?"

"Periodically. I was out there within the last ten days. Met up with him as he was tending to the burning of some carcasses of his herd that had been mysteriously dying off. I was with a friend and we took some time to ask about the problems he was encountering with the cattle. Pretty odd stuff," he shook his head with an air of slight bewilderment.

"I remember reading about that in the paper. Did he offer any information in regard to the die-off?"

"Evidently, he was fairly worried about the large number of losses but he wasn't exactly forthcoming as to the cause. But then, I don't think he knew."

"What brought you out to the accident scene?" The sheriff sharpened his gaze.

"This is all going to sound rather strange and unconnected. I'd been hearing a lot about some of the local landowners coming under different kinds of financial stress to the point where they've been forced to sell off their holdings. Most of them have been right up here between Marcasite and Lilliot. Just piqued my interest when I knew that Frank was also dealing with the enigmatic destruction of his herd." He shrugged his shoulders.

"What gave you the idea to examine the area of collapse for evidence of anything out of the ordinary?"

"A wild hair mostly, and my suspicious nature probably from too many years of dealing with the criminal mind. And Frank knew his land inside out. He'd never pull that close to the edge if he hadn't known it was solid and safe."

"Why'd you think there was anything to do with these other property owners and Frank's troubles?" He sat forward in his seat now, interested in Mathers' answer, because it didn't make sense to him.

"I'd read about the Stablers having to sell out to a conservancy and move because of crop failures and Mrs. Stabler's illness and subsequent death. Then I talked to Bob Powell and he was entertaining an offer to sell to the same conservancy. Then Frank had mentioned some conservation group having toured the ranch recently. Made me wonder."

"Pretty slim relationship," stated Stellenbeck.

"If there even is one. What can I say? This group has been quite visible in its acquisitions over the last year or so. Who knows? I just had to look."

Stellenbeck leaned across the desk and turned off the recorder.

"You may have saved me from overlooking some very important evidence, even if the circumstances of your inquisitive eye are a little suspect. I probably ought to thank you because I want to make sure Frank's family gets justice. You got any names related to this conservation group?"

"No individuals. Just the name of the organization: Nature's Wilds Conservancy. But you know, Frank didn't mention them by name," said Mathers realizing just how simple-minded the whole thing sounded. *I wouldn't take me seriously and I've been in his place.*

"Guess I'll have to ask Vera if she's heard anything about them," he muttered half under his breath.

"Anything else you need, today?" he asked, smoothing the fabric of his jeans over his thighs.

"Nope, that's it for now." Stellenbeck stood and shook hands with Mathers. "Thanks for coming in and you call me if you think of anything else."

"You bet." Mathers turned to leave, waving adieu at a smiling Annie and a surly Tolman.

Chapter 32

Rising up over the tree-lined ridge, a sleek golden-colored, customized Hughes, looking more like a flying limousine than anything else, rapidly swooped in to settle on the helipad.

Emblazoned with the sunburst of Solis Industries just forward of the tail rotor assembly, the helicopter, luxuriously outfitted to chauffeur up to a dozen guests in unmatched opulence, was making its first delivery to the newly christened Solis Ranch. Today it was ferrying eight visitors who were generously plied with champagne and canapés during their flight from the regional airport.

Landing with a gentle thump, a couple of the guests disembarked with some hesitancy, the alcohol having influenced them with a reticence they hadn't felt as they had boarded the aircraft. One of the travelers spouted some crack about fear and curiosity being interchangeable emotions and hustled the lollygaggers to the tarmac with laughter.

As they alighted, their heads coming up after passing outside the range of the whirling blades, they were dumbstruck by the dramatic landscape that rolled off to the horizon in every direction. One of the men, finding his larynx working again, still couldn't do more than gape at the expansive vista, uttering the word 'magnificent.'

Carl Chamberlain, who had clambered out of the helicopter last, stood with his hands on his hips, drinking in the praise as if it were for him and not their surroundings. In his mind it was the same, he owned it and it was a reflection of his ability to strike awe in the hearts of his guests, whom he viewed as lesser beings.

"My god, Carl," drawled a spikey-haired blond adonis in his well-known British inflection. "I can't believe what heaven you have here." The pop star, who regularly appeared at Amnesty International and Save the Rainforest events and concerts, let the envy drip from every pore.

Pride of ownership overpowering Chamberlain he boasted, "this is my Avalon. Welcome all!"

Turning away from their craft, the whump of the rotors easing as it powered down, Chamberlain led his entourage, trooping in his wake, up the main stairs to the wide veranda that encompassed the main house that was more reminiscent of a cedar sided manor than a residence. They were trailed by a group of stewards who had unloaded the baggage and were carting it to a side delivery entrance.

"Ms. Cane will introduce you to the house manager, Angelo, who will escort you to your rooms and have your luggage delivered promptly," Chamberlain explained as a teacher would to errant children. "You'll have an opportunity to freshen up and we can converge on the rear deck at 5:00 p.m. for cocktails. Thank you all for coming." He whipped around on his heel and disappeared into the recesses of his private study.

After seeing to the comfort of Chamberlain's visitors, Laura Cane knocked briskly on the door of his personal sanctuary. Staying seated in his leather wing back chair, feet propped on a matching ottoman and facing the French doors that opened out to an unimpeded view of the distant mountains, he called out his permission to enter.

Pulling open the door, she waltzed in with a tall, lanky, balding man in his mid-fifties in tow. The man thought to offer his hand but as he was confronted with the backside of Chamberlain's chair, he decided against what would only be a humiliating rebuff, since the host didn't have the good manners to even address his guest face-to-face.

"Well, Glen, are you being treated well?" asked Chamberlain, not bothering to turn around to see who stood behind him.

The man walked over to the side of the chair before answering.

"Yes, Carl. The staff has been most attentive. It was kind of you to invite me along on this junket. It's not often I have the good fortune to enjoy the fruits of our combined labors."

Chamberlain's head cocked at Glen's comments, a mask of disapproval descending over his features, knowing that this man was only a tool as opposed to any partner in trade. Letting it slide he said, "Well, just look at it as a thank you for a job well done. Our organizations can continue in this limited assistance capacity on future projects, yes?"

"Of a certainty, Carl." Chamberlain cringed at the informal address, as if they were equals, which most assuredly, in his mind, they were not. "This estate is well on its way to becoming landlocked by Conservancy acquisitions, guaranteeing privacy and halting public access to the national forest land you so enjoy viewing out that window."

Glen tried to gain a bit of an edge by reminding the host that his possession could not have been cemented without the complicity of his organization's status. It wasn't much of a jab in that Chamberlain's money funded most of the operations, but he wanted him to know that you need more than money to accomplish some goals, and people like himself were irreplaceable for such employment.

"We'll all be appreciative of the fact that we won't have to suffer the abomination of locals buzzing through this exquisite tranquility with their ATV's. They have other areas to haunt with their beer and hunting rifles."

"It is our intent to preserve this incredible beauty for future generations," added Glen.

"*Our* progeny. Respect for this land hasn't been bred into these country bumpkins. It's our duty to protect it from them," he slipped into a murmur at the end.

"The most sensible thing is to protect it from them in order to protect it for them," he agreed.

"Well, Glen, thanks again and we'll see you back in the civilized world," said Chamberlain, summarily dismissing him in such a way that Glen understood that he was to keep a low profile for the rest of his stay. Laura Cane had already tried to defuse his ego when she informed him that his presence was considered more of a business necessity rather than a social call. He was more or less an obsequious personality and wasn't about to fuss about being shoved into the shadows. With a nod to Chamberlain and then Cane, he slipped through the door.

Chamberlain pushed himself out of his chair, directing himself to the wet bar where he wrapped his fingers around the neck of a cut glass decanter that housed his favorite gin. Pouring a generous portion into a highball glass, he addressed Cane over his shoulder.

"Laura, do we have to deal with him face-to-face?" He added some tonic to his concoction and a slice of lime, "he's so odious to deal with, I'd prefer not to if we can avoid it in the future."

"It's best to keep him on our good side, though your rude handling of the meeting leaves a lot to be desired as far as that goes." She was a little ticked at his lack of sensitivity in working with someone like Glen Alison, who was an important cog in their very convoluted machine. "The acquisitions are heating up around the different states, and placating him isn't really all that difficult. I know that charm isn't your forté, but it couldn't hurt to try a little harder."

Blowing off her comments, he said, "He's replaceable, if it comes to that," and he took a stout swig of his drink.

"It doesn't make sense to complicate matters any more than they are, and irritating a relatively minor player like Alison could be more trouble than its worth." She sighed and rubbed her temple. "He's happy for the moment. The organization is expanding its holdings and we stand to benefit from the prize of pristine acreage set aside for our special usage."

"Fine then," he looked down his nose at her. "Just try to keep him as far away from me as possible. Now, why don't you kick back for a bit before the groupies descend on us with all their innocuous 'oohing' and 'aahing.'" He shook himself like a dog trying to dislodge a tick, then went back to the bar to mix her favorite cocktail.

Chapter 33

A midmorning knock sounded lightly on the back door and, Anthea, having just arrived from upriver, dropped her handbag on a counter and sauntered over to unlatch the slider while looking up into Lainie's inquisitive brown eyes.

"You didn't come home last night," she stated without heat but tinged slightly with the guilt-inducing tones any good Jewish mother would use.

"And you two keep track of my schedule?" Anthea quirked up an eyebrow with amusement.

"Someone has to watch out for you after what happened this last week." Lainie moved into the accusing attitude. "You should have called. We were worried."

"I didn't know that I was required to check in with my tenants every time I stayed out late." She crossed her arms over her chest and stood her ground as Lainie brushed past her, sweeping into the room and settling herself onto the couch. "Don't you need to be at work?"

"Just got out for a few hours and decided I *should* check on you. Make sure you got back all right. Who *knows* where you've been." She shot Anthea a sidelong look crafted to intimidate the most incorrigible youth. Anthea decided that Lainie would be a daunting force as a matron.

Anthea bent down a little to lock eyes with her young friend. "But you *do* know where I've been, don't you."

At this Lainie colored and lost ground with her older, and supposedly wiser, adversary. Though, at the moment Anthea felt anything but wise in the growing attraction to Gary Mathers. In fact, she felt defensive about her actions.

Lainie sat up, a big smile drawing across her lovely face. "Yeah, and did you get any?"

Anthea's mouth literally fell open. "Lainie! I'd like to think that you have a little more respect for my judgment than that!"

"It's time you found someone nice, and I gather that this guy is." She stated plainly and without remorse.

"Yes, he is nice," she backed down. "He's so nice that he isn't pushing me on the intimacy scale." She shook her head. "Not that it's any of your business, my dear."

"But it is. Cisco and I want you to be happy and I know you're getting tired of being alone all the time."

"Oh, you do, do you… You should know that I'm doing perfectly well on my own and I'm not ready to jump at any good-looking guy with charm."

"So, now he's handsome and charming." If it was possible, Lainie's smile got bigger. "Sounds good to me." She stood up. "When do we get to meet him?"

"I don't know if that's such a good idea. You two might scare him off and you know good men are hard to find. It gets tiring lifting all those rocks."

Lainie laughed outright and started moving toward the door. "So how 'bout lunch tomorrow? You can tell me all about your adventures in dating." She cocked an eyebrow and grinned.

"You're just dying to hear the details, aren't you?" and laughed along with Lainie. "Isn't this kind of like quizzing your mother on her love life?"

"Nah, she tells me everything anyway. Gets dull. *You* however, are a different story, Miss Priss."

"You got me. Well, I have to prepare to leave soon for a business meeting in L.A., but I think I can squeeze you into my book for tomorrow."

"Good. I'll be here at noon and you'll spill everything." She bussed Anthea on the cheek and strolled out the door and over to the guesthouse. Anthea just scratched her head and thought that there wasn't much to 'spill.'

•••••••

While Anthea was going through her files preparing them for the meeting she had set with a client in Los Angeles, she made the decision that she could expand her inquiries on Nature's Wilds during her jaunt south. She was mulling over her itinerary with her calendar open in front of her. Checking off the days she had allotted to visit with her brothers in L.A. over the weekend, she saw the opportunity available to simply add a stop to her travels by swinging through San Francisco. Fine, she thought to herself, she'll just call the main offices of the conservancy and see if she can't set up an interview with the director.

Digging through her notes, she found a sheet she had downloaded from the conservancy's website that listed the address and phone number as part of their contact information. *Here goes.*

She dialed the number and found herself speaking with the executive secretary. She was surprised, figuring that they'd have a receptionist, at the least. *Small office for such a big operation with so much money to buy up half the nation.* It didn't take much cajoling to get her to agree to an interview for the next week. She used her history as a newshound, indicating that she was doing a freelance article on the organization's good works.

After settling her schedule for next week, she sat back in her chair, contemplating her next move. After a few moments, she picked up the phone and called Mathers for an update on the Ahlsted situation.

He answered after three rings, "Mathers," was all he said in lieu of a greeting.

"Hello, Gary?"

His demeanor shifted immediately, his voice audibly softening. "Hey, Anthea. How's your day been?"

"Not half as interesting as yours, I expect. Did you learn anything from the sheriff?"

"I believe the idea was for him to get information from me, as opposed to what happened," he chuckled. "Unfortunately, I wasn't able to shed any light other than sounding like a conspiracy theorist when I told him why I needed to check the accident scene. Despite how crazy I think it sounded, he seemed a little intrigued by a possible connection with the conservancy."

"Speaking of which, I'm flying out in a couple of days to Los Angeles to see a client and spend a little time with my brothers. I just got off the phone with the executive secretary at Nature's Wilds and scheduled an interview with the director for the day after my L.A. meeting. So, I'll be swinging through San Francisco before I head home."

"San Francisco, eh?" Gary mused aloud.

"That's where Conservancy headquarters are located. So the mountain must go to Mohammed, or something like that. I have an appointment with the executive director, Mr. Glen Alison," she added.

"You realize that we have no idea how involved the upper eche-lons are in this thing, or if they are at all. And, actually, we don't even know if there is a 'thing' to begin with. You'll be careful about how you approach him, right?" he said, looking to allay the concern for her safety that was sneaking up in the back of his mind.

"Sure. I just told them I was doing an article for a magazine about their philanthropy. It shouldn't be a problem, and it could be true enough. I'll write something and submit it to an editor friend of mine. It's in their court as to whether they'll run it."

He mulled over her answer and decided to jump in with both feet.

"How would you like some company?" He heard her suck in her breath as he had obviously caught her off-guard. "A little protection goes a long way and I am trained to 'serve and protect,'" he quipped.

"Hmmm. Company sounds like it might be enjoyable. Have you got a yen for the big city?" He could hear the smile in her voice.

"For the big city? Not particularly. But to have an opportunity to take in the sights with you, that might be categorized as a 'yen.'" His voice took on a dulcet quality as he intoned the last thought. "What if I meet you in San Francisco?"

"But will you 'wear a flower in your hair,'" she sang. "Actually, that's not requisite. I'm booked at the Hyatt Regency at the Embarcadero Center for Tuesday. You're sure you want to come all the way down there for rest and relaxation? Because I don't remember San Francisco as being the most laid-back place," she was subtly try-ing to give him an out since he had offered his company without any forethought. *The last thing I need is for him to regret his impulsive - ness.*

Instead he came back immediately with, "Do I need to reserve another room?"

At this she flushed bright red. *Thank goodness we're talking on the phone...Now what do I say?* She almost panicked thinking how much she was really beginning to feel infected by some illness. *Well they call it 'lovesick,' don't they?* Her throat felt as dry as a desert and she couldn't even croak out an answer. Instead, she remained quiet for what seemed like an eternity. *You have to answer him.*

All she could do was hum an indistinct reply. "I'll be arriving around noon next Tuesday. See you then." She hung up the phone without saying anything else. All she could do was lay her head against the chair back and gulp in some fresh air, her heart flipping cartwheels inside her chest. *Oh boy, you've done it now.*

•••••••

The executive director of Nature's Wilds Conservancy was alone on a deserted section of the wide wooden veranda that encased the circumference of the massive cedar castle perched on the apex of a mountain meadow. Solis Ranch had been constructed in record time and ahead of the careful schedule Alison had sketched for Chamberlain. Nursing his drink and listening to the echo of the other guests cavorting at a distant part of the porch where it overlooked the falls, he brooded about the rush for Chamberlain to assuage his ego by inviting Hollywood tripe peddlers for a tour of the unsecured estate. In his mind, the ranch was exposed because the digital entertainment emperor simply couldn't wait until the conservancy had the opportunity to secure the neighboring properties.

Chamberlain had put them all in a very tenuous situation and Alison was worried and royally aggravated with the foolishness that had forced him to pull out all the stops in consolidating the surrounding holdings. He knew that moving the plan up by more than a year had placed them all in a fishbowl with Nature's Wilds as the conspicuous entity gathering unflattering attention. He shook his head in disgust even as he admired the fields of wildflowers, a riot of violet, sun drenched yellow and brilliant white blooms stretching over the fields to the knees of the nearby mountains.

He hoped that no one was particularly interested in investigating county records, particularly since he knew that farmers and ranchers across the country were being forced to sell out because they couldn't handle the burden of fiscal loss any longer. Well, that was a boon for him and his organization and if he had to coddle billionaires like Chamberlain in order to save the land then, so be it. There's a price for everything.

His reverie was interrupted by the ringing of his cell phone, Vivaldi's 'Four Seasons' softly playing at his hip in a tacky, tinny pitch. The noise took him a bit by surprise until he realized that the elevation made it possible for the signal to get through. Flipping open his credit card sized instrument, he pressed it to his ear and answered, "Alison."

The voice of his secretary, who was actually one of the only three employees that made up the core of Nature's Wilds office staff, of which he was one, cut across the airwaves in a digitized tone that faded slightly at intervals.

"Glen, I just called to let you know that you have a change in your schedule for early next week," she said.

"Oh?" was his only response.

"Yes. You'll need to come back to headquarters from Sacramento immediately after your meeting Monday because I've booked an interview for you at the office on Tuesday afternoon," she explained.

"You couldn't have made it later in the week? I was hoping to be able to spend some more time lobbying on that one Sierra issue," he whined.

"She's coming in from out of town and was only able to make it at this time. I think it could be a very beneficial article that will likely get national exposure. Seems to me we could use some positive press," she drawled the last sentence a little to cajole Alison into accepting his fate.

"All right," he conceded. "Who's the journalist? Anyone I know?" he asked hopefully, seeing Diane Sawyer seated across from him in his high-rise office, overlooking a view of the San Francisco skyline.

"I don't think you would recognize her name," she paused to look at her notepad. "Her name's Anthea Keller. She runs a PR agency, is a former publisher and often does freelance work for a number of publications."

Trying not to let his disappointment appear evident, he simply gave a blunt answer that the appointment would be fine with him and signed off with a slightly brusque, "See you Tuesday."

Chapter 34

Winging in from the south, Anthea scanned the murky depths of San Francisco Bay, viewing the mud flats and the spiked cityscape that spread below. Mentally, she traced back the years to figure out how long it had been since she had visited the area other than to change planes. She shocked herself when she realized that it had been almost twenty years. No wonder she recognized so little.

Trying to remember her last venture here, the only flashbacks that appeared were of a rowdy Super Bowl weekend when the 49ers had utterly trashed the Miami Dolphins. A slight smile crossed her lips when she remembered trying to move against the hordes that had blocked Columbus Avenue with whooping and hollering drunken revelers. The image of her idiot brother jokingly asking the mounted policeman for a 'horsey ride' made her laugh outright. No one else could be so charmingly stupid in the face of an officer and get away with it.

Unlike more recent celebratory displays following sports play-offs, that one had been nothing more than loud and relatively benign. She had trouble understanding how fans had left the realm of peaceful fun and crossed over to violent displays and near rioting that had become a common occurrence in the last ten years. The most vivid memory was that of being physically lifted off her feet by the press of the crowd, a feeling that would have been frightening if not for the fact that everyone was in an ecstatic haze.

She began to pack her personal effects in preparation for landing, stowing her laptop under the seat and cinching her seatbelt a little tighter.

Touchdown went smoothly and the taxi to the gate was a quick trip across the tarmac. She didn't fly often these days since she was able to handle most of her work out of her home office, and, in all truth, she felt as though she'd rather not fuss with all the hassle involved with the security checks anymore. This once however, she was thinking it would be worth the flight time. Her client in L.A. had been less trouble than expected and she now had him trained for telephone and internet connections as opposed to the requisite face-to-face, which would save her time and money in the future.

Her mind drifted to the fact that after this afternoon's interview with the enigmatic Nature's Wilds Conservancy, she'll actually get to relax for a bit. That thought made her blush as she started gathering up her carry-on items as she remembered that Gary was due to meet her this afternoon at the hotel. Her head whirled as she contemplated the probable consequences of her accepting his notion to join her in the city. *Am I a fool or what?* She berated herself yet again for the impulsive acquiescence to his company. Shaking herself free of the whole direction of rethinking her decision, or lack of one, she hoisted her laptop on her shoulder, grabbed her purse and added herself to the line of passengers deplaning.

The process of collecting her bag at the carousel and exiting the terminal was far less painful than boarding had been and she found herself on the curb hailing a taxi within twenty minutes of landing. The drive into the city was unfamiliar since she had driven into town from a different direction every time that she had visited in the past. The traffic was pretty much what she had expected for approaching the noon hour, which was heavy. Her only consolation was the fact that she wouldn't have to get behind the wheel this trip. Sitting back, she laid her head against the seat and started going back over the direction of questioning she wanted to follow with Mr. Glen Alison, hoping that he wouldn't clam up too much when she arrives at the subject of funding. She had a distinct feeling that it was going to be a sticking point with him.

Some forty minutes later, she climbed out of the cab at the entrance to the hotel. Because she had arrived almost exactly at noon, when she went to the reception desk she was informed that her room was not yet ready so she'd have to park her bags with the bell captain for the afternoon. Her appointment with Alison was set for two o'clock so she arranged to have the bellman take her luggage up to her suite when it came available. That way, everything would be ready for her when she came back from the conservancy offices.

With all the nuances handled in lieu of checking in until she could pick-up her key, she decided that she ought to get a bite to eat before heading over to conduct the interview. Standing at the hostess station waiting to be seated, she felt more than heard the approach of someone close behind her. Turning to see why her skin was tingling, she found herself situated only inches from Gary who was looking very cosmopolitan in his city casuals of pressed gray slacks and a blue silk shirt, open at the neck. He had maneuvered himself close enough to give the impression of a couple, which the hostess assumed as she led them to a table by the window. As they were shown to their seats, he slipped behind Anthea and pulled out her chair for her, bending over to buss her neck and whisper, "hello" as she caught herself just in time before she plumped indecorously into the plush upholstery.

Taking the seat opposite, he leaned across the table and inquired about her flight.

"It was uneventful," she replied with her voice husky with discomposure. "How was yours?"

"Did I say I was flying?" he raised his eyebrow with a touch of jocularity.

"You drove?" she asked, slightly incredulous.

"Yeah, call me a road warrior."

"Looks like we have something in common. Whenever possible, I prefer to drive than fly. Unfortunately, the planning of this trip didn't allow that choice. I had no choice but to join the jet set," she said, trying to keep herself from gawking at how good he looked to her. She hadn't realized how much she had been anticipating this time with him. *Lord, I hope I'm not making a mistake.*

"Unless you're in a real hurry to return, you now have the option to accompany me on the drive home." He waggled his eyebrows in feigned lasciviousness.

She cocked her head to the side as she contemplated the suggestion. "Thank you for the invitation, sir. Do you make a habit of assisting stranded women in this manner?"

"Only when they have piercing blue eyes that skewer my heart with unfettered ardor," he mocked.

Anthea felt herself flush and quickly lowered her eyes while mentally kicking herself for acting no more sophisticated than a country bumpkin at the debutante ball. Determined to bring her emotions into check, she sat back and stared directly into eyes the hue of stormy seas. "Well then, I'll definitely have to take your offer under consideration."

Laughing lightly, he squeezed her hand gently and asked if she was ready to order, which shut down her wild thoughts with the impact of a bucket of ice water. *I made a fool of myself for certain.* Instead of letting her discomfiture show, she carefully opened the menu and quickly settled on a Caesar salad, which decision she shared with the server who had practically materialized at her elbow.

•••••••

Lunch transformed into a leisurely experience as Anthea and Mathers fell into more comfortable chitchat sans innuendo. Realizing that time was slipping past, she checked her watch to be sure that she was allotting herself enough travel time to reach her 2 p.m. appointment.

Looking up from the remains of the meal as a busboy was clearing the dishes, she told Gary that she would need to leave in a few minutes.

"And where does the elusive conservancy keep their offices?" he inquired.

"Some swank address in the financial district," replied Anthea.

His brow furrowed in barely concealed surprise. "A fancy salon, eh?"

"So it seems."

"I'd be more than happy to drive you," he offered.

"Thank you, Gary. But I think it would be better all around if I take a taxi," she said, declining. "There's no knowing whether or not they think I'm worth scrutinizing. The whole reason for this visit is to learn whether or not we have any basis for our suspicions. If we're not nuts, which I wonder about, then it's best not to stir up any curiosity on their part."

"All right, low profile it is." They stood to leave and he walked around the table, faced her and gently placed his hands on her shoulders. "Then I'll meet you in the lobby bar at 6:00 p.m. Seeing you will definitely constitute 'happy' hour," and he leaned down to kiss her lips before escorting her to the exit.

•••••••

The cab hurtled down the avenue, flanked on either side by the concrete and glass sides of the urban canyon that comprised San Francisco's financial district. The peaks of the buildings were drenched in the slanting shafts of the early afternoon sun, reflections bouncing off the myriad windows redolent of liquid gold. Anthea half-consciously compared this metropolitan ravine with the natural basalt walls that formed the river valleys of home, realizing how man's ingenuity seems to mock the beauty of nature's creation. *Is this why people somehow believe that they have a special mission to preserve natural elements? Can they possibly think that man has the power to transform the earth into a caricature built of concrete and steel?* The thought that humans should have a little more faith in their capability as good stewards would help. As far as she was concerned, the other part of that equation is the lack of faith in God's ultimate wisdom and his creation, both man and earth. *Call me a dreamer.*

The taxi driver slammed on his brakes, pitching her forward hard enough that she almost connected with the backside of the front seat. Whiplash she didn't need. Checking the address of the glass encased structure that shot straight up forty stories, she noted the high-end rent that must be paid for the offices she was visiting today.

Anthea checked the meter as the driver told her the amount due and paid him, not bothering to add much for tip after the roller coaster ride he'd so generously provided. She disembarked from the car, thankful to be on solid ground. As she pulled herself upright, she compared the experience to her more hapless jaunts through cities like Naples, Mexico City and New York, wondering if San Francisco was doomed to the same fate of inundation with ill-trained drivers.

Her briefcase in hand, she pushed her way through the huge bronze doors embossed with a sunburst encircled with flames reminiscent of a corona. She almost fell through the entrance when the massive doors gave way with an ease that belied their obvious weight. Catching herself quickly before anyone noticed her loss of balance, she straightened her skirt and found the bank of elevators where she punched the up button. While waiting for a car to arrive, she scanned the lobby area, noting the multimedia art that dressed the walls with pastel tones and the long elegant runner that reflected the hues from the entryway floor.

The lift doors opened and she stepped inside. With no one else to share the car, she pressed the button for the 38th floor. The elevator shot up like a rocket, kicking into express mode with no other stops between the lobby and her destination. *Can you get vertical whiplash? Nah, probably just compression injuries.* The car stopped with the same impact and finesse of her cab driver. *Wonder if I can litigate?*

Vertigo notwithstanding, she exited the elevator slightly lightheaded and turned to examine the directory for the floor to see who were the conservancy's illustrious neighbors. The first and only other name on the directory was Fairbanks, Louden and Turnbull, the powerful, and infamous, law firm that was renowned for representing environmental causes. The offices apparently occupied the whole of the floor save for the one suite leased by the conservancy. *I ought to ask Alison if his organization is the guest of F, L and T.*

Looking down to the end of the hall, she saw it led directly to the law offices, so she began hunting around for the one suite number assigned to Nature's Wilds Conservancy. She turned to walk in the opposite direction from the attorneys' suites until she finally found the door number 3802 all the way at the other end of the floor.

Peering through the large plate glass window that composed part of the outer wall, Anthea saw a jungle of lush greenery blocking most of her view. She opened the door and walked purposefully to the receptionist who was fashionably attired in a Banana Republic pseudo-business suit. Khaki and desert dust flowing in leopard spots, or was it jaguar, wrapped around her trim waist and hung at odd angles from a carefully draped scarf that coated her shoulders. *Got to be ready for the instant safari. Just remember to take your camera instead of an elephant gun.*

The receptionist, who appeared to be all of fourteen, finally looked up as if she had become tired of dealing with the constant barrage of inquiries from a lobby full of ignorant clients. Anthea guessed she previously had worked either in an M.D.'s office or at the other end of the hall where she had perfected the 'I'm too busy to be bothered' air.

When she pulled her nose out of whatever important paperwork she had been pursuing, she plastered on a wide smile that didn't extend to her eyes, which remained mud brown.

"Ms. Keller?"

"Yes," acknowledged Anthea.

"Welcome to Nature's Wilds Conservancy. Mr. Alison just arrived a few minutes ago. If you don't mind making yourself comfortable for a bit, he'll be with you right away." The girl managed to express herself without too much condescension dripping from her voice, so Anthea answered with equal warmth.

"Thank you, Ms.," and she checked the nameplate, "Jordan. No problem." Placing herself in the center of the couch in order to avoid palm fronds poking her eyes, Anthea scanned the full extent of the small suite, noting the designation assigned to the few adjoining offices. The total was a meager four; the treasurer's office, executive director's office, the program director and executive secretary's office and a conference room. Small quarters for a multi-million dollar environmental concern that is buying up acreage, county by county. Compact but pricey.

Five minutes later, a tall, pale man, with an underfed appearance and receding hairline emerged from the director's office. *Not exactly the outdoorsy type. Vegan and allergic to sun,* she decreed.

He walked over as Anthea rose from her seat and offered her a weak, irresolute handshake.

"It's good of you to come all the way just to write a little story about our preservation efforts," he said, blandly. "My name is Glen Alison."

"Good to meet you, sir." Anthea let go of his clammy grip as soon as she could without appearing rude and forced herself not to wipe her hand on her skirt. "It's my pleasure to be here. Actually, I haven't been in the city for close to twenty years, so it's also a terrific opportunity to get reacquainted with some culture."

"Won't you join me in the office then," and he gestured toward the open door with a flourish, if a man with no panache could be said to do anything with a flourish. "You'll enjoy our little bird's eye view of San Francisco."

In this, he was not being coy, for the vista from his office was a sweeping scene of the city to the northeast, with the bay sparkling a few miles in the distance. *Now this is choice real estate.*

She took a seat in one of three half-round seats with a back that curved all the way around the sides, creating a semi-circular cell that made it a little difficult to get elbowroom to write. Anthea supposed some hare-brained interior designer, smitten with what they thought was a chic retro-Danish style circa 1958, had decorated the offices, hopefully at no charge.

Taking another gander out the window she said, "What a lovely office and the view, well, there's not much that needs to be said about that other than it's fantastic."

"Yes, we're very fortunate to occupy this space," he said proudly.

"Knowing that it's often customary for non-profits to have benefactors that offer them office space, may I ask if the law offices down the hall subsidize your suite?"

"Actually you'd be correct in your assumption as it is a common practice. It's convenient for them to take advantage of the tax benefit and definitely good luck for us."

"I'd agree on your good fortune. Probably not all the attorneys down the hall have quarters equal to this," she observed.

"You may be right," he smiled, rather like an anemic shark.

Getting down to the task at hand, Anthea opened her notebook and began with queries on the origin of the organization, when and who chartered it and its mission. On the whole, his answers were fairly concise, keeping to the basic meat of the subject without wandering too far afield unless Anthea had requested more detail.

The youth of the conservancy, although previously known to her, was of interest as Alison spoke about the rapid development of preservation holdings that had occurred, particularly in the last three years.

"The conservancy has definitely been a prolific agency in creating wilderness preserves," she commented.

"That is our purpose," said Alison, sagely. "We were created to sock away, if you will, some of the pristine acreage still available for the enjoyment of our posterity. Too much of public land is being desecrated and desolated by uncaring, and often greedy corporations. To use an overused axiom, the almighty dollar is at the heart of our nation's loss of precious wild lands." He shook his head, eyes closed, hands pressed together, as if praying to some earthbound gods to help save his planet. Gazing at him, Anthea wondered how sincere he was in his convictions, because he emanated an aura of someone truly convinced of his passion, not unlike a zealot.

"A noble cause, to be sure, but all good works need financing. What can you tell me about the funding in order to create these conservation areas."

There, she did it. She broached the subject, now she only hoped that he wouldn't hide behind the hedge of the noble cause being foremost, because they both knew that to fight corporate greed you needed corporate money. A real catch 22.

It didn't take long before she knew that he was only going to go the generic route in offering any information on funding. She couldn't get much more out of him beyond the usual answers, i.e. private donors ("who, of course, expect us to respect their privacy"), philanthropic foundations, of which he named a few – nothing new there, and public collection campaigns.

"We are always seeking new sources of funding although we have also been named as beneficiaries in some estates, situations like these can be a bit traumatic if there is still progeny with a vested interest. That sort of thing can engender rancor among the surviving family members and we don't encourage people to name the conservancy in their wills unless they have the support of their family members." He tapped his temple as he considered the consequences.

"Not too long ago I read of one of Hemingway's former homes being in the eye of controversy. It had been left to a conservancy, not ours, by his widow and they had not felt comfortable doing much with the estate until recently. Apparently, it's the house in Idaho where he resided when he ended his life and it had been left as a virtual mausoleum, with nothing changed since his demise. The organization wanted to conduct small tours and run it as a part-time museum, but the neighbors and some of the children and grandchildren weren't in favor of the plan. Everything comes into play in a scenario like that, from effects on neighboring property values to the sensibilities of family in having the house reopened as a virtual shrine to his death as opposed to his life's work.

"We try to sidestep situations that could be so volatile. I don't envy the curators of that estate," he said, wagging his head in simulated sorrow.

"I can definitely see your point in avoiding that type of bequest. However, I assume the conservancy has received bequests in the past."

"Oh yes, and we do encourage monetary infusions of the like and some land bequests if they fit our requirements," explained Alison.

Anthea moved on to the board of directors, since the website had been so vague.

He sketched out the same public list, which included captains of the corporate world, a couple of pop/movie stars and a former Russian head of state.

Figureheads, or puppets?

"Do they donate much to the cause?" she asked.

"Oh yes. A few of them have been very generous individually. Some of the businesses they represent give in-kind, such as advertising, building materials for the information centers, things of that nature," he said while his eyes moved around the room rather than focusing on her.

"What about their philanthropic foundations? Some of these people oversee corporate giving campaigns that mount into the millions," she pointed out.

"The corporate giving campaigns and the foundations are almost always handled via an independent staff. We must apply for grants the same as any other organization and hope that they feel our mission is compatible with theirs. Our board is not able to sway the independent directors as prescribed by law. They can lobby, yes, but they are not allowed undo influence." He sighed. "It's all very bureaucratic. Truthfully, government couldn't be any worse."

"So there's no direct connection from the board to finance within their companies." She made a statement rather than forming a question.

"No, we must conform to stringent regulations in order to maintain our nonprofit status." Alison firmly clamped his jaw closed on the issue.

Anthea changed tack and started on the issue of land acquisition. How does the conservancy identify land for preservation? How do they fund each purchase, is it a different set of funding circumstances with each new parcel? What does the conservancy do with the land once they have control of it?

Alison was not inclined to offer many details in this area of interest and he artfully evaded any revealing answers. He was rather obtuse in describing the areas identified for protection, as they might be parcels that communities are trying to preserve, or it might be an environmental group that lobbies for a particular area to be purchased. He only came down to the ideal of preserving pristine or unsullied forests, prairies and desert lands for future generations' enjoyment.

"So who has access to these reserves once they are established?" she tried again.

"School programs are developed in some areas where the children are given the opportunity to visit the preserves, sometimes as field trips and even overnight camping excursions for some programs. We have some developed campsites and nature walks throughout our inventory."

Her eyebrows rose slightly at the usage of the term 'inventory.' It struck her as an odd word choice to describe land that is being held in trust for posterity.

"What percentage of the property controlled by Nature's Wilds Conservancy is open for public use and educational activities?" She was really curious as to how much of their 'inventory' was being accessed by the public for whose benefit it was being preserved.

"Truthfully, I don't have that statistic at hand. I'll need to follow-up on that and give you a call," he smiled.

This one would have made an excellent politician, or an attorney. Very canny and unprepossessing. It was obvious that she wasn't going to get much more out of the guy so she started to wind down the interview.

"To finish, can you describe a particular project that is underway that you feel is worthy of specific focus within this article?" She thought she'd try to draw him out on a pet project.

"We are developing funding for a particularly wonderful tract of fifteen hundred acres in the Santa Cruz area, up near Ben Lomond. The redwood forest remains pretty much untouched and healthy. We'd like to develop a learning center there to service the Bay Area schools, perhaps with a retreat that would be available for lease by environmentally oriented organizations."

His face lit up with the remembrance of the delicate fronds of the evergreens, their tips dancing in the sunlight as they reached up for the warmth. The California redwood forests were one of Alison's passions and it shone in his eyes as he talked about the project.

"Do you know how far the conservancy is from closing the deal?" She noticed his intensity and envisioned some of his desire to fulfill his mission.

"It should be concluded within the month. We were absolutely floored when one of the former Apple Computer founders decided to back the effort with his foundation. Usually he gives to the arts, so we were really pleased."

Anthea made a few more notes to check the internet on the foundation he named. As she jotted the rest of her thoughts, she asked if there were any questions that she could answer for him.

He thought for a moment then asked simply, "What publication will this appear in and do you know when it will be published?"

"Actually, there are a number of magazines and newspapers to which I am a regular contributor. I'm doing this as a spec piece, but I believe that either Entertainment L.A. or Northwest Times will pick it up." She bent over her briefcase and rummaged a little bit until she came up with her digital camera.

"Would you mind if I got a couple of photos of you at your desk?"

Obviously loving the limelight, he said, "Absolutely, take your best shot." He almost giggled at his small joke.

"Great. How about you move over here and I'll catch a couple of profile images with you looking contemplative as you study the city view." She maneuvered him around so the light wouldn't be directly behind him. Anthea then placed him in a few other poses, one of which was in front of a map of the United States with Conservancy properties outlined in fluorescent green.

"Let's see…that ought to do it." She smiled as she packed away her notebook and camera. "Can you get me access to a couple of Conservancy preservation areas for photos?"

"Sure, there are a couple in this vicinity." He scratched his head as he went to the map and pointed out one by Bodega Bay and another near Calistoga, northeast of Santa Rosa. "These two are within a couple hour's drive," he suggested.

"Hmmm. Is there anything in Nevada? Something that I could swing through on my way back north?" she asked.

"We do have a property that has a newly completed visitor center outside of Lake Tahoe." He pointed at the map. "Would that be more suitable to your travel plans?"

"That would be perfect. I'm driving through Sacramento and that would be fairly close to my route. Thank you," she said appreciatively.

"Consider it finalized. I'll call ahead and let the project director know you're on your way."

"That's very generous of you. I'll enjoy having a guide to show me what the conservancy has been working on." She gathered up her satchel, shook his hand and went out the door.

Land Barons

Chapter 35

Pushing open the massive bronze doors, Anthea stepped back out into the sunshine and took a deep cleansing breath. Not that Alison had been unduly objectionable, but there had still been an air of corruption that infused her bones. Odd, considering these were people who prided themselves on supposedly saving the earth from man's evil ways. *It must be the way he evaded every other question I asked. All that time and virtually no real answers.* Sighing, she raised her arm and waved down an approaching cab.

Lord, I hope this guy has more control behind the wheel than that other misanthrope.

Tossing her bag into the vehicle, she fell onto the seat and, as pleasantly as possible, gave the cabbie instructions to return her to the Hyatt. She hoped that a sweet disposition might spare her another e-ticket ride through downtown. It didn't take long before she realized her misplaced hope as she was greeted with a grunt, an oath administered in some unknown language, and a blast-off that must have pulled three G's.

It seemed less than five minutes before the taxi slammed to a halt in front of the hotel, Anthea's bones rattling for the second time that day. So much for luck, or a lack thereof, she thought.

Peeling herself off the vinyl seat, she leaned in and paid the fare, barely extricating her hand from the window before the car rocketed off down the street. Anthea just watched in utter amazement at the rude behavior, wondering how people get by with attitudes like that. Briefcase in hand, the one that was nearly dismembered, she entered the lobby and stopped by the front desk to collect her key. While she waited for the clerk to program the keycard, she consulted her watch to see that she had more than an hour to freshen up and meet Gary in the lobby.

As she boarded the elevator, she began to mentally walk back through the afternoon's interview, wondering if she had gleaned anything of real interest. Flogging her brain didn't seem to be a fruitful endeavor…she was just too drained. Maybe later, going over her notes with Gary would help her put the information into some order. Two heads are better than one.

While she was in L.A. she had already called a friend about tracking down the financial statements for Nature's Wilds Conservancy, both public and, hopefully, private. His special abilities in skirting legal boundaries should give her information that put everything into perspective, since all trails are paved with money when it comes to big business, or big charity, as the case may be.

Readjusting the shoulder strap of her satchel, she exited the lift and locating her room, unlocked the door and let herself into the sunny suite. Glad that she hadn't spared herself any expense on this trip, she tossed her briefcase on the dresser, saw that her luggage had been neatly deposited by the closet, the suitcase perched on a rack, and plopped herself onto the bed.

Laying back, she took a few minutes to luxuriate in the accoutrements of the room. The soft pastels lulled her into a relaxing pose while letting her gaze drift over the original art that decorated the walls. Her mind began to ebb between two utterly divergent directions. On the one hand, she was considering the true purpose of Nature's Wilds, and on the other she began to wander through fancies of Gary accompanying her to this very room later tonight.

On the second vein, she was divided as to what she truly wanted, whether she was ready to take that fatal step toward letting another human being into her safe little world. The idea not only frightened her, but absolutely threatened the little control she had been able to forge in her life. This was a step that couldn't be approached as cavalierly as she might have in her younger, wilder days. Not that she would ever want to return to those times, but what she wouldn't give to have a few of the latest years shaved off her existence.

She pushed herself off of the oh-too-inviting mattress which called with it's siren song of rest, and peering at herself in the vanity mirror, she again wished for fewer gray hairs and fine lines that were beginning to give her face 'character.' As much as she hated that term, she knew it was true and she also knew it was a kinder description of the changes in her skin that spoke of age. *I certainly can't see what any man could find appealing in this visage.*

With that thought she ran the water in the shower with the intention of washing off the travel grime and starting anew for the evening.

Maybe a refreshing shower would reinvigorate her body if not her overall appearance. *Can't hurt to try.*

•••••••

Alison was on the phone with a representative of the conservancy's largest donor, giving her the good news about the article.

"Some good publicity would be a real boost right now since we've been encountering some resistance in some of the regions where acquisition has been heating up. I'm always for positive press. I would think you'd concur," he practically sniveled when her initial reaction had been lukewarm at best.

"So which publication will be carrying the piece?"

"She said she had two on the hook that she often freelances for. She said it was a spec piece but that she had already pitched the idea with Entertainment L.A. and Northwest Times. One of which should run it."

"Well, that does sound positive," she conceded. "What's the journalist's background?"

"She has a strong resumé and is regularly published, carries press credentials though she said she rarely covers real news anymore. My executive secretary did a bit of a check before confirming the appointment."

"Where's she from?"

"Apparently, she has two bases of operation. Her card lists an address in California and one in Idaho," he said as he read the business card.

"Hmm, you may want to double check those addresses. Since the conservancy activities have been somewhat accelerated in Idaho, you should be certain about the identity of your guests. Particularly nosey ones," she said in a clipped tone.

"You've made your point. I'll call my contact in the area as a safety net."

•••••••

Anthea emerged from the elevator, a filmy, gauze dress the color of seafoam flowing in her wake. She had a multi-tonal wrap of the

225

same diaphanous fabric encasing her shoulders, a drop necklace and earrings of matching sea washed glass. She made her way across the lobby to the lounge where her gaze immediately found Gary, leaning provocatively against the bar, eyes locked on her as she approached.

A slight shiver ran up her spine as they closed ranks, his smile spreading in a slow, sultry turn of his lips. Scanning his form, she was impressed all over again of his solid masculine presence. *They must be right. Some men definitely get better not older. Only wish they said that about women, too.* She sighed audibly as the idea flitted through her mind, which led her companion to raise an eyebrow silently questioning her thought.

Ignoring his openly inquisitive expression, she gave him her hand instead. Drawing her close, he kissed her lightly on the lips but sensing a quiver in her response, pushed for a deeper connection. Although the kiss was relatively brief, she was slightly flushed when he released her and led her to a table.

After helping her to her seat, he found the chair next to her and settled himself close enough to keep one of her hands in his own all the while a rakish grin played on his face.

"You look like icing on petit fours, delicate and delicious," he said in such a soft tone she had to lean forward to hear him. Which must have been his intent because he quickly moved in for another kiss, one hand holding her chin up to meet him.

Blushing like a teenager, she was again taken by surprise with his unexpected ardor. She blinked as he let her go.

"And you have not only the handsome cast of a Don Juan, but his demeanor as well." *Pretty lame... I definitely need work on this kind of reparteé.*

Although she felt utterly out of her league with this man, he laughed with a warmth that shared itself as a flash of heat through her limbs. All she could think was that this was going to be some night and she hoped she'd survive intact.

"What would you like to drink this evening?"

"Vodka Collins will suit me just fine, thank you."

He got the server's attention and ordered for Anthea and a Stoli for himself.

"Funny you don't look Russian," she said.

"No, but I speak it."

"Ah, s*drazvitye*,'" she said, "though I don't really remember what that means." She shrugged her shoulders.

"Fine. I'll instruct you in the language and the proper usage of the tongue," he offered playfully.

"That's right, I'd almost forgotten that you are a professor of foreign languages. How many do you speak?" She was interested now and happy to leave the innuendo behind.

"Let's see. I'm proficient in Spanish, Arabic, French and Russian and I can hold my own with Italian, Farsi and Vietnamese. English gives me the most trouble," he said eyes glinting in the soft light.

"There are times when the most difficult of modern languages, English, can be more of a hindrance than silence."

"I definitely agree," and he picked up her hand, turned it over and stroked her palm.

As their drinks arrived, he sipped his and commented, "Doesn't taste anywhere as good as you. Are you hungry?"

"Actually, very," she replied.

"What appeals to you tonight?"

"Besides your company? Frutta della mare," she said, tossing out the minuscule amount of Italian she could muster.

"I'm guessing that means Fisherman's Wharf or, if I remember, North Beach. Isn't that the Italian section?"

"It most certainly is and I haven't been there in years, goodness, almost decades. It's almost shameful to admit," she added.

"Which? That you haven't been or that the years have flown by?"

"Both," she admitted.

"I'm with you in each case." He stood and reached for her hand. "Let's go."

•••••••

After hanging up from his discussion with the donor's representative, Alison was stricken with a minor flash of uncertainty. He dialed the number of his contact in Idaho and sat forward at his desk, fingers drumming on the wood while he waited for someone to answer.

A clipped voice came across the line with one brusque word in greeting.

"Yes."

"It's Alison. I just have a couple of questions for you."

"I only have a few minutes before I've got to leave," the man on the other end said without emotion. "What do you need?"

"Has there been anyone snooping around the properties or checking out the activities of the conservancy in the area, lately? I'm particularly interested in a journalist," explained Alison.

"There's been one guy, a local, who seems to have been showing up at a couple of places, asking questions and, I believe he looked up some information at the assessor's office. But he isn't a reporter or anything, just a neighbor to some of the properties that have been changing hands."

"Has he been working with anyone that you know of?" Alison was beginning to fret over the idea that somebody was taking a real interest in Conservancy business.

"Actually, I've seen him with a woman from down river. She's been doing some research on your organization, but it didn't look like it amounted to much." He was beginning to lose patience because of a time constraint and the slightly panicky sound of Alison's voice.

"Do you know who she is? What she looks like?"

"Let me think. Ann something. No, it's an odd name. Sounds like a plant," he's silent for a moment while he accesses his memory. "Right, it's Anthea. Anthea Keller. She has some PR agency in town. Her interest seemed peripheral and we can't ascertain that she has actually gathered much information about the conservancy other than your land purchases. But that's public record. Why?"

"She just left my office not an hour ago," his breathing was becoming slightly labored as he worked through the implications of her visit. "She was interviewing me ostensibly for a magazine article that she's freelancing. It checked out with my secretary when she did a credential inquiry. She seemed on the up-and-up."

"She is who she says she is, but it sounds like she's taking a serious interest in the conservancy. What did you have in mind?" His voice was flat and expressionless.

"Maybe, you should expand your surveillance of *her* activities. We don't need any outside pressure. But if she's just writing an article, nothing needs to be done..." Alison left the thought dangling.

"Right. I'll get on it. I guess my plans have changed for tonight. Now, tell me what happened at the interview."

Chapter 36

Gary had wrapped his arm around Anthea's waist after helping her from the cab. They sauntered up the steps of a small *ristorante* that had been recommended by the concierge as a spot that she frequented. Entering the cozy lobby area, they were led to a table almost immediately.

After thanking the hostess, Gary pulled the chair out for Anthea.

"We must be in luck. I had expected to wait before being seated from what the concierge said about the popularity of this place," he noted as he pushed in her chair.

"Maybe they're a little slower on week nights," she clasped his hand as he sat across from her. "Good for us. More privacy and quieter."

He let his gaze wander around the room, taking in the continental ambience.

"This really reminds me of a little place I loved in Florence," he looked at her. "It was a favorite of the concierge at the hotel I stayed at there. The food was simple and it was beyond compare. We need to go there together sometime."

"Florence was one of my favorite cities in Italy," her blue eyes became incandescent as she remembered the river and the ageless art that seemed to drape the city's piazzas. "You springing for the airfare?"

His eyes turned to molten mercury as they slid over her features, settling on her mouth. "Do we leave tomorrow?"

Her laughter at his suggestion was a bright tinkling sound that brought him out of a fantasy that included a whirlwind tour from the cultural meccas to the rugged coastline of Sorrento.

"If reality wouldn't get in the way, your offer would be irresistible. Can we leave next week?"

"You're on," he said half seriously. "But tonight, 'Little Italy' will have to do."

They whiled away a couple of hours enjoying each other's company and a blissfully satisfying meal personally served by the owner, a native of Tuscany who regaled them with stories of his family back home.

Almost reluctant to take leave of their host, they thanked him profusely not only for the excellent meal, but for the engaging tales he had shared while they dined.

Standing on the street watching the evening traffic fly past, Anthea asked what Gary had in mind for the rest of the evening.

"It's still early, so let's catch a ride down to the tourist areas where we can stroll and window shop," he suggested.

"Considering that I haven't been here in twenty years, I guess I should consider myself a *turista* and act accordingly."

"May as well. We wouldn't want to be confused with the natives," he jibed.

Hailing a taxi, they followed the visitors' handbook and were deposited at Ghirardelli Square.

"My favorite namesake," said Anthea as she looked up at the large sign indicating their location. "Chocolate is my spiritual guide. No preaching, just a taste of the afterlife on earth."

Gary laughed lightly and, taking her hand, led her through the walkways where they roamed past the shop windows, occasionally feeling drawn to investigate some of the more interesting displays. The rest of the time they studied the other tourists, who were pursuing the same evening diversion of meandering the streets and peering into the windows.

As they discussed the wares in the various shops, they learned more about each other's tastes and opinions, discussed their personal histories and where they'd traveled around the world.

"There's one thing to be said about courting later in life," surmised Gary. "We've chronicled so much more than youngsters that it's unlikely we'll run out of material for conversation. Your experiences interest me no end and I know that it would take years to hear all the stories."

"Like I'd tell you everything," she sniffed. "Mystery is half the intrigue."

"Half the fun as well. What would Mata Hari's captivation be without mystery?"

"Frankly, I don't seem to have anywhere near the storytelling elements you've compiled over the years," observed Anthea. "Civilian life couldn't possibly offer the color that your military and law enforcement careers have."

"You'd be surprised how drab the usual day-to-day routine was. Of course, there were those times when you couldn't crank out enough adrenaline to keep up with events," he mused. "Most of the time, life was a schedule of meetings, following an ordinary pattern, almost a nine-to-five."

"There's the rub... 'almost' but not quite, eh, Officer? Or was it 'Detective?'"

"Lieutenant, actually." He smiled as she had nudged just a little more information out of him. "That was as far as I needed to go. It's 'Professor,' now." He stopped at the edge of the curb to look across the street. "What say we stroll over to one of those waterside cafes for a cappuccino before heading back to the hotel?"

"A fine idea." She hooked her arm inside his proffered elbow as they crossed the avenue.

●●●●●●●

The crisp late spring evening made Anthea thankful that she'd thought to bring a wrap. Pulling it a little closer around her shoulders, she let herself relax and watch the scant water traffic moving through the light chop of the bay.

"It's been so long since I was here, I hardly recognize the place," she said wistfully. "They were in the midst of renovating the Cannery at the time. It was quite a ways from being finished."

"When was that?"

"I don't know if I should say. It might reveal too much about my past," she looked at him earnestly. "It was during my college years."

"By looking at you, it certainly couldn't be that far back," he said warmly.

"Not that a lady gives away her age, but 'deadheads' were still aimlessly wandering the streets in ripped jeans and the air was redolent of a rather acrid, smoky scent."

"You could be describing today with all the retro mania."

"Well, it's not on this corner anymore. It looks like the 'hood has been reclaimed by the counter culture-cum-yuppies. Of course, even that term is dated. Money will out over free love every time," she philosophized.

"At least it puts you in an era that I can relate to," he smiled.

"Really? And I thought you pre-dated me by either the hippie epoch or maybe even the beatnik period," she teased.

"Not quite. The gray gives me that illusion of significant age."

"Hardly. What's the term applied to men of middle years? Ah yes, distinguished."

"I'll accept that. Distinguished is far more appealing than ancient by any standards."

"I often protest the fact that there is no equivalent term for women," she added. "Apparently, we simply do not get the benefit of the doubt with the accumulation of years."

"That's a matter of opinion," Gary stated. "There is an aura of sophistication and rare beauty that only a woman can exude, like an expensive perfume, and its allure isn't comparable to the superficial charms of youth."

He sipped the last of his coffee, catching Anthea in a soft blush that only enhanced the elegance that he had just described. Standing, he reached out his hand for her in invitation.

"Join me?"

Anthea rose and closing the distance between them, he placed his arm around her waist and led her out of the café and into the muted light cast by the street lamps.

•••••••

As Anthea and Gary stepped out of the cab and entered the lobby atrium, a shadowy figure left the darker penumbra of the building, following at a distance as they made their way to the bank of elevators. It was late enough that the couple were the only passengers in the car when the doors closed.

The tail watched the illuminated numbers climb until they stopped at the 19th floor. He then hopped into the elevator he'd been holding open across from the car he'd been observing and punched in the button for the 19th floor.

Taking advantage of the fact that they were alone in the elevator, Gary caught her attention, his gray eyes emanating the heat of a banked fire. The look alone sent a shiver up her spine, making her wonder yet again whether she was prepared for what she knew was an equal ardor within herself. As the upward movement stopped and the doors slid open, Gary flattened one hand on the frame, holding the doors ajar as he pulled her toward him with his other hand. Unable to wait any longer, he slipped Anthea through the door as he bent down to bring his lips to hers for a kiss that he had been anticipating for hours. Leaning against the wall as the elevator closed and hummed along its way, Gary tightened his arms around Anthea and pushed the envelope, forging her mouth open and probing deeper with his kiss.

Anthea's composure shattered as her knees weakened. She brought her hands up to stroke his neck and shoulders, following Gary over the edge. She felt herself slip into a new dimension where she surrendered part of her being. The intimacy of the kiss was overwhelming as she let herself go, taking what he offered and giving back in kind. Finally, he pulled away long enough to look into her azure eyes, both of them breathing rapidly in time with their accelerated pulse.

Clasping her close to him he turned them away from the steel doors.

"Which way?" he asked in a low voice, rough with gravel as he wrenched himself from the tender connection, struggling for control.

Without saying a word, she took his hand and led him down the corridor to her suite, her heart fluttering in anxiety and anticipation all at once.

You can stop now…you don't have to do this. Oh, but I want to. He's more than I could have asked for. She had an argument rattling through her mind as she walked to her door, knowing she was going to bring Gary into her room, knowing she was going to let him into her heart. Knowing that she was making another life-changing decision, right or wrong.

As she unlocked the door, sliding the card into the slot and pushing open the handle, he looked intently into her eyes, asking her with his smoldering gaze if she wanted this. She answered by grasping his hand and guiding him through the open door. She knew that the decision was already made.

•••••••

The shadow, who had followed them upstairs, emerged from the

233

elevator just as Gary and Anthea disappeared into the room. They hadn't seen him arrive and he was able to take his time walking down the hall to check the suite number his target was occupying.

He dialed a number on his cell phone as he moved back down the corridor. Holding it up to his ear, he heard a deep voice answer on the other end. After giving the other person his location within the hotel, he asked for instructions.

Chapter 37

Blinking in the shaft of sunlight that streamed through the window, Anthea blinked in the light that crossed her face and turned to relieve her eyes of the brightness. As she did, her gaze fell across the sleeping form next to her, sending a shock wave rippling through her body. She looked down at herself, tangled in the bed sheets, with Gary's arm thrown across her midsection, his thigh drawn up over her own.

Memory of her response to Gary's irresistible appeal set her skin aflame with embarrassment. *How long has it been since I've given myself to anyone. Oh my, what did I do now? Just given up your inde - pendence, stupid!* Her thoughts flipped through all kinds of gyrations. First berating herself for getting into this situation, then tenderly stroking her partner's arm as she relived the wonder of the evening and the incredible passion that she had been sure was beyond her ability to feel.

Unable to keep a coherent concept flowing through her mind, she gave up and rolled toward her bedmate, letting her fingers flutter softly over the outline of his whisker stubbled jaw.

As she drew her fingertip across his cheek, his eyes slowly opened, revealing a sharp, silver gaze that seemed to stab right through to her very soul. In spite of herself, she shuddered.

His eyes became concerned as he felt the tremor run through her body.

"Are you cold?" he asked, his voice barely audible and gruff with sleep.

"No, just amazed," she replied.

His brow raised in a puzzled expression. "Amazed?"

"At you. At me," she sighed, knowing that she hadn't adequately answered him. Instead she just let her hand drift across his chin and down his neck to his collarbone and around his strong shoulder. She gave him a languid smile. "You could use a shave," she said as she brought her hand back to his face, tracing his lips with her forefinger.

"Or I could give you an unforgettable whisker burn."

"I don't need a skin condition to remember an intoxicating tryst that I couldn't forget if I wanted to," she murmured.

"Intoxicating? That's probably the most romantic thing anyone's ever said to me." He brought himself up, looking intently into her eyes and lowered his lips over hers, firing both of their physical response memories of what they had just recently shared. He brushed the hair away from her forehead as he deepened the kiss, entwining his tongue with hers until they were lost in the renewed heat of passion, which delayed their rising for another hour.

• • • • • • •

When they finally emerged from their sensual haze, Gary dressed and giving Anthea one more good morning kiss, he started to leave.

"Where are your things?" asked Anthea as she prepared to get up.

"In my room."

"I don't know why, but I thought that you hadn't booked one," she said, mildly confused.

"Yes, I reserved a room," he replied, his gray eyes glinting with humor. "You never know where you're going to end up…your place or mine." He settled into a more serious tone. "I didn't want you to feel pressured to invite me in. Had you been hesitant, I would have said good night and left you on your doorstep, like the chivalrous gentleman that I apparently am not," he grinned.

"We're even then, because I left my goody-two shoes at the front door when I invited you in."

"Good enough," he said as he bent down to give her one last brush across her lips. "We're equally depraved. I'll be back in half an hour," and he swept through the door.

The door closed behind him and Anthea trod over to the bathroom, turned on the shower and slipped under the hot spray.

Outside the room, the dark figure from the night before, watched the elevator door close on Gary as he went to his room to get cleaned up and pack. As soon as the steel panels met, the shadow moved down the corridor to Anthea's suite, placed his ear on the door and hearing the water running, he unlocked the door using a key from housekeeping and cautiously opened it. He peered around the corner to be certain that the occupant was actually in the shower before he pressed the rest of the way into the room.

When he got inside, he moved quickly, intently focused on his goal. It didn't take him long to locate her satchel sitting by the desk where she had perched it the afternoon before. He opened it and rapidly clawed through the papers. Her laptop was also inside, but he knew that he wouldn't have time to boot it up and hunt through her files.

He was looking for a notebook. Alison had said that she had been scribbling her notes by hand during the interview. Quickly sorting through the contents, he came up with two notebooks. One, a full-sized, yellow legal pad and the other, a stenographer's book.

Flipping through the pages of the steno pad, he read the notes from her interview at the Nature's Wilds offices. He tossed it aside as being of little value since Alison pretty much knew what he had said and as he thought, she hadn't strayed from the essence of the meeting.

He glanced fleetingly through the handwritten notes on the legal pad and deciding that this was what he had come for, he ripped the used sheets off the book, folded them and stuffed them into his jacket.

He heard the water turn off in the shower and, without panicking he quietly closed the satchel and replaced it from where he had found it. Dashing across the carpet, he exited the room just as Anthea emerged from the bathroom, a towel wrapped around her. She didn't even notice the click as the door to the suite closed behind the intruder.

Standing in what seemed like a draft, she pulled the plush terry cloth closer around her body and swiveled her head to check out the room. A slight shiver ran through her as she assumed that the air conditioning had just kicked off. She shook her wet mane and decided that she was just being hypersensitive and probably a little bit foolish. Chalking up her anxiety to fatigue after a relatively sleep-deprived night, she went over to the closet to collect her clothes.

•••••••

Twenty more minutes elapsed before Gary rapped on the door. Anthea, dressed casually in jeans and an old L.A. Raiders t-shirt, peered through the spy aperture and seeing Gary's form on the other side of the barrier, opened the door to admit him.

Setting his duffle off to the side, he pulled her into his arms and solidly planted a smoking kiss on her lips, her eyes widening in surprise. Settling into the passion of the moment, she drew her arms around his waist and returned the kiss with a fervor equaling his own.

Finally managing to pull themselves apart, she was trembling with the heat engendered by the connection as they reluctantly disengaged. His own composure crumbling from the fiery bond as they broke apart, he clasped her to his chest as he looked down into her eyes.

"Unfortunately, we don't have the luxury of indulging ourselves any further than that decadently delicious kiss," she breathed softly against his neck.

"You have something more important planned for us?" he whispered against the soft curve of her ear. I missed you over the last," and he glanced at this watch, "forty minutes. I don't know if I can restrain myself around you." He brushed his lips across her forehead, eliciting a sigh from her as she collapsed against him.

"Alison made arrangements for me to tour one of the Nature's Wilds properties up at Lake Tahoe later this afternoon. I received his call while you were gone, just a few minutes ago. So, we're under a little bit of a time constraint since the drive is a good three and a half hours. But I thought you wouldn't mind doing double duty as chauffeur. I'm sorry," she apologized into the soft folds of his chambray shirt.

He peeled himself away from her and gazed at her open features that conveyed far more than she wanted. "Well, I guess we better hit the road then. Or is breakfast a possibility before we depart?" He slid a light kiss across her cheek as she slowly nodded her assent.

"We don't need to be there until 2:30." She ran her fingers down his clean shaven cheek. "We have time for a morning repast. Here or elsewhere?"

"Better be elsewhere, otherwise I'm apt to stay right here." He swung her around until her knees buckled against the edge of the bed, forcing her to sit on the mattress, gazing up into his smile which barely concealed the desire in his expression. "Do you want to call for the bellman?"

"No," she said as she picked up the phone to do exactly that.

•••••••

They met at the reception desk where Anthea was finalizing her check-out. Gary sidled up beside her as she finished her transaction. Feeling his proximity, she turned to ask him if he had already checked out.

"Hm-mmm," he hummed as he settled himself well inside her personal space, nodding affirmation. "The chariot is being delivered as we speak."

"What mode of transportation should I anticipate? Flight of fancy or down-to-earth carriage?"

"The simple pleasures of a pick-up truck," he shot back.

"Sounds like just my speed," she smiled her answer.

He wrapped his arm around her shoulders and leading her past the parking valet, asked them to hold their bags and the truck until they returned. Then he guided her down the street to a sidewalk café on the Embarcadero, where he pulled out a seat for her, taking a place across from her and ordering coffee for both of them.

The day was bright and clear and the breeze floated past with the light, brisk flavor of a salty, waterside tang. Enjoying the morning, they took their time over breakfast, Gary with a hearty appetite and Anthea hardly able to swallow a bite. Imagining that they had no cares other than for each other, they savored the coffee and finally moved to stroll back to the hotel and start their first leg of the road trip home.

Land Barons

Chapter 38

Bay area traffic met their expectations of clogged arteries and slow moving vehicles of every size and shape as the morning rush hour passed its peak but didn't offer any clearer roadways. Autos moved with a stop and go rhythm that didn't let up until they'd begun to wind their way out of Oakland and over the hills that ringed the metropolitan sector with spring green that was rapidly taking on the golden brown of summer grasses.

Splashes of orange fled up the side of the rounded highlands as poppies overtook whole fields, interspersed with bright yellow swatches of other native wildflowers vying for the same space. This was the tail-end of the season for California's state bloom, however, and they dominated the rolling landscape that stretched on either side of the highway.

The drive to Sacramento swept swiftly by as traffic flowed at well above the posted speed limit. Although Mathers kept a wary eye out for the highway patrol, there was nary a flash of black and white anywhere along the way until they reached the outskirts of the state's capital, at which point the traffic slowed as the road narrowed and the lanes became more crowded. With the ease of a city-bred driver, he maneuvered around the slogging semis and the speeding subcompacts that swerved in and out of the flow.

Making good time through the city, Mathers sped up with the general convoy as I-80 began its ascent up the Sierra Nevada. The golden hills slipped into more lush green as they gained elevation, deciduous trees ceding to the more numerous conifers as they approached the summit of Donner Pass.

It never failed to fascinate Anthea to think about the pioneers of the Gold Rush, struggling across the precipitous heights of the mountainous spine that severed west from east with a steep and rugged terrain that she assumed they must have found not only daunting, but death-defying. Gazing at the intimidating heights that surrounded the winding interstate, she knew that she would never have been brave or courageous enough to cross a continent as those intrepid trailblazers

241

had more than a hundred and fifty years ago. Shivering at the thought of the hardships they endured, she was thankful for the comfort and ease with which she was able to climb the summit, being pulled over the ridge by the modern version of horsepower.

Mathers caught the slight shudder that shook Anthea's shoulders out of the corner of his eye.

"Someone tromp across your grave?" he inquired.

"Just thinking about the graves left by the droves of fortune hunters that dot the mountainsides all through here," she replied. "I can't imagine the hardships they endured just for a chance to try their luck at trudging through mountain streams to catch a glimmer of golden flakes from the mother lode."

"I'd agree that you don't find that kind of intrepid soul in today's society," opined Mathers. "The most dangerous kind of gamble most people make these days is in deciding which dot com or junk bond they're going to trust with their retirement funds. I certainly can't conceive of many of us giving up our cushy lifestyles to trek into the wilderness like they did here and in Australia, the Yukon and South Africa more than a century ago."

"I suppose our choices are colored by the fact that our frontiers have changed so radically. The wilderness that Lewis and Clark hiked through is now riddled with asphalt making our adventures far less of a challenge. Perhaps that's why so many manufacture a frontier by suiting up in their outdoor gear and climbing Mount Everest or boarding a blow-up raft and fighting the white water of some relatively unspoiled river. Whatever their need is to find a new frontier, I'm perfectly happy to contemplate our forefathers' courage and drive while I take on the challenge of finding a new market for my clients." She shrugged as she peered out the window breathing in the fresh mountain air. "Guess I'm just lazy."

He smiled across the console separating them as she turned to look into his warm gray eyes.

"Hardly," he said. "Times have changed and so have the challenges that providence gives us. Hardy souls of today have other hurdles to leap. They're no less difficult to surmount in that it still takes heart and chutzpah."

"Well, I certainly know a few nervy types that push the envelope," she grinned. "You seem to fit the bill yourself, though I'll bet your mother never used the term 'chutzpah.'"

"You're right, she preferred the word 'gall.' But it wasn't beyond her to label a deserving body as a 'schmuck' or a 'putz' if the shoe fit, or pants, as the case may be."

"Oh, an Irish fishwife with a tongue for Yiddish, eh?"

"Nah, just a Brooklyner with Jewish friends."

"Is that why you developed such an ear for languages?" she wondered aloud.

"Don't know. Mother had a velvety alto and sang in five languages, Gaelic among them. I might have cultivated an interest while listening to her perform."

"Perform? She was a professional vocalist?" asked Anthea.

"In a way. Probably more along the lines of a cantor, if there were such a thing in the Christian faith," he replied. "She sang at services, weddings, funerals and sometimes performed in community theater. She'd been a music major at Oberlin before she had to leave college. She might have been a real star given other circumstances."

As he finished his short maternal history, he glided down the off-ramp, taking the exit to Truckee and the northern shore of Lake Tahoe.

•••••••

Wending their way off the freeway and onto the local Route 267, they met Highway 28 which circles the north shore of Tahoe's expansive, clear waters. Following the road east for some distance, they crossed the Nevada border and headed north toward Reno when they saw a sign on the right indicating the turnoff to the Nature's Wilds Conservancy Sierra Summit Preserve. Turning left, they pulled onto a restricted, paved road that wound around the mountain.

They followed the progressively narrowing way as it became little more than an asphalted path, which eventually turned into a small parking area fronting a well-designed facility constructed to resemble a frontier log cabin.

The lot was empty but for a relatively new Ford Explorer painted a puke green similar to the color sported by USFS vehicles. Pulling in next to the rig, which carried the Nature's Wilds emblem on the door, they climbed out of Mathers' truck and walked up the path. Gary tried the door and, finding it unlocked, pushed it open. He stepped aside to allow her entry and followed Anthea through the aperture.

They were surprised by the modern interior that confronted them in contrast to the rustic façade of the building. A small lobby area was well turned out with numerous wall displays and glass jewelry cases exhibiting high-end art pieces, most with a Native American motif. Crafts, books and clothing items were tastefully presented on shelves and racks for purchase at one side of the room. Beyond that was a compact museum with a fair amount of information on the area and the early settlers, Forty-niners and the indigenous Washoe Indians. Among the many displays was a section given over to the memorabilia from many of the local pioneer families who had originally settled the region.

Anthea and Gary wandered through the exhibits, carefully noting the care that had been given to the presentation of the artifacts until they came to an office which occupied a wing to the right and wasn't easily noticed upon entering the lobby area. A door with a sign that designated the office as being that of the director, stood open and occupied.

Seated behind a bulky, wood desk was a rather burly fellow with long dark locks that, were he not scrubbed and dressed in a natty uniform, gave him the appearance more of a logger than an environmentalist. Anthea shrugged her shoulders thinking, *go figure.*

As they walked toward the office, he noticed their approach, stood up from his desk and came out to meet them at the office entrance. Offering a handshake to Anthea, who stood in front of Mathers, he welcomed the two of them to Nature's Wilds preserve and introduced himself.

"Afternoon ma'am. My name is Brad Turnow, director of the Sierra Summit Preserve."

"Hi," said Anthea as she held out her own hand, "I'm Anthea Keller and this is my associate…" she let her sentence dangle so Gary could cut-in with his own introduction and replace her hand with his in meeting the director.

"Gary Mathers. Pleased to meet you."

Turnow appeared to be a genial fellow and after shaking hands, placed both of his on his hips and proceeded to ask what he could do to assist them.

"It's my understanding that Mr. Alison called ahead to inform you of my arrival," said Anthea, to which Turnow nodded. "I'm doing a piece on Nature's Wilds for a magazine and he seemed to think that you might be able to find a little time to give us a basic tour of the grounds and some background information about the preserve, it's purpose, the history of its development and how the land is currently being used." She tilted her head back and smiled, "that sort of thing."

"That sounds like something I can do," he acknowledged pleasantly.

"Great. So where would you like to start?"

"Well, if you haven't had the opportunity yet, why don't you go through the museum a little first and that way you'll have a little of the history under your belt before we tour the preserve," he suggested.

"That's fine. We've been through some of it already and maybe you could answer a few questions while we wander," she prompted.

"Sure, what've you got in mind?"

"Just a few little facts would be nice," she said as she pulled out her notebook. "How many acres does the preserve encompass here?"

"Oh, about a quarter million but it's mostly backcountry terrain that is of little use for development or agriculture," Turnow explained. At the mention of the huge number of acres, Gary turned his head and lifted his eyebrows in surprise at Anthea.

"Was it logged at one time?"

"Oh yes. This whole area was logged out and we're now seeing second and third growth forest. You can tell by the wide interspersion of deciduous trees among the native conifers. They always make inroads when the dense firs and pines are culled, changing the sunlight availability for the different kinds of growth needs. Anyway, we can start here."

He took them through a brief history of the area, describing the development of the native culture, while pointing out different artifacts in some of the displays as a visual aid. He then narrated some on their displacement by the European population in the mid to late 19th century.

"The gold rush changed the face of this country, the populace and the land use," he said. "Here, at this preserve, we're trying to restore some of the original feel of the forested mountains that the pioneers first saw when they crossed the passes of the High Sierras.

"I grew up in California and I've always been enamored of the

245

diversity of the geography. I've always felt that, because of the size of the state, there is no other place on the continent that offers so many vistas. What is true about California is that you can travel two hours in any direction and be greeted with a view that varies from an Alpine meadow to a seascape with rugged cliffs to a vast desert scene dotted with Joshua trees and scrub." He slowly shook his head from side-to-side. "Nope, no other place like it."

"My goodness, Mr. Turnow, how very poetic. Perhaps you should be writing this piece. I grew up here too, but I can't say that I've ever put it into words quite as you have just done."

He smiled a bit shyly. "I may not write, but I have been known to apply pencil to paper and sketch now and again."

"I'd say the soul of an artist has shown itself," she added. "With descriptions like that, I'm sure your art exhibits the same passion."

Gary had to turn away before the smirk that creased his face became too noticeable. He was in awe at how well Anthea could work her subject so they simply spilled their innermost thoughts and feelings. *Gotta give it to her...I don't think I had that much success in most of my interrogations.*

Figuring that it was time to move on before he became any more embarrassed by her praise, Turnow directed the couple to the green truck near which they had parked.

The director opened the passenger door for Anthea, assuming that she would take the gunfighter's seat so she could easily continue her questions. Mathers climbed in behind her and the both of them fastened their seatbelts as Turnow powered up the vehicle and sprinted up the gravel road leading off from the left of the visitor center. The path swung around through dense forests of pine and aspen that occasionally opened onto meadows dotted with spring blooms just making their appearance as the rest in the lower elevations were moving toward summer.

Turnow pulled up at an overlook where they climbed out to take in the view spread below them of the dark blue jewel of Lake Tahoe many hundreds of feet beneath their location.

With the magnificent panorama spread below, Anthea plied her art on the director once more by swinging into a few questions about funding. Noting with wonder the incredible vista before them, she asked how the conservancy could afford such a large and obviously costly piece of real estate.

Dodging the question, Turnow explained that he knew very little of the transactions that occurred in order to acquire the acreage.

"To the best of my knowledge, the land was both donated by private owners and some of it purchased via philanthropic foundations," he attempted to elucidate on the subject. "But, truthfully, I was brought in after the fact and the details of the acquisition were not divulged other than what I've just told you. I earn my keep running the preserve."

"And they brought you in as an ecological or environmental expert?" she asked.

"Actually, no. I'm an MBA who has an interest in environmental affairs. I left corporate America to come here," he added with a self-effacing smile.

At that confession, Anthea had real trouble keeping the shock from showing on her face. If anything, she thought this guy was just some good-natured environmental buffoon as opposed to a corporate business type. *Who'd have thought?*

So she returned to her inquiry by asking if the preserve was often visited by any of the conservancy board members or if he was pretty much left on his own to manage the land.

"Well, actually, there's a modest lodge up the mountain that is sometimes used for business meetings and corporate educational functions. Often the Nature's Wilds board will invite corporate donors out for a weekend to coax funding from them." He added after a slight pause, "You know, PR, wining and dining and all."

When she asked if they could visit the lodge he replied that it's kept under lock and key.

"I'm rarely allowed up there, being the on-site peon. It's simply my duty to make certain the preserve runs smoothly. They even have a special crew that comes in to prepare the lodge and do general upkeep. Although it's situated on the property I administer, it's outside of my jurisdiction," he said with a slight shrug. "So, in answer to your question, uh no, I'm afraid that I can't take you up there."

Disappointed, she just said, "Too bad. It would have been a nice sidebar on the facility."

"Sorry, but I was only given permission to take you around the general area and give you the basic tour. Is there anything else that I can tell you about Sierra Summit?"

"You wouldn't happen to know anything about the land donors for this facility or the foundations involved, would you?" She gave it one last effort.

" 'Fraid not. We don't have any of those records here and my knowledge in that department is minimal." He gestured toward the vehicle with an open hand. "Shall we?"

With that, the three of them climbed back in the rig and Turnow drove them around a bit more before heading back to the visitor center. Parking next to their truck he gave them some written material about the preserve before bidding them goodbye and turning back to his work inside the building.

As Turnow ambled back to his office, Anthea pulled out her briefcase in order to add her new notes from today to those that she had been compiling.

"Look at this, Gary," she said as she pulled a blank legal pad from her case.

"What is it?" He asked.

"More like, what isn't?"

He came around behind her and peering over her shoulder inquisitively, he said, "What? You're not making any sense."

She held up the pad from her briefcase. "Look. My pad…it's empty."

"Call me obtuse but, that means?"

She exhaled slowly. "That means somebody took my notes. All of my notes…pages of notes on Nature's Wilds."

"Important notes?" He asked, concerned.

"Depends on who you are and if you think information on the financial status of Nature's Wilds is important."

Now he was getting a little exasperated. "Be more plain. What do you mean by 'financial status?'"

"Well, who's funding what. How the money's being channeled for the acquisitions and who's benefiting from the purchases. Though nothing fingered any one individual or group yet." She paused to think, "Trouble is, this info is not irreplaceable and most of it I had already entered into my computer. So, why'd they take it? And who?"

"The why is simple. They want to see how much you know and what you're really interested in. As to who, is another question. No matter how you look at it, this could be a problem."

"How so? I'm not dangerous."

"No, but they must think that your investigation could be threatening to someone involved and apparently, whoever set this up is closely connected to the top of the heap at the conservancy since they're the only ones who knew you'd be here."

"Great," she huffed. "Now what?"

"We watch our backs and we check out the building permits for this parcel in town. It may lead us somewhere." He glanced at his watch. "And if we hurry, I think we have enough time to do it today."

With that nudge to rush, he helped her into the truck and quickly climbed in behind the wheel and roared off into town.

Land Barons

Chapter 39

Pulling back onto the highway, Mathers careened out of the turn and barreled around the mountain, trying to make time and reach the Washoe County offices before closing.

Threading his way through traffic and finally slipping into a parking space behind the Assesor's office, Anthea was surprised at their rapid descent and quick arrival.

"How did you know where we were going?" she asked incredulously.

"Been here before," he answered perfunctorily as he slid out of his seat and opened her door for her to climb down. "Let's go, we've only got about twenty minutes."

"I hope that's enough," she said, hurrying to keep up with his long stride.

Halting in front of the directory to double-check what room they needed, Gary hurried off to the elevator and held the door for Anthea.

Catching up with him, they rode the car up to their floor and exited.

Mathers reached the door first, and holding it open for her, said, "Lets see what we can find about this 'modest' little lodge they've constructed for entertainment purposes."

It didn't take long to check in with the clerk and receive instruction to locate the proper permits pulled for the Nature's Wilds Sierra Summit site and what they found hardly fit the description of 'modest.'

"This is more along the lines of what old time business barons back east called a 'cottage' down at the shore," observed Mathers. "Those were estates suited to house an army of servants and sycophants. Hardly a 'cottage' in the same fashion that this is hardly 'modest,' with some 10,000 square feet of living space with eight bathrooms and a couple 2,000 square foot outbuildings, ski trails and landing strip. I guess one of them must be the hangar." He stood hunched over Anthea's back in order to get a good view of the paperwork.

Land Barons

•••••••

As the two of them were taking a few notes of what the building permit allowed to be constructed at the Sierra Summit site, a figure furtively glanced at their computer screen while practically slithering by unnoticed by the engrossed sleuths. Carefully noting the object of their interest by file and page number, he managed to settle himself behind a nearby computer to quickly access the same page and take careful note of the subject now on his screen. Without gathering any attention from the duo, he closed out the file and left as unobtrusively as he had come.

"I guess that answers a few questions," said Mathers.

"Yeah, like why they built a big ass mansion on land that is supposedly held in the public trust?" said Anthea sarcastically. "A playhouse, at that, with all the accoutrements required by the rich and famous." She arched an eyebrow at her companion. "Who do they expect to entertain there, the royal family? Or just some corporate schlubs with a ton of money to drop into the eco-bucket to save the environment from the common man like you and me?"

Gary looked down at her with an expression drifting between amusement and slight alarm at the unexpected antipathy.

"You don't appear to have a very high opinion of these 'do-gooders,' do you?"

"Well, I'd hardly call them 'do-gooders' in that their only real interest so far, appears to be in retaining the good stuff for their own personal enjoyment." She turned to look up at him. "Has any of this made you feel as thought these folks are really humanitarians or more likely, gifted media manipulators?"

"Oh, I don't disagree with your conjecture. There's far more behind all the different entities that seem to back this single-minded consumption of vast acreage. I just haven't been able to figure out the purpose to it all," he mused.

He stood up as Anthea scooted back her chair and nodded in accord with his observation. "We still have some work to do to put all the pieces together, but for the moment, I'm clueless and ready to pack it all in for the rest of the day."

"That's the most sensible thing you've said in a while." He grinned widely as she placed her fists on her hips and glared at him briefly before breaking into a solid laugh.

"Damn right. Let's go do something fun."

With that determination, they left the building and decided to stay the night in Reno and round up a little entertainment of their own.

••••••

Leaving the two at their computer in the county offices, the shadow rounded the corner and waited for Anthea and Mathers to exit the building. Unseen, he followed them to their vehicle and carefully climbed into his own car in order to tag along as they drove to a hotel and registered for the night.

After ensuring that they were not leaving the city until the next morning, he found a coffee shop down the street, settled into a booth and pulled out his cell phone. The waitress plumped a steaming cup of strong coffee in front of him, and he dialed Alison's office to make a report of his activities for the day. Alison asked his subordinate for the hotel and room number of the subjects he had been following and upon receiving the information, summarily dismissed the tail, informing him that his services would no longer be needed.

••••••

When Anthea and Mathers returned from an evening spent dining at a steak house most frequented by the locals followed by a comic revue at one of the casinos, they didn't notice a discreet figure lounging in the lobby of their hotel. A strategically placed baseball cap obscured any identifying features. Sitting back in one of the overstuffed loveseats where he had been appearing to study the newspaper for the better part of an hour, the new shadow peered around the edge of the broadsheet, noting the floor where the elevator paused before descending back to the ground level. Confirming the facts given him with observation, he rose, folded the paper, tucked it under his arm and walked over to the reception desk. He requested a room near his targets, citing some innocuous rationale for preference. Throwing his own overnight bag over his shoulder, he smiled at the young woman behind the counter and made his own way toward the bank of elevators.

Land Barons

Chapter 40

Waking for a second day in a row with a man by her side, Anthea started at the sight before realizing where she was and who occupied the other side of the bed, his arm draped across her waist. *If only I could remember the most pertinent facts when I wake up, I could prob-ably get used to the company.* A smile spread across her face as she felt Mathers gather her closer to his chest, more fully engulfing her in his embrace. *I could definitely get used to this.*

Breathing softly in her ear, Gary asked when she'd be ready to leave.

"Never, if you keep that up," she said pulling his arms tighter around her.

"You know," he said softly, "we'd better get our act on the road."

She sighed. "All right, but you first."

He chuckled as he sat up and padded to the closet to grab some clothes. Anthea rolled over to watch him. "Nice view from here."

"Glad you're enjoying the scenery, because it's about to change," and he disappeared through the door where the next thing she heard was the shower. Following his lead, Anthea climbed out of bed to begin preparing for the trip home.

•••••••

Less than an hour later, coffee stop behind them, Gary and Anthea settled in for the first leg of the trip up I-80 to Winnemucca where US 95 left its conjoined course to proceed north. They were unaware of the pursuer that trailed them by a fair distance and kept them in sight as they continued along the interstate. Following them wasn't difficult despite the high rate of speed, but the stalker was careful to stay back since he understood that Mathers had been a seasoned police officer and might be on the alert for a tail.

They didn't make any stops until they reached the seat of Humboldt County where they pulled off to gas up and stop at the grocery store for a few snacks and water.

Slowly making their way across town at the well-enforced 25 mph speed limit, the shadow had to expand the distance between vehicles since once they left town to head up Highway 95, the lack of other traffic would make him more obvious. As they ascended the low summit outside town, he dropped back to a good mile behind his quarry, knowing that they wouldn't be going anywhere other than straight up the only route north in the region.

Even knowing that there was little traffic on their route, Mathers still kept an eye on the rearview mirror half-expecting to see someone suspicious behind them. Traffic was light except for the big rigs heading both directions on the lonely road, many of which he passed when it was safe to maneuver around them.

"Don't you worry about the local cops pulling you over for speeding? You know the limit is only 55 mph through this corner of Oregon, " baited Anthea.

"Right. And how many cruisers have you ever seen through here on your trips to California." It was a statement instead of a question. Then he looked over at her fidgeting fingers. "You're just itching to get your hands on the wheel and do your usual 85, aren't you?"

She peered over at him. "I'll have you know that I rarely go over 80 unless I'm in a dither to get somewhere fast. Then it's only 90."

"In a dither? I haven't heard that since Aunt Bea got flustered in Mayberry." He laughed. "Since when are you *ever* in a 'dither?'"

She didn't particularly care to go into any specifics about her marriage and the state of perpetual motion she'd lived in having a husband who expected a career-track wife, office manager and homebody/gourmet chef all in one. It was easier to let the past lie rather than moan about someone else's unattainable expectations. They were done and gone.

"No need for details. It was another life. And, for your information, Andy Griffith wasn't high on our viewing list. Nothing more than TV snobs in our house," she chuckled lightly.

"So, all dithering aside, I wonder if it'll be safe to put you behind the wheel with your penchant for speed." He grinned and she slid her eyelids half-closed and gave him the evil eye glint, which only made him laugh again.

"Well, if you've logged anywhere near as many hours driving across country as I have, you might find yourself in a road king (or queen as the case may be) duel. 'En garde' when you are."

"Doubtful that I could beat your record. For all I know you also had another life as a big rig jockey."

"Nah, just family on both coasts and a will to take the wheel." At that, she winked at him, dropped her seat back and let her gaze sweep across the expanse of the land stretching toward the horizon, the greens of spring slowly making way for the golden hues of summer's ripening grasses. Within minutes Anthea had drifted into a light doze.

More than an hour and a half later they rolled through a long, wide valley and Mathers began to slow the vehicle as he came into the little hamlet of Jordan Valley where she directed him to pull over in front of a quaint, old structure built of river rock.

"I expect you could use a cup of java about now, I sure know that I could and I wouldn't mind stretching my stumpy legs a bit, either," said Anthea as she opened the door and hopped down.

Coming around the back of the truck, Gary gave her a thorough examination. "I don't see anything remotely looking like stumps in your make-up," he yawned.

"If you had a brother who called you 'shrimps' you might picture yourself otherwise," she replied blandly and headed toward the porch.

Mathers brought up the rear. "You get coffee here, huh?"

"Yup, and good espresso at that. I'd rather call this place a blessing for its location out here in the relative wilds and thankfully, it's independently owned and operated. The Rock House is exactly where travelers up and down this road need it. It makes the last leg to Boise quite a bit more bearable."

As they entered the house, their shadow drove past them and parked toward the rear of the lot of the mini-market next door for his own pit stop. While purchasing a few items, he kept watch for Mathers and Anthea to continue their journey, making plans for the next leg since he knew that they would be stopping for gas at the next juncture of civilization. He also figured he'd have to have contingencies available in order to keep a low profile when they next decided to take a break, because even though he was well acquainted with the route, there was no way of knowing where they'd pull over next. The last thing he wanted to do was draw their attention.

The couple exited the shop some fifteen minutes later, ready to resume their trip after chatting with the owner who just happened to be manning the barista station that afternoon.

"This is one Northwest fad that's worth exporting. Finally, espresso bars are getting to be as commonplace as McDonald's," noted Mathers as he took a sip of his steaming brew. "Hmmm, this may be the most exotic roast I've ever found in a backwater stop. It sure beats the convenience store mud I used to drink. Come to think of it, even that has become more upscale with the coffee craze."

"I imagine you subsisted on the less-than-gourmet variety during all those years behind a badge," offered his companion who cradled her own cup as they walked back out to the truck.

"That was the worst. At least I usually managed to avoid the stale donuts," he flashed a sidelong grin at Anthea's sniff of disbelief.

"No cop turns down a donut...or so I heard," she smirked. "But I'll bet we had more donuts in production than the whole force ever laid eyes on."

"And you still managed to keep your figure. Stumpy legs and all." He eyed her with an exaggerated leer.

"Ha! I didn't say that *I* ate them, well, often. They were a bribe to promote a lagging morale at deadline."

"Did it work?"

"Pizza's better," she laughed and climbed into the cab.

•••••••

The road wound around and up the Owyhee Mountains before dropping down into the southern sweep of the Snake River watershed. Driving through the farmlands, Mathers made the decision to stop at a smaller gas station in order to maximize his ability to keep track of other patrons. Without being obvious he maneuvered their time around the rig to be certain that one or both of them had it in their field of vision at all times. They picked up a couple of fresh sandwiches and supplies for the road ahead and after fueling up, started back on their way.

"I had planned on this being a more leisurely trip but I'm fairly sure we've had a tagalong for the last few hours," he said as she turned the key in the ignition. Anthea had taken over the driver's seat to give Gary a break.

"I kind of wondered whether you had plans to make this a romantic weekend but at the rate you've been driving I gathered that you were more interested in making time," she observed as she pulled into traffic and headed out of town.

He looked over and winked. "The best of intentions gone awry. I'm afraid that outside influences have changed our circumstances. I don't think it would be safe to stop for the night where the truck would be unattended and vulnerable."

"Too bad. There are a few cozy bed and breakfasts along the route," sighed Anthea. "not to mention the camping opportunities."

"Somehow I don't see you poking your head out of a tent on a crisp morning."

"And you'd be right. I'm more the five-star resort type but there are times that the great outdoors calls even to the urban weenies who prefer indoor plumbing." She looked to the hills and envisioned the dramatic landscapes that they would be driving through for the rest of the trip.

"Guess we'll just have to put that on the to-do list because I think we'd best make it home before we lose the light. I don't want to be caught on the road with a potential hazard on our tail." Mathers checked his watch. "We're making good time. You concur with the plan?"

"Hey, in this you're the boss. I'm just along for the ride." She smiled at him as she gave the truck gas to meet, and pass, the speed limit. Belying her words, Anthea's eyes reflected worry at his voiced concerns. He wrapped his left hand around her fingers that played on the right side of the steering wheel, giving them a quick squeeze, saying nothing.

•••••••

Wending her way through small towns and past sprawling ranches, Anthea climbed over one pass and down into another river valley where she finally pulled over at a rest area that hugged the bank of the swift moving water. She and Mathers took the opportunity to briefly stretch their legs when he noticed a Ford sedan as it maneuvered into one of the parallel parking slots some distance behind their own vehicle. The driver and only occupant of the midnight blue car tugged a Mariners baseball cap down to obscure his facial features, at least the action looked surreptitious to Gary as he walked with a measured step to reach Anthea as she rounded the building.

As the driver dropped his seat back as if to take a catnap, Mathers was careful to indirectly check out the Ford as he approached Anthea and casually draped his arm around her shoulders to guide her gently back toward the truck.

"Gotta roll, huh?" she looked up inquiringly.

"Yup. I think our shadow just showed up to catch twenty winks." He furtively nodded at the blue Ford further back in the parking line-up.

"Do you recognize him?"

"He was careful to cover his face right away and I didn't want him to think I made him so a close inspection was out of the question. But I'm pretty sure I've seen that car a few times here and there over the last five hours. Looks like a rental." He kept his voice low in response to her question.

"Well, no time like the present to make time. You don't mind if I drive some more, do you? This is probably my favorite part of the road," she said.

"You've probably driven this road far more than I have so be my guest," he said grinning at her as she climbed back in behind the wheel. "Let's just hope he doesn't know the road as well as you."

"Rental or not, if he's from around here within 200 miles, he'll know this stretch of road better than me," she offered as a statement of fact. "All these good old boys know every inch of the highways and backroads."

"Then let's pray he's not from around here."

The next few miles didn't allow much opportunity for passing, but Anthea managed to put a few slower vehicles between them and their pursuer, though they hadn't seen whether or not he followed them out of the rest area immediately. She figured that it didn't make much difference if he were right behind them or half a mile back as there weren't many turnoffs around this part of Idaho unless you wanted to drive up a dead-end against the Seven Devils or someone's private property. There's only one logical route and they had to continue on their way. Playing tag would only waste daylight.

On the other side of the river as they reentered the Pacific Time Zone, the road flattened out into long sweeping curves that gave

Anthea a chance to pick-up some real distance between her and the blue Ford. Mathers had seen him exiting town trailing them by a good three quarters of a mile and advised her to increase the spread when she could, which didn't take long as two big rigs were quickly dispatched creating minor roadblocks for their tracker.

Pressing to make time, Anthea plied the accelerator while Gary watched the growing number of cars that formed a trail behind them. He switched his focus from the road to the river where rafters fought the white water rapids, the spring runoff splashing and roaring over the rocks.

His attention drifting back to the road, Mathers spotted the Ford sweeping around one of the semis like it was standing still.

"Looks like this guy definitely knows the road. He'll be on our tail in no time if that's his aim," he said.

"Whatever difference that'll make. There's no other real road to follow so we'll all end up in the same place anyway," said Anthea seemingly unbothered by the prospect of a hunter. "Just gives me a little bit of a challenge and let's me hone my rally skills."

"I didn't know you drove rallies." Gary seemed mystified. "When did you find time for racing?"

"I never raced," she explained. "I just had a boyfriend who was involved with European rally drivers. He followed the circuit in the French Alps for a couple of years and showed me some of the finer points of negotiating mountain roads. Comes in handy once in a while though a four-by Chevy isn't the best stock vehicle for the course," she turned to him and smiled. "As long as there's no real danger, we're good." She peeled off around a curve.

It didn't take long before they we're scaling up the steep hill that wound around the mountain before cresting the summit to drop onto the prairie. Mathers looked back over his shoulder to see that the Ford was a good mile to their rear. *Maybe it was nothing all along. This is basically the only north-south route through this side of the state.* Relaxing back in his seat, he allowed Anthea to handle the driving until they made their last stop before the final leg of the trip.

•••••••

Stopping at the Zip Trip on the route skirting town, Gary and

Anthea switched places in the driver's seat.

"That was enough to assuage my backseat driving tendencies," she said as she dangled the keys to the side for Mathers to grab. "That also handles my control issues for the day," she tilted her head and smiled sweetly as if to punctuate her propensity for displaying a micromanaging alter ego.

The sun was dipping low on the horizon as they pulled back onto the road. This was a cause for concern to Mathers as he picked up speed. If the Ford was truly a tracker with hostile ideas things could prove detrimental to their health, a lonely stretch of road wasn't the best scenario for a good defense. With another hour to go before reaching Anthea's, darkness would be falling and increase the potential for danger.

After driving twenty miles he had just about decided it wouldn't be too much trouble getting back to Lewiston without incident when he spotted the Ford again, this time gaining on their rear although he still kept some distance between them.

Could just be a coincidence.

"The Ford has arrived," stated Mathers matter-of-factly as he checked the rearview mirror. "But he seems to be hanging back. It's hard to tell."

"Maybe it's nothing but our paranoid impulses," offered Anthea as a reassurance, though she wasn't sure if it was meant more for herself than Mathers.

"Could be, but not likely since this guy has been with us since just outside Winnemucca."

"Are you sure? I never saw him until he pulled in at the rest area," she said. "I guess that cop-sense never really dies, huh?"

He chuckled slightly. "Guess not, though I could've sworn I was cured."

"Well, ya'd think after, how many years?" she added in an attempt to lighten the mood, even as the darkness descended across the high prairie.

"Apparently, not enough. And maybe that's a good thing." With that he decided to speed up a little to test his possible pursuer's intentions. The Ford picked up speed as Mathers did, which didn't improve his mood any. What was worse, was that the loss of daylight was making it harder for him to see anything more than his headlights.

"This guy either has a fondness for tailgating or he has ulterior motives for creeping closer." As he said that, they began their descent down the grade, a dangerous bit of road under the best of circumstances. This stretch of US 95 was notorious for seeing it's share of accidents.

The distance between the two vehicles rapidly lessened as the Ford gained on them. Mathers was uncomfortable with going much faster knowing how treacherous the road was at higher speeds, so he decided to give the guy an opportunity to pass, just in case he had misinterpreted the Ford's encroachment.

"Well, if he's gonna pass, now's his chance," said Mathers as the vehicle came right up on his bumper.

As soon as the words came out of his mouth there was a flash behind him, which was hard to see in the diminishing dusk, followed immediately by a sharp report that made Anthea jump.

"What was that? Did something backfire?" her voice raised in pitch.

"Doubt it. Looked like a muzzle flash from the driver's side window." Mathers kept his voice controlled.

There was another bang that sounded even closer, followed swiftly by two more reports.

"Looks like he's trying to shoot out our tires," said Mathers blandly.

Anthea twisted in her seat to stare at him. "Are you serious?" her words beginning to reach a piercing level. Hearing herself, she settled herself back in her seat and said more calmly and in carefully chosen words, "Then you'd better get us the hell out of here."

He shot her a grim smile and resumed his rapt attention to the, now dire, situation.

"Hold on, honey..." He swerved the truck side-to-side in an attempt to avoid any shots connecting to anything vital and then he gunned the engine and shot down the highway. They heard a few more shots in their wake as Mathers barely controlled the truck as he slid around the tightening curves. Anthea grabbed on to the "oh shit" bar and hung on for dear life as Mathers careened down the mountain, shots ringing out around them. When one blew off the passenger side rear view mirror, Anthea let out a yelp of fright. Mathers ignored her in his intense study of the headlight illumination on the road ahead,

263

which he knew he was overdriving in his desperate need to get away from his tracker.

Anthea peered back over her shoulder to see if she could discern their pursuer's intentions. In the glow surrounding the vehicles from the headlamps she could barely make out the other driver's silhouette.

"He's going to shoot!"

"Hang on, here we go again." Mathers swung the truck toward the center of the road and then, both hands clenching the wheel, heaved the truck to the outer edge of the macadam just as a semi approached from the other side, clearing the way and giving Anthea heart palpitations all in one instant.

The Ford was about to make an attempt to overtake Mathers but pulled back just before he would have been hit head-on by the rig coming up the mountain, whose driver pulled hard on the airhorn as he passed. A shot rang out and sounded like it connected somewhere with the back of the truck. That was enough for Anthea to audibly let out her breath, sounding like a punctured soccer ball.

"We're at the bottom of the grade, hold on…" Mathers said as he screamed around the sedan in front of him and pulling out of traffic just before getting creamed by another big rig who also blared his horn. Mathers crammed down the accelerator and plunged down the road at 90 leaving his pursuer stuck waiting for the line of oncoming traffic to pass. Anthea watched as he tried to pull out but had to swing back in behind the slower car before he collided head-on with a Dodge Ram.

Pressing his luck, Mathers blew through the small town hoping the highway patrol didn't catch him. He didn't let up on the gas until he reached the four-lane highway on the other side of the Clearwater River where he finally slowed to 70 mph.

The Ford finally gave up the pursuit when he reached the bridge, writing off the episode as a lost opportunity since he couldn't very well fire a weapon in the vicinity of the weigh station where law enforcement was always present.

As Mathers took the turn toward town he watched the Ford continue north on 95 toward Spokane, at which point he breathed a sigh of real relief. Feeling his heartrate finally slow as the adrenaline rush subsided, he set a course for Anthea's hoping that the worst was passed for the night.

Chapter 41

Neither of them spoke as Mathers drove a circuitous route through the neighborhood before arriving at Anthea's door. After pulling into the driveway she simply felt paralyzed as she tried to steady her breathing. Gary took her hand and clasped it tightly then reached across her to open the glovebox. Anthea's brows slid up to her hairline as he extracted a gun from the compartment, took the safety off and chambered a round.

"I didn't know that was there," she observed with a small voice.

"Would it have made any difference if you had?' He asked her seriously as he leaned forward and stowed it under his waistband at the small of his back.

"Guess not. I wouldn't have known what to do with it and you had both hands on the wheel."

He nodded assent and brusquely ordered her to stay put before climbing out of the rig. He adjusted the weapon for comfort and availability if needed. He then walked around to the end of the driveway to check traffic and see if they might have been followed or if a suspicious vehicle were parked anywhere nearby.

Walking up to Anthea's window, he said, "Do you recognize all the cars on the street?"

She swiveled her head around, glancing up and down the road and replied, "Yes. They all appear to belong here. Looks like the kids are home, too," and she nodded at the Honda on the street. "I'll never figure how the two of them can fit in that thing."

Mathers gave her a puzzled look and she offered a brief explanation about Lainie and Cisco, her tenants.

He opened the door and lifted her to the ground, after which he poked his hand under the passenger seat and grabbed his Maglite.

"No cop travels without one," chuckled Anthea, whose sense of humor was returning as the fright wore off.

"Yup, the perfect multi-purpose tool. You can see the perp before you either beat him senseless with it or shoot him with the gun in your other hand." At that he flicked on the light and looked at the place where the rearview mirror used to be. He then went back around the truck slowly, examining it for damage. Stopping at the left side of the cargo box, he spotted the end of the bumper, which was twisted and deformed by another of their assailant's wild shots.

"At least I can get this fixed without having to make a gunshot report."

"Why wouldn't you report the attack?" asked Anthea, who stood looking over Mathers' shoulder as he squatted to look at the buckled bumper.

He turned to peer up at her. "I'm not sure that I want anyone sticking their nose into this before I have a better idea as to who's stalking us and why. I have a feeling that retribution would be more than just an attempt to blow out a tire."

"Not like a blow-out on that grade couldn't have killed us anyway." She screwed up her face with a bitter grimace. "Dead is dead, by indirect means or not."

"Not that I don't agree with you," he said standing up. "But I think we'd best keep this low profile for now. If they think they've scared us off, they may figure their job is done and then it's back to business as usual. In which case there'll be activity to track down. Otherwise they might go underground and we'll never find out what's going on."

She shrugged, shouldered her purse and started walking toward the front door but found Mathers blocking her way as soon as she took a step forward.

"Give me your key," and he held his hand out.

A little perplexed, she handed over her keychain.

"I want you to stay behind me and wait just outside the door while I check the house to make sure you don't have any uninvited guests wandering the halls or hiding behind any doors."

An expression of understanding swept her features as she followed him to the entry and waited obligingly on the stoop while he went through the interior.

"It's clear. You can come in now," he called as he was walking back toward the front hall.

"Yeah, welcome home," she muttered half under her breath.

He came up next to her and enclosed her in a long, sheltering hug, which diffused her uneasiness.

"It comes in handy to have a big, strong man around," she

quipped. "Particularly one that smells this good." She looked up and smiled.

"I could've sworn I smelled more like fear. Any dog would go for my jugular, so it's a good thing there isn't one around."

"Is that a nice way of saying I'm not a bitch?" she said laughing.

"No way, no how." And he pulled her close for a lingering kiss.

"Does this mean you're staying?" she asked once she had caught her breath.

"There's no way I'd leave you alone tonight." With that he kicked the front door closed, turned the locks and drew her deeper inside.

•••••••

Next morning they were awakened by a rattling knock on the sliding glass doors. Pulling herself out of Gary's arms, Anthea got up and started hunting for her robe. She pulled it on as she half-stumbled down the hall toward the living room, trying to wipe the sleep from her eyes. She was pulled up short by a naked Mathers, who grabbed her shoulders and stopped her forward progress in mid-step. She looked back at him and scanned his nude form with an amused grin.

"What are you doing? The kids'll never let me live it down if I show up at the door with a naked man standing behind me, training a gun on them."

"You can't be sure that's who it is. Wait 'til I pull on some pants and I'll go out with you. We have to be careful. I think that last night was a lesson in caution." His voice lilted up a little at the end of his statement to enforce the point.

She nodded her agreement and waited patiently while he donned his jeans but didn't bother with a shirt. He told her okay and then followed her, his arm at his side concealing the gun by his leg.

If eyes could get any wider, Anthea was sure she'd never seen it. The two tall Indians stood at the back door, looking into the interior with surprised faces that swiftly turned to beaming mirth that was rapidly replaced by stoic stares at Mathers. Anthea unlocked the door and slid it open.

"I *was* trying to sleep in this morning," she said in greeting. At which Lainie couldn't resist the straight-faced rejoinder, "I can see why."

Anthea swallowed her embarrassment and asked them what they needed at this hour.

"The obvious point is," explained Cisco, "that there's a strange vehicle in the driveway, no sign of your car and someone in the house. We wanted to check to make sure everything was on the up-and-up, so to speak," he gave in to a half-smile at his gibe.

Anthea groaned, Lainie jabbed him with her elbow and Mathers broke into a solid laugh as he slid the gun into the back of his waistband. Noticing the repositioning of Mathers' arm and the reason for it, definitely raised Cisco's eyebrows.

"So there was a reason for us to assume something might be wrong," he said flatly.

"Why do you say that," Anthea asked in answer, to which Cisco merely nodded his head toward Mathers' right hand that was now shoved in his back pocket.

"Kid's got two good eyes," acknowledged Mathers while taking his hand out and offering to shake with Cisco. "Gary Mathers."

His hand was accepted. "Cisco and Lainie Rafael."

"So, did you make coffee yet?" Lainie brushed past Anthea and Gary going directly to the kitchen to start a pot since she could see the answer to her question would be an obvious "no." Anthea just shrugged her shoulders at Mathers' querulous look and let both Lainie and Cisco past them and into the house.

"I see that I'm not going to get the opportunity to get a little extra sleep now," she grumbled.

"Or anything else," whispered Gary in her ear, which made her smile widen and the young ones turn to smirk at each other while poking around in the kitchen for coffee makings.

It wasn't long before the four of them were seated around the table, steaming mugs in hand and muffins on the table that Lainie had sent Cisco back across the yard to get from their apartment. Gary had dressed in a t-shirt that he had gone back to dig out of Anthea's closet while depositing the gun in her room. She caught him in a puckish grin as he tucked in the shirt, which proclaimed serving thousands at a California beach community bed and breakfast, i.e. the local jail.

"So, are you going to tell us what's going on?" Lainie asked bluntly as she placed her coffee back on the table.

Anthea and Mathers exchanged looks that said "you handle it" to one another, at which point, she pressed the issue by turning toward the kids and nodding to her companion. "He'll tell you." She looked back at him and smiled.

With a flat expression, Mathers launched into an explanation that, in the end, revealed very little of the situation since he didn't want to scare them with the possibility that there could be any real danger.

"Hmmm, so you make it a habit of sleeping with a gun," offered Cisco with a healthy dose of skepticism.

"Old habits die hard, I'm afraid." Mathers had told them that he was a retired cop from the city and after an unusual incident on the road home…he hadn't mentioned the shooter as such, but rather as a "drunk on a mission"…he felt inclined to keep a firearm at hand.

"I'm sure." He brought the mug to his mouth, training a hard look at Mathers over the lip as he drank.

Anthea was having a tough time keeping a smile off her face at the grilling the couple was trying to give a man who was used to sidestepping particulars when necessary.

Not to be cowed by Lainie and Cisco's vain attempt to use grim stares to get answers, Mathers shrugged and bit into one of the muffins, effusively praising the flavor and texture. It didn't take any more than that to soften up the young lady who had baked them that morning and she wasn't shy about supplying that information.

"I really appreciate you sharing your breakfast with us. I'm not sure what I've got in the pantry," said Anthea as she took another bite.

"Zip." Lainie said. "Your pantry and fridge are just about empty." When Anthea gave her a questioning look, she added in a matter-of-fact tone, "I noticed when I was hunting for the coffee stuff."

"Oh." She paused then asked, "don't you have class today?" hoping that she might move her visitors out the door soon. Despite how pleasant the breakfast club had been, she and Gary needed to get to work.

"No. School's out but we do have to get to P'lahka's for the weekend. There's a big family gathering. I guess we should be getting our things together." With that she glanced over at her husband who stood up, picked up both of their cups and put them on the counter. Lainie came around the table and wrapping her arms around Anthea's shoulders, gave her a hug. "I'm glad you're back safe. It's not a bad idea to have a bodyguard with you for protection." She gave Anthea an intent gaze that just hinted of humor before taking Cisco by the arm and leading him to the door.

"Keep the rest of the muffins. I made enough for the whole family." They slid through the door and closed it behind them.

Anthea moved her attention to the man seated beside her, indolently leaning back in his chair, legs stretched out under the table, lazily sipping coffee. "A drunk on a mission?" she asked incredulously.

"Someone high on drugs or alcohol takes a dislike to a stranger and follows them home, even trying to run them off the road. Not unheard of."

"Yeah, and cows dance in the moonlight."

"It could happen," was his short reply as a corner of his mouth twisted slightly upward.

She smiled, gave him a peck on the cheek and rose from her seat. "Time to get in gear," and she disappeared down the hall to get ready for the day.

•••••••

When she emerged after a shower and wasted fifteen minutes trying to manage her hair, which ended up roped into an unruly ponytail at the nape of her neck, she found Mathers hunched over some paperwork at the table.

"I decided a second pot of caffeine was in order for this morning since we've moved from playtime to work mode." He hefted a fresh cup in her direction without rising from his seat. His hair was damp from the shower he'd taken while she had wrestled with her locks, and was now more suitably attired in Eddie Bauer casual.

I just don't get how guys run through the shower in record time and it takes me forever just to control some wayward curls. And *he made it out to the truck to get the luggage,* she added to her thought as she noticed his clean clothes.

She took the mug from his hand and settled into a chair opposite him. Mathers watched her from over the frames of his reading glasses, a glint of regret in his eye at the prospect of trying to reconstruct the last few days' activities instead of following other pursuits.

"So, where do we start? And, by the way, what are we doing?"

inquired Anthea after a sip of coffee.

"We're trying to piece together what happened over the last week and why this guy tried to deflate our tires and, presumably, end our illustrious careers."

"I didn't know I had any such thing that needed to be terminated, but you're right that someone else seems to think so. Like I said, where do we start?" She sat forward expecting him to devise a theory out of the available facts, just like any well-trained detective.

"Good question," to which she quirked up an eyebrow.

"Hey, I thought you were the professional here. I, personally, don't have a clue where to begin," she said throwing it back to him.

"I don't think we have to rehash the incidents before leaving on your fateful fact-finding flight."

"Is that supposed to be a tongue twister?" She arched her brow in feigned annoyance.

He grinned and moved on. "Did you notice anyone who struck you as odd or out of place before we started the drive home?"

"Not that I can recall. Somebody must've been watching, though, since he managed to abscond with my notes."

"When do you think that could have happened?" he asked, looking across the table at her, pen poised to jot down anything pertinent.

"Hmm. I took the notes during the meeting with Alison, went to my room, got changed and met you for dinner. I *don't* think I looked at them, or for them, until we were in Tahoe." She raised her eyes and stared out the window at the river while she ran over the timeline in her mind.

"That means that someone knew where you'd been and where you were staying."

"It wasn't exactly a secret." She looked back at him. "I'm sure I told the Nature's Wilds folks where I'd be."

"Who else knew?"

"Besides you?"

"Yeah, besides me."

"I think I told my brothers, though I didn't tell them what I was doing other than writing a story. Aa..and, no one. The kids didn't even know where I was going, except to L.A. I'm pretty sure."

"That certainly narrows our field of suspects on one level. We know that I didn't take your notes. No reason to. I doubt that your brothers would have any reason to follow you and run off with them, either. So, I'd say it leaves Nature's Wilds and some crony or hired hand as the culprit. Agreed?" He raised his head from his scribbles.

"Unless I'm missing something."

"All right. So, what did they want with a bunch of relatively useless notes," he seemed to ask the room in general.

"Probably the same thing they wanted with the other notes they grabbed from my office…information on what our interest is and who we're talking to. They still don't have a why," she enumerated.

"Which is the reason for their abortive attempt to end the so-called investigation," he offered in an expressionless voice. "Okay, so we've got someone following us around San Francisco, appropriating your notes and tailing us on the road to Idaho. They must think that we're on to something."

"Yes, but what?"

"We obviously struck a nerve by your delving into the Nature's Wilds connection, so let's start there." He looked up again. "Didn't you say that you had a friend piecing together some intel?"

"I guess it's time to check my e-mail." With that she put down her empty cup and went into her office. She plopped down into the executive chair, a relic from her days as a newspaper honcho before the new management put the operation into a tailspin, disposing of her position along with the publication which met an ignominious demise soon after, and started typing away at the keyboard. It wasn't long before Dan Rennselaer's lengthy message opened on the screen.

"Whoa, did we hit paydirt," she mumbled.

Mathers noticed that she had stopped tapping keys and came down the hall to investigate. "Got something?"

"Looks like. Apparently it took some digging but Dan sure hasn't been idle this last week," she noted while she continued to read.

"What did he come up with?"

"Boy, it sure helps to have someone who knows their way around corporate rigmarole and philanthropic foundations. You know how they say 'follow the money?' It works pretty much every time. This money trail goes backwards from Nature's Wilds to a number of corporate and private foundations, all of which have one of two of the same people on their board of directors."

"And the winners are?"

"Carl Chamberlain and his second lieutenant, Laura Cane, attorney-at-large."

"Carl Chamberlain," and he mulled over the name. "Solis Industries Carl Chamberlain?"

"Now *you're* the prize winner," she said. "The ubiquitous Chamberlain and his vast empire of computer software and digital entertainment are deeply involved in seven major gifting foundations that have been the core donors to Nature's Wilds for the past five years. In fact, according to IRS documents, not only do they fund the conservancy, but it is almost *exclusively* funded by Solis alter-egos that look to have eluded being named as such by the tax wizards in D.C." She was amazed at the complexity of the money trail as she read down the e-mail.

"Then how did your pal manage to unearth all this gold when the IRS can't figure it out?"

"Let's see...banking tracks from the U.S. to the Caymans and Bahamas and, let us not forget, Belize."

"What, no Swiss accounts?"

"Nope. Must be old hat. Anyway, the convoluted movement of money was more than I could understand, but he got the goods."

"Legally?"

She turned to look up at him as he bent over to read the screen from behind her shoulder. "I doubt hackers ever do this sort of thing through proper channels, which means we have nothing if it ever came down to needing evidence of some illicit activity. The government would have to trace the money trail themselves with the appropriate warrants in place. But it gives us something to work on. We now know that the real Hydra's head is Carl Chamberlain. What we don't know is why he's buying up all this land via Nature's Wilds."

"Or why he may be advocating the convenient disposal of folks who get in the way." He stood up straight and thought for a moment. "Do we have a number of acres that this 'consortium' is acquiring?"

"Acres? You mean square miles, right?"

"Square miles?" he looked perplexed.

"It appears to be in the neighborhood of a quarter million."

"Square miles?" He was dumbfounded by the concept.

"And growing," she sang the commercial ditty. "Not only that...did you look at the papers today?"

"Not really."

She pulled out the local daily and pointed to an article.

"Look here. This environmental organization, Friends of the Land, lobbied for passage of legislation in King County to restrict rural property owners' land use. They've passed something called the Critical Areas Ordinance that allows owners the ability to develop only 35% of their private property, and even that would be regulated. It would virtually halt development so that landowners would be forced to keep their own property in its 'natural' state for the benefit of 'others.' And to top that, there's already an ordinance in place that restricts a large part of the county to keeping 65% of their property in an undeveloped state."

"Let me see that," he said as he reached for the paper.

"Can you believe that?" Anthea was incensed. "Not only do some folks think they have the right to force people off their land by subverting their livelihood and then buying them out, but they've been passing legislation to impose land use according to their idea of what's proper management. It's incredible, the utter gall," she sputtered then took a deep breath.

He read further down the article. "Looks like the ordinance was instituted by the Metropolitan King County Council. It's not even an initiative that the people had the opportunity to vote for or against even though a lot of folks protested. All in the name of saving the wetlands which, anymore, seem to be arbitrarily designated and not according to what was historically described as such." He looked over at her. "You know, I understand wanting to protect the watershed but not when the interpretation of the term is debatable depending on who's in power. I've had too many encounters with anecdotal accounts on how private property rights were lost because a government agency waved a wand and called land a 'wetland,' that was temporarily underwater due to a newly constructed beaver dam or some other unnatural obstruction, like a dead log blocking the course of a small stream. Then they interfered with the removal of the temporary barrier. Abracadabra and the property is now under new jurisdiction and the owners have no more control on how they can use their land. Makes you wonder why you have a deed."

"This ordinance isn't even targeted to keep developers out of the rural areas but to restrict legitimate land use, like building a cattle kraal for a couple of milkers or clearing a horse pasture," Anthea tapped her finger at a paragraph in the story.

He took a minute to mull over the implications.

"Thank God I live in Idaho. Not that that seems to be any saving grace with wealthy elitists buying up everything in sight." It was the first time that he thought of outsiders, and he was considered one himself to a large degree, as undermining the fabric of the community in the name of environmentalism. He pulled up another chair and sat down.

"All of these years I just assumed that all environmentalists were pretty much on the same page...keep the public wilderness intact for posterity to enjoy. It never really occurred to me that private property could be lined up in the sights of over-enthusiastic do-gooders, if that's what they are."

"I wouldn't argue that environmentalism serves an important role and most of the people I've met in the rural districts do their best to keep their land in a productive state that enhances life for everyone in the community. I've yet to meet someone who trashes their farm or timber stand in order to get rich though there's always got to be some idiot out there. But that's no cause for a few to expect that they should regulate general land use, bypassing the concept of private property" She sighed and rubbed her temples. "Damn, the whole idea makes me tired, and frustrated."

"At this point, we just need to find out what Chamberlain is really doing, and why." He sat up. "Somehow I doubt that he truly has the good of 'mother earth' at heart."

"Whatever he's up to, I just don't want to be flattened by his steamroller."

Land Barons

Chapter 42

They climbed back into Mathers' truck to drive up to the airport and reclaim Anthea's car from where she'd parked it in the long-term lot before flying to L.A. As they pulled up behind the vehicle, he dropped back into his recurring cop-mode and abruptly told her to keep her seat.

"Now what?" She was a tad put out by the command and wondered what else could be problematic. After yesterday's narrow escape down the grade, followed by a restless night, her nerves had frazzled more than she'd anticipated.

As he dropped to the ground, he looked across the cab at her with a serious tilt to his head.

"I think we should take every precaution since these guys obviously know so much about you. I just want to make sure that there are no surprises lurking in or under the Expedition."

"I can't imagine anyone would bother to mess with the truck. I mean, it's sitting here in plain view. But if you think there could be a problem, go for it. I'm not averse to having my life saved more than once." *Hell, the man is just watching out for me. You'd think I could be pleasant,* and she slapped a tired smile on her face in an attempt to be better humored.

A minute later Mathers pushed off the ground where he had been kneeling to examine the back wheels. "I truly hate to be a told-you-so kind of guy," he said as the grim look on his face deepened the creases between his brows. "Looks like you need to be concerned because there seems to be an awful lot of brake fluid puddling under your rig. I'm going to take a closer look."

Squatting down again to get a better view of the inside of the wheels, he checked more thoroughly to be sure that the puddles weren't just from a vehicle that had parked there previously.

"What's the prognosis?"

"Cut brake lines. It's a good thing you didn't come back from your evening flight and just drive off because the result might have been a nasty accident."

She shivered at the thought and recanted her impatience, which she followed with a silent prayer of thanks.

"You'd better call Triple A and have this baby towed. You won't be driving it today." He got back up and brushed the dirt off his hands and bent over to smack the dust from the knees of his jeans. She popped out of the cab to join him by her car, where she gazed down at the red fluid pooling on the ground inside the tires.

"Guess not," she concurred with his estimation of the damage.

• • • • • • •

It must have been a slow morning for roadside service since they only waited ten minutes before the wrecker arrived, at which point she went through the basic paperwork. They formed a miniature cavalcade as they followed the tow truck down the hill to leave the Ford with her regular mechanic.

The explanation was a bit sticky as Anthea and Gary tried to evade questions about how the brake lines had been severed. In the end, it came down to simply not answering the mechanic rather than making up some lame excuse about vandals or whatever else they could have devised.

"It was enough to try to mislead the kids this morning with your rather imaginative scenario, but I certainly wasn't up to topping that with some other barely believable story," she said as they left the shop. "He can think what he wants just so long as he fixes it."

"There are times when details only get you in deeper," he agreed. "Guess you're with me now," he added.

"I probably should rent a car."

He opened the door and helped her up. "Nah," he grinned, "I like this arrangement better."

* * * * * *

Exiting the airport arrival area, a man dressed in flannel and jeans waited as his buddy drove up to the curb and rolled down the passenger side window, popping the trunk at the same time.

"Thanks for coming up to get me," offered the outdoorsman reluctantly. He wasn't a particularly genial character.

"No prob. Tough luck about your vacation, man," the driver added without a lick of real compassion. Whatever his reason for helping out, it wasn't out of consideration for anyone other than himself.

"Yeah, well, that's what happens when your fishing partners are workaholics and an emergency call signals the end of the world. I suppose I could've driven his rig back, but he'll need it when he comes back into town. Just let me get my gear into the back." He wasn't about to discuss why he really needed the lift back to Idaho. Dropping off the rental car in Spokane had left him stranded and in need of concocting some story to cover the fact that he didn't have another fall-back plan. It ticked him off to have to cover Alison's stupid ass when the conservancy director should have done his homework in the first place.

Trying to readjust his attitude away from the anger that had been pulsing through his system since his quickly laid plan had backfired the night before, the outdoorsman finished loading in his things and dropped down into the passenger seat. He was exhausted after catching a redeye and dogging a couple of part-time sleuths for 500 miles.

"You get the day off?"

"It wasn't easy. The boss is a slave driver for the environment. Figures the world will self-destruct if we're not there to save it, but they didn't have anything pressing today that my pal couldn't handle so I told her I had to do a favor for a friend," he explained his absence. "And that leaves me free for mischief. Got anything in the works?"

"You've got nothing better to do than make trouble?" he looked over at the younger man disapprovingly.

"I just like a little excitement now and then. That's why I answer your calls. You've usually got something interesting on the burner." He grinned unabashedly across at his passenger, obviously expecting to be pulled into another caper.

The outdoorsman gave him a discouraging stare that was rapidly turning to fury again, so he turned to face the window to watch the swiftly passing acres of wheat fields. Ignoring his companion, his thoughts took a new tack as he considered that this guy was nothing more than a loose cannon, which could be dangerous to his own interests.

•••••••

An old black Bronco clambered over a jeep trail that barely

279

deserved that much of a designation, the washboard often being so bad that the driver was jolted in his seat as he hunted for the smoothest surface he could find. Finally locating the hardly perceptible turnout, he drove another quarter mile until he had to pull the truck up short before it plunged into a small cleft where spring runoff had cut through the track.

Opening the door, Billy Brogus examined the ground before setting foot into what could be solid-packed dirt or knee-deep mud. Satisfying himself that the earth was dry, he got out and followed the twisting, semi-track another 100 yards to find what he was looking for, which was virtually nothing. At least, that's what he expected and, to his approval, that's what he found.

He walked around the widely spaced tree stand, checking the ground for any sign of cultivation and saw only the natural deposit of old leaf detritus amid the undergrowth. He kicked through the molding accumulation until he was sure that there was no sign of his operation ever having been there. *Well, there might be something, but the feds would have to use a forensic team to locate it* and since he'd been able to avoid suspicion so far, he assumed that there would be no reason for anyone to investigate.

Pleased with the work of his crew, he decided to follow the elk trail that meandered from the clearing until he found himself within sight of the road leading to the Solis estate. He hadn't been there long before he heard the rumbling of a large diesel engine approaching. Not taking any chances of being spotted trespassing, he backtracked enough to conceal himself behind a cluster of pines.

Less than a minute later a beat-up yellow school bus trundled past. Looking closely, he saw that it was filled with the laborers that had been boarded on the grounds while constructing the manor house and outbuildings.

Guess that clinches it if they're finished. Apparently it was time to quietly shuttle the illegal work crew out of the country. Once they were gone he'd no longer have any leverage. He'd known the time was coming, he just hadn't expected it so soon. *The decision's made for me, then. It must be time to close-up shop.*

Hiking back to his rig, he determined that he would call his lieutenants together to plan the final strategy for shutting down. He reached the Bronco, fired up the engine and, waiting until after the dust had settled, followed the bus down the hill.

Land Barons

Chapter 43

Having made up his mind the day before, Brogus called a meeting of his management team. Joe Santos and Charlie Weeble sauntered into the room and helped themselves to the coffee pot before settling into chairs around a small conference table.

"Hey boss, when you gonna get an espresso machine in here?" mocked Weeble. "Class outfit like this, we should have capuccino when we take a meeting." He tossed his neatly groomed ponytail across his shoulder as he lifted the coffee mug with his pinky outstretched.

Santos laughed.

"Maybe when we institute the final changes an espresso machine will be installed in the executive meeting room." Brogus was blasé.

"Changes? What's in the works, Billy?" Santos immediately turned serious.

"We're downsizing the operation, boys."

Weeble lowered his mug, eyebrows moving up his forehead. "Downsizing? That's a term I hadn't expected to hear around these parts."

"The time has come, my friends. We have to disassemble the clandestine operation."

"Seems a shame to shut down such a lucrative business," lamented Santos. "What's the rush?"

"There have been some developments that make it clear we no longer have a safe haven for continuing the forest cultivation enterprise."

"Did you lie awake last night thinking up that euphemism?" asked Weeble.

"Hey, just want to flaunt my education for you backwoods yahoos," he grinned. "Seriously, the cash crop side of the business has to be dismantled. We have no choice."

"So, something's going on. Can you at least give us a little info?" Santos was beginning to worry at his boss' demeanor.

"This stuff is beyond anything we want to get near. Just take my word for it that it's time to make this disappear, quietly, completely and quickly."

"Are the feds onto us?" A slight current of panic fled through Weeble's frame.

"No, nothing like that. Just believe me, we need to take our profit and move on." Brogus sighed with more relief than regret.

"Whatever you say, boss." Weeble accepted Brogus' assessment of the situation since his business acumen had steered them so far as to make a pretty comfortable retirement.

"The first harvest is underway right now, it'll just have to be the last. We'll package the product, get it to market, restore the rest of the fields to a natural state and make sure everyone is handsomely compensated. You know, a nice severance package." He smiled at the promise.

"Thanks Billy. I hope you know what you're doing." Santos was a little skeptical at the sudden development but had done well trusting Brogus' intuition.

Brogus rubbed the back of his neck as he sat with his legs stretched out under the table. "I know what I'm doing. We get greedy and keep this going, we'll lose it all. We don't have any more protection.

"So, finish your coffee and get back to work. Next time we convene it will be to reconstruct the operations around the *legitimate* natural herb packaging business of Pinesap Farms and we'll do it over lattés." He leaned forward, placing his elbows on the table and shooed them off.

"Surright!" saluted Weeble for what he figured might be one of the last times.

•••••••

After he dismissed his two commanders in the field, as he liked to call them, his phone rang over at his desk. He raised himself up heavily after having to close out the meeting with a feeling skirting gloom.

"Brogus. Can I help you?"

"It's Carrie, I didn't know who else to call."

He was about to offer some glib comment, but realizing she sounded distressed, he switched to a more soothing tone instead.

"What's the matter?"

"One of my student interns, Sully Tyson, he's missing."

"Are you sure of that?" Brogus was trying to understand her panic. "How long has it been since you've heard from him?"

"The other kid who works here, Gordon Curry…he says he hasn't seen him since yesterday. They room together and he says that Tyson may stay out late on occasion but he always shows up in time for work."

"Maybe he just went to Lathrop without saying anything, he's a college kid, after all. Reliability isn't one of their best qualities," he placated. "Why are you so sure he's gone missing? It hasn't been 24 hours."

"I just know. No, this guy doesn't just up and vanish. He's wild but punctual. At the least, he always calls if he's run into a problem." She stopped to catch her breath. "He always manages to be where he's supposed to be, and he was supposed to be here hours ago."

A responsible party boy? That sounded like an oxymoron to Billy.

"You know something you're not telling me?" he sounded slightly suspicious. "Or have a reason to believe something's happened?"

"No! No… I don't know," her denial petering out with her voice. "Can you help?"

"I don't know what I can do, but I'll come down to your office and we'll figure things out."

Feeling unsettled and a little manipulated, he hopped into the Bronco and headed down to Marcasite and the Rural Resources office.

•••••••

Brogus parked in front of Carrie's office surprised to see her pacing the sidewalk in front of the big, plate glass windows fronting the street. The clever displays of a simulated mountain stream flowing amid the variety of indigenous flora usually drew pedestrians to stop and gawk at the lifelike reproduction. Today, Carrie's frantic presence not only obscured the window, but discouraged anyone from lingering by the storefront to check out the model.

Before he could even open the door to step down, she pulled wide the passenger door and jumped in.

"I have to go look for him," she blurted out before she had even buckled the seatbelt properly, which was a challenge in her agitated state as she kept missing the catch.

He looked over at her struggling with the apparatus and leaned across to take the restraint from her shaking hands, securely shoving the ends together.

She looked up sheepishly, "Thanks."

"So where do we begin our search?"

Trying to calm herself down enough to think, she leaned her head back against the headrest and said simply, "I don't know…"

"Let's start with the basics," he laid his hand over her slightly trembling one. "Go through his routine. Do you know what it is?"

"Sort of. Gordon told me a little when I talked to him."

"And was he worried about," he grasped around the air, trying to remember the name she'd given him earlier, "what's his name… Sully?"

"Yes and no." Her breathing was becoming more regular. "He just said that he hadn't seen him. Curry assumed that Sully was asleep and couldn't, or wouldn't, wake up when he banged on his bedroom door this morning. Occasionally he likes to ignore Gordon and then comes bombing in at the last minute, though they often drive together." The words flew out in her haste to get going.

"Slow down. It always helps to have a plan when looking for someone."

"You've done this before?"

"It was only once when a kid got lost up on the mountain. Wandered off from the hunting camp while his dad was getting water at the creek. Now, *he* was frantic with worry. Even though the kid was 15 and knew the drill, he also knew that he wasn't supposed to leave camp by himself." Brogus stared out the windshield at nothing.

"Did you find him?"

"Yeah, we found him the next day not a mile from the camp, ensconced by his own little fire, keeping watch over a ten-point buck that he'd followed and nailed with his new rifle. He was freezing his tail but wasn't about to leave his prize to the cougars and wolves." He put the truck in gear as he peered over at Carrie. "His dad would've brained him if he hadn't been so proud of the boy's kill. It was enough meat to feed the family for a month or more." He grinned as he backed out of the space.

She grimaced at the thought of someone taking the life of a beautiful denizen of the forest, but moved on. "So they taught you search tactics?"

"Yeah, you get a crash course in search and rescue when you go out to find lost hikers and such. It's usually the inexperienced ones that get themselves in trouble. You know, day trekkers from the city. Hunters rarely end up in a mire, they're careful, well, most of the time. They know just how dangerous the wilderness is."

He pulled into traffic and asked her where the boys lived. Steering him back onto the highway, she gave him directions to the rental property a few miles out of town.

As he came around a curve, the landscape opened up into a wide, flat zone that harbored a mobile home park and a few houses bunched together on the right side of the road. She pointed to a little cottage that was situated at the back of a larger house with some grand, old sugar maples marching up the drive.

She frowned at the trunks as they drove by.

"What's wrong now?"

"They could have at least planted trees native to the area," she said, disapproving of the grandparents' choice of tree.

That earned her a hearty guffaw from Brogus. "Maybe they just wanted some fall color or something to remind them of their roots back east. You can take your environmental agenda too far at times. Ease up, girl."

She shook her head like she was coming up from a dive, gasping for air. "Hunh? Oh yeah. But even these things can affect the eco-system."

"Well, apparently these haven't because I don't see any wild maples of this species hereabout, do you?"

"No. Never mind. We need to check to see what's happened to Sully, not discuss environmental practices of the locals."

"I'd say," he agreed good-humoredly as he parked in front of the cottage.

Before she could unhook her seatbelt, he was out of the truck and wandering around the premises, looking for anything unusual.

"Do you know whose car this is?" He pointed to a twelve-year old Subaru that had seen better days.

"It's Sully's." She poked around the side and back of the building. "His bike isn't here," she called out from the other side of the house.

"Looks like we can assume that he did come home last night and simply decided to sleep in or couldn't be wakened by his roommate's knocking, then took his bike when he was ready to go." He walked up and checked the front door handle. It turned easily so he walked inside. "Suppose there isn't much reason to lock up around here."

She followed him inside. "Do you think we should be in here?"

"Just don't touch anything. I want to make sure that there's nothing weird going on. Then we'll know whether or not our hypothesis holds water." He wandered through the small edifice, noting the dirty dishes in the sink and the discarded clothes on the floor of one of the bedrooms.

"Any idea whose room is which?" he asked.

"If I had to guess, I'd say that Sully's room would be the messy one. He doesn't seem like a real tidy sort though he's always presentable," she ventured.

"Another uncommon trait among single male college students...hygiene." He smirked as he scratched his ginger colored beard thoughtfully.

"You would know," she said recalling a past life.

"Was I that bad?" he asked, a little hurt at her tone.

"No. Though there was one comedian who put it rather well back then. What was it he said? Oh yeah, 'you can always tell a bachelor pad. They live like bears in a cave.' Or something like that."

He rolled his eyes and laughed. "Looks like you haven't visited often enough. I don't think my *pad* looks anything like a shabby cave."

"Yeah, well this does. But I don't see anything here."

"No. Do you know his bike route? Does it deviate from the road, anywhere?" He moved the conversation back to the matter at hand.

"Don't think so. Is there any other way down the hill besides the road?"

"Not really. We'd better drive back to town and take our time checking the side of the road," he put in nonchalantly, which didn't work because her panic meter immediately elevated.

"Why? What are you thinking?" Her voice began to get a little shrill.

"I'm not thinking anything. Let's just check the road for sign."

Not wanting to contemplate anything along the lines of where she thought Brogus was going with his comments, she darted out of the cottage and climbed back into the Bronco, fastening the seatbelt without problem this time.

•••••••

He turned back onto the highway and started driving south slower than the posted speed limit.

"What are we looking for?"

"Keep your eyes open for anything odd," replied Brogus.

"Like what?" Her vision was scanning the highway and the shoulder, not knowing what to focus on.

"Look for skid marks, breaks in the brush or dents in the guardrail," he stated without inflection, hoping to keep her calm enough to look.

"But what if you were right and he just went down the hill to Lathrop or something?"

"What did you tell me? That he would've called. So, however distressing this might be, we'd better assume that he might have had an accident." He thought for a minute. "Does he have a cell phone?"

"If he does, he doesn't bother with it here. You know how crummy the service is."

"Particularly if you have one from out of the area," he agreed. "Just keep looking."

As they rounded a curve that required traffic to slow to 25 mph, Carrie yelled out something incomprehensible.

She caught him off-guard enough that he almost slammed on the brakes, but instead pulled over to the side and stopped by the crest of the outside turn. Looking at her face, which seemed to have drained of blood giving her the pallor of a vampire, all he could say was, "what did you see?"

"I don't know if I saw anything," she replied in a small voice. "I *thought* I saw a crumpled span of the guardrail right back there." She pointed back about 20 yards.

He took her hand and gently clasped it. "Don't get too excited. A lot of people have taken this bend too fast and banged into the railing." Letting go of her, he got out of the Bronco and walked back up the shoulder to examine the stretch of metal railing. What he saw were some relatively fresh skid marks made by thin tires - bicycle tires - and they led directly over the edge of a 200-foot drop.

Carrie came running up beside him to look at the disturbed gravel and the scratches and buckling of the white guardrail that lay in a direct line from the skids. She followed Brogus to the edge of the precipice and the two of them looked down the rocky side of the mountain.

A hundred feet down the side of the hill, lodged in the scree, they saw the crumpled, twisted frame of a racing green road bike. Thirty feet beyond the remains of the bicycle lay a figure outfitted in red and black, sprawled across the loose rock of the slope like a broken toy action figure.

"Oh God," she murmured and turned her head into Brogus' chest, tears soaking his shirt while he soothingly combed his fingers through her hair. Using his free hand, he fished out his cell phone and checking that he had a signal, dialed 911.

•••••••

It took twenty minutes for the sheriff's deputy to arrive with the rescue crew on its way, still fifteen minutes down the road. By that time Carrie had been re-deposited in the passenger seat of the Bronco, a sheaf of napkins from a fast food place, taking the place of tissues, were clutched in her fist.

Deputy Tolman dropped down from the four-wheel drive cruiser and approached Brogus, who stood by his rig's open door, offering what little comfort he could to Carrie as she sniffled uncontrollably.

"The dispatcher didn't have any real information for me other than there was an accident?" he inquired carefully, noting how distraught the passenger was. "Was this vehicle involved?" He scanned the rig for obvious damage.

Brogus sighed and motioned the deputy away from the car and Carrie's hearing.

"No. I'm afraid that a bicyclist has gone over the side here and we found him not half an hour ago." He drew Tolman to the point where Sully had apparently gone off the road.

Leaning over the guardrail, the deputy noted the bike and the fractured form of a man lying some distance down the side of the mountain.

"Did you see him go over?"

Brogus shook his head 'no.' "We assume that this is Sully Tyson, who was working as a summer intern for Carrie, Ms. DiMarco," and he gestured back toward the Bronco. "He didn't show up for work this morning and knowing him to be prompt, she got worried and called me to find out what to do. We went to his house to look for him and, seeing that he wasn't there, we started looking along the road for sign of his passage. She spotted the damage to the guardrail and, well, you get the picture." He shrugged.

Tolman wagged his head at the wastage. "We won't know for sure who it is until the EMT's get here. They were called at the same time but it takes them longer to scramble being a volunteer unit. I just happened to be on my way up to Marcasite as it was. All we can do is wait right now."

He went back over to the edge of the cliff to assess the position of the casualty. Looking back toward Brogus' rig he said, "It's going to take a while to recover the body - it looks like he's pretty obviously dead - and the bike. She looks like she's pretty upset so you'd be better off to take her back to town and wait for the sheriff to call. Is there anyone else who can make the identification? It might be good to spare her the trauma."

"I don't think so. He has a roommate but Tyson was her employee and charge, in a manner of speaking. I think she'll insist on taking responsibility for as much as she can," he said sadly, wishing that he could help Carrie more. He'd had one of his own workers get hurt badly on the job once and tried to do whatever he could to alleviate some of the anguish of the man's family. He didn't envy Carrie's position.

Tolman went to his truck and retrieved a pen and pad. "Why don't you give me your name and hers, contact number and the probable name of the victim again. I've called the sheriff to come up and examine the scene. He'll also want you to make an official statement later."

Brogus gave him the information and went back to the Bronco to drive Carrie back down to Marcasite just as the ambulance came up the hill. He checked back over his shoulder to see the deputy jotting down notes as he greeted the rescue squad to fill them in on the situation. She wasn't ready to go back to the office yet and insisted on waiting while they watched the rescue team rig their equipment to support a climber and the lowering of a stretcher down the slope to retrieve Sully, or who they thought was Sully.

Although they were waiting for the sheriff's appearance, one of the team was preparing to rappel down the slope to ascertain the state of the victim and undertake rescue if the bicyclist was still alive. The activity prompted Brogus to convince Carrie to leave the experts to their work and return to the office to wait for Sheriff Stellenbeck's call. He didn't want her sitting by the roadside and witnessing the state of the victim when they brought him to the top.

She acquiesced without argument so he started the truck and drove back to town.

•••••••

Forty-five minutes later, Carrie was standing by the window, staring out into space and Brogus, tilted back in a secretarial chair, feet on her desk with ankles crossed, was staring at her.

Finally deciding to break the uneasy silence, he asked point blank, "What do you know about this?"

"Nothing." The answer was monotone but unconvincing.

"Un-unh. Don't give me that. You guessed something. That's why you were so anxious." He paused for a few moments. "What have you been up to here?"

"Nothing."

"I don't believe that. I'll bet Sully was something of a troublemaker and I think he was involved in raising some hell. I also think that you knew about it or at the least, suspected something."

She refused to turn around and he just bored holes into her back with his unyielding stare. Getting no response, he got out of his chair and walked up behind her thinking that it might intimidate her enough to own up to whatever was going on. Instead she just lowered her gaze, so he put his hand under her chin while he stepped around to look directly into her eyes.

"Tell me. You're so frightened you must believe that something else could happen."

"You're wrong. Nothing's been going on." But her voice quivered slightly, giving her away.

"You're lying. You've never been a good liar." He let go of her and just stood next to her looking out the window. "You never cultivated the art form.

"He was involved in the Powell arson fires, wasn't he."

She tried to conceal her shock at his guess.

"No!"

He didn't think she was credible despite her exclamation.

"Yes. I thought it was just a little too pat with these landowners having financial problems and the other catastrophes falling out of the sky so suddenly…and you know, or think you know, something about it."

Carrie couldn't stand feeling so naked and turned away, her eyes brimming with tears from the pain of Sully's demise and her growing apprehension. All she could do was shake her head trying to negate his statements.

For the time being he dropped the interrogation and started wandering aimlessly around the office.

"I'm going to get some coffee," he finally said. "You want anything?"

She just continued to shake her head side-to-side while he pulled open the door and left.

•••••••

Two hours later the ringing of the phone broke the uneasy silence. Brogus reached over and picked up the handset since Carrie didn't seem inclined to move from her frozen stance gazing into space.

The voice of Sheriff Stellenbeck betrayed surprise in response to Brogus' manner of answering the Rural Resources office phone, which was a brusque "Brogus here."

"Billy? What are you doing there? I thought I'd dialed the wrong number."

"'Fraid not, Sheriff. Ms. DiMarco is a little too upset to handle calls right now and the other kid, Curry, is still out at the school. I gather he's helping them with the garden," he said in lieu of explanation.

"I didn't know you two knew each other."

"Oddly enough, we went to college together. Have you got any

293

information for us?" He was wary of asking too much in Carrie's presence.

"The bicyclist that went off the road had his driver's license in his backpack, which we found another 20 feet or so from the body…"

Brogus interrupted him. "So he was dead?" He had turned away from Carrie and lowered his voice.

"Oh. Yes. He had already been dead for a number of hours, killed when he vaulted over the edge. Neck broken in two places." He took a breath. "The license identified him as Sullivan Tyson and he carried papers that indicated he was working at Rural Resources there. Is Ms. DiMarco in any shape to come down and make a positive I.D.?"

Brogus turned around to see Carrie hadn't moved or acknowledged the conversation going on behind her.

"I think she can manage it. Probably better to get it over with." He sighed and rubbed his temple with his other hand. "Where do we go?"

"I'll meet you at Marcasite County Hospital. Go into the Emergency entrance and they'll direct you to the morgue." He was about to hang up when Brogus asked another question.

"Sheriff? Did they retrieve the bike?"

"Yeah, not having to rush the victim back to the hospital, they took the time right then to bring the bike up the hill. Why?" Now he was curious about Brogus' interest.

"Do you know if they happened to find anything out of the ordinary?"

"Have you been talking to Gary Mathers?" the sheriff asked incredulously.

"Who? No, why?"

"Never mind." He was quiet a few seconds while he digested the implications of Brogus' question. "But, yeah, it looks as if the brake lines were jimmied."

"Jimmied?"

"Hmm, maybe not the right word. They were disconnected, like they had come loose. I don't think it could've happened without a little outside help. The ends were just dangling. Since the bike showed signs of regular maintenance and we found a well-used tool set in the backpack, I imagine he kept the brakes in good condition too, unless he was just plain stupid."

"From what I've heard, Sully was a hellion but definitely not dumb. Thanks, Sheriff, we'll see you shortly."

Land Barons

Chapter 44

After seeing the body, Carrie turned away and just started crying. Brogus wrapped her in his arms and led her to the anteroom of the morgue.

The sheriff, who had been standing at the foot of the gurney while the attendant had uncovered Sully's face, followed them through the ceiling-high double doors. Earlier, the medical examiner had made an effort to realign the unnatural angle of the neck so the image wouldn't be such a shock when viewing the dead man.

"Do you recognize him as Sullivan Tyson?" the sheriff asked once the doors swung closed behind him with a whoosh.

Carrie nodded her head almost imperceptibly and answered, "yes,' in a bare whisper.

"Is that all you need for now, Sheriff?" Brogus wanted to get Carrie as far away from the hospital as possible.

"For now, but I will need to get statements from both of you about how you came to find him." He was trying to be sympathetic but realized that he needed as much information as he could get as soon as he could get it.

"Sure. We'll be in your office first thing in the morning. Will that do?"

"I'd like to have answers sooner but I don't think we'd get too far tonight," he said as he looked at the pitiable form cradled in Brogus' arms. "You oughtta just take her home," and he turned to exit the building.

"Thanks, Sheriff." Stellenbeck waved backwards, acknowledging Brogus as he strode down the hall.

•••••••

On the drive back up to Marcasite, Brogus couldn't help but to ponder why Sully had been targeted for death. He was having trouble connecting up the misfortunes of the local landowners and any possible motive, let alone Sully's or Carrie's involvement. His gut was telling him there was a connection, nonetheless. *But what the hell is it?* He was getting frustrated even though he'd managed to add up Sully with the fires, which Carrie's reaction at the office showed that he was right on track. She either knew or suspected the same thing.

He just couldn't understand how or why she would be mixed up in any skullduggery, but it made him wonder if she had any involvement with the death of the rancher the week before. He didn't like thinking that she would get tangled up in some outlandish plot, but her foolish 'right' thinking had always made her vulnerable to committing some stupid exploits at someone else's behest.

At least, every dumbass move he'd ever made had been for his own reasons and no one else's, and just about every one of them had boiled down to a profit line. *Well, you gotta have your priorities*, he thought bitterly. *At least Carrie has always tried to follow some high - er calling, however misguided.* But he still couldn't figure out why some people thought they knew more than others about how they should live their lives. *Damn the whole lot of over-educated assholes.* The entire set of circumstances just pissed him off as he looked over at her dejected figure peering listlessly out the Bronco's window.

Tired of his line of reflection, particularly since no answers were forthcoming, he told her that he was taking her home.

"No, I need to go back to the office."

"It's already locked up. What do you need there? You've already talked to the other kid, Curry."

"I have to call Sully's parents," she said without enthusiasm.

"No," he stated bluntly. "You can do that tomorrow when you're more in control of your emotions. The sheriff is taking care of the notification. That's his job." He went on without sympathy, "you need to figure out how deeply involved you are in this mess and what you have to do to extricate yourself."

She snapped her head up and whipped it around to glare at him.

"What do you mean 'involved,'" she spat.

"It's pretty obvious you have some clue as to what's going on here and I think you're just dumb enough to be involved, even if it is peripherally," and he glared back at her. "You're always busy telling people what's right, but I think you took your self-righteous environmentalism too far this time."

"What the hell do you know," she said in a voice low and hard, swinging her eyes back to the window. "I didn't have anything to do with Sully's misfortune."

He was livid now.

"Didn't you hear me talking to the sheriff? It was no accident." He paused to let the information sink in. "I'm taking you home so you can get your story straight for tomorrow when you make your statement. He's not going to be as easy on you as I am."

She barked an indignant laugh. "Yeah, you've been the epitome of compassion."

They descended into an uneasy silence for the rest of the trip. He pulled into her carport, and when he got out, walked briskly around the car, opened the door before she could do it herself and offered to help her down. She just pushed his hands away and brushed past him to the side door. Her hands were steady as she turned the key in the lock and was too slow in attempting to slam the door in his face. He just bullied past her and closed the door behind him, standing in the mudroom with his hands on his hips, daring her to stand her ground instead of running into the interior of the house.

To her credit, she stood with her arms stiffly at her sides and glowered at him murderously.

"You're going to stay put and I'll take you back to your car in the morning after we see the sheriff to make our statements. Then we're going to figure out what we're going to do." He dared her to defy him.

"What do you mean we? I thought this was my mess." She softened her stance a little.

"Obviously, two heads are better than one so I'm volunteering to be the extra cranium in this caper."

Carrie couldn't help herself but gave into the relief with a visible collapse of her shoulders and unclenching her hands. He dropped his own belligerent posture and came over to her, smoothing her hair from her brow and bending down to lightly kiss her forehead.

"Do you want me to stay?"

"No."

"Fine, I'll be back in an hour with some dinner," and he steered her into the living room.

"I'm not hungry."

"Too bad. You haven't eaten all day and you're no good to me weak and weepy," he spun her into the sofa and sat her down. She just gave him a dirty look.

"See you in a bit and," he bent over and gave her a no-nonsense look, "don't go anywhere."

•••••••

Turned out she didn't have to go anyplace, he found her there.

She finally picked up the phone on the sixth ring. The voice on the other end was cool and deep.

"For a minute there, I thought you weren't going to answer the phone."

"I almost didn't," she said trying to appear composed when she felt as if her stomach was going to turn inside out.

"It's better that you did. Tell me what your friend knows."

"He doesn't know anything. For that matter, neither do I," she sounded slightly acerbic in her response. "He was just helping me try to find my employee, who, unfortunately, we found after the fact."

"I heard." He was quiet for a beat. "Are you sure that's all there is?"

Trying to grasp the idea that this man already knew about Sully, she fell into a momentary silence.

"Carrie…"

"Uh," she climbed back to the surface. "Yes. Positive."

"You make sure he stays out of this. You don't need anyone poking around your activities."

"I don't have any *activities,* so there's nothing to worry about,' she said flatly.

"You just keep that mantra, because I know differently." The phone went dead.

Carrie set the receiver back in its cradle and sank back into the couch, hugging her knees to her chest, rocking back and forth.

Chapter 45

It was fairly early when Carrie and Brogus made their way back down to Lathrop to meet the sheriff. Stellenbeck had caught her at home at 8:00 a.m. to inquire as to when they'd be in to give their statements regarding Sully's accident the previous day. Although she tried prevaricating, he was firm in stating his requirements since the accident appeared to be anything but, not that he actually voiced that opinion during the brief conversation. Billy, having listened to her side of the call, understood her attempt to put off the inevitable after her erratic behavior the day before, careening between belligerence, terror and despair. After he had returned with supper in hand, she had been even less forthcoming on what he deduced was her unwitting role in Sully's death. Watching her flip from one extreme to another he had insisted on spending the night to make sure she didn't try anything desperate. Though he hadn't really believed Carrie capable of doing herself serious damage, he wasn't willing to take any chances either. There was also the possibility that she might be in danger, which only doubled his determination to camp out for the night.

Now, as he steered down the road, he frequently cast an eye across the console at Carrie, but she just remained statue-like in the passenger seat, her gaze unmoving from the centerline as they drove. Unwilling to open a dialogue that would only exacerbate the situation, he kept his mouth shut and his hands on the wheel.

•••••••

Brogus tugged open the heavy glass and metal door of the sheriff's office, thinking it could use a better counter-weight, and stood aside to allow Carrie to enter. They walked up to the reception area and were promptly met by the deputy, Tolman, who had insisted on being present despite the fact that it was his Sunday rotation to be off work. He leaned back against the dispatcher's desk and hitched his thumbs in his belt and looked down at Carrie.

"How are you doing, Miss DiMarco?" His query was made in a

301

somewhat frosty manner. Brogus' back stiffened.

"I'm fine, thanks." She replied without noticing the deputy's attitude.

"Well, I'm sure it was a shock seeing your boy down at the bottom of the cliff."

This time she bristled a little in response. Billy noticed and squeezed her shoulder in warning.

"It's hardly what I wanted to find."

"You seemed to know where to look for him…" he let the insinuation trail off.

"What's your point, Deputy," Brogus jumped in before Carrie lost her composure under his scrutiny.

"Just that it appears awfully convenient that Miss DiMarco took you right to the scene of the accident." He dared Brogus to challenge his assumption.

"It also seemed the most likely place where someone could lose control of a bike or a car. That part of the road is notorious."

Sheriff Stellenbeck emerged from his office and indicating to Tolman that he would conduct the questioning, walked up, shook both their hands and invited them into his sanctum. Pointing to the chairs in front of his desk, he settled himself behind the scarred metal surface and asked if they minded him recording the interview.

"I don't take very good notes and this way I won't miss anything," he offered in explanation.

"No problem, Sheriff. Just hope that we can help," replied Brogus. Carrie simply nodded her head in agreement, a sad smile pasted on her face.

Stellenbeck started off by noting the date, time and place of the interview, adding the identification of both of the people seated across from him as well as himself.

"Just tell me the sequence of events to the best of your recollection, starting at the beginning."

Carrie started talking about waiting on the arrival of her employee for several hours before calling Billy in a panic.

The sheriff stopped her there for more detail.

"Do you normally keep hours on Saturday?"

"We often have special projects going. Yesterday, the boys were supposed to help the teacher at the elementary school who oversees the garden. It was the only day he had to prepare the soil for the children to plant their summer flower garden on Monday. The summer school classes will be watching the progress as a science project," she elucidated and would have kept going except for the sheriff's indication that the information she'd provided was sufficient.

"Except Sullivan Tyson never showed," he stated.

She shook her head. "No, he never got there and Gordon called to ask me when he was coming to help with the rototiller. I had simply assumed that he'd gone directly to the school but Gordon told me he hadn't shown up. That's when I started to get worried."

Stellenbeck indicated that she should continue and the tale went back and forth between her and Brogus until they reached the point where the deputy had arrived on the scene.

As they finished, the sheriff depressed the 'stop' button and thanked them for coming into the office. He was about to stand up when Brogus broached the subject of the bicycle.

"Have you confirmed that the brakes didn't come apart accidentally?"

The sheriff's brow crinkled in concern. "The state police took the bike and backpack as evidence and have a forensic team checking them out," he told them.

"Will you let us know what the final determination is?" Brogus asked while Carrie sat with her head down, uncomfortable listening to the possible circumstances of Sully's untimely demise.

"Sure," he said rising from his seat. He held out his hand to Brogus, then came around the desk to take Carrie's arm, kindly escorting her from the office. "We'll be in touch. I may have some other questions down the line."

Tolman sat on the edge of the dispatcher's desk, stoically watching as Brogus nodded and the couple exited the building.

•••••••

Having exhausted their investigative pursuits via the internet the day before, Anthea and Mathers decided it was time he checked out the homestead with a planned stop at the Miner's Gap for breakfast and the latest scuttlebutt first.

The café was experiencing a minor lull between the early after-church crowd and the late service attendees. Marcasite might be a small town, but the Methodist, Presbyterian, First Assembly of God, Catholic and Lutheran churches all had healthy membership rolls and the few cafés in the area all did a booming business on Sundays. The Miner's Gap, one of the few places that offered everything from bite-size to freshly baked gourmet treats *and* espresso (the Northwest staple), was a favorite for locals and visitors. Being such a popular restaurant, the two were lucky to be shown to an empty booth within five minutes of walking in the door.

Grabbing a discarded copy of the Sunday paper, Gary sat across from Anthea and parceled out the sections between them.

"This won't give us what we're looking for, but hopefully we'll hear what's been going on from the usual gossip mongers," he said leaning over and giving a sideways nod toward a couple of tables situated fairly close by.

She smiled in response as she unfolded the front page to scan the headlines which were more concerned with occurrences downriver, some 30 miles away.

The owner came by with a coffee pot in hand and a couple of mugs. While she approached, she raised the pot in the air as if to ask him if they were interested. Mathers gestured toward her that they'd be happy to indulge so she settled the cups on the table and filled them quickly and neatly.

"Thanks, Pat," he said gratefully. Anthea followed suit with her own words of thanks before taking her first sip. "Busy morning as usual, I see," he added hoping that he'd get a little feedback.

"Sure is…back in a minute for your orders," and she winked as she hurried off to take care of another customer who was signaling her.

"You'll have to try your charm on her a little later," Anthea turned sideways and copied Pat's wink. He ignored the dig and serenely drank his coffee.

It wasn't long before they overheard more news than they had anticipated. The buzz around town was the bicycle accident on Lilliot Road and it was flying from table to table as neighbors shared rumors. Their own talk having been kept to a minimum, it didn't take much to catch the gist of the jabber, which was that some college student had ridden his bike off the cliff at 'the curve.'

"I don't know how the kid managed it. He came down that road almost every day. Don't know how many times I had to avoid him on that bike of his," said a beefy fellow sitting down with two other men who looked like they'd just come in from some early morning fishing.

"I heard that he lost his brakes on the curve," filled in one of the other two guys who pulled off his ball cap and dropped it in the empty seat beside him.

"That still don't make any sense," added the beefy one. "He checked that contraption all the time. I used to see him messin' with that thing in front of the office like every other day."

"Guess he missed something the last time he worked on it," the third one lifted his mug for a drink and scratched his chin. "Too bad. Not that he wasn't kind of obnoxious. But then, we weren't much better at his age," he mused a little regretfully.

"Yeah, this must be killin' his parents. I know I'd be dyin' if that had happened to any of my kids," said the guy who'd removed his cap as he ran his fingers through his graying locks, unconsciously trying to lessen the look of hathair.

When Pat came back by after delivering an order, Mathers asked her who they were talking about at the other table.

"Oh, hadn't you heard? Yesterday morning, that Sully, who was working up here for the summer at Rural Resources… it's really terrible, but he died when his bike went over the side of Lilliot Road at the curve." She shook her head sadly. "Okay kid, liked to flirt with all the ladies. Kind of cute, you know?" she looked at Anthea as she asked, figuring another woman would understand how young men could be playful.

Anthea cocked her head. "What's 'the curve'?"

"Oh, that bend in the road outside of town that just sneaks up on you if you're not paying attention," she clarified. "Lot of accidents there."

"Does the sheriff think he just wasn't paying attention?" Mathers thought he'd find out if more than one person was talking about mechanical failure.

"Don't think so…heard it was the brakes went out, or some such. They found him yesterday around noon."

"Who did," Anthea asked, "do you know?"

"His boss and Billy."

"Billy?" Mathers probed further.

"Yeah." Turning back to look directly at him, her inflection went up, "Don't you know Billy? He runs Pinesap Farms, not that he comes into town all that much during the spring…too busy with the business."

"That's probably why we haven't met. Real sorry to hear the news, though." Gary looked down at his coffee cup for a second. "Thanks for the lowdown, Pat," he said as he raised his eyes again.

"No trouble. Your breakfast ought to be up soon. More coffee?"

Anthea smiled a little, "Sure, thanks."

She and Mathers exchanged looks across the table as Pat walked off to retrieve the coffee pot, and mouthed to each other, "brakes?"

Chapter 46

Returning to Marcasite, Brogus and Carrie discussed the strange attitude of Deputy Tolman.

"I don't understand what he was getting at," Carrie wagged her head in dismay. "That guy was just plain rude and purposefully cruel."

"He seems to think that you could have some kind of involvement in the accident. Remember, the sheriff said that the brakes were intentionally disconnected." He took a breath. "This 'accident' took planning on someone's part. I expect they'll be questioning the roommate too," he added.

Carrie started in alarm. "Gordon wouldn't have done anything like that. There wasn't any reason," her voiced raised a little in pitch. "He's a good kid, works hard at school and doing what he can to help protect the environment." She relaxed some. "No, he had nothing to do with it. I'm sure."

Billy just shrugged. "They have to find the culprit, if there is one, though I doubt Sully loosened the brakes himself. So they have to talk to everyone who might have had access to the bike."

"Yeah, I know," she calmed visibly. "I just hate to see anyone put through the wringer to no purpose. The whole thing is tough enough as it is."

"That's true but the sheriff's job is to ask questions and solve the riddle," he finished his sentence as he pulled into a slot right in front of the building. "You'd better expect to be grilled further because Tolman can't be the only one thinking there's something fishy going on at Rural Resources. I know I do." He let that dangle as he started to climb down from the Bronco.

She pinned him with an angry glare that was tinged with panic. "I already told you there's nothing going on."

"Right. And Bullwinkle is joining us for tea," he glared back.

She just clammed up and stared hatefully at his back until he turned after stepping down, and looked back accusingly. "If you haven't done anything, why are you so terrified?"

"I'm not," she backpedaled. "I'm just whipped." She sighed.

"With everything that's been happening these past few weeks, I'm an emotional zombie."

"What 'everything'?"

"Oh just the general uproar with the lumber mill, the rancher getting killed and now Sully," she said lamely. "That's an awful lot for a sleepy, little burg like this."

Unwilling to let her move from her seat just yet, he added more to the fire.

"You know as well as I do that sleepy, little burgs like this are a hotbed of passion. How do you think 'Peyton Place' made such a splash that now it's slang for exactly what we're talking about?"

"Look, Billy. I'm relatively new here, remember? And I don't know what usually goes on but I'm willing to bet arson and murder aren't part of it."

There, she said it. It's finally sinking in that this is not *normal.*

"Fine, let's just get you into the office," he made to close the door. "You now have the unpleasant duty of calling Sully's parents. I don't envy you."

Carrie unlocked the front door and pulled it open. She was ticked enough that she didn't bother to hold it open for Brogus but just kept walking, letting him catch the metal frame on his own.

Wanting to get the onerous task of having to call Sully's family with her condolences over with, Carrie went directly to her desk and started flipping through an old fashioned rolodex that sat in the upper left-hand corner.

"I didn't think anybody used those things anymore," Billy said in an attempt to cut the rancor in the air.

"It's actually faster than having to boot up the computer to look up a phone number and I'm not quite in the PDA mode yet." She started to reach for the phone and noticed a screwdriver sitting smack in the middle of the oversized calendar she used as a desk blotter.

"Billy."

He turned around to see what she wanted.

"Did you put this here?"

"No. Would the other kid, Curry, leave it there?"

"He hasn't been in since yesterday morning. He doesn't have a key." She reached to pick-up the object.

"Don't touch that." Brogus commanded as he came across the

room. "Someone left that there as a warning."

"What are you talking about?" Carrie was flustered and flopped down into the chair behind her desk.

"I think we'd better not touch anything else, either."

She just looked at him, puzzled. "What did you mean warning?"

"You know they think that the accident was not an accident and that the brakes went out, apparently not of their own volition," he gave her a meaningful look.

"But how does that relate to this," and she pointed at the offending implement on the desk.

"The sheriff told me that there was a tool kit in Sully's backpack and, if someone messed with the brakes, well…" he let the idea gel.

"You think this may be Sully's…" she just slumped back deeper into the chair and put her hands at her temples, pushing her chestnut hair to the top of her head and holding it there for a moment before dropping her arms and letting the bangs fall back across her forehead.

"And if it's not a message, it may have been left there to implicate you," he added in an undertone.

She bent over at the waist, her head on her knees. "Oh God…now what do I do," the desperation poured off her.

He came around to her side of the desk and, crouching down, put his hands on her shoulders.

"Just tell me what you know. I need to hear everything, you understand?"

She weakly nodded her head into her thighs, moaning with the burden of it all.

"We'll work it out from there."

•••••••

The last hour in the Miner's Gap gave Anthea and Gary more to chew on than their meal. They spent a little extra time mulling over their coffee to see if any of the new wave of diners had anything of interest to add to the general knowledge about the accident. After a while it became evident that no other information had hit the rumor mill, so they deemed it time to collect the scattered newspaper sections and head toward the cashier to pay the bill.

Pat flashed Gary a very friendly smile, which Anthea caught out of the corner of her eye, as he dropped the paper sections on top of the stack by the door. As they exited and he held the door for Anthea, she was about to bait him when a fellow with two espressos to go followed him to leave. Gary continued to hold the door open for him as well.

The man turned to thank Gary for his courtesy and stopped in his tracks. He stacked one cup on top of the other and holding out his right hand, he said, "You're Gary Mathers, right?"

Mathers was a tad surprised at the recognition and the outstretched offering of a handshake from a perfect stranger but responded with a polite grip and a simple, "Yes. We haven't met before…"

"No, but I saw you with the volunteer fire crew at the Powell fire a couple of weeks back. I'm Billy Brogus," he released Mathers' hand and redistributed the to go cups between his own.

Speak of the devil… thought Anthea as she slipped across the street and out of earshot. She wondered what this might be about but quickly concluded that her presence might hinder the conversation and fled unnoticed.

"We're all neighbors here. I know that everyone would come to my assistance under the same circumstances. I'm just sorry that we weren't able to make a difference." He hesitated a moment. "We heard about the bicycle accident just a little bit ago. That's a sad situation in itself." He let the subject lie.

"Yeah, don't like being the one to make that kind of discovery." He fastened his eyes on Mathers' as if deciding whether or not to plow ahead. "I heard that you were out at Ahlsted's place when he had his accident."

"I came by after I'd heard about the incident to see if I could be of any help since I live right down the road from them." He considered Brogus' interest in his past whereabouts and determined to throw out a hook for some fishing of his own. "You seem to be pretty well-informed on my activities, any reason for that?"

"It seems odd that there's been such a spate of destruction and accidental deaths lately, don't you think? I got the idea from the sheriff that you were the suspicious sort."

"And you mean that, how?" he arched an eyebrow. "That I suspect something nefarious or that I'm a nefarious suspect?" and he quirked up a corner of his mouth, sardonically.

"Both," replied Brogus with a straight face that belied the odd humor behind his eyes.

"So, what are you suggesting, Mr. Brogus?"

"Would you mind if I dropped by your place later today? It looks to me like we could have a pretty stimulating discussion on recent events."

Gary considered the man and his request. This guy looked like he harbored a dangerous streak underneath his backwoodsy look and general good ol' boy appeal. His curiosity took precedence over his wariness in the end.

"Sure," he said. "I'm up Lilliot Road two miles on the left. Name's on the mailbox."

"I'll find it. Thanks," and he nodded his head as if tipping his non-existent hat as he walked back up the street to the Rural Resources office.

Mathers went out to the truck, which was parked across the way. Anthea had watched the exchange from her vantage point standing next to the open passenger door. Since she had decided not to interfere with the men's meeting, she had just gone on ahead to the rig without looking back. When he reached the truck he came around to her side and helped her up, then went around to get in himself before he said anything.

"That was a strange encounter," he noted as he turned the key in the ignition.

"And why is that?" inquired Anthea calmly even though she was chomping at the bit for information. Seeing his pensive mood she didn't want to seem too eager.

"That was the infamous Billy Brogus, himself."

"Ah, the man of the hour," she added. "What did he want?" Now she was really interested.

"He just wants to chat." He looked over at her as she clipped her seatbelt in place. "I think he has some idea about the odd occurrences around here and he's coming to the house to 'discuss' them later."

It was her turn to arch her eyebrows in curiosity.

Land Barons

Chapter 47

A couple of hours later, Billy Brogus showed up on Mathers' front porch. He knocked on the solid oak door, and was examining the carved panel, standing with his hands stuck in his back pockets when it opened wide. Expecting to see the tall form of the owner in the doorjamb, he was surprised to have to lower his gaze almost a full foot to lock eyes with the petite woman that he had barely noticed when he stopped Mathers on the street earlier.

"Mr. Brogus?" she inquired in a voice that was a little lower in register than he had anticipated, her blue eyes slicing through him incisively.

Guy's full of surprises. Somehow I don't think she's the maid. At which thought a smile flickered across his lips, not quite hidden beneath his beard.

"That'd be me, ma'am," he said pleasantly.

She flashed him a lesser version of stinkeye at mention of the 'm' word, almost immediately replacing it with a broad smile. "Anthea will do just fine. Why don't you come in," and she stepped aside for him to enter.

Mathers approached from the direction of the kitchen, though he had been hovering just out of view of the doorway in order to check Brogus for any indication of malicious intent. Seeing nothing to raise his hackles, he stepped forward and welcomed his guest into his home.

"Why don't we sit around the table," he led the way to the informal dining area. "Can I get you anything to drink? We seem to be on an unending coffee kick. There's some fresh in the kitchen."

"Why not? It's not likely I'll get any sleep tonight anyway," accepted Brogus.

"Oh?"

"That's what I'm here to discuss with you," he said.

"Right, broken sleep patterns," mocked Mathers, leading the way.

Brogus sat down and then thanked Anthea who brought over a steaming cup and set it in front of him. Both she and Gary settled into their own chairs and, cradling their mugs, patiently waited for Brogus to take the first step.

Leaning back and crossing one ankle over his other knee, Brogus balanced the mug on his thigh. "You seem to have managed to show up just about everywhere at the most convenient, or is it 'inconvenient,' time lately. Pretty coincidental." He just let the words hang while he sipped his coffee.

"And your point?" Gary had his elbows on the table, and although he wasn't being confrontational, he wasn't particularly pleased with the insinuation, either.

"Got any clues as to what's going on?"

"You mean to suggest that something out of the ordinary is afoot?"

Brogus smiled at the dated term. "You don't think so?"

Gary looked across the table at Anthea, who thought she was going to be more of a spectator at this meeting. She shrugged, in effect telling him that he may as well continue.

"We've had our suspicions. We're just having trouble putting all the pieces together."

"I may be able to help with some parts of the puzzle," said Brogus as he took another swallow. "By the way, this is pretty good stuff," he said with a disarming grin aimed at Anthea.

"Hey, he's the brewmaster, I just class up the joint," she said straight-faced.

The standoff abruptly at an end, Brogus, who answered her comment with a grin, went into a detailed explanation of what he knew about the involvement of the Rural Resources employees. It boiled down to the director, Carrie DiMarco, being pressured to keep a close eye on some properties that she was led to believe would be coming onto the market soon. It seemed that someone supposedly representing Rural Resources' largest donor was demanding that she send out feelers to make inquiries about the operations at the properties of interest to them. As a result, she sent one of her interns to Ahlsted's place as a shill to gather information about the ranch. There was also the Powell lumber mill that burned along with a stand of timber they were preparing to log after an injunction to stop them had been overturned in court. At that point, she began to think that one intern, Tyson, might have actually torched the place though she didn't have any proof. When the kid met his end on the other side of the guardrail, she completely collapsed under the strain, particularly when she received another phone call from her 'handler' threatening her to keep quiet even though she really had no evidence or direct knowledge of any wrongdoing. He paused to get up and help himself to more coffee.

"You don't mind, do you?" he asked after he'd already begun to pour.

"Nah, make yourself at home. I do," replied Gary as he rose to refill his own cup.

"Did the intern ride down at the Riverside Trail very often, do you know?" asked Anthea. Gary caught her eye and immediately understood where she was going.

"I know this Sully was a bicycle enthusiast and he rode wherever he could, according to Carrie. Why?" Brogus looked across the counter at her as he made his way back to the table.

"I wonder if he was the one who ran into me down at the river," she said half to herself.

Billy looked at Mathers. "What's she talking about?"

"Seems that someone threatened Anthea not to meddle in their business and followed it up with a physical assault by bicycle when she went for her regular walk on the Riverside Trail. Whoever it was must have been watching her, and me, as we began to innocently arrive at scenes rather inconsiderately, to somebody's thinking." He turned his own thoughts inward while Brogus sat back and sipped at his coffee.

"Could your friend have sent her young goon to do any burgling, you think?" Mathers finally asked Brogus.

"Well, she did say that the voice on the phone had her keeping tabs on persons of interest." He stopped to think. "Now I know why she wouldn't elaborate. She was supposed to be watching you, wasn't she? Now why would the guy want that?" He threw the question at Mathers, holding the mug to his lips and skimming his eyes across the top to spear his host.

Gary ignored the crack. "Probably because we were getting suspicious about an organization called Nature's Wilds Conservancy and," he paused for effect, "from the sound of what you've brought to the table today…" Anthea choked on her coffee at the deadpan pun. "…he was right to be concerned."

Despite the heavy subject they were discussing, Brogus threw back his head and laughed. "Is this how all you old cops handled your investigations? You'd think that you didn't have an ounce of compassion." He smothered his laugh by taking another sip.

Gary gave him a hard stare. "Who told you I'd been a cop?"

"Are you kidding? Even if Sheriff Stellenbeck hadn't let it slip, your posture gives you away. Once a cop, always a cop."

"Spoken like a true outlaw." Mathers trained his eye on his guest. "You still skirting the legal system?"

Brogus wasn't bothered a bit by the implication. "What's it to you?"

"Actually, nothing. It's just good to know that I haven't lost my flair for pigeonholing hooligans," he said with a wry smile.

"Damn, could you two stick to the business at hand?" Anthea said, exasperated with their banter.

"Hey, guys will be guys," offered Billy in contrition.

"You mean 'boys'?" She knew she was being reeled in.

"We're too old for that."

"Yeah, and this insufferable wit, too," she said disgustedly. "I thought somebody had died, or was it two or three people." She skewered the two of them with a schoolmarm glare. The following silence was deafening.

Properly penitent they resumed comparing notes.

"Whatever the case, it looks like they did away with their messenger. Since it seems pretty certain that Tyson's brakes were tampered with," Brogus said acting as if they had never strayed from the original conversation.

"That's the talk around town," said Gary. "Do you have a reliable source?"

"Not only that, we have the murder weapon," Brogus stated flatly.

Both Anthea and Gary sat up and carefully placed their mugs on the table, looking hard at Brogus.

"Say what?" Mathers was instantly attentive.

"Looks like a simple phone call to my friend wasn't considered to be sufficient to get the idea across that she was to hold her tongue." He exhaled before going forward. "We found a screwdriver carefully deposited on her desk when we returned from the sheriff's office this morning. Believe me, it was enough to give both of us heart failure." He put his own mug on the placemat and propped his elbows on the tabletop.

"You called the sheriff, didn't you?" Mathers asked.

"I may have a healthy dislike of law enforcement but I'm not crazy. Of course we called Stellenbeck. Last thing either of us wanted was to be caught withholding evidence. Even at the risk of incurring the displeasure of the 'voice.'"

"There seems to be a pattern with this 'voice.' He seems to have a penchant for disabling brakes. Anthea's rig is in the shop now for repairs," explained Mathers.

Brogus just looked at him, disbelieving. "When did this happen?"

"Saturday morning. It's a long story but had she picked up her car Thursday night as expected, she would have gone off the edge of the road herself." He looked over at Anthea, her hair slipping out of its clip, letting tendrils trail down her neck. "It was damn lucky I checked under her rig before she drove off."

"The scale of this thing just gets bigger and bigger," Anthea added to the mix. "But we're still no closer to knowing why all this has been happening." Her frustration showed visibly on her face.

"I was hoping that putting our facts together might bring us closer to a solution because Carrie is scared out of her mind. It was enough that this guy called her and told her point blank that I should butt out of their business. Because, if these jokers weren't trying to frighten her with the screwdriver, then they were trying to implicate her, which wouldn't be too hard since she's already considered a suspect at this point." Brogus rubbed his forehead with concern.

"She should be scared." Anthea looked him directly in the eye. "Since someone tried to shoot out our tires as we were coming down Winchester Grade a couple of nights ago."

"What?"

"We were driving back from San Francisco." Mathers made the determination to lay all of it out in case Brogus was holding something back. He wanted him to understand the real nature of these bozos and how far they were willing to go. "Anthea was down there making a visit to the national headquarters of Nature's Wilds Conservancy and interviewing the director, ostensibly for an article she was writing." He stopped to draw a breath and then swallow some coffee, which was tasteless when he remembered how close he'd been to losing her and the promise of a new life. Without revealing the dark nature of his thoughts, he continued the narrative.

"Short story is that we were followed from Nevada until the guy made his move at sunset to try to force us off the road by taking pot-shots at the truck. Luckily his aim was off. Someone thinks we're onto their secret." He gazed directly at Brogus. "Are we?"

"Hell if I know. Looks like they've been putting pressure on local ranchers and others to sell property that appears to ring that lodge that Chamberlain built up on that mountain. At least, that's what it looks like in this light." He coolly applied himself to the work of enjoying more coffee but the name triggered a reaction he didn't expect.

"Chamberlain, the Solis exec?" Anthea's attention was intensified. "Wait, we hadn't gotten that far. Who owns that land? It's not Nature's Wilds I don't think, I thought that was national forest up there." She got up and started to dig into her portfolio, looking through paper-work.

Brogus put in a little more. "To my knowledge, it technically is, or was. You know there have been some land swaps made between some big developers and the forest service over the last few years. Like that one that happened down near Vegas where the USFS made a deal on an exchange, only this one was really low-key."

Anthea quit rummaging. "We know that Chamberlain has a num-ber of front corporations and philanthropic foundations through which he's been funneling funds to Nature's Wilds for land acquisition. We assumed something like that was going on here, but maybe they went a lot further this time and swapped this pristine area for some other lesser property in one of the conservancy's land caches." She looked at Mathers. "We didn't think of that." She muttered the next thought, "but why wouldn't it be recorded?" which slipped by unnoticed by the other two.

"So what'd he want with this location?" Mathers asked the gener-al audience.

"Are you kidding?" Brogus was amazed at their lack of compre-hension. "This lodge is an absolute palace with a heliport and landing strip. Not to mention snowmobile and ski trails. It commands an unheard of view of the waterfall and it's totally off the books and out-side of public knowledge. He can do anything he wants up there in absolute safety, not that I have any idea why he'd need that kind of pri-vacy…"

"You've been there?" Again Anthea was rocked by the goings-on

318

right under everyone's nose.

Not wanting to offer too much detail, considering he was yakking with an ex-cop, Brogus explained as best he could by trying to paint himself more as a witness.

"I had a little agreement with the, mmm, management that was to my advantage for a while," he said. "It was a give and take until they moved the workers out this last week. Looks like they've finished building." He mulled over how much to say, then just threw away caution. People were dying and Carrie could be on their hit list, not to mention himself.

"They've had illegal aliens making up their construction crew. They secretly bus them in from Mexico and then shuttle them back over the border. It's kept the work under the radar. So far as I know, no one knows what's being built on the mountain. Basically, they're trafficking in illegal labor in order to avoid the prying eyes of the county or even the feds. It backs federal land and it looks like they've swapped a good chunk of that real estate for land elsewhere, if you add in your information. I'm pretty sure they have some legislators in their pockets on this, though I'm not sure who. Except, wait… I could almost swear that I saw Congressman Heubert there once. How else can you build a castle without a fanfare?"

The room was quiet while Gary and Anthea digested the new data.

"You'd think that some locals would stumble across the construction site," Mathers said half aloud.

"Not unless they were up there illegally," began Brogus, matter-of-factly. "Access has been cut-off since the Roadless Act went into affect. The USFS doesn't even go up there, not since they returned the road to its 'natural' state. It's been a growing practice in a number of areas of national forest."

"So how did you know about it?" asked Anthea.

"I was up there. Illegally, of course," he smiled roguishly.

"Man, this just gets worse the more doors we open." Mathers massaged his temples as he tried to absorb the enormity of the iceberg they'd just plowed into.

The three simply sat and cogitated over the facts they'd compiled until Anthea got up to make another pot of coffee.

"I thought you said he was the barista?" asked Billy in an attempt to assuage the heavy atmosphere.

"He's a pretty good teacher," and she continued with her small stab at domesticity.

"We have to decide where this is all going," Mathers said after listening to the coffeemaker drip for a while. "Is this as big a scam as I think and if it is we need real evidence to blow a hole in their plans."

"Yeah, if we can figure out what *those* are," added Brogus humorlessly.

"Such optimism," observed Anthea.

"Well, what have we got so far beyond alleged bad deeds to unsuspecting members of the community who otherwise just look like they've had a run of rotten luck?"

"Good point, but," and she went back to her portfolio to extract a yellow legal pad that had pages of handwritten notes from their most recent research, "there are numerous financial ties between Chamberlain/Solis and Nature's Wilds. Many that may be illegal donations, i.e. money laundering activities – particularly if he's using conservancy trust land for personal benefit, a definite no-no. Remember what brought down the Tyco chief, Kozlowski," she said looking up from her notes. "That $2 million toga party and resultant mutual fund scandal was penny ante in comparison to what it looks like this character is pulling off. This is far more convoluted and could run into *hundreds* of millions of detoured funds."

As she continued, Brogus went to the kitchen to grab the coffee pot and refill everyone's mug. Gary accepted with surprise as he poured.

"Hey, we all gotta pitch in, right?" Billy said, chuckling, to which Mathers nodded in acceptance, allowing Anthea to continue her monologue.

"We also found evidence of that at another chalet the man has erected at Lake Tahoe and from what the gatekeeper had to say, that spot is pretty much for personal use as well, or, at the least, Solis business use. Still not kosher." She leafed through her notes, "Let's see what else. Right, looks pretty certain that they used strong-arm tactics to accelerate land acquisition. That's circumstantial but each of the properties in question were bought by the conservancy at a firesale due to a series of unfortunate events. They've been dealing in illegal labor and transporting aliens across the border. Corporate coyotes," she shook her head in disgust. "Oh, and let us not forget that they even stooped to building without a permit."

The last charge in the list brought about light laughter from everyone. "So we can sic the union and the building inspector on them," said Brogus sarcastically.

"Trouble is, none of it is really solid aside from the last issue, which is also the least serious infraction." Mathers brought the mood back to earth. "We still don't have a direct tie to any henchman other than what we suspect, with Tyson gone and only your director friend's word that she's been receiving calls. Who knows if the two are even related?"

"And there's no way I'll let her open her mouth. From my perspective it would be a death sentence. You need to find another way to prove their intent to defraud landowners," Brogus set aside the jolly good fellow role and let the steel show through. Mathers had been expecting it sooner or later. The guy was no pushover, nor was he a fool.

Mathers decided to line it out. "Let's see what they've done? The arson...the probable perpetrator is dead and nothing but hearsay or conjecture to tie him to Nature's Wilds, let alone Chamberlain. Ahlsted's so-called accident...no real leads. The police have no idea who might have engineered that beaut, though they're working all the angles. So far we have two deaths that appear to be related, maybe, and both appear to be murder but no apparent motive. Then we have the Stablers and I'm convinced that their selling out was also manipulated."

"How can that be?" Brogus was confused on that score.

"I was up there two weeks after the family moved and the whole kit 'n' caboodle had been dismantled, board by board and sold off at a profit. One of the 'hotheads' chased me off with a rifle as opposed to simply, and politely, I might add, escorting me off the property. What were they trying to hide?"

"Those poor folks had bad harvests for three years running. The canola fields were ravaged by pests that simply couldn't be eradicated. I never really thought about it but it's almost like the buggers were reintroduced after every treatment, because what they used was standard and works most everywhere else." Brogus became pensive. "And then Mary got ill so quickly. She didn't last six months and the doctors never did diagnose the problem."

"Poison?" Anthea threw it out without thinking.

"Never occurred to me. She was the epitome of health beforehand. Always working in the garden, that was her passion. She wouldn't let anyone touch her herb patch, not even to water. That was forbidden territory."

"I doubt that anyone even thought of poison and I'd lay money that there was no post-mortem either, let alone toxicology testing," said Mathers.

Anthea asked if there was any way to introduce a poison that wouldn't affect the plants.

"Could be, I guess" Brogus replied, "but it's nothing I know anything about. The thing is that she's the only one who got sick. Not the kids and not her husband and it didn't take six months to put her in the grave."

"They got tired of waiting on the repeated crop failures, same as they were too impatient to wait for Ahlsted's cattle losses to cripple him enough to sell," surmised Mathers. "But they made a mistake in Ahlsted's case. Looks like they may not have done their homework because I heard that his life insurance is more than sufficient to keep the ranch in family hands."

"Aha, foiled again," and Billy tried to look villainous by twisting the ends of his short mustache. Oddly enough, he was fairly successful despite the idiocy of the joke.

"Lord, who let him in?" queried Anthea.

"You have no one to blame but yourself," said Brogus with a smile.

"Back to the point," said Mathers. "How badly do they want that land and how far are they willing to go now?"

"We'll have to get some real evidence before they get a chance to do anything else," Brogus stated, setting aside all comedic tendencies. "What you need is the poison, if that's what it was, that killed Mary Stabler and the element that's killing Ahlsted's beef. Think they used the same thing?"

"No idea," said Mathers. "I don't know a damn thing about the subject. I can assume that either they haven't determined Ahlsted's problem or someone's covering up the results."

"Okay, so how do we find out?" Anthea asked pragmatically.

"You do what you have to. My involvement ends here," Brogus stood to go. "I just had to make sure someone else was on the same page."

"So why not take it to the sheriff?" said Gary.

"No. I'm not sending Carrie into harm's way. Nor am I sticking my neck out."

Gary's curiosity kicked in. "Too much to hide?"

Billy pushed in his chair and grinned, "Just a fondness for privacy." Shaking Mathers' hand once more, he was escorted to the door and wished them good luck as it closed behind him.

•••••••

Sometime during the afternoon as the three volleyed the facts back and forth playing 'pin the crime on the felon,' Deputy Tolman drove by on his way back to town. What caught his attention was that he recognized the black Bronco parked next to Mathers' rig at his house. The sight definitely set his imagination running as to what those two could possibly have in common.

Land Barons

Chapter 48

While cleaning up the coffee paraphernalia, Anthea asked Gary if he was very familiar with the Stabler place.

"Sort of. I'd been to visit a few times." He looked at her quizzically, "Why?"

"I was wondering if you know where Mary Stabler's garden was located."

"Yes," he looked at her harder. "Again, why?"

"I'm not sure yet," she said as she grabbed a towel and began drying her hands. "We need to reassess our information and see where to go next." She hung the towel on the oven handle and walked back over to the table where her notes were lying. Standing with her hands flat on the tabletop on either side of her pad, she leaned forward and began to pore over the scribbles that only she could decipher.

After a few minutes of silence she looked up at Gary who was leaning against a cabinet watching her intense scrutiny of the pad, a look of bewilderment on her face.

"I still can't figure how Sully was involved other than by way of Brogus' girlfriend," she said.

"He made it crystal clear that she didn't give the kid any orders to burn Powell's place, let alone set fire to part of the local forest." He stared into space for a moment. "I think I believe him. There's no reason she'd want to burn trees if she's as hardcore an environmentalist as he suggested," he shook his head. "Un-unh, there's no motive for her to order a forest fire though she might be wacko enough to destroy a business that she thought was ravaging nature."

"Even that takes having a real screw loose," she concurred. "I doubt this gal is that far gone. It sounds more like she was coerced to go along with some spying but I don't think she has a particularly larcenous disposition." She raised her eyes to Mathers' with a mischievous glint, "though I'll bet your buddy Brogus does."

He laughed. "Oh, I'm sure of that. He, however, has a very healthy respect for private property." He cogitated a minute. "Those two must be a pair, the heathen and the true-believer."

It was Anthea's turn to laugh and nod in agreement. "I'll bet, but which one's which?" she asked which made him chuckle more.

"Love really is blind, I guess," said Gary.

Still smiling, she returned her attention to her notes and asked, "So, do you think that this Sully character would take it on himself to become a firebug?"

"I doubt it. He may have been a real rabble-rouser and if he ran you down, who ordered that? I somehow don't think that his boss at Rural Resources would call for inflicting any injury, though she was probably behind the file being stolen." He came over to stand next to her and peer down at her legal pad, though the scratches and squiggles were an utter mystery to him.

"Let's take another tack." He twisted one of the curls dangling down her neck around his finger. Ignoring the slight shudder that went through her at this touch, he continued. "What about their history. Do we know anything about the players? Do their lives intersect any-where in the past?"

She turned to gaze up at him over her shoulder. "We can see. I'll have to get on the computer and plug into a search engine. I can start by googling the kids and the director of Rural Resources. Where's your setup?"

He grimaced knowing how antiquated his system was and how he was also totally devoid of skill in using it. "Walk this way," he said, waving her down the hall to his makeshift office. "I'm warning you that the system is slower than slow and older than dirt."

"Does it work?"

"That it does. My daughter managed to get this mismatched pile of junk to operate in a barely satisfactory manner," he apologized.

"Hey, I have a friend who had an old Apple Lisa up and running 15 years beyond its lifespan with up-to-date software," she grinned. "Now, *that* was a miracle comparable to bringing Lazarus back to life."

"I'm sure I'd agree if I knew what a 'Lisa' was," he grinned back.

"Never mind. It's a computer from 'long ago and a galaxy far, far away.'"

"That, I get," he laughed as he showed her into a room that was piled high with papers on almost every flat surface.

She scanned the scene. "And I thought you were a neat-freak."

"They're neatly stacked," he said defensively, indicating the individual mounds.

"I'll grant you that. Now where is this computer buried?"

He picked up a short stack of books from the chair that was facing the computer desk and laid them atop a nearby pile of file folders. She checked the book titles quickly before sitting down and noted language texts in Spanish and German and an odd title that looked like Arabic on the spine.

"I'd almost forgotten that you were a linguist. I'm impressed."

"Sure, I speak every damn language except computereze."

She rapidly booted up his machine and quickly looked over the components. "As long as you're connected to the internet, I think I can handle this translation." It didn't take anywhere near as long to get online and navigating the search as he had expected. He paid attention to some of the shortcuts she utilized that were new to him.

A few minutes later she had zeroed in on a Sullivan Tyson and a news article that had just been posted on the daily's website giving the basics of his accident on the Lilliot Road the day before.

"That was quick. He just died yesterday," said Gary as he read from beyond her shoulder.

"Yeah, well they pick things up off the police scanner and if the sheriff had already notified the family, the name of the victim would be released to the press. Lucky for us, they already did our homework." She scrolled down the screen. "It says here that he was a law student at Greenfield College of International Studies in Wisconsin."

"Never heard of the place. Must be small."

"It is and I'm surprised you haven't heard of it." She talked as she pulled up another window and punched in the college name to search. Locating their website she said aloud. "It's a small liberal arts college with a renowned law school that focuses on environmental and international law. The Southern Poverty Law Center is a big supporter of their program and employs a number of students as interns." She stopped and thought. "Interesting that Tyson would opt to intern for a little rural environmental organization all the way out here." She typed some more. "Let's see if the other kid is also enrolled there."

It didn't take long before she came up with the positive answer. "Okay both boys were in the same pre-law program at Greenfield. Now let's check on Miss Carrie DiMarco," and she went to work locating her history. There were actually a couple of pages of references on Google for the director of the local Rural Resources office.

"Hmmm," murmured Mathers from behind Anthea. "Looks like that's been one busy lady."

Anthea nodded as she scrolled down the screen after choosing an article that had run in a southern Oregon regional newspaper. She wasn't overly interested in the details of the story that talked about developing a nature center at a state park near Klamath Falls. Instead she zeroed in on DiMarco's history as an environmental activist that, at one point in the tale, even pitted her against a tribal government. It seemed she and a radical group were opposing development of a fishery as being an aberration of the natural diversion of a salmon run. The local tribe's intent was to rebuild the fish population that had diminished over the last century due to over-fishing.

As she read further down the page she said, "I've heard of purists before, but this one is definitely walking the edge of silliness if she thinks that creating a salmon fishery to improve fish numbers is dinking with the natural process."

"I thought all environmentalists were on the side of supporting Native American land use and fishing rights." Mathers was bemused.

"I guess some folks think they know better than the combined wisdom of tribal elders who revere their people's past and their historical connection to the earth." She finished the article. "Their protests didn't come to much anyway. The tribal fishery was built and has since tripled the salmon population on that river. I was looking for her school…let's see. Yes, here it is. It mentions her graduating from Humboldt State. I had friends who went there and none of them walked away with that warped an idea of saving the environment that I know of."

"Whatever. It's still a bust in terms of tying the schools together." He stood up straight and thought. "What about that fella you went to interview. There may be some connection between Nature's Wilds and Rural Resources."

"I'm pretty sure that I've got his history in with my notes in the portfolio among the stuff we downloaded a while ago." She closed the program and shut down the machine. Mathers was already looking through the papers when she reached his side at the kitchen counter.

He pulled out a paper-clipped batch of pages. "This looks like it," and started sifting through the press releases, maps and miniscule amount of real information hidden in the flowery language. He found a sheet of biographies of the few officers and board members. Sliding it free, he quickly read over the history of Glen Alison, the director of the conservancy.

"Woo-hoo, here we go…a former professor of environmental studies at Greenfield."

"Woo-hoo? Is that a war-whoop from your cop years?" she laughed at hearing the local slang.

He gave her a slightly disparaging look. "I watch football with some of the guys here and I have a tendency to pick-up linguistic anomalies. Is there a problem with that?" He eyed her more closely and she only laughed again.

"Hardly," and she pulled him down to plant a quick kiss on his mouth. "Just unexpected, but kind of cute."

"Oh lord, I've digressed to 'cute,'" and he captured her for a proper kiss. When he released her he said, "I hope that dispels any misapprehensions about my being 'cute.'"

"It certainly does," she said after catching her breath.

Rapidly switching gears, he turned back to their research. "What do you wanna bet that Alison is somehow tied to this little mess?"

"I presume he is, but here it says that he left his post seven years ago, so it isn't as a direct influence on any current students unless he occasionally teaches special programs or workshops."

"Let's just keep that in mind as we move on. We can check that out later."

They were both quiet for a minute trying to piece any of the facts together.

"This doesn't seem to be leading us anywhere," Mathers finally broke the silence. "We need to start somewhere else. You mentioned Mary Stabler's garden. What were you thinking?"

"It's kind of off-the-wall but I was considering the poison angle and thought maybe we should get some soil samples."

"You're right, it's pretty out there but I can't think of much else since we seem to have hit a wall for any real connections." He considered her idea. "It certainly couldn't hurt to check out the garden though I doubt there's anything to be found." He looked up to check the ship's clock he had hanging by a bookcase. "It's still early enough.

I'll run up the road and do that now," and he started moving toward the door, stopping to fetch his keys. As he did so, her hand fell across his.

"I think you mean 'we,' right?" She pierced him with a defiant glare, daring him to cross the threshold without her. "I believe you'll need corroboration as to where these samples were collected. You know, like a witness?" She turned the corners of her mouth up into an enticing smile.

"It could be dangerous. Remember those turkeys and how they chased me with a loaded rifle? What if they're still hanging out at the property," he wasn't giving in to her logic.

"Highly unlikely. They finished their work over a week ago. You saw most of those trucks haul off the wood yourself." She knew he was relenting. "All we need is a camera to record your evidence collection. Video would be best."

"Just so happens my daughter got me a digital video camera for Christmas. The computer queen, she said she wanted to make sure I had something here when she visited with the baby."

"Good girl, always thinking ahead, considering she was what, three-four months pregnant? I do believe we have something in common."

He stopped short, eyes wide. Anthea broke out laughing so hard she squeezed Mathers' hand around his keys so they bit into his palm.

"Some detective. Thinking ahead, boy…thinking ahead."

Chapter 49

Since the evenings could still get nippy, Anthea grabbed a light jacket while Mathers went into his bedroom. He opened a floor safe he had in his closet and drew out an ankle holster that encased a small caliber gun. He pulled it out of it's leather housing and checked it to be sure it was properly loaded, then positioned it on the inside of his left ankle. Mathers then went over to his dresser and withdrew a wrist sheathe with a nasty looking knife and strapped it in place on his forearm. Though he wasn't expecting any real trouble, he planned on being as prepared as possible in case they got cornered. His last experience at the farm had left him just a little bit paranoid so he figured that it couldn't hurt to be equipped to handle the worst scenario. *But why does Anthea have to be so damned stubborn. It's hard enough to watch my own back let alone keep a protective eye on her tail, nice as it is.* Giving in to the fact that she had a point about verifying the soil collection and that there was no way she'd let him go alone, he just muttered, "Hell. I didn't sign up for this."

Meeting her back in the hallway, he asked, "Do you have anything to protect yourself with?"

"What, isn't my rapier wit weapon enough?" She said sardonically as she tilted her head to look up at him. "Never really expected I'd need a real sword. Besides, dangerous acquaintances didn't come along with *my* job description, unlike you white knight types."

"Hmmm." He gave her a slight smile in spite of his reservations of hauling her into potential peril. "In that case, would you prefer the vicarious pleasure of shooting a perp or a more hands-on method of inflicting pain and suffering?"

"Years ago I decided that if someone came after me, I'd probably succumb to rage. So I concluded that if I had a gun I'd be more apt to beat the guy with it than shoot him," she said half-seriously.

He looked at her small frame with a barely concealed smirk trying hard to break through the gravity of the moment. Instead he said, "All right, then let's go the old Maglite route since they're dual purpose for illumination and clubbing bad guys." He went into the closet to find the extra one he kept next to the umbrella. He handed it to her. "Remind me not to tick you off."

•••••••

It was nearing sunset when they climbed into his truck and drove up the old road to the Stabler place. The appearance of a once productive farm as it now stood desolate and empty except for the few trees scattered here and there among the untended fields, was a depressing scenario as they approached. Deciding that he didn't want to draw too much notice to their visit, Mathers left his rig parked by a tall stand of pines that bordered the long drive more than a quarter mile from where the house had been. They didn't see any sign of the fifth wheel that had seemed to serve as the operations office a couple weeks earlier.

As he put the truck in 'park,' he commented on the lack of anyone around.

"Looks like we may have lucked out and are sole guests at the newest of Nature's Wilds' appropriated properties,"

"The emptiness would be inviting if it weren't for the thought of the displaced family coping with the loss of their mom. This should still be a warm home filled with everyday sounds… kids getting ready for school, the tractor rumbling to work and a mother nurturing her garden," said Anthea as Mathers assisted her down from her elevated perch.

He arched an eyebrow, "Waxing poetic, are we?" But there wasn't any humor in his tone as he added his own observation. "This was a pretty happy place even with the challenges they were facing, you know? I only visited with them a few times before Mary really declined, but the feeling was always hopeful." He looked around after half-lifting her to the ground. "It'll never feel right around here, now. Too barren. Maybe it's the memories."

He grabbed the bag that held the camera and made sure that Anthea had her flashlight. "It's not dark yet but this may come in handy. Don't turn it on unless we really need it, I'd rather not call attention to ourselves." Hoisting the bag over his shoulder, he added, "We'd better get going while we still have plenty of light for the camera"

She didn't answer but just picked up the pace as he began walking up to where he saw the stones of the path leading up to the ghost of a demolished house and dismantled dreams.

"Well, let's see if I can locate the garden," he said as he started to follow the line of the river rock foundation that had not yet been removed, although they had filled in the basement with stony soil. "I hope they didn't obliterate the garden space when they were backfilling the cellar," he remarked as he eyeballed a line from the house to where he thought Mary's pride and joy had been. A mound caught his eye to the right and he made his way over to find that it was the remains of the compost pile. Checking out the general area, he knelt down to find that he was standing in the midst of spongy, loamy soil that didn't match the rest of the hardened clay that was beginning to show cracks with the drying season.

"I'll take some samples from a couple places in this patch and from the compost. Can you get the camera out and pan the area a little before zooming in to film the soil collection? Don't turn the camera off in between shots so it's obvious that everything took place at this location."

Anthea was occupied with opening the bag and extricating the camera while Gary was readying bags for samples when he felt a cold, hard object apply pressure to his back. Recognizing the sensation as the muzzle of a rifle being placed firmly right about where his heart would be, he stiffened.

"I wasn't expecting company, were you dear?" He said to Anthea as her eyes widened in surprise and fear. *Damn... I knew this wasn't going to be as easy as it looked.* He immediately regretted bringing her with him.

"Hands behind your head." It was Hothead. "What the hell are you doing here, asshole?"

"Apparently, not the same thing as you." Mathers turned slightly to better examine his adversary. "We're digging worms and you, looks like you're hunting game, though I'm sure you know its not hunting season."

"Stand up slowly and don't dick around," he said as he backed off a few steps to make sure Mathers wouldn't have the opportunity to take a swipe at his gun. "You too, lady."

At least he didn't use the 'm' word, thought Anthea as she straightened up. *That might piss me off.* He didn't seem to take her too seriously as a threat and although he kept his distance from Mathers, wasn't as careful about his proximity to her. As she stood up she swung the Maglite around and batted the rifle away from Gary, giving him the opportunity to lunge forward and make a grab for the barrel.

A shot rang out and Hothead crumpled to the ground, blood pooling around his head and neck. Mathers just stood stock still, his hands still wrapped around the barrel of the gun pointing it away from himself and Anthea, a blank look of shock on his face.

"Sometimes you just gotta take out the trash."

Anthea and Mathers turned around to see Deputy Tolman standing off to their left. He held a handgun securely gripped in his hand, which he slowly brought to bear on Mathers' chest. *What now? How many gun-happy good ol' boys do we have around here?* With one hand Mathers pushed Anthea behind him as he lowered the rifle stock to the ground.

"You can give that to me now," Tolman motioned to a spot in the tilled earth. "Just lay it down over there."

Realizing he had no choice but to comply, he laid the rifle on the ground a few feet away and backed up to where he could shield Anthea.

"You *are* going to call in the shooting and get someone up here to assist at the scene, right?" asked Mathers. "It obviously occurred in defense of a victim. He could easily have killed one or both of us and he had the temper to do it."

"Sorry pal, that's not in the plan."

"This is part of a plan?" Mathers' tone implied derision.

Looking down at Hothead's limp form, Tolman directed his remarks to Mathers. "No idea what his plans were, but mine don't jive with his since he's been unfortunate enough to meet his maker." Never having wavered in directing his gun at Mathers' chest, Tolman caught his eye. "Now, just do what I tell you and don't get cute or you'll be joining him in repose."

"Yeah, I'm just as happy to avoid any new holes in my head, thank you."

Tolman tossed a small packet at Mathers, which he recognized as a space blanket. "Get that out, wrap the guy up and carry him over to your truck."

"Wouldn't it be easier just to bring the truck over here?" offered

Mathers, trying to maneuver some advantage in the situation.

"For you maybe, but I'd rather you had your hands full so I can keep an eye on both of you." He motioned toward the small package. "Now, just do what I said."

Following directions, Mathers extracted the folded material that resembled a swath of aluminum foil more than any kind of blanket. Laying it on relatively clean, grassy ground next to the loamy soil, Mathers dragged the body close to the blanket then lifted it onto the sheet and rolled the rapidly cooling Hothead inside.

"Pick him up and let's go." Tolman motioned him onward with the rifle now in hand, having holstered the pistol. Gesturing for Anthea to follow Mathers, who had shouldered the body in a fireman's carry, their abbreviated train marched back to where Mathers had parked his Chevy. As they approached the pines and Mathers' truck sheltered beneath the boughs, they saw another rig parked next to his Silverado. Tolman had anticipated some bloody outcome, it seemed, since the bed of Gary's truck was already lined with a large blue tarp.

"Just dump him in your truck bed and wrap the tarp around him securely," instructed Tolman. He pulled a pair of handcuffs from his belt and tossed them to Anthea, who surprised herself by quickly reacting and catching them. "Okay pal, turn toward your girlfriend and let her put the cuffs on you, hands in front."

They followed directions carefully to avoid Tolman assuming that they were trying anything sneaky. They just exchanged looks and performed the duty without incident.

Opening the driver side door of his truck, he pulled another pair of handcuffs out and told Anthea to approach him.

"Get out your keys and get behind the wheel, Mathers," said Tolman.

"I can't drive with my hands cuffed like this," he held them up and pulled on the shackles.

"Yeah, you can. You've got an automatic. It won't be comfortable but it isn't far and you're plenty capable, probably one of those guys can drive with his knees. This is what you're gonna do…you follow me up the road at a three-car distance. Your lady here is gonna drive the other rig and I'll have a gun pointed at her head. If you follow too far back or too close, I shoot her and you'll see it. We'll be going slow enough that I can control the vehicle if you make it necessary for me to shoot her, so don't try anything stupid."

Gary kept his face expressionless as he studied Anthea, who was keeping her cool despite the pressure of the circumstances. He realized that Tolman was as good as his words…ruthless and determined. He just didn't know the 'why' of his actions.

"Get in and wait for my signal to move or I'll shoot her right now." He turned his attention to her briefly as Mathers climbed behind the wheel and inserted the keys in the ignition. "Come with me, Ma'am." Gary heard the designation and saw a brief flicker of annoyance flit across Anthea's features as she walked to where he pointed.

Opening the driver's side door Tolman directed her to get in and then cuffed her left hand to the handle on the door before closing it. He then circled the front end of the truck, keeping the rifle trained on Anthea over the hood as he passed and climbed in the passenger side, at which point he unholstered the pistol and leveled it to target her head. Mathers could easily see the whole scenario unfold next to him including the handover of keys from Tolman to Anthea.

"Okay, move out."

With Mathers following at the prescribed distance, they drove up the private road more than a mile before they turned onto a gravel road that led them up the mountain another few miles. They reached a smaller dirt track that turned off to the right and they continued to climb up a fairly steep slope over roughening surfaces that rocked the rigs now and again as they slowed to maneuver over the increasingly uneven terrain. Finally, the road leveled out but it was little more than a glorified four-wheel trail winding through the trees that was just wide enough at intervals to accommodate two passing vehicles, maybe.

After a while they exited the woods and Anthea saw a barracks on the left in the dwindling daylight. It looked rustic but well maintained to her as she pulled up and Tolman instructed her to park and turn on the headlights to better illuminate the entrance.

While Tolman got out and walked back around the front of the vehicle to unload his driver, Mathers pulled up behind the other truck, keeping a little distance. He quickly leaned over to open his glovebox and search the interior for his gun, which he had left inside.

All of a sudden the driver's side door was yanked open, revealing Mathers in an awkward position with one hand trying to steady himself by gripping the edge of the glove compartment and his right hand half-buried inside.

Tolman said evenly, "What're you looking for? Could it be this?" and he brandished the gun he had used to shoot Hothead, which Mathers recognized as his own. Tolman then stood back and used the pistol to wave Mathers to get out of the truck.

Pulling himself upright and stepping down from the rig, Mathers stumbled as he climbed down. Muttering "clumsy," he landed in a crouch, and palmed his pea-shooter from his ankle, pocketing it as he straightened up as if he were adjusting his pants. Pulling himself to his full height, he looked over the top of the door to see Anthea standing with her hand still manacled to the handle.

The deputy turned back to Mathers, having been distracted by Anthea's yelp when Mathers looked like he'd taken a fall. Tolman directed him to collect the body in the truck bed and waited for him to be encumbered by the weight before he unlocked Anthea from the door and motioned her inside with Gary following close behind.

"Just put him down by the woodstove," said Tolman, "and both of you take a seat on those bunks over there, one on each bed."

He moved within six feet of Mathers and, gun in one hand, told him to stretch his hands out for Anthea to unlock the handcuffs with the key he'd handed her. He then told her to tie Mathers' hands to the bedpost with a rope he threw to her. He watched her and gave her instructions on exactly how to make the knots in order to be certain that the bindings were tight enough. Then Tolman removed her hand-cuffs and tied her hands to the bedpost of a bunk opposite Mathers. The two of them locked eyes across the short distance separating them as if to ask one another, "what now?" to which Mathers just shrugged his shoulders while he tried to figure a way out of their dilemma.

Pacing back and forth, Tolman had relegated the physical presence of his two captives to the back of his mind as he sketched over his plans, checking to be sure he'd covered his bases. Mathers watched him intently from his vantage point, noting the flickering of expressions traveling across Tolman's face. He was bemused by the switch-es from uncertainty to confidence as his captor strode from one end of the barracks to the other.

In Tolman's mind the whole scenario was uncomfortable despite his conviction to follow through with his strategy. He contemplated how the other situations were more remote and far easier to implement because he didn't have to deal with the doomed individuals up close and personal. He just told himself to suck it up, the time for choices was long gone.

He stopped in his tracks and turned to catch Mathers examining his every move.

"Studying me isn't going to help you out of this one," he addressed his prisoner. "Your little love triangle has met a tragic end."

"You're kidding, right?"

"Not hardly, pal. You've shown up in the wrong place too many times for it to be considered coincidental. You've gotten in the way too often and are a real liability."

Mathers was genuinely confused. "Gotten in the way of who? Of what?"

"Your sniffing around has already supplied the answer to that. Flying down to California to "investigate," he sneered. "You're a lucky driver managing to stick to the road like glue coming down that mountain." The two hostages exchanged quick, puzzled glances. "What were you doing up at the old Stabler place? Planting petunias? Don't insult me by acting stupid."

Tolman walked to the end of the room and back again. "You don't belong here, either of you," he said, half distracted.

"And you do?" Mathers inquired as much out of real curiosity about Tolman's motives as attempting to ascertain his state of mind which seemed to be swinging between two poles.

"Damn right I do!" he spat. "This place and all up along Lilliot Creek belonged to my family until it was stolen!"

Mathers took a moment before responding, debating whether or not to goad him further. "If the government took your property, then why are you helping Nature's Wilds to steal more land?" he asked taking an intuitive leap, right or wrong.

"It wasn't the government that snatched my family's heritage. A few bad harvests and we were forced out by the bank. Our neighbors were right behind them. The vultures swooped in and bought up our farm for nothing. You expect community to pull together, instead they were hiding behind the bank's shirttails to expand their own fortunes." He was so agitated over the memory that his face suffused red, making his blond flattop look like the bristles of a shorn wheat field.

"And those neighbors were…" Mathers left it open-ended to see if Tolman would implicate himself in what looked like a twist to the motive that he'd originally assumed was behind the local crime spree, if that's what it was.

"Ahlsted for one. Stabler's dad for the other," Tolman supplied in a now flat and angry tone. "The government moved in afterward to stake its own claim and whisked off this part of the acreage as protected watershed. Dad couldn't even get the bank to back him to log some of this to make the payments. He was just a simple farmer in a panic, not a wheeler-dealer who knew how to handle the moneychangers and rip-off artists. *They* obviously had another agenda." He shot Mathers a milk-curdling glare, "the scavengers were everywhere. They still are"

He took a deep breath in an effort to regain control of his blood pressure. "Now those greedy bastards can all suffer for what they did. The conservancy calls itself a 'protector of the land,' and whether or not it really is, all of this will be kept out of the hands of the vandals. It will all finally be protected from the self-serving land hogs."

"Sorry to be the bearer of worse news, but that isn't really true," Mathers thought he'd try a few facts to wake up his captor. "Do you know what this bunkhouse is?"

Tolman looked at him like he had a third eye. "Abandoned forestry workers quarters. What're you getting at?"

"The fact that you are misinformed. This is where the illegal laborers were billeted while they constructed the multi-million dollar chalet that graces the other side of the ridge up there…" he nodded his head in the general direction of a rise in the land that wasn't visible in the dark. "…all at the behest of your so-called environmental advocates under the guise of saving the land for posterity."

"What the hell are you talking about. There's nothing up here but you, me and your date with a bullet."

"I really hate to be the one to burst your bubble, *pal*, but Solis Industries, which underwrites your favorite charity, has just shipped out the workers that completed the private castle of one Carl Chamberlain who plans to make this, and millions of pristine acres around the country, his personal playground." Mathers gave him a narrow look. "Didn't it strike you odd at how well-tended these barracks are? There's even fresh-cut wood by the stove and not a bit of dust anywhere. Pretty damn clean for an abandoned forestry outfit."

"Who the hell cares? You're still shit out of luck, because no matter what this was used for, the two of you are going away. You put me in this predicament and you'll have to pay the same ultimate price that the others did."

"You're a fool if you think you've got a way out of this. It's not going to take a genius to figure out who sent Sully and Ahlsted to their deaths." He waited to see if his assumptions would prompt any reaction from Tolman.

"Why would anyone connect this to a couple of tragic accidents? They haven't come up with anything so far and who would ever link this, a foiled rape of your sweetie, here, by that neanderthal," and he pointed his gun briefly at the still bundled Hothead, "that turned deadly times three."

Mathers shrugged. "I'd say it looks a little too theatrical, but what do I know?"

"Doesn't matter what you know, or don't, after this is cleaned up. If you and that Brogus asshole hadn't managed to insert yourselves onto the scene of those other incidents, both those accidents would have been shuffled into the 'closed' file in record time. Folks up here don't go looking for conspiracies."

"I'm guessing it's because they don't know much about their law enforcement officers. Or is it that they think they know them just because they grew up together?"

"Assumptions can be dangerous," answered Tolman as he bent over to begin unrolling the tarp that encased the unfortunate, and unpleasant, Hothead.

The bunkhouse door slowly began to swing inward, squealing slightly on hinges that should have been oiled. Tolman, hearing the noise swept around on his heels, bringing the rifle up but not being fully anchored in his squatting position, he couldn't aim quickly enough. The double barrel of a shotgun had already entered the room in the grip of Billy Brogus, who had it pointed at Tolman's gut.

Mathers used the diversion to snag his own small caliber weapon from his pocket, having to contort himself in order to get his hand to his pocket. Luckily, Tolman had attention only for his new adversary framed in the open doorway.

"No need to hurt anyone else, man. Just put the gun down,"

Brogus said as he calmly kept his own weapon at the ready. "Your role in the land scam has already been confirmed. There's nowhere to run."

"You're full of shit. You aren't about to take any of this to authorities and certainly didn't have time to since your little confab with Mathers here this afternoon." He was surreptitiously maneuvering his gun to a firing angle. "I get rid of you and I'm home free and done with all the thieves."

"Sorry you think so, man, but it's not gonna go down that way. Drop the gun."

"I'm done talking to all of you…"

Mathers saw his finger move to the trigger and immediately twisted around to aim his pistol awkwardly in Tolman's direction. Not waiting for any more provocation, Mathers fired, catching Tolman in the arm so the rifle shot went wild.

Brogus swung his shotgun around and swiped Tolman across the temple with the butt of the gun, but it glanced off at an angle as Tolman squirmed to grab Brogus' legs and felled him with a strong tug. The two of them struggled on the ground as Mathers, watching, tried to find a way to fire another shot at Tolman.

Before long, Tolman got the upper hand in the fight and shoved the stock of his gun hard into Brogus' midsection, depriving him of air, which gave Tolman the opportunity to roll away, turn and bash Brogus again with the gun butt, knocking him unconscious. He whipped around and faced Mathers, who, with his little gun in his hand, tried shooting again but couldn't angle himself properly to strike Tolman. As the bullet whizzed past Tolman, he jumped forward and kicked the weapon to the floor.

He just stood menacingly over Mathers, catching his breath. "You're making this far too difficult." He looked down at the blood running down his arm from the one shot Mathers had gotten off that connected and strode over to the cupboards to rummage through them for something to staunch the flow.

He found a pillowcase and tried to wrap it around his arm but couldn't manage alone, so he untied Anthea, warning her to just follow directions or he'd shoot her. Unwilling to make any moves without having a back-up strategy, she took the fabric and fixed up a makeshift tourniquet.

"Now back off and sit down." He bound her hands again. Standing back up and wielding the rifle with one hand, he laid Mathers gun next to the dead man by the woodstove and checked to be sure that Brogus was still out cold. Making a last minute decision to make sure Brogus couldn't interfere any further should he wake up, Tolman hog-tied him.

"It looks like we've got a change in plan. Since you can't cooperate we're just going to have to do this the hard way and let you fry in hell." Leaving them tied to their separate bedposts, he spun on his heel and went out to his truck. When he returned he had some unexpected tools under one arm…those of an arsonist.

Anthea's face displayed her surprise and obvious dismay at the implication when he lowered the fuel can and implements to the floor.

"So it wasn't Sully who started the forest fire, was it?" she riveted Tolman's gaze with her own. "He just set the mill's office on fire but you did the rest. I'll bet you added to his work to make certain the whole operation burned."

"You're smarter than I thought."

"Doubtful as I am that you mean it to be, I'll take that as a compliment." She continued to watch him as he went about laying the base for an inferno. "Why'd you burn the mill? What did Powell do to you?"

He looked up from his work with a hate so intense she felt her skin burn before the fire was even set. "Nothing more than refuse to hire my dad when he was destitute and losing his farm."

"If he was a solid worker, why would he do that? Powell seems like a fair man," Mathers added his two cents.

"At the time Powell said they were cutting back production because of cheap competition from the Canadian softwood industry and were already laying off…no demand for lumber, no job. He shot himself and the rest was gone in a month. Mom moved north to her sister's and I had to leave school. She died a year later." He turned to stare past both of them seeing something that had dissolved years ago. "First the land, then the family. All gone. Now you'll be gone too," and he returned to his chore pouring kerosene on the bunks and around the base of the walls.

Anthea dropped her eyes, feeling a certain amount of pity despite the circumstances of her own imminent demise. At least she was beginning to understand his twisted idea of justice, however warped.

Mathers reentered the dialogue. "They're going to come looking for the arsonist in this incident. No one's going to believe this was an accident."

"No, but they have a perfectly good suspect in Ms. DiMarco since she was complicit, if even tacitly, in the other eco-terrorist activities. It shouldn't be too much of a stretch to see her take the blame for everything from the kid's bike accident to masterminding the Powell fire and Ahlsted's death. She'll have a tough time denying it or disproving her guilt."

Anthea furrowed her brows and whispered to Gary, "you're not helping matters."

As Tolman continued to pull out combustibles and throw them around the floor of the barracks, dousing them liberally with kerosene, Mathers was contorting his hands around in an attempt to release his knife from the wrist sheath. Finally freeing the weapon from its housing, he furtively began to saw through his bindings, silently blessing their good fortune in Tolman's foresight of using rope instead of handcuffs to avoid suspicion.

Tolman reached the entryway of the quarters and stepping outside, he struck a match and threw it toward a bunk fully soaked with kerosene, which immediately began to blaze with quickly growing flames.

"Warm yourselves by the fire, guys." And he slammed the door shut behind him.

Mathers' efforts were rewarded with success as he was able to cut through the last of the fibers while the fire grew just yards away from their perch. Jumping to his feet he ran over to Anthea and quickly sliced through her bonds just as the fire ran down the legs of the bunk to reach the wooden floorboards within a foot of the kerosene trail that traced the base of the wall. The place was rapidly being engulfed in flames while he stooped to saw Brogus' ropes.

"Get out now!"

"I can't leave you here," she yelled back over the sound of the snapping flames.

"You can't help. Just get out and try to call for help."

She ran to the door and tried to pull it open. "Damn it! He locked it!"

"Come here and cut him free while I get us the hell out of here."

She replaced him at the job of sawing through ropes as he grabbed a sheet from the cabinet and wrapping it around his hand and forearm, looked away from the window and punched through the glass. Swiftly clearing as much of the jagged edges as he could he rushed back to Brogus and Anthea, just as she slashed through the last strand.

"Climb out the window, now!"

Seeing no point in arguing, she ran to the window and scrambled through the opening, cutting her hands and knees as she clambered over the sill and tumbled onto the grass outside.

Mathers was quick to follow by pushing Brogus' limp form through the broken window, with Anthea pulling on his arms to help him reach the ground without any further injury other than some cuts. Gary climbed out behind the unconscious man and dragged him away from the building until he could shoulder his weight, with Anthea under Brogus' other arm, to carry him as far as they could from the growing blaze. They hadn't gotten more than a hundred feet away when the flames reached the propane heater that stood at the other end of the bunkhouse and the whole barracks exploded in a fireball.

Chapter 50

They found themselves sprawled in the dirt where they had been hurled by the concussion of the blast, an unconscious Brogus between them. They quickly heaved themselves to their feet and hauled their inert companion over to the truck, the opposite direction of their escape.

They half-carried, half-dragged Brogus to the far side of the rig to put some distance between them and the now raging fire. Laying down their charge, Anthea sat down beside him to monitor his recovery while Mathers checked out the vehicle.

The Chevy was standing close enough to the burning building to have sustained considerable damage by the explosion but, after inspection, not beyond being serviceable. Tolman's truck, which had been parked in front of Mathers,' was long gone.

Pulling open the door, he hunted for his cell phone and finding it under the passenger seat, turned it on to find that he had a weak signal. Blessing the stars for the mountain's altitude in this backwater, he depressed the buttons for 911 and reported the fire.

After some prodding, Brogus groaned and raised his hand to rub his head where Tolman had whacked him with the gunstock. Opening his eyes, he tried to sit upright and being unsuccessful in the attempt, looked around and asked what happened.

"There was an explosion," was as far as Anthea got before he interrupted her explanation with, "Oh God. Where's Mathers?"

"Calling in the fire. Tolman got away before the bunkhouse blew and we're lucky to have gotten out with our skin."

"I can tell." He scanned her from his prone position. "You look like a half-burnt chicken with ashes for feathers."

"You're no great shakes yourself, boy. And you've probably got a monster headache to match." He was trying to sit up, so she pressed him back into the earth. "Just lay back and catch your breath. I'll bet you've got a concussion on top of everything else."

"No. I've got to go. I can't be seen here." He was resolute as he grabbed her arm and drilled her with a grave look. He rolled over and pushed himself onto his knees and painfully stood up.

"You should take some time and recuperate a little."

He started to shake his head but stopped abruptly when a sharp pain shot up the side of his temple. "Don't tell anyone I was here." He turned and ambled toward his Bronco at a fairly quick pace, despite the aches racking his body.

Mathers was striding back to Anthea when he caught sight of Brogus' back as he finally upped his speed to an awkward run to reach his rig that he had left parked under some trees. He tried to run and catch their erstwhile rescuer but didn't get far before the Bronco's engine fired up and leaped back down the trail. Bending at the waist, half-crouched with his hands on his thighs, Gary stopped short to catch his breath. He coughed and slowly straightened up before turning back to Anthea.

"He was pretty adamant about us not letting on that he was up here," said Anthea. "What's that all about?"

"Probably doesn't want anyone checking on his movements or asking questions." He looked down at her as he wiped some of the soot from his brow and looked at the black smudge it left on his fingers. "His timing couldn't have been better for our sake, but he's not exactly a law-abiding citizen. I think that we ought to follow his wishes and not mention that he was here. It may come out later, but when the time comes, we can just claim stress of the situation." He paused to cough and spit to the side. "I doubt Tolman will be offering any information to the contrary when they catch up with him. He'll have enough charges to face."

"Right. And what's one extra indictment for attempted murder on top of the bodies he's already collected." She waved Gary to the ground. "Damn, I feel like I've been hit by a truck." Checking his hands and face for injuries, she added, "how do *you* feel?"

"Same as you. That blast knocked us flat. I wouldn't be surprised if one or both of us were concussed." He finally turned to examine her eyes, taking both her hands in his own. Suddenly he just gathered her onto his lap and brushed her hair away from her face with his fingers. "Thank God you're all right," he muttered under his breath. "Thank God…"

●●●●●●●

It was another half hour or more before the fire fighters arrived. The crew jumped down before the truck had pulled to a complete stop and ran to take what little action they could to douse the flames. Fortunately, the barracks had been standing in a clearing lessening the chances of fire spreading through the trees and causing a major blaze in the isolated sector of forest.

Sheriff Stellenbeck pulled in right behind the engine, practically bounding out of the truck cab, leaving the door ajar in his hurry. He rushed over to check on the two casualties seated at a safe distance from the fully engulfed building. Just as he hunkered down and began to ask what the hell was going on, the roof of the cabin fell in with a huge crash causing Anthea to duck her head into Gary's shoulder. They all turned to watch the edifice crumble with the sound of breaking timbers and the sight of flames shooting thirty feet into the air.

"Let's get you out of here," said Stellenbeck as he pulled Anthea to her feet and helped Mathers gain his balance. The ambulance drove up just as they were steadying themselves and walking toward the sheriff's vehicle. Turning them aside to the new arrival, the EMTs hurried over to assist the ash-coated duo to the back of the rig.

As soon as the noise abated enough that they could hear one another, Gary told the sheriff that Tolman was on the run with a gunshot wound in his arm. Before he could exclaim his disbelief, Mathers waved his argument aside.

Over the ministrations of the EMTs, Gary tried to rapidly explain the basics of the incident without going into any detail and omitting the presence of Brogus.

"You'd better call out the reserves, because he's responsible for at least three deaths that we know of."

"Any clue where he took off to?"

Mathers just shook his head. "No, but that wound in his arm will give him some trouble, though not enough to stop whatever it is he has in mind." He looked into the sheriff's eyes. "He believes we're dead, so he's continuing on his mission, who knows what that is."

"Look, I'm loading you two off to the hospital in Lathrop." He skewered Mathers with a deadly look. "You damn well better stay put until I can get down there to take a proper statement." He stood back while the techs loaded them into the back of the ambulance. "I'll have that rig of yours brought down the mountain if its drivable." He gave them one more stern order, "Be there when I get there or I'll put out a warrant for your arrest." With that he slammed the doors closed.

•••••••

After calling out for an APB on Tolman and putting Deputy Sonia Newsome in charge of the scene, Stellenbeck swiped his hand through his hair and consulted with the fire chief, who had just arrived and was clambering out of his truck. It took a bit of doing to extricate himself from the cab and climb down. Not standing much taller than the female deputy, but twice as wide, Chief Ray Geisner adjusted his belt, which had the hazardous duty of keeping his trousers barely situated above his hips.

"What in hell's name happened here?" he blustered at the sheriff. "A perfectly nice evening all gone to shit in a firestorm," he spluttered as he waddled over, pulling on a lightweight jacket.

"Yeah, well I hate to interrupt your repose, Ray, but we've got a bit of a problem up here, and I sure as shit wish I knew what to do about it." Stellenbeck was in no mood to hear the complaints of Lathrop's overfed fire chief. He towered over the shorter man with his hands planted firmly on either side of his waist, ticked off enough to be toying with the snap on his holster.

"I'm leaving the deputy here in charge of this mess which is a crime scene. There's a dead body burnt to a nub in that wreckage, so keep your boys away from the building except to make sure the fire's out."

Geisner's eyes opened wide. "The hell you say… Sure, Dave, I'll keep 'em in check."

The sheriff gave some last minute instructions to Deputy Newsome, who was putting her hat back on after pushing her bangs out of the way. She nodded assent to his brusque words and trotted after Chief Geisner to keep an eye on the situation while the sheriff hopped back into his patrol vehicle and whipped a u-turn, flying back down the mountain at record speed.

•••••••

Striding into the emergency room at the hospital, Stellenbeck removed his hat and rolled his right shoulder, which always gave him steady spasms when he was stressed out. The old football injury is what kept him from going any further than one year as starting quarterback at Washington State back in his heyday. Tonight he was anything but happy about the turn of events with his own deputy out shooting up the countryside and apparently responsible for the demise of his neighbors, if Mathers' story held any truth.

The emergency room was a fairly small area with only six beds, so it didn't take any time at all to swing his gaze onto the two troublemakers, as he viewed them, who were occupying adjacent beds. They were sitting up and fully dressed, Mathers with his legs over the side and Keller with her legs outstretched on the mattress, talking about the implications of the events of the evening.

"Don't get any ideas about heading out of here just yet," said Stellenbeck as he stationed himself at the foot of Mathers' cot. Leaning down, he laid one hand on the metal rail and tucked the back of his other hand on his hip, still gripping his hat. He gave them both a weary glare that disguised his startle at their disheveled appearance. They both looked like they'd been barbecued and served up overly crisp and sunburnt from the heat of the fire they'd escaped. Nor were they any too pleased about wasting time in the emergency ward. *Well, join the damn crowd,* thought Stellenbeck. Looking at their haggard expressions just made him roll his shoulder again.

"You want to tell me what in the Lord's name is going on?" His exasperation was palpable in the close quarters.

Mathers and Anthea sighed in unison. Gary undertook the recitation of occurrences, being familiar with police procedure and more able to sketch the important information in a fashion that was brief but detailed enough for the sheriff's report.

After his description of events and the involvement of Stellenbeck's underling, Mathers took a drink of water and asked if that was enough for now.

The sheriff switched his attention to Anthea who had sat calmly by, nodding on occasion as Gary went through their experiences and asked her if she had anything to add.

"No. Gary's account is pretty complete. We weren't separated for any time other then the drive up to the barracks and Tolman wasn't inclined to share during that pleasant little outing."

"Is there anything else that you need to know tonight?" asked Mathers. "We'd be just as thrilled as you to get out of here and," pulling at his soot covered shirt, "get cleaned up."

"Nah, you may as well get on home. I can't think of anything else for now, though I'll likely call you if anything comes up." He placed his hat on his head. "I'm guessing that you'll be safe enough for the time being since Tolman believes you dead."

Mathers just bobbed his head once then inquired, "Is the truck outside?"

It was Stellenbeck's turn to sigh.

"Yeah. It looks like you drove it through an erupting volcano, but it'll get you home. Are they ready to release you?"

Mathers stood stiffly. "Like I care. There wasn't much they could do for us anyway. Just a few bangs and bruises." He assisted Anthea to her feet and guided her out the door, turning to look back at the sheriff. "Thanks for your help, Sheriff. Keys?"

"In the ignition. No one's gonna steal that burnt out shell."

Chapter 51

The ride back to Gary's place was made in exhausted silence. Filthy and worn out by the night's unexpected activities, he and Anthea just managed to park themselves inside the door. They stood there for a few moments deciding what to do next.

"You're getting in the shower while I make some coffee," Gary stated as he pulled her jacket from her shoulders and tossed it on the laundry room floor. "We're both fatigued but I'm not ready for sleep yet." He started maneuvering her through the hall and into the bedroom. Walking through to the bath, he reached inside the roomy shower stall and turned on the water. "I've got to figure out where Tolman took off to."

"*You*," said Anthea as she walked into the bathroom, "need a shower and rest as much as I do."

He stuck his head in the door and kissed her cheek as she stood half undressed. "Yeah, but not yet."

Anthea peeled the rest of her grimy clothes off and stepped under the spray of warm water, relishing the feel of the clean, pure stream as it flowed over her skin, washing away the remnants of a fiery night.

Gary couldn't wait for a shower to change his shirt, so he pulled one out of the bureau, buttoned up and went into the kitchen to put on a pot of coffee. He stood brooding, his back to the counter, and stared out the window into the darkness. The thought of Tolman loose in the area was a real problem. It wouldn't be long before he found out that he left the job unfinished. Granted, there were no all night radio stations so even if he had a decent receiver, he wouldn't hear about the results of his little conflagration until morning. Even Gary knew that news traveled faster than wildfire in small towns, though. Whether or not the guy was injured and keeping out of sight, he'd find out before long and that meant that Gary and Anthea were both in danger. *Just like a wounded bear*, thought Gary. *This guy is gonna charge what he thinks is most threatening.*

He continued to ruminate as the coffee dripped into the carafe and the machine burbled.

So, what's he think is the greatest danger to his survival? Or is he just out for revenge? Well, Gary knew that Tolman's plan, or supposed plan, was to wreak vengeance on whoever had wronged him. *But we were supposed to be the last on his list...until we told him about the Solis chalet.*

"That's gotta be it. He can't go home with a bullet in his arm."

Anthea came into the kitchen wrapped up in his oversized terrycloth robe. She looked like a mouse burrowed in a blanket as opposed to the burnt chicken Brogus had compared her to. Wet hair curling around her cheeks, Mathers pulled her into his arms and hugged her tightly against his chest. Then he set her down and plunked a cup of fresh coffee in front of her and deposited the telephone handset next to it.

She cast him an arched eyebrow. "Why do I need this?"

"Because you're going to wake up and call the sheriff."

Both eyebrows went up. "And?"

"And, you're going to tell him that I think Tolman went up to the Castle-on-the-Mount past the barracks he torched tonight."

"What makes you think Tolman went there? He didn't even believe us and we're pretty sure he was working for Nature's Wilds as a contractor to produce this havoc." She looked up at him as she sipped the coffee.

"Oh, I think he took our news to heart and he can't go home or get medical attention for a gunshot wound. His only option, in his state of mind, is to take out his frustrations on the people who made hay off of his dirty deeds." He shook his head. "Oh yeah, he's got to be livid with rage after finding out that those folks have built an empire using him. Shades of his father – that's what he sees."

Anthea stood up and pulling the robe around her, started to pad off to the bedroom.

"Where are you going?"

"I'm going to get dressed because you're going up there, aren't you." She stated it as a matter-of-fact. "And I'm going with you."

"No, you're not," and he caught her around the waist and pulled her back into the kitchen. "You're going to call the sheriff and tell him just what we talked about and that he needs to meet me up there with back-up."

She looked up at him and wrapped her arms around him, returning the embrace.

"You don't have to go. You shouldn't go. You have no idea what's up there and you could get hurt."

"I'll be careful. You remember that this kind of reconnaissance work was my stock and trade for years. You, on the other hand," he caught her gaze with serious intent, "are wholly inexperienced and, as much as I love having you with me, you'd be a liability." He squeezed her. "Call the sheriff."

With that, he let her go and went to collect his tools and a minor arsenal in preparation for what could be a nasty encounter. *I damn sure hope the sheriff makes it up there with a full brigade in tow.*

Unlocking his gun safe, Gary grabbed his little-used hunting rifle and his other pistol, since the one used to down Hothead was caught in the flames where it lay next to its victim. He also put on a belt sheathe for his knife, deciding that he'd have support for this go-round and hidden weapons weren't as necessary.

When he came back out to the living area, Anthea checked how he was armed. "Aren't you forgetting the warpaint?" she quipped in an attempt to lighten the mood.

"I think the ashes will suffice, don't you?" He leaned down and kissed her, expecting to get past with a chaste buss. Instead, she pulled him toward her and kissed him soundly then pushed him toward the door.

"You'd better come back in one piece, with everything intact," she snapped though her eyes softly belied the threat of her words.

"No question. One working piece, it is."

"Yeah, or a 'piece of work' might be more apt."

He laughed as he closed the door behind him and she dialed the phone.

•••••••

Driving back up the road, where earlier that night Mathers had maneuvered over the rocks and ruts with his hands manacled, brought back the fear he had suffered as he had followed Tolman's vehicle up the grade knowing that a gun was aimed at Anthea. Shaking his head to rid himself of the vision, he continued past the smoldering remnants of the collapsed workers' quarters that had almost become their gravesite. Gary was amazed when he thought of the fortuitous arrival of their unlikely savior and how incredibly lucky they'd been to survive at all. He also gave silent thanks that Anthea didn't fight him about coming along on this outing, particularly since he had no idea what to expect or how he was going to deal with the situation, *except to stay alive, of course.*

He saw a sheriff's SUV parked near the remains of the building, which was roped off in yellow tape. Gary figured that the deputy was dozing while she waited for the crime scene techs to arrive. No need to be overly vigilant up here in the middle of nowhere and in the middle of the night. Though he would have thought that Sheriff Stellenbeck would have let Deputy Newsome know that her colleague was probably on the run and in the area.

Deciding that he couldn't worry about that now, he was happy enough that she wasn't yelling at him to pull over and explain himself. *Guess it's been a long day for everyone.* So he just drove past as slowly as he could, parking lights on, in hopes of avoiding waking sleeping beauty.

If Stellenbeck thinks about it, she'll probably catch hell anyway.

Not knowing exactly where he was going, he flipped his headlights back on, thinking that it's surprising that everything still worked. He just kept following the slightly improved road, trusting that it would eventually lead him to the estate.

As he crested the ridge, he was rewarded with a starlit vision of a multi-story 'hunting' lodge perched on the top of the rise about a mile away. It appeared there were lights filtering through some of the windows, but he couldn't be certain at that distance. If so, however, it looked like the place was not only occupied but someone was entertaining company. Coming closer, he went back to using parking lights and came around by a five-car garage noting that Tolman's vehicle was parked near the outbuilding.

Not wanting to be easily noticed, Gary parked the blistered Silverado on the edge of a copse standing about a tenth of a mile from the house. Just in case Tolman felt a need for a rapid escape he didn't want to be caught in the line of retreat. He carefully climbed out, quickly grabbing his firearms and closing the door before anyone would notice the inside cab light winking on and off. Then he checked the rifle and, holding it with his left hand, snugged the handgun in his waistband at the small of his back with his right, making certain safeties were off and they were loaded and ready for the action that he hoped wouldn't come.

He took his time reaching the oversized manse so he didn't trip in some ditch or over a rock or root lying unseen in the dark. Although he was tired, the familiar adrenaline he remembered from his terrorist tracking days coursed through his veins feeding him the energy he knew he would need to finish tonight's work, whatever that was to be.

As he approached, he noticed that the only lights burning were downstairs and appeared to be indirectly shining from the back of the building. He went around to the side entrance of the house where he took hold of the doorknob, which turned silently. *Who would lock up out here? Unless they were afraid of bears.* he thought as he began to ease open the door. *Guess they should have been since it looks like they've got a wounded one in their midst.*

Just as he was about to push the door inward, he was startled by a sound to his right. He stopped abruptly and reached around his back, pulling his gun free from his belt and turning to get the building behind him so he could face the threat.

"You'd better lower that thing before you hurt someone... like me."

The voice came from his right, so close to his ear that he felt like he was going to jump out of his skin. Instead, he retained his grip on his gun and swiveled to face the interloper. The ambient light from beyond the corner of the lodge was dim, but the size of his unexpected companion along with the recognizable lilt of his deep voice gave him away.

"Cisco, what the hell are you doing here?" Gary asked sotto voce in an attempt to keep their presence unknown to the lodge's occupants. He readily discerned the outline of a shotgun in the young man's grip.

"I might ask you the same, except that I have a good idea what an ex-cop...it is 'ex,' right?... is doing skulking around the perimeter of another man's home." Even though it was too dark to see Cisco's features, the teasing in his voice made it evident what he thought of the predicament.

"Well, since you've apparently already reconnoitered the place, why don't you fill me in on the details, and don't leave out the reason for your own 'skulking.'" The use of Cisco's phrase tossed back at him evoked a low chuckle.

"We were down by the river north of the barracks picking plums in a patch of wild trees when we saw the smoke and came up the ravine to investigate. We saw the sheriff's truck taking off up the road when we heard the explosion coming from the direction of the smoke."

"You knew about the camp?" Mathers was beginning to think that everyone but the authorities knew about this little retreat.

"Sure. We've been coming up here forever, family gathering place for berries and wild fruit. Sweetest plums you'll ever eat," and he pulled one out of a fanny pack and offered it to Gary who just wagged his head to decline the fruit.

Families of the plateau tribes have continued the tradition of seasonal rounds over millennia. Gathering fruits, nuts and roots in season; following game in autumn; fishing salmon in the spring. Semi-nomadic in their past lifestyle, traditional camps are spread throughout the region, convenient for the harvests. Many of the families still utilized the long-standing sites for weekend, vacation and holiday outings to carry forward the old ways, teaching the young ones how life was for their ancestors and how the land still gives its bounty. Cisco's family had a number of different camps that they would visit each year to collect huckleberries, camas and other traditional foods. Woven into the cycle of gathering and hunting were the many milestones reached by children as they cross into puberty when they take their first white tail or dig their first water potato. These landmarks in life are commemorated by sharing the harvest with those too aged or infirm to hunt for themselves and it would all begin by returning to the traditional camps, where parents juggled jobs in the city with finding time to train the new generation in ancient lore..

"Later. So, why are you hanging around here?"

"I left Lainie and the rest of the ladies down at the river and decided to investigate a little on my own. That sheriff's truck heading up the mountain like a maniac was driving caught my attention, so," Gary could just barely see the big Indian's shoulders shrug, "I followed at a distance."

Mathers stared at him hard, not certain whether Cisco could see his eyes in the near pitch-blackness. "Do you have any idea what kind of a man you were tailing? He's a murderer." He kept his tone low, but the import of his message was clear.

"Yeah, all the signs were there that this guy is dangerous, which is why I brought some protection and was real careful not to be seen. I've been waiting to see who would show up to save the day, Dudley."

The slight mocking in his voice almost made Mathers burst out laughing but managed to retain his stoneface. "You couldn't have expected me, of all people."

"Actually, although I've been here for hours, I could. It *was* your truck parked out by the cabin." Gary could hear the smirk. "I saw it when I went back to get my rig to follow. So now, what would the RCMP do?"

"Leave the rookie by the door to guard the entrance and wait for back-up, while the ranking officer goes inside to investigate."

Cisco shrugged again. "You're the boss. I've been tracking and hunting game all my life, but homicidal criminals are out of my league."

"Good. The sheriff is due to meet me here anytime. You just hold the fort and make sure he doesn't mistake you for the bad guy." He turned and reapplied pressure to the knob, pushing the door open and entering the lodge.

He found himself in a large mudroom that lay off a long hallway. He followed the wide passage past the kitchen and stopping to check inside, made note that it was equipped like a restaurant with two refrigerators, ovens and sinks and a huge stovetop that was black, flat and cold. If there were any serving staff around, Gary assumed they'd been bunked down in one of the smaller buildings for hours, having no clue that a warped deputy was lurking nearby.

He slid cautiously down the hall, keeping his back close to the wall until he found himself on the verge of a vast entryway that was basically rustic in the use of cedar paneling but emanated the feel of a Gothic cathedral with its arching heights. A large, stained glass window depicting a free flowing waterfall graced the full length of the massive doors on one side. Gary could imagine the play of colors across the marble floor in the daylight.

Giving the architecture no more thought than locating where the echoing voices were coming from, he noiselessly crossed the space to find a dramatic, sweepingly large entertainment area. A wall of windows that stretched from floor to ceiling overlooked a landscape that was drenched in darkness this time of night, only allowing the occupants to see several feet beyond the house where the projected light dispersed. Five people were scattered among the comfortable but stylish furnishings… Tolman and his hostages.

The deputy's complexion was wan in the lamplight. He stood with his back turned to the entry, unheeding of any unannounced guests, although he was one himself. Mathers assumed Tolman felt safe enough in these remote environs that he thought he wouldn't need to be overly wary. The other occupants appeared to be frightened and definitely didn't pose a threat to their captor, by the looks of them. Well, all but one man who appeared relaxed if not slightly annoyed, sitting cross-legged in a silk dressing gown and calfskin slippers. He was holding a crystal snifter, delicately swirling a golden liquid around the bottom of the glass.

The woman was curled up in a fetal position on the leather couch, desperately hugging a tapestry pillow to her chest. The other two men were sleepily sprawled on a chair and adjacent loveseat, half-dressed and trying to appear visibly calm.

Aside from the open bar, the only other provision Tolman had made for his victims' ease was the fire blazing in a hearth that was large enough to turn a boar's carcass on a spit.

Mathers moved away from the scenario and crouched down back by the hall exit leading to the kitchen after noting the layout of the room. Assessing the situation, he figured that if he waited too long the sheriff would be arriving to find dead bodies, judging from the gist of the conversation he was overhearing.

It didn't take much to start adding it all up once he saw and heard Tolman railing against the arrogant ass sitting primly in what he probably viewed as a makeshift throne, peering down his nose at the irate man. Tolman was clenching his wounded arm to his side while training his weapon on the twit with the liqueur who obviously felt completely removed from his assailant's tirade.

Tolman, on the other hand, turning a deepening shade of crimson with what little blood he had left in his system, was tossing a number of choice and definitely unflattering epithets at his hostage for having used the Protect Our Planet organization for his own personal gain.

"I simply can't understand why you're so disgruntled," the dressing gown fluttered as he switched legs. "It's not as if some mining operation moved in to excavate an open pit. That would make even me angry. Instead we're preserving the integrity of the environment." He sniffed the fragrance emanating from the glass and sipped a little of the amber liquid.

"You knew these students were on a genuine crusade and I am the *last* person who would be helping assholes like you create a personal pleasure palace," spat Tolman. "You're the worst of the gravediggers who destroyed my family." He began raising the gun as if to take aim. "It wouldn't take much to put you out of my misery. No reason to give you the satisfaction of thinking you own that waterfall and all this," and he waved the gun as if to encompass the whole of the outdoors that was hidden from view by the darkness.

"Oh, but I do own it. What else could possibly be the purpose behind buying up all this pristine acreage except to save it from the greasy, redneck hunters and mishandling of crude industry that rapes the land for profit?"

"That profit would at least go toward feeding more than one man's ego."

"Do you really think that Nature's Wilds was created to save the land for 'Joe Six-Pack? Figure it out, they're as destructive as the conglomerates that strip the forests and poison the rivers."

"So a king should be crowned and you seem to believe the title is yours for the taking."

Dressing Gown sipped his liqueur and laughed. Mathers couldn't believe the stupidity of this guy in goading on a desperate and proven killer. Did he have a death wish? He sounded like some British blueblood from Empire days who assumed the heathen would know better than to gut him.

"You inferior chucks can haul the furniture. Are you expecting a thank you or respect from me for having done the nasty job of chasing those families off their farms? The families that you stated were evildoers in their own right." He lifted the glass to examine the exquisite color of the liqueur in the soft light of the table lamp. "Nothing buys respect but money and money buys power, even a kingdom. But revenge does serve its purpose," he mused aloud before taking another drink.

"Shut the fuck up." Tolman didn't raise his voice but stated the command in a low and menacing voice. "You're nothing more than a leech. I ought to just shoot you where you sit and let that Courvoisier spill all over that expensive silk robe you're wearing." He slumped back against the mantle. "It doesn't matter, your career of using people like me as pawns is ending tonight anyway."

Unruffled, the seated man straightened the leg of his pajamas showing from beneath the robe, then sat up again. "Then what? Where are you going to go? If you were thinking halfway straight you would accept my offer and be done with it." He swirled the cordial, watching the play of light through the crystal. "The money's here and Laura, there," he flicked his other hand toward the woman cowering on the sofa, "can have you papers and reservations ready in less than an hour." He looked over the rim of the snifter at Tolman, "Don't be a fool. Escape while you can. Your work is done here."

"Sure. I accept your proposition and then, in the next heartbeat, you turn me in."

"How can I? We've gone to a great deal of trouble to keep this little retreat off the map. I can't very well call the authorities and divulge Nature's Wilds little secret, now can I?" He arched an eyebrow in his disdain for Tolman, who he obviously considered to be no more than a lackey.

The deputy sat heavily onto an ottoman that was situated across from the hearth, on the other side of a buffalo hide rug that took the place of the more conventional bearskin floor covering. Another buffalo hide hung above the bar. That one was painted with a rich scene of Plains Indians hunting the animal that had given its pelt as a canvas for a well-known Native artist. The hanging was worth several thousand dollars but both of the men engaged in the conversation ignored their surroundings in favor of their personal desires and dilemmas of the moment.

He dropped his head into the hand of his injured arm, sighing while continuing to keep his weapon directed at the arrogant one, who simply waggled his foot back and forth impatiently.

"All right. I'm not really left with much choice at this point. Just get on the phone and set it up. I want out of here." He looked up at the man in the silk wrapper. "You people make me sick."

Utterly disregarding Tolman's last comment, the man simply smiled triumphantly and told his assistant to get the satellite phone and make the call. The woman, who had been keeping her head down in hopes of avoiding attention, raised only her eyes to her boss, loathing evident in her gaze — not that he noticed or cared.

Tolman caught the man's eyes menacingly. "Don't mess with me. Just one call and I want to check the number, see who you're calling. Dial it, then give me the phone so I can hear who answers."

"Whatever you wish," he said in a tone intended to denote the fact that he had no interest in Tolman or his concerns.

Although Tolman was still silently seething, Mathers determined that the tension was dissipating since a decision had been made to deal with the manipulative jerk holding the snifter who, apparently concurring with Mathers' appraisal of the circumstances, went over to the bar for a refill. Tolman appeared to be a little less jumpy, but Gary wasn't willing to take any chances with his volatile temper, a sample of which he and Anthea had seen earlier that night. He crept back down the hall to await the arrival of the sheriff, which after checking his watch, he assumed should be any time now, he hoped.

Standing off to the side of the door from the hallway, Mathers kept vigil in the mudroom. It wasn't long before he heard a number of vehicles drive up at a high rate of speed. Despite the fact that the reinforcements had arrived without sirens or the lightbars flashing, the noise of the rigs' engines alerted Tolman.

Mathers was pulling open the door to check on Cisco when he heard Tolman roar expletives at the man in the chair, followed by the blast of a gunshot that echoed inside the house.

Instead of exiting the building and joining the sheriff outside at the front entrance, he sped down the passage, reaching the foyer just as the front door flew wide and before Stellenbeck could rush in, Tolman laid down a rash of shots at the gaping door. Gary watched the sheriff jump back, the state police who followed him immediately backed up to give him space.

With Tolman concentrating on the front door, Mathers was able to sidle up along the opposite wall of the entryway, aim and shoot him in the thigh. Yelling at the top of his lungs, Tolman dropped his weapon and collapsed, clutching the wound in his leg. Stellenbeck careened through the door, flanked by the state troopers, while Gary who was closer to the downed offender, flew over to kick the gun out of Tolman's reach.

Standing out of the way, Gary made room for the sheriff to hurry in and, flip Tolman onto his stomach, slapping handcuffs around his wrists. As he grabbed his captive under his good arm and twisted him back up to sitting, Tolman spotted Mathers standing off to the side, with Cisco standing right behind him.

"How'd you get here and who let the bear in?" The glazed look in his eyes indicated that the pain from his multiple wounds along with the loss of blood was affecting his grasp on reality.

"You burned up, man. You're burning…in hell," and his head flopped forward. He would have pitched sideways in a dead faint if one of the troopers hadn't grabbed him and laid him on his uninjured side before heading back outside to call an ambulance.

"Not quite yet, my friend," muttered Mathers as he turned to catch Cisco's eyes. "I thought 'the bear' was protecting the back egress."

Cisco shrugged again. "Hey, all the action was in here. Couldn't miss out on a good story, y'know?"

Stellenbeck straightened up and looked at Mathers. "You took a lot of chances tonight. I'll get the information on your sidekick later." With that he sauntered over to better examine his surroundings.

"Nice place you got here, Mr. …" he left the sentence hanging expecting the character with the snifter, who seemed to be nothing more than irritated by all the commotion, to oblige by filling in the blank.

Hearing no response from the man who continued to hover beside the wet bar, Stellenbeck strolled through the room toward the foyer.

"Hm-hmmm, nice place you got here," he repeated a little louder. Stellenbeck looked up at the ethereal arches that reminded him of the transepts gracing cathedrals he'd visited in Germany during his tour of duty. "Never even knew about this little resort." He turned to look back at the man who leaned indolently against the bar. "Y'ever get a building permit? Must've been a bitch to get this estate built way out here. 'Cause I know castles like this don't normally fall out of the sky, but that's exactly what you'd think happened. Powerful piece of luck for you, wouldn't you say?" For some reason the sheriff caught on to the proprietor's abhorrence of hicks and instinctively accentuated his backcountry twang even though he'd spent most of his life in the city. Apparently, the ruse was enough to get a rise out of the snob.

"You can just turn yourself around and take your leave now, Sheriff," he sneered. "I'm sure you noticed that this is private property before you crashed through the front door, uninvited, I might add. And we would prefer our privacy, if you please. So, just collect your trash and take it with you when you go."

"Sorry, Bubba," and he looked directly in the man's eyes to see the spark of fire flash at the name. "You may have noticed that this is a crime scene and "you all" are material witnesses. We'll be roping off the premises to investigate."

"You must be mistaken. No crime has been committed here." He swept his arm to encompass the room in his domain as he walked forward without haste. "Just a gathering of friends and this one," he used his toe to nudge the unconscious Tolman, "has lost his welcome."

"Sorry you feel that way, but we'll be transporting all of you down to the county offices for questioning." He looked over at Mathers who nodded in agreement.

"Obviously a hostage situation, Sheriff," said Gary as he drilled the man in the silk robe with a stare that challenged him to contradict his statement. "The discharge of a gun was heard by everyone in the vicinity," and he turned back to face the property owner, "which was why we all ran to your aid," and he raised his eyebrows inviting defiance of his assertion.

The sheriff rounded on the man again. "Was anyone else hurt?"

"Of course not. This man was just waving the gun around and it went off." He went back on the offensive. "Leave now and I'll have my attorney reach you with all the necessary information regarding your inquiry."

Everyone else in the room had retained their peace throughout the confrontation. The two men frozen by fear were moving as little as possible, but one of the troopers had walked back in the room and turned his attention to them. "An ambulance is on the way," he reported. "What's wrong with her?" In all the tumult no one had noticed that the woman was still lying on her side.

Mathers' and the sheriff's attention was drawn down to the sofa that had been partially obscured by the bodies rushing to and fro. Being closest to the couch, Gary hurried over to check the figure who had appeared to be cowering on the sofa, a phone clasped in her hand. He squatted down and moved her hair away from her face. Her eyes were open and staring.

"She's dead. Shot."

The man brought his gaze down to really look at his assistant, taking notice of her for the first time since Tolman went down.

"That's not possible. She was making a telephone call and obviously cancelled the transmission when the guns went off." He was aggravated with the turn of events, finally beginning to notice the complexity of the situation but waving aside the problem, all the same. "She's obviously just frightened. Laura never did have a backbone," he said as he turned back to the bar and his Courvoisier.

Gary looked over his shoulder in utter astonishment. "Man, you definitely need a reality check. Your associate is killed right in front of you and either you don't care or can't." He caught Stellenbeck's gaze. "From what I see, this reptile is as guilty as your prisoner, there. Living in denial, notwithstanding."

Stellenbeck sighed and took off his hat, wiping his brow with his sleeve.

"Take them all in. We'll straighten it out at the station."

Chapter 52

After making sure that Cisco was back in his rig and heading down the mountain to rejoin his party, whom he had left at their campsite near the thicket of wild plums, Gary climbed wearily back into his truck and just laid his forehead against the steering wheel.

A few minutes later, he was startled awake by the sound of the passenger door being opened as the sheriff ducked his head inside the cab.

"Dozing off are we?" Gary could hear the mocking in his voice, which was gravelly with fatigue. "You really could use your beauty sleep. Gonna be able to find your way home?"

"Yeah, it's been way too long a day...*and* night." He studied the sheriff who appeared disheveled as well, sans ashes. "Got the place locked down?"

"Yup. Mr. More-Important-Than-God squawked an awful lot, but he'll be cooling his heels in the hoosegow until his attorney flies in. That whole sorry bunch are on their way down to the station now. Want me to follow you down, make sure you don't drive off the road?" he smirked slightly.

"Thanks for your concern, Sheriff, but I think I'll make it home."

"Just don't forget to come into the station first thing. I want this a-hole gone and oughtta my jurisdiction. I have a feeling he's gonna be entertaining federal charges before the day's out."

"How appropriate. See you at sun-up," he said as Stellenbeck closed the door.

Looking at the scene, Mathers watched the EMTs finish loading their patients, even though one was already beyond their help, in the multicolored hues of their flashing lights. He decided to wait for them to start down the road before leaving himself, which only took another few moments before he heard them shut the rear door. A state trooper was stationed at the entrance of the lodge, taking his turn to await the crime scene techs, who Gary assumed were already combing through the barracks a few miles back down the road.

Time to go and get what little rest I can before the next round. He turned the key in the ignition and followed the ambulance down the mountain.

·······

It didn't take as long as he'd expected to negotiate the road home and the fact that he didn't really remember much of the trip made him wonder how much of a trance he'd been in while maneuvering through the switchbacks. Deciding not to worry about that minor problem, he pulled into his own drive and was greeted by Anthea before he'd even shut down the engine.

She pulled open the truck door and waited for him to practically fall out of the cab into her arms.

"You're dead on your feet, babe," she said as she hauled him through the door and settled him on the bed.

"I need a shower."

"Do you think you can stand up long enough to take one?" she asked, disbelieving his capabilities to do more than keel over into a sound sleep.

"I have to get clean. Too much filth up there…gotta wash it off," he mumbled as he began pulling off his clothes. Accepting his decision, she helped him out of his boots then went to turn on the water.

Chapter 53

It wasn't more than four hours later that the two of them were back on the road headed to Lathrop and what was sure to be a grueling morning of answering yet more questions. Anthea hadn't broached the subject of the night's events, partially because as soon as he'd cleansed himself of the ash and dirt from his nocturnal prowling he'd fallen into an exhausted slumber. The morning had left them little time to get dressed and jump into the truck with nothing more than a cup of coffee each in travel mugs. Now that they were on their way, she was reticent to open the topic. Just looking at him as she drove to town gave her enough information to know that the experience was still rather raw.

"You can quit looking at me like I'm going to collapse from strain, Anthea." Gary could hardly miss her concerned looks from behind the wheel. "It was more a lesson in how old men shouldn't be doing recon work than anything else. I'm just not up to this level of exertion anymore." He sighed. "Even though those folks are beyond belief when it comes to greed and ego, the circumstances were certainly not anything to compare to a battlefield, so you needn't worry for my state of mind."

"That's good to know," she relaxed a little. "I just hated sending you back out after all you'd already been through yesterday. Damn near getting blown up isn't exactly a picnic."

"And I came back with all my parts in good working order, like you commanded," he managed a grin as he sipped the hot coffee.

"We both fared a lot better than this heap. Hard to believe she looked like new a few days ago."

"Yeah, well, better the truck than us. I can't trade you in for another model. Some things you just can't replace."

"I know you're still half asleep so I'll take that as the flattery I know it was meant to be," she smiled across at him as they slowed down with the morning traffic as they entered town. "Whattaya say we butter up the sheriff with some donuts. I know I could sure use some sugar."

"It just may be the way to his heart. I have a feeling he's not apt to be particularly happy with us, even if we did manage to help him break the case."

Ten minutes later they entered the sheriff's station to behold a full house, including Cisco who managed to wrest two pastries from the box before Anthea saw him. "Man, you are good. Who taught you prestidigitation? Can you pull a rabbit out of the sheriff's hat?" she quipped while he downed the donut in almost one bite. "You made that disappear pretty damn quick."

Cisco just grinned back at her before biting into the second sugary puff.

"Good thing I got a couple dozen. What a crowd," she said surveying the occupied chairs at every desk, including the one in the sheriff's personal office where a man dressed for bed sat indignantly wriggling his foot as if it were motorized.

With his mouth half-full, Cisco clued them into the current news.

"That guy," he nodded his head sideways to indicate the man in the Sheriff's office, "is the one-and-only Carl Chamberlain, that Solis computer billionaire."

Gary didn't say anything but Anthea's eyes widened in surprise. "The big man himself?"

"Yup, but I'll bet Mr. Mathers here, knew that," and he polished off the rest of his donut, wiping the powdered sugar on his pants.

Anthea looked again at the man. "Not exactly dressed to give an audience, is he," she noted his costly silk robe and slippers.

"He kind of had his dreamtime interrupted and ended up being hauled down here in the middle of the night," Gary provided.

"The sheriff didn't give him time to grab any clothes?"

"He wasn't being exactly cooperative and I think Sheriff Stellenbeck wasn't particularly inclined to offer him any perks. It was a crime scene and I believe the sheriff was right not to allow him back into his rooms where he might have contaminated, or even destroyed, evidence," said Mathers.

"So, dignity be damned, huh?" Anthea noticed Gary's dour stare that was directed at Chamberlain's back.

"After what I witnessed, I doubt that lounging in his robe in a sheriff's station disturbs him. Dignity is something this guy doesn't understand."

Cisco bobbed his head concurring with Gary's assessment of the man's character. "He could care less what anyone thinks anyway. I'd venture to say he's a sociopath."

Anthea looked up at him, eyebrows going up in amusement. "And would you diagnose megalomania as well, doctor?"

Cisco laughed, which drew the attention of some of the others in the office. "You know, you could be on to something." The little bit of jocularity hadn't lightened Gary's mood nor had it affected the sheriff who finally made his appearance.

"Glad you can find something funny in this whole mess, kid."

"The lack of emotion observed from your prime suspect, or witness, was cause for some speculation, Sheriff," Anthea said in explanation.

"You have managed to be pretty perceptive. The circumstances are kind of vague as to why Tolman went after this guy and his entourage in the first place. But the fact that he was sitting pretty in a mansion that looks like it was erected illegally on public land was enough to call the U.S. attorney earlier. Feds're due anytime."

"Good to know and I think we can shed some light on what he was doing up there," offered Mathers. "But you're right, none of it is particularly funny. Pathetic and despicable would be the words I'd use."

"You've got my attention now. Unfortunately, my office is occupied so we'll have to find another corner to chat."

"Sheriff, I'd recommend placing Chamberlain in a more secure area and keeping him under lock and key. He's apt to just up and walk out the door and I doubt that your deputies would stop him."

"Oh, and what excuse could I use for that?"

"Well, you've a good case for obstructing justice but he's also probably guilty of grand larceny and fraud. Not to mention conspiracy to murder," Gary stated unemotionally, "I'd suggest finding something to detain him since I wouldn't be surprised if the feds don't start looking at RICO charges."

"I'm sure you have good reason for your assumption of his culpability. Care to let me in on it?"

"Before or after you lock him away?"

"Think he's a flight risk, huh," asked the sheriff.

"Absolutely. I assume he's just waiting for his attorney, at which time you'd better have some facts backing your assertions." Mathers bored his eyes into the sheriff's. "And that is what we can help you with."

"Good enough," and he waved over a large deputy, giving him directions to take Mr. Chamberlain to other quarters, i.e. the holding cell. "Tell him it's for his own protection."

After freeing up the sheriff's inner sanctum, he ushered Anthea and Mathers inside, closing the door behind him. The tape recorder made another appearance on the desktop and the two sketched out the evidence garnered from their investigation, near death experience and Gary's eavesdropping at the lodge during the standoff.

"It's obvious that there was a middleman directing Tolman in his engineering of the 'accidents' that occurred to the Ahlsteds, Sully and, we believe, Mary Stabler," Gary began tying the strands of the story together.

Stellenbeck's head popped up at the mention of Mary Stabler. "What makes you think he had anything to do with that? She died of natural causes."

"We have reason to believe otherwise, which is how we ended up as Tolman's first set of hostages for the evening," and Mathers went on to describe why they were at the Stabler's farm when the deputy killed the Nature's Wilds employee, otherwise known as 'Hothead.'

After they'd finished recounting that part of their adventure, the sheriff directed them back to the original topic – that of the middleman. "So you have a suspicion as to who was orchestrating Tolman's activities?"

Mathers and Anthea both nodded. "Glen Alison, the director of the now infamous Nature's Wilds Conservancy," said Mathers.

"He's apparently the missing link between Tolman and Chamberlain," added Anthea. "It also appears that he was behind some of the mischievous activities of the Rural Resources folks. Look, I brought some of our research delineating the financial ties between Nature's Wilds and Chamberlain."

"I think you can establish a strong enough tie between the entities and alter-egos to keep Chamberlain from disappearing before you can get the justice department involved. You've got to contain the information long enough to get the feds on board so they can apprehend Alison, otherwise, he gets wind of this and he's gone. Both these guys have all the resources to cut and run and never be found."

It took an hour to go over all the facts and clarify the paper trail that led to Tolman's connection to Chamberlain and Nature's Wilds, not to mention all the arrows pointing every which way but always coming back to roost at Chamberlain's chicken coop.

Land Barons

Chapter 54

Finally sapped of the adrenaline fueled by the life and death struggles that had devolved into a three-ring circus, Anthea and Gary crashed to sleep off the night's after-effects. They awakened in the same prone positions in which they'd lain down hours earlier, somewhat refreshed by the hiatus in crises.

Even the sleep of the dead didn't completely shake the battle fatigue and they congregated in the kitchen to make coffee.

"When all else fails, rely on caffeine for a booster shot. That's my motto," yawned a half-awake Gary as he filled the coffeemaker by rote. He looked at his watch. "Past dinner time. Guess we'll make do with coffee and crumbs."

"No problem. I'm not hungry anyway," supplied Anthea from her curled-up position on a dining chair. "This whole escapade had drained me of every last ounce of energy, not to mention faith in the underlying good of mankind in general."

"Hey, don't be so morose. We got the bad guys," he perked up. "It's just the downhill run of an unholy shot of epinephrine talking."

She looked up at him over the tops of her knees, around which she had wrapped her arms. "I guess you oughtta know. Me, I could do with a whole lot less excitement and a nice week on a tropical beach to recuperate." She arched an eyebrow at him. "You're ready to go again, aren't you?" she accused.

Gary laughed for what seemed like the first time in weeks.

"No way, Babalouie... I'm ready to hang up "el kabong" for good."

"And I thought you weren't musical," she replied, envisioning the 60's cartoon character and his battered guitar that he used to bash outlaws. "Moving on are you, Queeks-draw?"

"Only if my faithful sidekick thinks I should."

"Oh yeah, it's time. I don't think I could handle another night like last night wondering if you were all right, let alone lying dead or wounded under some pine tree like coyote-bait." She grimaced at the thought.

Mathers left the kitchen and came to stoop behind her chair, pulling her back into his chest in an awkward embrace. "Believe me, that was the last time for playing in that band. I'm too damn old." He kissed the top of her head.

"Good," she stated with finality. "Now that that's settled, what happens next?"

"It's time, my girl, to try to piece this puzzle together."

Grabbing a mug of coffee each, Anthea settled to the task of jotting down details that pertained to their mini think tank. They had left a fact file with the sheriff, but after having notes stolen not once, but twice, she had set aside a second file for easy updating should someone become light fingered again. Extracting that folder from her briefcase, they started sifting through the papers once again.

"It's amazing to me what havoc someone can wreak when they feel so justified by social victimization, or at least believing that's what they'd suffered," mused Anthea aloud as she culled the personal histories from the rather large stack of printouts.

"I assume you're referring to Tolman," said Gary as he sat down at the table to help Anthea. "To me, it's a wonder that anyone can go so far in this life nurturing a hate so bitter that all his aspirations are only to accomplish final revenge." He looked up at his partner. "What do we do to our children to make them think that they're entitled to have things 'their way?' I understand desperation and devastation when a family is ruined by circumstances the way his was. But what is it that makes someone like him think that justice is served by doling out death to your neighbors?"

"Frankly, Tolman is pitiable in his feeling of abandonment, but he was what, fifteen, sixteen at the time his father died? I'd like to think that that's old enough to begin to get a grip on the harsh realities of life, pleasant or not." Under her breath she muttered, "I did."

"You did what?" and he laid his hand over hers.

"Oh nothing. Our family suffered quite a few setbacks as I was growing up and I didn't become a mass murderer," and she cocked her gaze teasingly. "Or did I?"

"I knew there was something behind that "I'd rather clobber the bastard than shoot him" thing."

Anthea laughed, letting go the tension that had been building steadily for the better part of a month. "Yeah, I've got a mean streak, all right." She supposed there'd be plenty of time in the future to particularize her history that led to her feisty attitude. Thoughts slipping into her own past she pondered why people make the life-changing decisions that herald a future of promise or, often enough, heartache.

Her family had weathered decades of seesaw fortunes as many do. Surviving a suicidal mother – whose medical bills for psychiatric care plunged her father into bankruptcy after she finally succumbed to her fatal inclinations – was a part of coming of age. As the oldest and still a teen, Anthea had trained in the journalistic trenches of the L.A. news scene to assist the family by putting food on the table while her father struggled with spiraling finances, wayward sons, and a rebellious niece that he'd rescued from his alcoholic sister.

So what family's perfect? Despite the challenges every one of her siblings confronted, they managed to turn out all right and become upstanding, contributing members of society… a small source of pride for her that her father and brothers had carved a niche for themselves and established real success. Not to mention her niece's landing a position as full professor in the history department of a renowned university. Okay, so her personal failing was a poor choice of marriage partners but, in her estimation, even that isn't a block wall that couldn't be scaled. Experiences like theirs could either build your survival skills or destroy your faith. Luckily, her family never lost that faith or hope for the future. Lousy circumstances certainly weren't a reason for pity or a rationale to obliterate enemy offenders. *Too bad Tolman didn't have the wherewithal to move on, too. Makes the rest of your life far more palatable.*

Getting back to the topic, she shook off her brief reverie and said, "It still seems odd how someone can be transfigured from a hard-headed kid to a dupe for over-achieving environmentalists turned terrorists. Because that's what we're dealing with here, pure and simple." She looked up again, a light of epiphany shining in her eyes. "Didn't you work anti-terrorism in your law enforcement heyday?"

"Yes, but more as an interpreter and translating text. Physically busting up the cells was someone else's be-knighted duty, thank God.

"Look Thea. I was wondering the same as you, how Tolman made a drastic turn to crime and we have to consider finding a link. I'm not sure that it's in here," and he made a sweeping gesture to encompass the shifting maze of paper. "Aside from the fact that had his father been better able to cope with the family's misfortunes, and I am no way belittling those...particularly when he had to watch everything crumble around him even to the point that the local economy couldn't offer a simple job for his dad...it comes down to influences in Tolman's life. And I don't see anything here telling us what those were." He plumped back down in the chair.

"Thinking about why people become activists or apathetic makes you take another look at the involvement of Carrie. Was she completely unwitting in her role or did she have an idea as to how she was contributing to families losing their heritage? How could she be so misguided as to think that her vision of the ultimate good was worth the misery these people are enduring. I'll never understand how people can be so brainwashed to believe that they have the ultimate capacity to make decisions for others."

"Come on now," said Gary, "politicians do it all the time. Why not a self-righteous do-gooder in some backwater who has 'superior' knowledge? Face it. There are elitists everywhere you turn. Maybe we are too because we think people should be able to make informed decisions for themselves."

"Now, there's the rub, *me boy*. Informed is a word that doesn't describe everyone, not even you and me in terms of having all the facts. Which is precisely why we can't yet put this jigsaw together." She sipped her coffee. "You did hit on something, though. There has to be a political connection. No way does a land swap of this magnitude get waltzed through the system without a sponsor. We need to be looking at the big picture."

"Wasn't one of the attendees at last night's party Congressman Heubert?"

"Yeah, and I think he was whisked off before we arrived this morning. I'm guessing this is going to be one big hullabaloo for him and his cronies. They've locked away legislators for less."

While they had slipped into silence, mulling over the implications, the phone rang, jangling their nerves, which hadn't had time for full restoration.

Gary reached over and lifted the handset. Eyebrows rising at the answer he received when inquiring as to who was calling, he gave Anthea a look that indicated a new development. Thanking the caller for letting him know, he hung up and turned back to Anthea.

"We've been summoned to the summit," he grinned.

"And that means?"

"Sheriff Stellenbeck has asked us to come down to the office. Apparently Tolman has been answering questions."

"Yes?"

"Yes. Looks like the dosages of painkillers loosened his tongue. Let's go."

•••••••

When they entered the sheriff's office this time there was a noticeable change in the atmosphere. It was no longer hectic and charged with kinetic energy from bodies running to and fro. Instead the feeling was of a calm bordering on catatonic. Annie was at her post at reception and Deputy Newsome was back at the desk previously occupied by Tolman, but no other bodies were clogging the hallways or cluttering up the other two offices.

Annie, usually perky to the point of being annoying, was subdued and looking a little ragged around the edges.

"Been a long day, has it?" asked Gary as they closed the door behind them.

She shot him an uncharacteristically venomous glare. "That's an understatement, doncha think?"

He chuckled lightly. "Probably." Glancing around and seeing no one else but Deputy Newsome he asked if the sheriff was still around.

"Oh yeah, he won't be going home for awhile yet. And he's lost his sense of humor. So I'd caution you to be on your guard," threw in Sonia from the other side of the room. "You're pretty much the bane of everyone's existence right now."

"Me? What'd I do? Damn, I thought I'd be at the top of the sheriff's list for a civilian commendation." He tried to get a rise out of the glum audience, to no avail. Shrugging his shoulders he just asked. "So, where's he want us?"

"I wouldn't ask him that either, if I were you," smirked the deputy. "He might just tell you where to go."

"Thanks for the warning. I guess we'll wait here then. Is that good for you?" he asked her.

Newsome just waggled her head noncommittally, letting Gary

377

know what she thought of his interference in the whole mess. It seemed pretty apparent that she'd been reamed for letting him slide past her in the dead of night even if he *had* managed to round up a roomful of land thieves.

Settling back into the couple of chairs lining the wall, Gary and Anthea awaited Stellenbeck's appearance.

It came from an unexpected quarter, in that the sheriff pushed wide the front door, entering from the street. Gary shot to his feet to offer his hand as Stellenbeck marched into the anteroom. He took Mathers' hand in a grip that was a little weaker than earlier in the day. Looking haggard from too many hours on the run without even a catnap, the sheriff was ready to call it a day.

Stellenbeck just stood there for a moment scratching his day's growth of beard, examining the two would-be sleuths that ended up dumping this mess in his backyard. Not that it was their fault, he had to admit, and the fact that he'd be nowhere in investigating a number of suspicious deaths if it weren't for their curiosity. Sighing, he flicked his big paw toward his office, indicating that they should follow him inside.

Landing hard on his chair, he leaned back and glowered at Gary and Anthea for a few moments before opening the conversation.

"Figured you'd want to know what your meddling 'hath wrought.'"

Anthea's head came up to meet a half-hearted smile on the sheriff's face. "I didn't know you were interested in classical literature, Sheriff Stellenbeck."

"It's Dave. And by now you oughtta know that the only thing I'm interested in is putting this entire, sordid tragedy to rest."

"So, what's the deal, Dave? And don't we get the tape recorder?" inquired Gary, hoping to move this along with a little humor before Stellenbeck's mood turned and they were charged with some misdemeanor, or worse, rather than being considered part of the team.

Ignoring the remark, Stellenbeck just forged ahead. "They picked up your buddy Alison an hour ago. Somehow he'd gotten wind of the developments and he was getting ready to board a plane for Rio when the feds caught up with him. They're starting with lesser charges along the lines of conspiracy to defraud and racketeering.

"Lesser charges?" Anthea was slightly astonished. "Those sound pretty formidable."

"Yup, but conspiracy to murder is a lot more heinous, I'd say."

"Tolman has been talking then," cut in Mathers.

"That is *no* joke." Stellenbeck leaned back in the chair and clasped his hands behind his head, mussing his already unruly ruff of hair. "Seems this Alison character has been filling students full of spleen for years and Tolman was only one of his hapless pawns. You'd found that Alison had been faculty at Greenfield College and low and behold, guess who ended up in his class years ago?"

"Your former deputy?"

Stellenbeck nodded.

"Turns out this guy had been Tolman's professor some years back, after Tolman did a stint in the army. Allison apparently spearheaded some little secret student organization called Protect Our Planet at Greenfield, where he inducted saps like Tolman into the underworld of environmental activism. This P.O.P., as they liked to call it began rearing its ugly head about fifteen years ago mostly as minor players in demonstrations and the like. It seems though, that this *purveyor of wis - dom*," and he nearly spat out the words, "was practically conducting para-military training."

Anthea piped up, "That greasy weasel?"

He just nodded again and went on. "Alison continued to mentor, if you want to call it that, and teach special workshops at the college every year, taking environmental studies groups into the forest and other natural areas, filling their heads full of 'how you can be a savior of the world' bullshit. Some of the more impressionable ones signed up for P.O.P. and were infiltrated, sort of, into community organizations like Rural Resources in areas where it looks like Chamberlain wanted to acquire land."

Stellenbeck stopped to take a breath and shake his head. "This guy is good because it may take years to unravel all the elaborate money schemes he set up. Through all kinds of sophisticated financial gyrations he put in place, he funded the land acquisitions with Solis money and the P.O.P. group provided the strong-arm tactics if simple coercion didn't work. Though it isn't clear yet whether he was actually complicit in the little *accidental* death plots that Tolman devised."

"What a pair," said Gary, almost under his breath.

"Oh, there's more. You already heard Tolman's history straight from the horse's mouth. You know, a farm boy whose daddy lost his grip after losing the family farm. And he was right. It was no fault of his dad's other than too many years of bad crops and an unethical local banker who eventually ended up in jail, by the way. I heartily doubt that the elder Stabler and Ahlsted had purposefully taken advantage of the Tolmans' lousy luck. I knew both of them and they were honorable men. Who knows what tale the banker gave them when they purchased the divvied up parcels. I do know that there was a real pride in old man Tolman and he began having real personal troubles when he had to go to work for the neighboring farms, who did take the family in according to some of the oldtimers. You know how kids are. They see things in a different light and our friendly deputy certainly doesn't remember circumstances the way the rest of the community does.

"Whatever the case, when he came back to town he was already a full-fledged member of this Protect Our Planet organization and hell-bent on revenge. He targeted the Stablers first and as I said, growing up on a farm, had a good bit of knowledge when it came to crop management practices including pesticides. Turns out he managed to get his hands on one of the more virulent poisons and introduced it into Mary Stabler's perfume. So she managed to dose herself everyday without anyone suspecting the nature of her illness. With Chamberlain apparently leaning on Alison to get a handle on that land and the repeated crop failures, which were also engineered, it looks like, not working to force them out soon enough…Tolman seemed to think that the time was right and just stepped over the edge. The family knew him from way back when and had opened their home to him pretty often. Guess he took advantage of that trust." The sheriff just let his voice trail off remembering Mary and her last few months struggling with an unknown affliction. He shook his head again. "And this was all happening right under my nose."

"You could hardly have seen it coming, Dave," said Gary. "How well did you know Tolman?"

"Actually, I didn't. I didn't grow up here and hired him on the merits of his resumé."

"What about the cattle at the Ahlsted's? Was he responsible for that, too?" asked Anthea.

Stellenbeck sighed again. "Yeah, looks like. Seems he used the same toxin he put in Mary's perfume." He looked up at the ceiling.

"So simple, yet so deadly. Damn, none of those folks should have died."

"But, I would have thought that the investigators would have looked for a foreign agent in the water at the Ahlsted's," said Anthea.

"They did. It's just that Frank raised organic beef and he didn't farm or spray any of the hayfields. Why would he? So they overlooked a poison of this nature in the tests they conducted on the water source. It's not commonly used anymore because it's such a strong neurotoxin and you have to suspect it in order to test for it. Pretty ingenious however simple."

"I guess he rigged the lip of the canyon too, huh?" asked Gary.

"Hmmm," Stellenbeck hummed in assent. "Tolman had some training in the field in the army and even Alison had pulled in ex-military mercenaries to teach some rather unorthodox warfare methods. P.O.P. is just one of a handful of groups that use this kind of violent means to reach their goal of controlling wilderness use. Their agenda is pretty straight forward from what the feds said today." He looked at the other two. "They brought in members of a domestic anti-terrorism task force. One of the guys actually filled me in on some of this info. Anyway, these eco-terrorists are completely set on saving the earth by keeping folks like you and me from ruining it with our cheap thrills like hunting, and even the necessary evils of farming, logging and ranching. It's suspected that the rash of wildfires in the west over the past few years also might be arson attributed to eco-terrorist cells similar to this Protect Our Planet group though no one's claimed credit. Better to burn the chaparral and forest rather than let rich folks destroy it for luxury homes," he added bitterly. "Instead they devastate the lives of a lot of retirees and hard-working folks who have everything sunk into their property." He planted his elbows on the desk and scrubbed his scalp in fatigue.

"It doesn't take a brain surgeon to follow how Solis starts the indoctrination process with the kids by making them think that no one but environmentalists and government have the ability to understand how to take care of the land."

He snapped up and looked them in the eye. "Have you seen the extent of Solis Industries 'entertainment' empire?"

"We were talking about this not too long ago, come to think of it," said Gary. "I brought it up when we first connected Chamberlain's name to Nature's Wilds Conservancy. I'd been brought up short when I started examining some of their products earlier this year, being a new granddad and all."

Stellenbeck bobbed his head in understanding. "Yeah, looking for computer games for the kids, right?"

"Yup."

"This is something Annie got online to download for me after the feds mentioned the 'environmental education' relationship. Take a look at the list of games and heroes there are. Here," and he picked up some printouts from his desk, handing them over to Anthea.

The list of games had names like Earth Nexus (saving the earth from evil corporations), Rainforest Corps (saving the trees) and SeaScape (saving the oceans); all games with animal heroes that wipe out the evil humans who are destroying their habitat for personal gain. The printout also included a number of movie titles, mostly animated, centered around these animal heroes that had been blockbusters in the theaters over the last five years. And then there were two cable stations with children's programming, and a network that Solis had purchased two years before.

"And you wonder why kids are afraid of their own shadows. Hell, they could think shadows are 'carbon footprints' for all they know," the sheriff said disgustedly.

"I'd noticed the environmental bent on the news carried by CNB but I hadn't realized how well this guy was undermining the thought processes of our young minds. Some of these games and computer programs have been instituted into school curricula," added Anthea.

"It's gone that far?" Gary found it hard to believe.

"'Fraid so."

"Can you imagine the damage this guy has done? Children around the world are being trained to think that humans are a plague on the earth, following the Lord Snowden school of thought." He was referring to the man who headed the World Wildlife Fund, who has been ascribed with quoted sentiments referring to humanity as little more than a pestilence that should be eradicated from the earth.

Mathers looked over at Anthea with a teasing grin on his face, in an attempt to lighten the mood. "I'm guessing you've got quite a job in front of you."

"Me? What are you talking about?"

"You do PR right? It's going to take a lot of professionals like you to counteract the damage Solis Industries has already done to the next generation."

"Haven't you been paying attention? I'm the minority in the press today. Everyone is sponging up this stuff. I couldn't make a dent in the overall scheme of things. But," continued Anthea, "a lot of that will be done for us when this guy is indicted and his empire is brought down around his knees in order to pay retribution."

"Lord, I hope so."

"Yeah, well don't hold your breath, son," Stellenbeck cautioned.

Land Barons

Epilogue

The warm weather brought out legions of boaters and water skiers to enjoy the last of September's late summer weather before leaves turn and fall sets in. Gary and Anthea had been enjoying the day lounging on the deck overlooking the swarm of spirited activity on the Snake River.

They were sitting side-by-side on a swing, rocking back and forth in the breeze watching the sunset sweep vermilion and magenta cloud fragments across the otherwise azure sky.

"I find it interesting that the 'good ol' boys' up here don't seem to engage in anywhere near the level of outrageous hell-raising I used to see on the Colorado River. There's plenty of noise but its not full of drunken swearing and screaming for the purpose of making yourself a miserable pain in the ass to everyone else on the water," said Anthea, sliding a little further down on the porch swing. "What a relief. 'Course it could just be the numbers factor. You know, more folks from the city out for the weekend causing havoc. We just can't compete with the amount of jerks from a major population center like L.A. or Las Vegas."

"That's one way of looking at it," chuckled Mathers. "It's all in the ratio of idiots to the general populace. Maybe it's the same, just smaller population so less of 'em here."

"Hey, don't burst my bubble," and she elbowed him in the ribs. "I like to think that this is the good life in the sticks."

"Well, it is and this isn't quite the sticks anymore."

"Talk to any Angelino and you'd be laughed off the planet."

"I don't hear even a giggle," he noted as he looked down at her.

"I gave up that citizenship awhile ago."

"Good thing or I might not have stumbled across your trail."

"You know that was a set-up, right?" she asked referring to his good buddy, Azy's machinations.

"What are you talking about?" and he looked genuinely perplexed.

"Oh," Anthea groaned. "Absolutely clueless," she muttered under her breath.

"What?" He gave her a cock-eyed look.

"Nothing, detective." She dropped the subject and handed him a postcard.

"What's this?"

"A mutual friend seems to be sending along his good wishes," she said pokerfaced.

Turning the card over, he read the inscription aloud: " 'Wish you were here.' Well, that's original." He checked the postmark. "Belize. Who do we know in Belize? Someone take a vacation? It's not signed."

"Have you already forgotten your comrade in arms? Well, even if he was kind of an outlaw."

"Billy?" Gary was surprised and flipped the card over a few times looking for something that wasn't there. "What do you figure he's doing down there..." he mused.

"Living happily ever after, I suspect. You remember that he and Carrie both took off without a word. I believe they are enjoying his ill-gotten gains and frolicking by the sea."

"Good thing, too," and he gave her a little kiss on the forehead.

Gary lifted his eyes to check the horizon again as he added to the information pool. "You know Brogus left Pinesap Farms to Lissa Ahlsted and Joe Santos, his manager, right?"

Anthea shook her head. "Nope."

"Yeah and word is they're tying the knot next year." She let her gaze settle back on the river tableau below. "You know, we never did find out who was behind *the voice* that she purportedly received threatening phone calls from during that whole ordeal. Do you think she was really being manipulated by a disembodied caller or just using it as a convenient excuse to take the focus off of her ?"

"That's something we'll never know but I have a hunch that Alison was behind that little drama."

"Are you kidding? That guy was a slimy rodent," and she visibly shuddered. "If sewer rats had lesser cousins, he's it."

"I rather think he was a passive-aggressive that could put the fear of hellfire into some poor souls like any brimstone spouting preacher worth his salt on Sunday." And he just gazed off into the distance.

"What are you, an anti-Christ?" she laughed under her breath. "You'd foist a character like that on good church-going folk?"

"Nah, proper Christian upbringing here. I'm just saying that he had that type of charisma or he wouldn't have been able to sway all those empty-headed 'younguns' at the U's." He looked down at her. "Evidently you were immune to his charms."

"Thank heaven for that. I like to think I've developed a little bit of discernment since my college days."

"Well, 'my stars,'" she did her best Aunt Bea impression.

"I thought you said you didn't watch Andy Griffith."

"No, I believe I said I couldn't stand the show," she elucidated. "Anyway, it's good to hear that some things are ending better than expected. As to Brogus, I imagine he's been able to mend Ms. DiMarco's criminal tendencies."

Gary threw back his head and laughed. "If they haven't been sharing trade secrets instead or throttling one another over environmental politics."

"She's probably working hard to save the Caribbean reef. Keep her out of trouble."

"I just hope they're happy." He looked over at his daughter playing with the baby on the grass. "I know I am."

Anthea just leaned her head on his shoulder and listened to the giggling of his granddaughter being tickled by her mother, their right hands clasped together in their lap. Their left hands were entwined, draped over her left shoulder and there was a sparkle of new gold circling their fingers.

– 30 –

ABOUT THE AUTHOR

Former newspaper publisher and editor, A. Dru Kristenev has more than three decades of experience in periodicals. Kristenev grew up in the publishing industry working every angle of a paper, from ad sales and production to writing and overseeing editorial content. The author carries a Bachelor of Arts degree, a Master of Science and a California Community Colleges Lifetime Teaching Credential and taught at the foremost colleges and universities in the Inland Northwest.

Since 2010, Kristenev has been on the road as an independent Christian missionary, crossing the United States more than ten times. She has also been a columnist for CanadaFreePress.com since 2014.

THE BARON SERIES

Four books in the series of stand-alone novels based on current, factual occurrences, the relationship of characters leads from one story to the next, weaving an ongoing tale of journalists running across criminally tainted philanthropy and politics. Caught by their own curiosity to uncover the truth, they are pulled deeper and deeper into the investigations, unexpectedly putting their lives at risk…

Land Barons- the first book in the Baron Series of romantic suspense novels that rely on solid research of environmentalist influence on American lifestyles, touching on the long reach of government regulation and media/corporate power. Anthea Keller is seeking a peaceful place to ply her trade as a PR agent. Instead, she finds herself in the center of a land scam, drawn in by Gary Mathers, an ex-cop who just can't reconcile the deadly misfortunes of local property owners forced to sell off assets. And who is waiting in the wings to snap up the firesale deals?

Gold Baron- the second work in the series. Fact meets fiction in the election process of the 2008 presidential campaign season, drawing on the reality driving the candidacies - who's influencing who and to what end with global markets and politics as the backdrop. Solana Greyfisher returns home to Idaho only to be snagged by a fascinating story that leads her to Toddy Littman, researcher extraordinaire.

Together they dig through the morass of campaign funding paper trails only to attract the murderous ire of power brokers working the system to their own benefit.

Energy Barons - the third novel, whirls around political manipulation of the environmental movement causing economic upheaval in the West and endangering lives of the innocent. Ambitious Allie Maitland is caught by surprise while investigating what appears to be anything but an accident at the new power plant. Sawyer Aleman, former marine, wheedles his way into the FBI inquiry, under Allie's skin and into the role of guardian. Before they know it, the story rolls from Wyoming to Alaska and everyone involved is walking a perilous tightrope of greed, murder and mayhem.

BLOOD BARONS - the fourth novel in the Baron Series brings the tale full circle.

NYC: a metropolis of 8 million people; 500 disappear each year. Of those, three dead end case files lie open on Special Agent Roy Esteban's desk. Who are they? Why doesn't anyone know they're gone and why does no one care?

Lack of leads and an ASAC that wants the cases closed drives the FBI agent to take on an unorthodox partner in Researcher Debra Chorister. Together they track an unwholesome alliance between corporate science and government healthcare. And those three lone individuals? They're not the only ones who can't be found.

UNKNOWN PREDATOR

Hands tied by regulations, what does a rancher do to forestall the concocted destruction of a traditional way of life by officials cowering behind an "unknown predator?" Not what you'd think.

When neighboring landowners take action, dropping them into the middle of a legal quagmire, individuals obsessed with their own righteous cause threaten the ranchers' livelihood... and their lives.

A. Dru Kristenev
ChangingWind Ministries
changingwind@earthlink.net

Scripture Led Politics: Mutual Exclusivity Be Damned

Wonder how Scripture relates to the political atmosphere in which we live?

Numerous legislative, judicial and regulatory decrees have altered life in America to a degree that our parents' generation would find it unrecognizable. To what end? Who benefits from the draconian coding that now cages the free thinker, particularly the faithful?

As government draws each new line in the sand, Author A. Dru Kristenev has taken a scriptural view of the cascading legal enactments, noting how they are fundamentally changing the American Dream. These commentaries open a deep discussion of how believers must tap their intellect and view the shifting political landscape in the historical light of the Bible, contemplating its significant lessons and their application.

··········

Read all of A.Dru Kristenev's books available on Amazon.com...

THE BARON SERIES Political Suspense novels:

Land Barons

Gold Baron

Energy Barons

BLOOD BARONS

UNKNOWN PREDATOR

Non-fiction Books:

Scripture Led Politics: Mutual Exclusivity Be Damned

Pay Attention!! ...your life, family and nation depend on it

A. Dru Kristenev